Edward Hunter has it all—a beautiful wife and daughter, a great job, a bright future . . . and a very dark past.

Twenty years ago, a serial killer was caught, convicted, and locked away in the country's most hellish of penitentiaries. That man was Edward's father. Edward has struggled his entire life to put the nightmares of his childhood behind him. But a week before Christmas, violence once again makes an unwelcome appearance in his world. Suddenly he's going to need the help of his father, a man he hasn't seen since he was a boy. Is Edward destined to be just like him, to become a man of blood?

Blood Men is "relentlessly gripping, deliciously twisted, and shot through with a vein of humor that's as dark as hell" (Mark Billingham). A true master of the genre, who only comes along once in a generation, Cleave unveils a brutally vivid picture of a killer's mind and a city of fallen angels captured at the ends of the earth.

ALSO BY PAUL CLEAVE

Cemetery Lake
The Killing Hour
The Cleaner

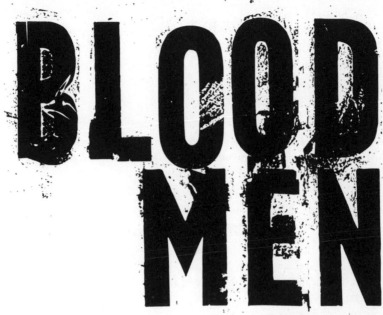

BLOOD MEN

A THRILLER

PAUL CLEAVE

ATRIA PAPERBACK
New York   London   Toronto   Sydney

ATRIA PAPERBACK
A Division of Simon & Schuster, Inc.
1230 Avenue of the Americas
New York, NY 10020

Originally published in New Zealand by Random House New Zealand

First Atria Paperback edition July 2010

ATRIA PAPERBACK and colophon are trademarks of
Simon & Schuster, Inc.

For information about special discounts for bulk purchases, please contact Simon & Schuster Special Sales at 1-866-506-1949 or business@simonandschuster.com.

The Simon & Schuster Speakers Bureau can bring authors to your live event. For more information or to book an event contact the Simon & Schuster Speakers Bureau at 1-866-248-3049 or visit our website at www.simonspeakers.com.

Manufactured in the United States of America

10 9 8 7 6 5 4 3 2 1

Library of Congress Cataloging-in-Publication Data

Cleave, Paul, date.
    Blood men : a thriller / by Paul Cleave. — 1st Atria paperback ed.
      p. cm.
1. Serial murderers—Fiction. 2. Christchurch (N.Z.)—Fiction.
I. Title.
    PR9639.4.C54B56 2010
    823'.92—dc22

                                      2009052483

ISBN 978-1-4391-8961-0
ISBN 978-1-4391-8963-4 (ebook)

For my mum, who I love—I've always been proud
and lucky to have such a great mother

prologue

"I first made the newspapers when I was nine years old. I made them in every city across the country, most of them on the first page. I even made them internationally. In them I was black and white, blurred a little, my face turned into my father's chest, people surrounding us. From then on I was shown on TV, in magazines, in more and more papers, always the same photo. I never wanted any of it, I tried to avoid it, but the option wasn't mine.

"My dad, well, he made the papers too. He was also on the front pages. There were more photos of him than of me, because he was the one being arrested. I was just along for the ride, trying to fight off the police as they came to take him away. I didn't know any better. Mum peeled me away from his side as I cried. The police handcuffed him, and I never saw him again until this week. He was my dad, sure, but it was pretty easy to stop loving the guy when it turned out he was never really the man we thought he was. Dad got himself arrested because he had tastes other people didn't look too kindly on—not even the people of Christchurch.

"Mum was dead a year later. She took cocktails of poisons and pills to escape the hate and the accusations from the public. That left me with the doctors and psychiatrists to study me. They were curious about me. Everybody was. My dad was a man of blood. He had murdered eleven prostitutes over a period of twenty-five years, and that got some of the good people of Christchurch wondering whether I'd turn out the same way. Dad was so subtle nobody even realized Christchurch had a serial killer. He didn't advertise the fact, he just did his thing, no fuss, no real mess, sometimes they were found and sometimes they weren't, and those that weren't were never reported missing. He was a family man who loved us, who would do everything for us. He never laid a finger on my mother or my sister or me, he worked hard to put food on our table, to provide what he could to make our lives better than his was growing up. The monster inside him never came home, it was left hidden in the darkness with the blood and the flesh of those it killed, but sometimes—at least eleven times that he admitted to—Dad'd go out at night and meet up with that monster. He wasn't my dad in those moments, he was something else. I never asked what, exactly. In the beginning I couldn't. In the beginning I wasn't allowed to see him, then, when I was old enough to make my own decisions, I didn't want to.

"I was ten years old when the trial began. It was a circus. My mum was still alive, but my sister and I were struggling. Mum was always yelling at us when she was sober, and crying when she was drunk, and whatever of those two states she was in, you always wished it was the other. Soon the pills and the booze took their toll, but not as quick as she wanted, and when they couldn't finish the job she used a razor blade. I don't know how long it took for her to bleed out. She might still have been alive when we found her. I held my sister's hand and we watched her pale body, the yelling and the crying gone now.

"My mum's family wanted nothing to do with us, but my dad's parents took us in. The kids at school would tease me, they'd beat me up, they'd steal my bag at least once a week and jam it down a toilet somewhere. The psychiatrist came around every few months with his tests and questions. My photo came up in the papers every now and then, always the same one, though the distance between those occurrences started to stretch. I was almost a celebrity. I was also the son of a serial killer—and some of those good Christchurch people thought I would follow in his footsteps.

"My sister, Belinda, she took the direction of Dad's victims. She was out fucking for money when she was fourteen. By sixteen she was an addict; her tastes ran to the liquids that could be scored cheap and injected into her veins. By nineteen she was dead. I was the last of my family—Dad's monster took them all away.

"Of course little Eddie grew up, I have my own family now. A wife. A child. I told my wife who I was not long after we met. It frightened her in the beginning. Thankfully she got to know me. She saw I had no monsters.

"There are those who think what my dad had was a gene, that he's passed it on to me. There are people who think that I'm destined to be a man of blood too," I say, and I look at the blood soaking into the upholstery from the woman slumped in the passenger seat, "that the same blood runs through both of us. They're wrong," I say, and I take the car up to sixty kilometers an hour and drive straight into the wall.

seven days earlier

chapter one

The alarm clock dragging me into the Friday morning before the Christmas break sounds like laser fire from an old sci-fi movie, the kind where the special effects budget runs the production company up about a hundred bucks. I manage to open my eyes about halfway. I feel like I have a hangover even though I haven't had a drink in ages. I reach out and shut off the alarm and am almost asleep when Jodie pushes me in the back. Hopefully this year Santa will bring me an alarm clock that doesn't make any noise.

"You have to get up," she says.

It takes a few seconds to focus on her words, and I let them slide with me toward the dark hole of sleep. "I don't want to," I hear myself saying.

"You have to. It's your job to get up and then drag me out of bed."

"I thought it was your turn to drag me out." I roll over to face her. The sun is bright behind the curtains, beams of light shining onto the ceiling. I close my eyes so I don't have to see them. I squeeze them tight and pretend it's nighttime all over again. "Five more minutes. I promise."

"That's what you said five minutes ago when you turned it off the first time."

"There was a first time?"

"Come on. It's Friday. We've got the whole weekend ahead of us."

"It's Christmas," I say. "We've got two weeks ahead of us."

"But not yet," she reminds me, and she pushes me again.

I sit on the edge of the bed and yawn for ten seconds before grabbing her hands and trying to drag her out as well, not wanting to go through this nightmare of waking up alone. She hides under the sheets and starts laughing. Sam comes into the room and starts laughing too.

"Mummy's a ghost," she says, and jumps on top of her.

From beneath the sheet comes an "oomph," then more laughing. I leave them to it and go and take a shower, the hot water bringing me fully around. I'm finished and halfway through shaving when Jodie comes in and climbs into the shower behind me.

"Just four more days of work," she says, then yawns.

"I know."

"It's almost the weekend. Then three more days. Not even that. The last day is always a short one."

"Sounds like you can add."

"It's an occupational bonus."

The occupational bonus comes about from the fact Jodie is an accountant. Being married to an accountant isn't the end of the world, but that's probably because I'm an accountant too. It is, of course, how we met. Accountants are the punch line of a thousand jokes, and our relationship might contribute to those stereotypes—I don't know.

Jodie turns on the small bathroom radio which is styled as a penguin. She twists its flipper until she finds a station with something decent to listen to, then its other flipper to increase the volume. She sings along to a Paul Simon song about fifty ways to leave your lover, and the accountant in me wonders how he came to that number, how many he tried out. My dad had his own ways of leaving his lovers—and I'm pretty sure they're ways that Paul Simon—*Slit her wrists, Chris*—never factored in. Jodie doesn't know all the words and fills in the blanks with loud humming.

I get dressed and head out to the living room. Toys and schoolbooks are scattered across the floor and the TV is going, gay-looking cartoon characters dancing across the screen. Sam is finishing off her homework while watching the TV, developing the whole multitasking skill at the tender age where homework is done mostly with crayons and markers—all kinds of colorful things that make all kinds of colorful messes. The living room is small, especially with the Christmas tree taking up one whole corner. The entire house is getting too cramped, which is why we're buying a new one. Today is Sam's last day of school until the end of January and she's acting like a kid who just discovered caffeine.

I open up the curtains and sunlight pours into the living room and the kitchen, bouncing off every metal surface and making the sun appear to be about as far away as my next-door neighbor. The poplar trees lining the street have been defeated by the heat, the burned leaves drooping, front lawns turning crispy brown as the sun beats down on it all. The air-conditioning is working overtime, separating the outside world from the inside by a dozen degrees. Sam's holidays kick in in about seven hours and her excitement levels are high and my stress levels are high and Jodie has high levels of both. I'm pretty sure the house has a poltergeist living in it; it comes through at night and does its best to make sure there are no straight lines anywhere.

I get the kitchen smelling of coffee. Our kitchen is full of modern appliances, most of them were in style back in the fifties and are back in style now, lots of stainless steel and curves everywhere. I pour Sam a bowl of cereal and she works her way through it, and I'm on my second piece of toast when Jodie comes down the hallway into the dining room. Her dark hair hanging around her shoulders is still slightly damp and her skin smells of body wash. She leans in, kisses me on the cheek, and steals the rest of my toast.

"Payment for the kiss," she whispers, and winks at me.

"I should have made you pancakes. They'd have cost you more."

Our cat, Mogo, gets under Jodie's feet before jumping up on the table and staring at me. Mogo is a tabby with way too much personality and nowhere near enough patience. I sometimes think he has similar thoughts to what my dad must have had all those years ago. He never eats when I feed him, and he always waits for Jodie to take care of him. He never hangs around me or wants me to pat him either—but cats never approach me—there's something about me that they don't like. Dogs too.

We finish up breakfast and get our gear together. Jodie has her briefcase, Sam her backpack, I have a satchel, and it's time to go. It's eight thirty and the Paul Simon song is stuck in my head and heading outside is like walking into a wall of heat. It's Jodie's turn to drop Sam at school. There are kisses all around and hugs, then car doors closing and engines turning over and we leave in different directions. The inside of my car is an oven. Neighbors wave while getting their own kids off to school, others out walking before the day gets too hot, some working in the garden. The houses in the neighborhood have recycling bins parked out front, the week's trash all ready to be picked up and emptied, green bins with yellow lids lining the streets. On the way into town I pass vans on the side of the road with trailers—people in collapsible chairs reading magazines while selling Christmas trees and Christmas lilies.

The central city is bordered away from the suburbs by four long avenues creating a giant box, within it a network of parallel streets made up in a checkerboard style, the buildings planted among them blending into one of two types—ugly ones built a hundred years ago, and slightly less ugly ones built in the years since. Most of the scenery could be picked up and spliced into a Sherlock Holmes novel without anybody noticing much difference, except for Holmes himself, who would wonder why Baker Street had suddenly turned from a loitering ground for pickpockets and heroin addicts to one of gang members and glue sniffers.

The drive-time routines are slipping out of whack as the city crawls toward Christmas, the traffic is thicker than yesterday, but not as thick as it will be tomorrow. There are a few early-morning—or perhaps ultra-late-night—hookers on the corners in town; their lifeless eyes follow me as I drive past, fake smiles on their faces, the makeup smudged and worn after a long night, their clothes short and scented with exhaust fumes and spent exhaustion. I've never seen anybody pull over and pick one up at this time of the morning—it would be like screwing something out of *Dawn of the Dead*. I wonder if they take the holidays off, whether Christmas is a merry time for them, whether they go home and slip into Santa hats and listen to carols and put up decorations.

I turn on the radio and have to flick through four stations until I can find a pair of DJs who aren't laughing at the tired old sex jokes DJs have been making for the last twenty years. The station I settle on mentions it's already twenty-seven degrees and is only going to get hotter; reminds us all that water restrictions are in place, that global warming is coming, and that Christmas is only seven days away and counting.

I strike nearly every red light on the way into town, people sitting in their cars cooking as the temperature rises. It takes me twenty-five minutes to get to the parking building, having survived all the Christchurch Christmas road rage. I drive up to the eighth floor, negotiating the narrow ramps as they wind upward between floors, some drivers taking them more carefully than I do, others treating it as a racecourse. I take the stairs down, breaking into a sweat, and pass a homeless man named Henry at the base of the stairs who tells me I'm a saint after I give him a couple of bucks. Henry has a Bible in his hand so maybe he really does have a keen eye for that kind of thing, or maybe it's coming from the bottle of cheap vodka in his other hand. From there it's only a two-minute walk to work. The sidewalks are full of grim-looking people all resigned to the day ahead, in office buildings, retail outlets, or sleeping under park benches. Some of them are waiting for Christmas, some of them excited, some of them probably not even aware of its approach. The sun keeps climbing. There is blue sky in every direction and the overwhelming sense we won't be seeing any more clouds this year.

The accountant firm employs almost fifty people, and is one of the bigger and certainly more expensive ones in town—its prestige made obvious by the important-sounding partner names—Goodwin, Devereux & Barclay—and prominent location watching down over the city. It's in one of the more modern Christchurch buildings, sharing it mostly with lawyers and insurance firms. Our company takes up the top three floors of fifteen—the biggest firm in the building. The foyer is throwing out cold air and people are lining up for the elevator. I take the stairs where the air smells stale and break into even more of a sweat.

I work on the thirteenth floor, where the view isn't as good as the bosses' above, but better than the lawyers' below. I go through the early-morning hellos with a few people once I reach my floor, which takes longer this time of the year because people always seem to want to know what everybody else is doing for Christmas. The ones who ask the most seem to be the people with great plans.

Most of us are lucky enough to have our own office—with a few using cubicles. I'm one of the lucky ones, plus my office is at the end of a corridor that doesn't get a lot of foot traffic. It's here I deal with taxes and not so much with people. I dump my satchel on my desk and slump in my seat and pull my already damp shirt away from my body. My office is big enough to fit a desk and a person sitting either side of it and not much more. Most spare wall space on the entire floor is covered in school drawings the parents have brought in from their kids—crayon-purple Christmas trees and dogs with seven legs reminding us all we'd rather be somewhere else but here—and my office is the same. I stare at a couple of the drawings Sam has done, taking a few minutes to cool down before throwing myself into the file I've been working on—the firm has been hired by a bottled water company, McClintoch Spring Water, searching for tax breaks. It's a company whose advertising campaign used images of Jesus to make it a lot of money last year.

I meet Jodie for lunch at twelve thirty outside a café down The Strip, a line of café/bars that double as nightclubs at night, with indoor-outdoor flow and tables spilling out onto the sidewalks. I'm called "sir" because I'm almost thirty years old, but if I came here tonight I'd probably get asked to leave for being too old. The cafés are all at about 90 percent full, some people turning red in the sun, others sitting in the shade of giant umbrellas, the smell of food and cologne thickening the air. The waitresses are all wearing tight black T-shirts. Most of them have their hair pulled back in ponytails that bounce as they walk. On the other side of the road the Avon River is almost at a standstill, bugs attracted by the smell of stagnant river weed and a dead eel floating along belly-up.

We talk while we eat, the only subject the new house we're trying to buy. Jodie picks at a chicken salad which is probably only chicken in name; she can't seem to find any meat in it. I work at a plate of nachos, the food okay, not great, but priced as if it were the best in the city. Maybe we're paying a premium to stare at the waitresses in their T-shirts.

The new house will have a spare room big enough for me to put a pool table in, and Jodie wants some aerobic equipment. We'll probably use neither, but the fun part at this stage is the dreaming. A new house will be exciting for Sam too. But before that we still have to get through the excitement of Christmas. Sam is the perfect age for Christmas—she still believes in Santa.

The waitress comes by when both our mouths are full and asks how the meal is and neither of us can answer. She seems to take that as a good sign and moves on to the next table. It's probably only a couple of degrees away from hitting thirty-five and the waitress is ready to melt into a fleshy puddle when one o'clock rolls around, the umbrellas in danger of catching alight. We pay the bill, and the waitress gives us the smile of the damned.

It's only a five-minute walk to the bank. One side of the road is warm in the shade, the other almost white hot. The sidewalks are covered in melted chewing gum and teenagers on skateboards wearing loose clothes with hoodies, perfecting the rapist image kids these days love and clothes designers are making millions off. I wonder how hot it has to get before they take their hoodies off. We get stopped every hundred meters or so by people trying to convince us to sign up to save the whales, save the environment, solve world hunger. There's tinsel hanging from streetlights and building frontages, decorated trees and fake snow on the window-display floors, plastic Santas and reindeer everywhere. People are rushing about on their lunch breaks trying to squeeze in some shopping, some carrying packages and gifts, others wearing lost looks on their faces.

The bank is pretty much slap bang in the middle of town, a tall building with the ground floor for the public and on the other floors—nobody really knows. It has air-conditioning and about fifty potted plants and a security guard who keeps glancing at his watch. We end up arriving early and are led to a group of comfortable chairs to kill time in. Nobody offers us anything to drink. There are racks full of banking brochures on the wall next to us, plenty of posters advertising interest rates; young families with new homes and new kids and big smiles is the image of choice—which is fine with us. But once you've seen one poster there isn't much more to look at: just more floating and fixed interest rate packages and more smiles from people thrilled to be a slave to their mortgage. There are percentage symbols plastered everywhere.

Then, at thirteen minutes past one—two minutes until our appointment with the mortgage consultant—six men carrying shotguns walk calmly through the door.

chapter two

Crime is escalating. Domestic abuse, adolescent street racers running down innocent pedestrians, people stealing and killing—this is the norm in Christchurch, everyday acts happening in an everyday city. Crime escalates like every other statistic, like inflation, cost of living, it ebbs and flows along with gas prices and the real estate market. Same with the murder rate—it can't be plotted and predicted on a graph, but it stays in line with other crime, a statistic, a percentage.

But this . . .

He's not even sure what this is.

Detective Inspector Schroder brings the car to a stop. There are two unmarked patrol cars blocking off the entrance to the alleyway but he can still see the body beyond it. Detective Landry is leaning against one of the cars, jotting down notes and pausing occasionally to cough into his hand as the medical examiner conveys the details with as many hand gestures as he does words. Schroder gets out of the car and walks over.

"Hell of a show, Carl," Landry says.

"And you figured I'd want to come take a look."

"Well, sure I did. I thought you could use the fresh air."

"Some air. It must be forty degrees out here."

"These nor'west winds—don't know what it is, but they make the crazy even crazier," Sheldon, the medical examiner, sighs, before taking off his glasses and wiping them with the tail of his shirt. "Don't discount it," he adds, "I've been doing this long enough to know."

"So what have we got?" Schroder asks, stepping into the alleyway. The body doesn't look any better than it did from behind his steering wheel. Landry and the ME follow him.

Blood has puddled around the dead man, creating a perimeter of about a meter that Schroder can't cross without contaminating the scene; the footprints already in it are from Sheldon. The victim's limbs are all twisted up, especially the legs—the left one has bent forward and snapped somewhere in the knee joint so the ankle is tucked up against the front of the groin.

The guy has three suction cups attached to him—one strapped on each hand, the third secured around his right knee. The fourth is resting on the ground about half a meter from the body, the strap broken in the fall.

The alleyway is cooler than the street, and in complete shade, but the top nine storeys of the ten-storey building are in direct sunlight. Even in this heat the alleyway smells damp. There are recycling bins lining one of the walls, broken wooden pallets and cardboard boxes lining the other. Christchurch alleyways are always full of something—just normally not bodies. He looks up, shielding his eyes against the bright reflection from the windows, then back down at the dead man's face. A guy with big Vegas-style Elvis sideburns and busted-up features and head wounds that have leaked all over the cracked tarmac.

"See, told you it was a show," Landry says. "Ain't much for us to do except wrap Batman up in a bag and take him to the morgue."

"I think he was trying to be more like Spiderman," Schroder says.

"Either way, the fact he's naked except for a trench coat tells us he's a piece of crap."

"Maybe."

"What's that supposed to mean? For all we know he was on his way to rape somebody," Landry says. "Dressed like this—he certainly wasn't trying to watch cable TV for free. I'm thinking he got what he deserved."

Schroder nods. Still, if he was planning on peeking into somebody's apartment—surely there was an easier way.

They all turn as one as the media vans begin their assault on the scene, all pulling up at the same time. The cameramen and reporters climb out and move around the barriers to get closer. Police constables push them back. Cameras are hoisted up onto shoulders and the sun glints off the lenses.

"And the show gets an audience," Landry says.

"We should cover him up," Schroder says, glancing up at the other tall buildings surrounding them. Landry is right—this is a hell of a show. People are standing in the windows, all staring down and pointing, their faces full of excitement. The reporters scan the buildings for better vantage points to invade the dead man's privacy from. A constable comes over and goes about covering the victim, a white sheet of canvas hiding the view away from the public. Not all the blood has dried and some of it seeps into the material.

"Anything in his pockets?" Schroder asks.

"Nothing."

"I'm all done with him," Sheldon says. "Pretty obvious what happened, but I'll know more once we get him back to the morgue. Messed up the way he is, he must have gotten pretty high."

"I'm not so sure," Schroder says. "All of this—something here doesn't add up."

Landry and Sheldon glance at the body, at the building, at the body again, then back at Schroder. "You want to elaborate on that, Carl? What exactly are we missing here? A mostly naked dead man with suction cups strapped to him at the base of an apartment building with a couple of hundred windows—what doesn't add up?"

"I don't get it," Schroder says. "I mean, it seems a hell of an effort to go to just to peep through some windows. Problem is, all the effort in the world wouldn't have helped him out. This whole suction cup thing, it's a myth. You can't scale buildings like that. Can't be done."

Schroder takes a step back to reduce the glare and gazes up the side of the building. None of the floors have balconies.

"All that means is he started climbing from higher up. Maybe he has an apartment here," Landry says. "He probably climbed out on the sixth or seventh floor, and fell from the sixth or the seventh floor. Come on, Carl, we didn't call you down here to try and make us look like idiots—there's no crime here."

"If there's no crime, why did you call me down?"

Landry rolls his shoulders back, and when he talks, a vein pops out in his forehead and starts throbbing. "For once the victim is someone who deserved it. For once the victim isn't some girl who smiled at the wrong guy and got sliced up for it. Come on, Carl, how many times have we seen that, huh? And this time—well, this time it's score one for the good guys."

"How come nobody found him earlier?" Schroder asks.

"There was a car parked at the front of the alley, blocking the view. Belonged to one of the tenants. He normally leaves it parked here overnight. He only came to move it half an hour ago."

"Time of death is about twelve hours," Sheldon says.

"Tell me, when he climbed out last night, before he fell, do you think he closed the window?"

"What?" Landry asks.

"None of the windows are open."

They all study the side of the building. There's no way the victim climbed out and made the effort to close the window behind him. There's no way he could have gone more than a meter before the suction cups gave way.

"Shit," Landry says. He pulls a packet of cigarettes out of his pocket and dances one across his fingers.

"Maybe he managed to climb all the way up from the ground," Sheldon suggests.

"It can't happen," Schroder says. "Look it up. Try it out. Do whatever you need to, but it doesn't work."

"How do you know for sure?" Landry asks.

"I saw it on the Discovery Channel."

"Maybe he took the elevator to the roof and climbed down," Landry says.

"Take another look," Schroder says. Between the roof and the top apartments is about a two-meter strip of concrete. "This isn't what it seems. This guy was a victim of something."

"I still don't get it," Landry says, putting the cigarette back. "What you're saying makes sense, I see that, but there are other alternatives."

"Like what?" Schroder asks, reaching into his pocket for his ringing cell phone.

"Like maybe the suction cups worked."

"Or maybe somebody dressed him up," Schroder points out, "and threw him off the roof." He takes the call. The woman on the other end of the phone talks quickly, and thirty seconds later he's back in his car, racing toward the bank, fighting for position with the reporters making their way in the same direction.

chapter three

It's a moment in a movie. Something so incredibly implausible and so far away from what I'm thinking about that I can't even comprehend it. I actually look away for a second, just this normal slice of life in this everyday normal bank where abnormal things don't happen, back to the family-oriented posters and floating interest rates, back to Jodie sitting opposite me—and then, somehow, somehow, it all becomes real.

The doors are two large side-by-side glass doors that open automatically as indiscriminately for these men as they did for me and my wife. The six men enter in three groups of two. The first group goes left, the second, right, and the third, straight ahead. It's all happening behind Jodie and she has no idea what's going on. She keeps talking. Most of the people are still talking. Some glance up at the men for a second before returning to what they were doing, then the realization of what they saw kicks in, the disbelief on their faces perhaps comical under other circumstances. Others seem to be noticing immediately, perhaps people who have seen this kind of thing on TV enough times to figure out what happens next. They're dropping out of sight behind desks. All this and the men haven't even made a sound.

Jodie watches my face. She hears the collective gasp from everybody else. She twists her head to see what's happening. A woman screams.

The six men are all wearing balaclavas. They're all wearing black jerseys and black jeans and could all have just come from a heavy metal concert. They move calmly but forcefully forward, surrounded by an air of confidence the six shotguns provide. They look like they own the bank. They look like never in their lives have they been said no to. The police station is a five-minute walk from here, which means the clock is ticking. Jodie reaches out and I take her hand.

"Next person to move gets their head taken off," one of them yells, and most people come to a dead stop, a few more keep running, others are hiding behind anything that remotely covers their bodies. The security guard's face turns about as white as his shirt. He's absolutely motionless. He's armed with a radio and the knowledge he's not earning anything more than minimum wage to be here, and he's trying to figure out what good either of those things are going to do against six men with shotguns. He doesn't get far in his figuring, unless he was figuring on inaction, which he does down to perfection. He raises his hands in the air but doesn't manage to do anything else, including duck, before one of the two men that went in his direction turns the stock of the shotgun and smashes it hard into his jaw. The guard's head snaps back with a sick crack. He hits the floor, his body slumping in a heap, limbs twisted everywhere. All this and only fifteen seconds have passed. A silent alarm may have been tripped, or maybe the bank cut back on a few of those features so they could offer the competitive interest rates the posters are going on about. The bank staff have open mouths and wide eyes and any training they've been given is all shot to hell, a snapshot in a moment of time, like somebody pressed the pause button on life.

"It's going to be okay," I say, and I squeeze Jodie's hand tight. She gives me a look that suggests she doesn't think things are going to be okay. She's pale and scared and I'm the same way and I wish we'd ordered something for lunch that would have taken longer to prepare.

The same guy who yelled moves closer to the bank tellers. "Everybody on this side of the counter move over there," he says, and he points to the far left of the line of counters. Nobody moves. "Now! And get down on the ground!"

We all move as one, footsteps shuffling on the floor, everybody hunched over and moving awkwardly, like old folks in a retirement home running from the Reaper. I don't let go of Jodie's hand. We sit on the ground, maybe twenty-five of us, all scared, all thinking the same thing—that we should have made more of Christmas last year.

The six men, in three teams of two, spread further out to the sides. One of them turns and points his gun at the door, ready for more customers to wander on in, even though the whole front of the bank is made up of glass and everybody outside is staring at us. The man barking the instructions reaches the counter.

"You," he yells, and he points his shotgun at a woman behind the counter. All the makeup in the world couldn't hide the tightening of her features. "Take these back to the vault and fill them." He throws some bags at her. They hit her counter and she doesn't move. "Now!" he says.

"What?"

"Fill them or die. The choice is yours."

She gets it. She picks up the bags.

"Help her," he says, pointing at another of the bank tellers. "You as well," he says, glaring at a third. "And you too," he adds, waving the gun at a fourth. "And if all four of you aren't back here in two minutes we open fire on everybody else. Get that?"

As soon as the four disappear, an office door opens. We all turn toward it. A man with a pink tie and his shirtsleeves rolled up stands there with his hands raised in the air, and his head tilted and hunched down slightly, as if trying to avoid sniper fire.

"P . . . p . . . please, I'm the manager, please don't hurt anybody and—"

He doesn't get to say any more. The shotgun barks and people cry out. The manager isn't thrown backward like in movies. He just stands where he was shot. His head hangs down so he seems to study the angry wound in his chest, seems to notice his shirt has blossomed red, and gravity pulls at the features on his face, making him appear sad. Then he folds at the waist, his ass going backwards, his feet staying in the same place, so when he hits the ground he's folded in half, his legs out straight, his face against his knees, and he stays in that position with his arms by his side. The wall behind where he stood is streaked in blood, the window next to the door is shattered, other small pellets are buried into the wall. The manager looks like he's stretching, warming up for yoga.

"Jesus," I whisper, and I can see other people mouthing the same word but can't hear it because my ears are still ringing. People are raising their hands to their faces. Others are crying. A man in his late sixties or early seventies has wet himself. A woman has passed out, her face pressing into the floor, looking far more relaxed than anybody else here.

Jodie's grip is almost breaking my fingers.

"Stay calm," I say, "just stay calm."

"Everybody shut up!" one of the men yells, then he fires another shot, this one into the ceiling. Plaster dust rains down, it settles on his shoulders like dandruff.

The four people return from the vault. The bags are bulging with cash and obviously heavy. They manage to lift them up onto the counter.

"Too slow," the man says, talking to the bank teller he first singled out. He pumps the shotgun and levels it at her chest. "You're coming with us," he says.

"No, no," she says.

"Wait!"

Everybody turns to the voice. It takes a moment to realize that they've all turned toward me, and a longer moment to figure out the reason for that—I'm the one who spoke. The man holding the shotgun on the bank teller turns his head toward me.

"What?" he says.

"Eddie," Jodie says, "what are you doing?"

I have no idea. People are staring at me like I'm an anomaly, like they haven't seen a twenty-nine-year-old white guy speaking in a bank before. I get onto my knees, then onto my feet, swaying slightly, with still no idea what I'm doing or why I called out. "I said wait," I say, and my voice is firm.

"We all heard what you said," he says, "and I think we're all curious now as to what you're planning on doing next."

"You've got what you came for," I say, and the girl with the gun pointed at her takes the distraction to duck down behind the counter. Everybody back there does.

The man turns back to where she just was. "Hey, get back up here."

She doesn't answer.

"Please. You don't have to hurt anybody else," I say.

"I didn't realize you were giving the orders here," he says, looking over the counter for the woman. He can't get an angle on her.

"Eddie," Jodie says.

"It's okay, Jodie."

"We have to go," another of them says, his finger pressed against his ear, listening to something small. "The police are only two minutes away."

"Shit," the first guy says, and he's staring at me now. "Okay, buddy, you're volunteering."

"I'll do what you want as long as you don't hurt anybody else," I say.

He offers a short, cold laugh. "No, you got it all wrong. You didn't volunteer yourself, you went ahead and volunteered that pretty little thing next to you."

"Don't," I say, and I step toward the man coming toward me and put my hand out in a stopping gesture. He doesn't even slow down. He comes in around my arm and hits me with the gun in the side of my face, hard enough to knock me down.

"Eddie . . ." Jodie is pulled to her feet.

Things are out of focus. I've fallen onto my side. I get my hands onto the ground and push up. There are two Jodies. Twelve gunmen.

They pick up the bags of cash and head for the door. Nobody else is moving. Nobody else is helping. The twelve men turn back into six, they're at the door and they have Jodie with them. I figure if the police are only two minutes away they're probably driving and the Friday lunchtime traffic has brought them to a crawl.

"Eddie," Jodie screams, reaching toward me, and it takes two of them to drag her through the door. I get to my feet, wobbling left and right somewhat. I stumble over my feet and trip myself up, hitting the floor hard with my palms. They toss the bags of money inside a van and five of them climb in right alongside it. The sixth guy keeps holding my wife.

I get outside. Nobody follows me. There are people on the street, but they're all ducked down behind parked cars and huddling in shop doorways. Shopwindows painted over with Christmas scenes have faces pressed against the glass. The kids in the hoodies are popping their heads up from behind a row of motorbikes and pointing cell phones at us. I can't hear any sirens or see any police. Cars have stopped about twenty meters away in both directions. The guy pushes Jodie toward me. She cries out and stumbles. She reaches out for balance and I can tell she's going down, she's going to hit the sidewalk.

He raises the shotgun. He points it right at her. He doesn't even hesitate, just pulls the trigger. *Shoot her in the back, Jack.*

"No," I scream, but the word is lost over the explosion. My wife hits the road. The shooter jumps into the back of the van and closes the door. The driver accelerates hard, the engine revs loudly and smoke drifts up off the tires. I reach my wife as the van turns the corner, running a red light and leaving us alone.

chapter four

Keep her alive, Clive.

I have no idea why I keep thinking of the song Jodie sang this morning, perhaps the last song she'll ever get to sing, steam from the shower thick in the air, the penguin radio launching out classic songs from a classic hits station. The words are in my head but they don't even feel like mine, as though somebody put them there, an English teacher or a bad comedian having reached out somehow and implanted them.

She's dead, Fred—and don't worry, you'll be hearing from me soon.

I scream for help but the only thing people are brave enough to do is step out from whatever hole they hid in and point cell phone cameras at me while others make calls. I try to hold the blood inside her, but it keeps flowing.

"Jodie, oh God, Jodie, it's going to be okay," I say, and I roll her onto her side so I can see her face while keeping pressure on her back. There is so much blood. Way too much blood. It's seeping between my fingers. It's like water. I need more hands. More help.

I need a miracle.

Jodie's eyes are open and she turns them toward me but focuses beyond me, somewhere a thousand miles away.

"It's going to be okay," I say. "I promise."

"My shoes hurt," she says, and she smiles, and she keeps staring past me and a moment later I realize she's no longer seeing anything at all.

"Jodie . . ."

There are too many holes in her, I can't stem them all. Her face is pale, except around her nose which has been broken and flattened when she fell. Blood is smeared there, there's a deep cut in her upper lip where it's been sliced by her teeth.

"Please, please, Jodie, don't do this, don't do this," I say. "Don't leave me alone."

But Jodie is doing this.

"Jodie, please," I say, but my words are only whispers now.

People move closer to get a better look, to get a better angle, a clearer photo. Nobody offers to help. Maybe they can see there is no point. Nobody has come out of the bank—either they're in too much shock or maybe they're trying to save the manager and the security guard. Sirens appear in the distance and get louder, and soon they appear, police cars and ambulances, all of them too late. The safety they bring with them allows more bystanders to come forward and watch and point and revel in the drama. Two paramedics rush over to Jodie, each of them carrying a case of lifesaving tools.

"Out of the way," one of them says.

"She's . . ."

"Move," he repeats.

I move aside. The two men crouch down over her. One of them slides a pair of scissors up her shirt and exposes the wounds. His expression doesn't change. He's seen it all before.

"No pulse," the other one says. "It doesn't look . . ."

"I know, I know," the first one says.

He pulls padding out from his case and jams it against the wound as if trying to pack the hole. They roll her onto her back and while one begins CPR, the other fires up a defibrillator. They hold off on using it, pursuing the CPR which—for the moment—couldn't be any more useless.

"Shock her," the first one says.

For a moment the two men stare at each other, the words unspoken, but I can see what they're saying. They both know there's no point. Both think it's too late. One of them figures it's best to at least put on a show because I'm watching.

They attach large pads to her chest, but they work slowly, methodically, their body language admitting defeat. Jodie's body arches upward as the volts go through her, putting tension on her spine. The pool of blood on the ground beneath her grows as the holes in her back widen and close like small apertures.

"Again."

They try it again. Then a third time. Then they go about packing everything away.

"I'm sorry," one of them says.

"Do something else," I say.

"There is nothing else."

"There has to be."

"There's too much damage. She's too far gone. Even if we'd been here sooner there's nothing we could have done. The gunshot—I'm sorry, mate," he says, slowly shaking his head.

"She can't die like this."

"She's already dead. She's been dead from the moment she got hit."

"No, no, you're wrong. She's supposed to die in another fifty years. We're going to grow old together."

"Sorry, mate, I truly wish there was something we could do."

I take a step toward him. He steps back. "You can do something," I say. "You can save her."

His partner comes over. They've been in this situation before.

"I said help her."

"I'm sorry, mate. We've done all we can."

Armed police officers are filling the street. One of them heads toward us.

"Please," I say. "There has to be something."

"I wish there was, I truly do," he says, and then they walk away and head toward the bank, where two other paramedics are coming out, wheeling a gurney with the security guard on it who at the moment is still alive. The armed officer stops coming over and decides to give another officer a hand to string yellow police tape all over the place, making the street a lot more colorful, blending the crime scene into the Christmas atmosphere of town—tinsel, fake Santas, candy canes, fake snow, and real blood.

I sit on the ground and hold my wife. I cradle her head in my lap and stroke her hair. I close her eyes but they keep opening up about halfway. The ground is blotted in blood and bandaging, there's a bloody latex glove lying on her leg. A man in a suit comes up to me and crouches down. "I'm sorry for your loss," he says, and I doubt he really understands the word "sorry" or the word "loss." Nobody can. "The van, did you see a license plate? Did you see anything?"

"They killed her."

"Please, sir, this is important. If you . . ."

"They wanted a volunteer. Got to be twenty-five people in that bank. They could have taken anybody but they took Jodie. That's a four percent chance. Calculate in that one person who was already dead, and that's what? What?" I look up at him. "What the hell does that make it? Tell me!" I shout. "Tell me!"

"The van. Did you see it?"

"All I could see was Jodie. I wish I saw more. I wish we'd never come here today. I wish . . ." I run out of words.

"Okay, okay, sir. You should step away from her now, you have to let us do our job."

"Get away from me," I say, and the words come out evenly and forcefully and he doesn't argue. He steps away and I don't watch where he goes. For a while nobody else approaches me. They see my dead wife and they know I didn't shoot her so they leave me be. Somewhere else in the city they're chasing the van, maybe they've caught it already. There's been a shoot-out and all six bank robbers are dead. They're all dying slowly from horrible, horrible gunshot wounds.

I want these people to be dead. I need them to be dead. Media vans speed into the street and brake heavily behind the barriers that have been set up. They jump out of their vans as if they're on fire. Dozens of lenses and hundreds of eyes all staring at me, I'm sure some of them are making the connection, their synapses firing, thinking, we know that guy, we know that guy, their hunger for the story evident in the way their eyes almost bug out of their skulls as they stare in excitement, evident in the way they try to push past the officers forming a perimeter. I want to walk among them, wipe my wife's blood on their faces, over their hands, I want to make them part of the story and ask them how it feels, ask how they can thrive on such suffering.

I don't have the strength, and if I did, it would only add to their frenzy, offer up sound bites and make them more money. All I can do is cradle my wife and watch her become blurry as the anger and despair take their toll and the tears fall freely, dripping onto Jodie's face.

Police push the barriers further back. They try clearing the street but the show is too good for these people to miss. Arguments turn into shouting matches. Some of the reporters yell questions at me. In the end the police are outnumbered. The police are always outnumbered. Reporters appear at the windows of neighboring buildings, filming us from the floors above.

A woman comes over and touches my shoulder and tells me it's time to let Jodie go. I don't want to, but I know I have to.

"Get me something," I say, "to put over her."

"Sir . . ."

"Please."

She comes back with a thick white sheet. I bunch up a corner of it into as good a pillow as I can make and prop it under Jodie's head. I spread the rest over her. I step back and can't pull myself away from the shape beneath it. I can still taste the lunch in my mouth, can still feel her hand in my hand as we walked to the bank.

"We'll take care of her," the woman says, and she puts her hands on my arm. "Please, it's time to come inside," she says, and I let her lead me, my wife left outside, my wife an item now, a piece of evidence, and I crouch over and throw up before stepping back into the bank.

chapter five

Where there is room, the cars pull over for him, his siren warning of the urgency. The problem is there isn't always room and he gets caught up at intersections, boxed in by traffic that on Friday afternoons takes on a life of its own. Cars that try to pull over for him end up blocking the way, people panicking and almost causing accidents. Schroder's already heard the bank robbers made a clean exit. Heard about the victims. There are plenty of armed officers on the scene but it's all too late.

The entire block is cordoned off. Suction Cup Guy is out of Schroder's mind as he parks outside the barriers, ducks under the police tape, and walks into the carnage. There's a body in the middle of the street with a sheet over it. The woman. There are hundreds of onlookers and dozens of media and he figures, as bad as this is for the people who were in the bank, as bad as it is for the dead woman in the street, today is turning out to be a great day for the media and sightseers. A bad day for the cops is gold for the six o'clock news. A couple of street performers are hanging out behind everybody else, juggling bright-colored objects and trying to cash in on the gathering crowd.

Inside the bank people are pale, they're lost and confused and there is streaked makeup from tears and swollen eyes. He's the third detective on the scene, and he's quickly given updates from the other two. There's a body lying outside an office, this one exposed. He gives an instruction to cover it, hoping it will go some way to calming the witnesses.

The husband of the woman killed is sitting in another office.

"Edward Hunter," one of the detectives says, pointing toward him.

"Hunter?"

"Yeah. Why? You recognize him?"

"I think so, but the name doesn't line up. Anybody spoken to him yet?" Schroder asks.

"He only just came inside. We almost had to pull him away from his wife."

The office has new furniture and a rubber plant in the corner with leaves coated in dust. Schroder steps inside and closes the door and Edward Hunter looks up from the desk and watches him with eyes that are bloodshot.

"It's colder in here than before," Edward says, then pulls his shirt away from his body. It's covered in blood and sticking against him.

Outside the office more people are arriving, other detectives to take statements. Men in white nylon suits are scouring the scene for evidence—the problem is the scene has been trampled over by too many people already.

"My name is Carl Schroder," he says, sitting down opposite Edward and not offering to shake hands, "and I know this is difficult, I know answering questions is the last thing you want to do right now, but you . . ."

"Not difficult," Edward answers. "Impossible."

"You're right. It is impossible." He pauses, taking in the impossibility of the situation. He isn't the one who woke up today and lost his wife.

"Are you married?" Edward asks.

"Please, we need to focus . . ."

"You imagine what it'd be like if that was your wife out there?"

"I'd want the men who did this caught."

"You mean you haven't found them yet?"

"We're working on it, Edward. It is Edward, right? Not Jack?"

"I didn't give you my name."

"I know."

"Jack's my father's name, not mine, not anymore. Which means you recognize me. Everybody recognizes me."

"Well, I don't know about that."

"It's true. You recognized me. You didn't know whether to call me Jack or Edward, so you knew. Everybody knows."

"I recognized you because I was there the day your dad was arrested."

"Yeah?"

"Yeah," he answers. It was his first year on the force. He hadn't spoken to Jack Hunter Sr., or really been anywhere near him. He'd been one of the constables who'd come along for the ride. He got a real good look at Jack Hunter Junior, the young boy, full of tears and pain.

"I remember you," Jack—now Edward—says. "But not from then. From the year after. You were the one who came when Mum died."

"I know," Schroder answers. That was his second year on the force. He and his partner had gone inside and found the woman in the bathtub. He can still recall exactly how she looked, how the bathroom felt, can picture the emptiness in her eyes. Edward and his sister were sitting on the bathroom floor, the sister with her arm around Edward, both of them leaning against the wall, Edward unable to take his eyes from the floor. Schroder and his partner had gone in and taken the children out before examining the body. The sister had told them what had happened. Edward never said a word.

"You're always there when my family is hurting," Edward says, and Schroder can see the little boy all those years ago in this man now. "And you've never made it any better. Am I a suspect in this, now that you know who I am?" his voice getting louder. Angrier.

"Of course not. Why would you think that?"

"People always think weird shit like that. I've grown up with it."

"What I need from you is to focus, Edward. I know this is hard," he says, "but this is the time where you can help the most."

"They just, they just came into the bank," Edward says, shaking his head as he talks and turning his palms up, "you know? Just came in like they owned the place. The way they shot the manager, they didn't care. They didn't have to kill anybody. They were getting their money and . . . I mean, why do that? Why take the time to do that? Even when it was all done, they took Jodie with them. Why would they do that?"

"We've heard from other witnesses the men said they wanted a volunteer."

"I tried to get them to take me."

"I know you did. They also said you saved one of the tellers from being taken, maybe even saving her life."

"What?"

"They say you called out. They say the men were going to take her, and you stopped them. That was a brave thing," he says, trying to prompt Edward. "A brave thing, risking your life."

"Yeah, it wasn't my life I risked in the end, was it? They were going to take her and they took Jodie instead."

"You couldn't have known that."

"You think?"

"It's a fact. It's a bad situation, Edward, a bad situation and people died, and you're the only one in that bank who had the balls to try and do something about it, to try and save somebody's life, and that woman is alive thanks to you."

"It's a shitty flip side, right? She's alive because of me and my wife is dead for the same reason. It's no different from me pulling the trigger myself."

"It's very different," he says.

"All the people in here and they took her. They didn't need to take anybody."

Schroder knows exactly why they took her. They wanted somebody dead out on the road. They wanted to use up more police resources.

It creates confusion and panic and gives them more of a lead time. It shuts down traffic into the street, creates congestion, slows down the roads in and out of town, the cars that had stopped outside the bank are still out there, blocked in. He doesn't tell Edward any of this. Doesn't tell him that his wife was a tool, a device they used to help them escape.

"There was nothing you could have done," Schroder says.

"You're wrong on that. There was everything I could have done. I could have made the appointment for a different time. I could have kept my mouth shut and let that other woman get taken. Maybe they wouldn't have killed her. I could have fought more, could have insisted they take me instead."

"It's not your fault."

"Then why does it feel like it is?"

"We have to focus, Edward, on finding the men who did this."

"I know. I know."

"Then it's time to tell me what happened. Start at the beginning," he says.

"Okay," Edward says, tears slowly sliding down his face. Schroder takes out his notebook and writes it all down.

chapter six

I'm given a lift home. The sun is past its peak and the city seems darker now. The shadows cast by the tired buildings are small but ominous, the people on the streets appear defeated, those caught in half shadows are dazed, the trees and plants and flowers that make up the garden city have all lost their vibrancy—the life is draining out of the world. We pass rundown fruit stalls on the side of the road, FOR SALE signs in front of houses that people want to leave. The blood on my clothes is drying, the color fading from bright red to deep maroon, my body itchy where the stains are stiff and scratchy. With every passing second the distance between me and Jodie stretches, and the hope of getting her back finally turns into the despair it was the moment I saw her gunned down. This is my city, my home, the place I loved but love no more. Now I don't know what it is. Certainly not my home. Not now. Now it's the place that killed my wife and took my daughter's mother away. Now it's a hellhole and I don't see any future here.

The officer driving doesn't say anything. He's never gotten around to preparing any rhetorical conversation for this exact situation. It's a thirty-minute drive in busy traffic in which the world goes by and I wonder how I can change it. He's relieved when he lets me out in my driveway. I've taken a car ride away from one reality to a new one. There aren't any neighbors walking about or working in their gardens. The houses are all dirty, the plants and trees all too dry, the cars old and the sidewalks cracked, the colors everywhere seem so diluted. There are brief moments—less than a second—where I'm distracted and Jodie is still alive, small lifetime moments like putting my key in the door—*bang!* A distraction—and the world is okay. Then that split second passes and reality floods back in, crushing me.

It's almost four o'clock and Sam has been picked up from school by Jodie's parents. One of the detectives arranged it. One of them made the call so I didn't have to, and I don't know who broke the news to them first, the detective or the media. From a stranger they learned their daughter had the misfortune of getting herself gunned down this afternoon, had the misfortune of being married to a man who couldn't keep his mouth shut, and they'd need to pick their granddaughter up from school.

My house has become a museum, everything inside a relic of my past, happy memories all turning to dust. The air-conditioning was switched off this morning so the house is stuffy. Jodie has been dead for three hours and I'm stepping into a different place, the ghost of the house that it was this morning. I wander through it, not really knowing what to do. Jodie's stuff is everywhere and I can't see myself ever packing any of it away. Her coffee cup is still on the bench, the bottom 10 percent still there, cold and manky. Toast crumbs form a trail across the kitchen floor. Makeup on the bathroom vanity, her towel, still damp, hanging on the rail. Jodie is missing and she's here all at the same time, the house waiting for her to walk in, her husband waiting for the same thing. There's an outfit lying on the bed; she must have been ready to wear one thing, then changed her mind. Jodie is always like that, she's always one minute deciding to . . .

Was. It's "was" now.

"Jesus," I whisper, and sit down on the edge of the bed. I pick up her top and hold it against my face and cry into it. What do I do with her clothes? Keep them? Give them away?

I don't know when I'm supposed to think those kind of things, what kind of person it makes me for realizing it now. Do I do the washing and hang her clothes back up? Do I go to work next week? Do I leave Jodie's clothes lying about the floor until after the funeral, then pack them up? My bosses at work don't even know what's happened. They know I went for lunch and haven't come back.

I walk up and down the hallway—I just need somebody to tell me what to do.

I take off my clothes and lay them on the bed next to Jodie's. A more creative man might study the bloodstains and find patterns in them, shapes of animals or boats, but all I see is my wife as she lay on the ground bleeding. They're ruined. I roll them into a ball, then find myself coming to a complete standstill. I stare at them for a while. The cuffs are the bloodiest, then the arms, then the front. One of the buttons is missing. There isn't any blood on the back at all. I straighten them out and hang them up.

I take a long shower, blood streaking off my skin, the penguin shower radio quiet as it watches me. I stare in the mirror at the large bruise on my face from the blow I took. The skin is slightly torn up, and one of my eyes doesn't open fully—which I hadn't even noticed until now. I don't want to know this man anymore because this man got his wife killed. I picture it all happening over and over. I think about the bank teller, the way the shooter leveled his gun at her. Then I think about the 4 percent chance I came up with earlier when figuring the odds of Jodie being the volunteer, and realize it's a false statistic since there wasn't any probability involved. There would have been, if I hadn't shouted out. If I'd kept quiet then Jodie would have had as much chance as anybody of living or dying—but I took that chance and turned it into a certainty. And why? Why the hell did I shout out? Schroder said it was to save somebody. Maybe that was it. Maybe I thought I could make a difference. Only thing I know is I was as surprised as everybody else—it didn't sound like me and wasn't the kind of thing I thought I'd ever do. Probably not the kind of thing anybody thought I'd ever do—the son of a serial killer trying to save a life. Well, Mission Accomplished. That woman is alive and Jodie is dead—I traded one life for another. This is what it's like to play God, I suppose—but without the ability to do any good.

When the phone rings it turns out to be a reporter. So does the second call. And the third. Before taking it off the hook I phone Nathaniel and Diana—Jodie's parents. Nat answers and he's already crying before I can say much.

"I don't really know what to say, Eddie," he says, his voice close to breaking. I've never heard him cry before. Nat, this solid, near-retirement-age man who could break a man in half, is weeping into the phone, he sounds like a child. "But we've been talking, and we think, we think that both you and Sam might, um, might be best staying with us tonight. Then she can stay with us tomorrow to give you a chance to . . . to get things organized."

"I don't know. I think I need her here. All I know is that I have to hold her and tell her everything is going to be okay."

"It's not going to be okay."

"What the hell would you have me tell her?" I ask, the emotion on its way, pissed off at Nat now—but of course he doesn't know what to say or do either, he's just trying his best. "That our lives are going to fall apart?"

He doesn't answer.

Five seconds go by. "Shit, I'm sorry, Nat," I say, and I exhale loudly. "I didn't mean . . . I . . . hell, I don't know."

"None of us know."

"I'm going to come and get her."

"Are you in any state to look after her? Think about what's best for her, Eddie. Come and stay with us tonight. It's for the best. Then, then tomorrow you can . . . we can, together, we can . . ." He doesn't finish.

"She doesn't know yet, does she," I say, my heart sinking even more.

"We wanted to tell her. And we were going to, but . . . I don't know. It's not that it was too hard, it's . . . well, we thought you'd be the one who'd want to tell her. Diana and me, we thought it was best that way, if we were all together when we told her. For everybody."

"You did the right thing," I say, and I can hardly breathe now, it feels like a golf ball is lodged down my throat. "I'm on my way," I say, and I hang up then take the phone off the hook.

My car isn't here. Jodie's isn't either. I phone a taxi company and a woman with no patience answers the phone and snaps at me, asking where I am and where I want to go.

I can't seem to get any words out.

"Yes? Yes? You want to go somewhere, don't you?" she says. "Or are you wasting my time?"

"Umm, I, I . . . I don't know," I say.

"Weirdo," she says, then hangs up. I take a moment to gather my thoughts before calling another company, and this time I'm able to put sounds to the names of the places.

"Somebody will be there in ten minutes," the woman says. "Have a nice day," she adds, and I almost burst into tears.

The taxi takes me into the city. The traffic is heavy; people are all following each other too closely and trying to change lanes. The driver gives me a funny stare, and I know the one, it's the one where he's thinking, *Is that the little boy, the one whose dad preyed on this city twenty and thirty and forty years earlier before and during and after he was born?* Henry the homeless guy is still outside the parking building, a sandwich instead of a vodka bottle in his hand, the Bible still in the other hand.

"Spare change?" he asks. He's dressed in clothes made twenty years ago, with a baseball cap made from recycled cardboard, and there's something about him that suddenly disgusts me even though he never has before. I have the urge to kick him. I look away and move quickly past before I can give in to the temptation. I run up the stairs all the way to where my car is.

I make my way out of the building, almost crippling a couple of other cars, almost clipping a couple of walls, driving perhaps too fast, perhaps even almost clipping a couple of people. I get onto the street and I'm two blocks away from the bank. I head in the opposite direction. Traffic is thick. I don't see a single police car anywhere. I drive alongside the Avon where the grassy banks are heavy with food wrappers and empty drink cans, broken up by the occasional homeless person sniffing glue in the sun while working on his tan. The breeze is coming from that direction, picking up some cool air off the dark water. Traffic lights have broken down at a few of the bigger intersections, the orange lights flashing, drivers fending for themselves as they don't know whether to give way or drive through.

It takes me forty minutes to get to my in-laws. They look awful. They look like some creature came around and reached inside of them and ripped out every happy memory they've ever had. They give me tight hugs and tell me that we'll all get through this. I hug them back and tell them nothing.

Jodie's parents have never approved of me. It's not that I ever did anything wrong, or treated Jodie badly. It's because of my father's past. Her parents have always seen me as a loaded gun. They've always feared for their daughter. They tried to be pleasant, but they could never hide the fear that I've seen on other faces growing up— the one of suspicion. It's been twenty years since my father was arrested for murder—that's twenty years of having people around me always wondering, wondering, when's Eddie going to become his father's son? What is Eddie capable of? Jodie's parents thought I was capable of slicing their daughter and granddaughter into a hundred pieces. Sum it all up, put a bottom line on it, and their fear their daughter would die at my hands came true.

Sam is asleep on the couch in the living room. I've seen plenty of photos of Jodie when she was a small girl, and right now Sam looks exactly the same. Her favorite teddy bear is clutched under her chin, her arm folded over it, holding it tight. I stand in the doorway and stare at her and my in-laws stand next to me and stare at her too. Nat has a key to my house—they must have swung by there first to pick up the teddy bear and probably some clothes. The plan all along had been for Sam to stay here anyway, so Jodie and I could go to my work Christmas party tonight.

"Let me make some dinner," Diana says, and the words seem out of place and she knows it. I have no intention of eating. Probably none of us do. She has to do something, anything but stand still and let the terror get hold of her.

Sam wakes up. It's slow at first, and then she sees me, and her face lights up. "Daddy!" she says, and she jumps up and has halved the distance between us. She's six years old and that's all she needs to be to immediately know something is horribly wrong. She can see it in our faces. "Where's Mummy?" she asks, and her approach is cautious now.

I break down in tears and we do our best to explain.

chapter seven

The street has cleared somewhat, the onlookers having thinned out from lack of excitement. The media presence is still heavy, reporters desperate to catch more nuggets of gold with their cameras, probably the bodies being loaded onto stretchers. There is blood and glass and pieces of drywall and splinters scattered over the floor of the bank. Detective Schroder steps around them to the other side of the counter; Dean Wellington, the South Island manager for South Pacific Banks, follows him.

"I still can't believe this has happened," Wellington says, his face flushed with the disbelief he's feeling. "I mean, Jesus, what a mess. We're talking about all that money, we've got damage to the building, we've got staff members ready to hand in their resignations, and this whole thing is a press nightmare. People aren't going to want to walk through these doors for some time. James was a good manager, a good man, we won't be able to replace him until after the holiday season. The timing of all this . . ."

"People died," Schroder says.

Wellington adjusts his tie, pulling down on the knot and tightening it. "I know that, Jesus, don't you think I know that? But this bank services thousands and thousands of people. We still have a responsibility to them, and you have a responsibility to find the men who did this. The bank wants its money back."

Schroder stares at him for a few seconds. "Just take me to the vault."

The vault is near the back of the bank in a downstairs basement, two doors in between requiring swipe cards to enter. The metal door is about half a meter higher and half a meter wider than any normal door and made from solid steel. Inside, the vault is the size of a single bedroom. There are shelves stacked neatly with blocks of cash.

"How much does this vault hold?"

"Well, normally we'll have a float of around a million dollars," Wellington answers, "but this time of year, we stock up on more cash. We have to reload the ATM machine four to five times more often and people are always coming in for cash. Christmas is still a cash business," he says. "Not everybody has a credit card."

"So how much?"

"About five million."

"And how much was taken?"

"We still have to add up what's here—but if you want a quick estimate, we think we're talking somewhere around three million dollars."

"And the procedure in a bank robbery?"

"It's simple. Do what the robbers tell you to do. Press the silent alarm, and if you have to come out to the vault, make sure you load in the dye packs."

"And they loaded them?"

"Yes. They would have gone off by now."

"How do they work?"

"They're magnetic. We store them next to a magnetic plate that controls them. You take them away from that, and it activates a timer. They explode five minutes after they've been moved. It ruins

44

all the money, covers it all in red ink. Covers the robbers in ink too."

"How long until you can get an amount?"

"An hour. Two at the most."

The blocks of remaining cash vary between orange, blue, green, and purple—fives, tens, twenties, and fifties. Schroder wonders exactly what three million in cash would look like physically. He wonders how heavy the bags would have been.

"So the tellers loaded the bags," he says, thinking out loud.

"Yeah. Nobody else came back here."

"The robbers never examined the bags, right? According to witnesses, and looking at the footage, they grabbed the bags and another victim and left."

"So?"

"So why load the bags with hundreds?"

"What?"

"I don't see any red blocks of cash—the hundreds. The bank tellers could have loaded the bags with any amount. The bags would have weighed the same. Why not load them up with five- or ten-dollar notes?"

"Maybe they thought the robbers would check."

"Even so, they could have loaded the smaller amounts on the bottom. The robbers would never have known unless they tipped it all out."

"Maybe they were scared and thought that was the way to go."

"Maybe," Schroder says.

"It's a good point though," Wellington says, "and something we might consider implementing in case, god forbid, this ever happens again."

"You do that," Schroder says. "And get me some amounts," he says, and turns his back on the vault and heads upstairs.

chapter eight

I was eight years old when I had the urge to kill my first animal. I was nine before I finally did it. It was about a month before my dad got taken away. I don't know what created the urge. I think it'd been there all along, sleeping deep inside me, hidden—then one day woken.

The police showed up at the house on a cold July day. The sun was out but had lost the battle to winter; the air was so icy cold, the mist that formed in front of your face when you exhaled could almost be snatched up and broken in two. It was the kind of day you didn't want to get out of bed for. The trees were bare and the leaves had turned to slush on the ground, slush that would stick to your shoes, then get left behind on the carpet inside. It was a Wednesday morning. Usually the most exciting thing about Wednesdays was that they weren't Mondays. Of course this Wednesday started out a whole lot different. It began with me standing at the window in my school uniform watching the police cars pull up, sure they were there for me, that somehow, in some way, somebody had found out it'd been me who'd killed the neighbor's dog. I watched the cars come to a stop and men spill into the driveway, and I thought about running, just heading out the back door and jumping the fence, only I didn't know where I'd go. No, rather than run, I would lie.

The police surrounded the house. They came up to the front door. I was crying when my mother answered it. I had moved into my bedroom and was standing behind the door, listening, shaking. The men came inside and spoke to my dad. I didn't understand what was going on, why the police were coming to take my dad away for something I had done, and as hard as I tried to tell them the truth, I was too scared to say the words.

I came out from the bedroom in time to see them put handcuffs on my dad. I cried harder. I wanted to confess but didn't. I didn't understand at the time, but the police had come for an entirely different reason—a reason that involved the niche my father had carved out for himself, one that included a list of prostitutes and a very specific hobby.

I didn't go to school that day. Instead my mum's sister came to sit with me and Belinda while Mum went to the police station to learn what was going on. She was gone all day. A year later, after she was dead, her sister didn't want anything to do with me or Belinda ever again.

I don't know what kind of dog it was I killed in that month before Dad got taken away. It was certainly big enough, and dark enough, and most of the time angry enough. All it ever seemed to do was make noise. It'd howl at the moon and bark at the sun and growl at the breeze. The barks were high-pitched yaps that kept on coming, one after the other, scratching into my head like nails. The growls were low and threatening, scary, and the howls were long and painful. My neighbor never did anything to shut it up. Most times my neighbor wasn't there. He'd leave this dog of his chained to a rusty old stake hammered deep into the backyard. If the dog was lucky he'd sometimes get food and if he was extra lucky then sometimes he'd get water for company. Neighbors would open windows and doors and yell at the dog to shut up, but the frequency dropped off over the years as they gave up. In the summer the yard was hard-baked dirt, cracked into jigsaw patterns, and in the winter it was dark with mud and cold with frost. The dog was too hot in the summer and too cold in the winter and one or the other during the months between. I didn't know who to hate more, the dog or the owner, and in the end I hated them pretty much equally. The dog was hardwired to bark at things, and my neighbor was hardwired to treat the dog badly.

The urge grew slowly. I'd be at school staring at a math problem then suddenly I'd think about him, that dog, and I'd think about how great it would be if that dog could be divided into two. I'd get that thought a few times at school, and I'd get it plenty more times at home, and the thought never made me sick. At night I'd shake, my hands twitching as the dog barked, wondering why my dad didn't go and do something. Of course I didn't know it—but my dad couldn't do anything about it. He couldn't draw any attention to himself.

The urge kept growing. It reached a point where it was never far from my thoughts. It affected my schoolwork. My marks were slipping, my homework was suffering—if things didn't change I'd end up leaving school when I was fifteen and spend my life bouncing between being unemployed and unemployable. It seemed to me that the thing standing between me having the life I wanted and the life of cashing unemployment benefits was that dog. No matter what angle I attacked the problem from, I knew that as long as that dog barked I had no real future. I had to stop thinking about it.

Day and night this desire to see the dog dead grew stronger inside of me, gestating, becoming a deep-seated need that was ruling my life.

I told the urge I didn't know how to kill a dog.

The urge, one night, found a voice and whispered back. It told me it was easy. It told me everything was going to be okay now. Then it told me how.

My mother was the kind of woman who, when shopping for groceries, would stray from the list she had made and add what was on special, even if we already had plenty of the same thing at home.

We'd have cupboards full of paper towels and flour and tins of food that wouldn't fit in the pantry. Meat wasn't excluded from this list—the freezer was always full, the exact quantity within its depths an unknown. I took a piece of meat from the freezer knowing it wouldn't be missed. I hid it in the garage one morning before school, wrapped in an old rag and stuffed inside an empty paint container with a twisted lid. It thawed out while I studied at school and while the dog went about using up the rest of his barks. When I got home the steak was soft and felt fresh. My dad was at work, my mother was on the phone to her sister, and my own sister didn't have any intention of shifting from in front of the TV. The dog was barking from two doors down. It was loud and consistent, but painful-sounding too, the barking of a dog who didn't understand why it was suffering but didn't know anything else.

It took me only a few minutes to prepare the meat, another twenty seconds to walk to the neighbor's house. I walked up the driveway and knocked on the door, the piece of steak wrapped in plastic and tucked into my schoolbag. I knew nobody was home, but I had a story planned in case somebody was, one of those "my ball went over your fence" kind of stories people hear every day in every neighborhood all over the world. Nobody answered. The dog was barking like crazy. I went around to the side gate and the dog lurched forward on his chain, lunging forward over and over, the chain snapping tight on his neck, strangling him as it pulled him back. Sometimes it'd pull him off balance and he'd fall over, but he kept on getting up and charging forward again.

I took the steak out of the bag and threw it at the dog and he caught it in midair. He ripped into it immediately. He paused after a few seconds, took a step back, then sniffed at it, his suspicion of this last meal obvious in the way his jaw moved as if searching for what was wrong. It was the dog's bad luck to be as hungry as he was, his bad luck to have an instinct tell him he needed to eat because he never knew when his next meal would come. He lunged back into the steak and, even as blood dotted the short fur on the side of his mouth, he kept chewing. The steak disappeared in only a few bites. Then the dog started running in circles. He carried on barking, but the barks weren't as loud, and soon they turned into yelps. Still he kept running.

I ran too.

The police were called the next day. The dog had died that night. Its owner had come home from a hard day of ignoring his dog only to find it lying in the backyard, quiet, its muzzle bloody—and in death the dog was shown a mercy it was never shown in life: it was taken to a vet. The vet took one look at the blood, opened the dog up, and went searching for answers and found plenty of them in the form of fishhooks and nails and thumbtacks that I'd squeezed deep into the steak. The police went up and down the street, knocking on doors, knowing somebody in our neighborhood had done it— hearing very quickly, I imagine, from the neighbors that everybody in the neighborhood had wanted to do it. It came down to who turned the fantasy into a reality. They came to our door and spoke to my parents, and I was scared then, but not as scared as I was when they came for my dad. They asked to speak to me and my sister, and I stood there with Belinda and told my parents and the police that I'd seen nothing, and the police thanked us all for our time and moved on to the next house.

Nobody ever questioned it. Not ever. Not even my mum. I was sure she'd notice the missing steak and figure it all out. I thought she'd call the police and they'd take me to a room somewhere and leave me alone until I pissed myself and cried and confessed. But she never did. Nobody ever did.

Four weeks later my dad was arrested. A month after that my neighbor got another dog—he probably figured my dad had killed the last one so this one would be safe. And it would have been safe too if it hadn't barked as much as the first one. He only had it a month before the same thing happened. The police came up and down the street and learned the same amount of nothing they'd learned the first time. My neighbor had had his fill of dead dogs by then and didn't go about getting another.

I have no idea why this story is in my mind as I drive home, or what it means. My psychiatrist way back then would have gone through entire prescription pads keeping me medicated if he knew.

Seeing the way that dog died—that frightened me. I vowed that day as I ran home that I would never, ever do that kind of thing again. I made the same vow the second time too—and that time the promise stuck. I never told anybody about the urges. Certainly I never told my wife.

Sam is asleep in the passenger seat. The school holidays have begun and I don't know whether it'll be easier on her not going to school next week, or harder now that her mum is dead. I don't know if the distraction of the classroom would have been a healthy thing or not. I don't know how I can look after her during the weekend, during the holidays, during the next ten or more years until she moves out of home and begins her own life.

When I get home I'm hit with the expectation that something will be different. It's as though all that happened today was a movie that's rolled to the end, the gunmen only actors, the wounds on my wife manufactured with stage blood. If not that, then at least Jodie will be here somewhere, released from the hospital—on the way to the morgue somebody found her breathing and they saved her. I expect the police to be here, to tell me they've caught the men who did this. I expect life to have moved forward.

What I get defies all my expectation—everything is exactly how I left it. Nobody has been; nobody is here, even the poltergeist who visits at night to mess things around hasn't shown up. I step inside and between the time I left a few hours ago and now, nothing has altered other than the angle of the sun. It's got lower in the sky, barely coming through the living room windows now, picking out dust floating in the air, and the temperature has cooled—but that's about it. Mogo is somewhere else, outside somewhere, doing whatever it is that crazy cat does. Sometimes the voice from twenty years ago tells me there is a solution to getting rid of that cat. I wonder if Mogo senses that. I wonder, now that Jodie isn't here, whether Mogo will ever come back.

Sam wakes up when I carry her inside, but falls back asleep within about a minute. I get her tucked into bed and head out to the living room. I turn on the TV but the next news bulletin is still over an hour away. I tidy up the kitchen, putting the phone back on the hook, packing everything into the dishwasher, killing time, killing time—rinse a plate and—*bang*—another distraction but only for a split second before my world comes crashing back down. Doing the housework seems the wrong thing to be doing—but what is the right thing? It turns out the right thing is throwing a couple of dinner plates really hard into the wall. They both shatter. A small tooth-sized piece bites into the wall and stays there, the other shards raining down on the floor. I pick up a glass and it follows the same trajectory. Next thing I know half a dozen of them are down there, a cocktail of broken glass and ceramic shards, and I tip out the cutlery drawer and add to it before sitting down and leaning against the fridge.

Sam is standing outside the kitchen. There are tears on her face and her teddy bear is tucked against her chest.

"Did you and mummy have a fight?" she asks, looking at all the broken dishes.

"No, baby."

"Then why did she go?"

I get to my feet and hug my daughter before taking her back to bed. I sit with her until she falls asleep, and I sit with her for a bit after too. I don't know how to make it through the weekend. Don't know how to plan the funeral. Don't know how to plan my future with Sam. The truth is Sam's the only reason right now I'm not picking up one of those shards off the kitchen floor and fishing for the veins in my forearm.

I clean the kitchen up, watching my wife reaching out over and over, the man behind her raising the gun, then I go back a few minutes earlier and watch us in the bank, I watch the men coming in behind her, different pairs going in different directions. I stand up and fight them, taking the guns off them, struggling with them, six gunshots and six gunmen all lying dead on the floor. People swarm around me and hug me, they recognize me, but the gene my dad gave me doesn't scare them, in fact it excites them. The serial killer gene just saved all their lives.

Another time I grab Jodie and pull her back from the action, locking us into a nearby bathroom until they've gone. Then I watch as the men come in and the security guard takes action and he grabs the first guy, twists him toward the others, guns going off, the bad guys all shooting each other as smoke and blood fill the air. Then I picture us at lunch, laughing, planning, the time slipping away and suddenly we've missed our appointment at the bank, disappointed but alive.

I picture getting a flat tire on the way to work this morning. I picture work piling up and me unable to get away. I picture a power cut, an earthquake, somebody choking on a piece of chicken at the restaurant, a car accident right outside work. I picture ringing Jodie and telling her I can't make it, that it'll have to be next week, and Jodie tells me what a pain in the ass I am and it's obvious she'll be pissed at me all weekend. I picture Jodie in the living room right now getting Sam ready for bed. The TV is on. Sam is asking for some cookies. Jodie is saying no, and Sam is getting upset. I picture reading Sam a bedtime story, something about elves and princesses, then Jodie and me sitting up watching TV, my arm around her, holding her, rubbing her shoulder and then she touches my thigh, I kiss her and then . . . she is gone. Dead. Her body bloody and empty lying on the road as the black van speeds away.

The phone rings. I stare at it but don't want to talk to anybody. After eight rings the machine picks it up. Jodie recorded the outgoing message. Her voice in the silent house does two things simultaneously—it makes me think she's still alive, and it makes me think her ghost is here. Two completely opposite things—and it does a third thing too—it makes me shiver.

"You've reached Eddie and Jodie and Sam, but we're all out or pretending to be out, so please leave a message after the beep."

The machine beeps. I'll never change that outgoing message.

"Ah, hi, Edward, it's John Morgan here, umm . . . I'm calling because we heard about what happened, and, um . . . all of us here at the firm are feeling for you, we really are, and, and, ah, we wanted to cancel the Christmas party tonight out of respect—I mean, none of us want to celebrate anything at the moment now—but the place is already booked and paid for and most of us were already here when the news came in. Okay, I guess that's it . . . well, there is one more thing, and I hate to ask, but this McClintoch file you're

working on, it really needs to be wrapped up before the break, you know what it's like, and nobody else can really step in and take over because you've invested so much work in it, and we'd end up chasing our tails for the week, so, umm, what I'm saying is I need you to . . . no, wait, I mean I'm asking if you can make it in next week to get it completed? After the funeral, of course, I mean, there's no way I'd expect you to come in before then—unless of course you really wanted to, say, if you needed work to distract you or something. Thanks, Edward. Well . . . ah, see you later."

He hangs up and the line beeps a couple of times and I delete the message. I hate my job. Sometimes I can sense the people there wondering about me, trying to figure how many people I've killed, or how many I'll one day kill, accountants inside all of them crunching the numbers.

I slump in front of the TV. I have to wait until 10:30 for the news to come on. It opens with the bank robbery. The anchorwoman looks like she's just come from modeling at a car show. She has only two expressions—the one she has for bad news, and the one for happy human interest stories. She composes herself with her bad-news face and recaps the highlight of the day, then says, "Some of these scenes may disturb."

There are images from the security cameras. There is footage of the "after" by the camera crews that arrived. And there's cell phone video footage from people too panicked to act but courageous enough to film what they could. The angle it's shot from reminds me of the teenagers in the hoodies, and I'm pretty sure this is their footage, and I wonder how much they got paid for it, how excited they were about it all. It shows Jodie being dragged out of the bank, and even though I know what's coming up, I still pray for it to go differently. Then it shows me coming out, chasing the men, five of them in the van, the sixth one with the gun, and late-night news being what it is these days where standards have relaxed enough where you can say "fuck" without being bleeped out; you can also see your wife getting shot too, because the footage doesn't stop, it carries on as ratings are more important than and certainly more profitable than ethics, so the country gets to watch the blood spray from Jodie just as I got to watch it today, they get to see her knocked

54

down, they get to put themselves in my shoes and see what I saw without feeling what I felt, and then they get to see it again in slow motion, the cell phone capturing everything in cell phone detail—not high quality, but high enough.

It goes back to the anchorwoman who, to her credit, appears momentarily uncomfortable by what the network aired. When she goes to speak she stutters over the first word. Thankfully for her career she recovers, and she's able to offer up other details before segueing back to footage from the bank. There are sweeping shots of people in the street staring at the scene, shots of the police scouring the area, a nice, tight-cropped shot of me holding my wife, and no shots anywhere of the men who did this.

Then, when there is nothing left to show, it cuts to the people nearby when it happened—*"we heard gunshots and ran," "we didn't know what to do," "seemed unbelievable it was happening right here," "we were almost killed."* Then come the interviews from people who were inside the bank. I recognize some of them. *"They came out of nowhere," "it was so scary," "those poor people, my God, those poor people did nothing and got shot anyway."* A photo of a man comes up, he was the bank manager, he was fifty-six years old and had worked at that branch for nine years. It shows the bank teller whose life apparently I saved, her name is Marcy Croft and she's twenty-four years old and has worked at the bank for nine weeks, and she's shaking as the cameraman zooms in on her, and she says *"He was going to kill me. I know that as sure as I know I'm never working here again. And that man, oh my God, that man distracted him and saved my life, and his wife, his wife . . .,"* she says, and she breaks down in tears and can't finish but the camera doesn't break away from her, it focuses on her pain and relief and the country watches her cry for another ten seconds before it goes back to the anchor.

After the interviews a picture of my wife that I have no idea how they got—maybe from her work somewhere—comes up. Both victims have families, pain, and despair filling the spaces these people left. Then there's me again, covered in blood, being led away from Jodie's body. Edward Hunter, twenty-nine-year-old son of a serial killer. The anchorwoman mentions it.

The footage turns to a live feed from outside the bank. There's still yellow crime-scene tape fluttering in the slight breeze. The spot where Jodie was killed has tape around it, and she's been moved, and I have an image of her lying on a steel slab in a morgue, pale, grey, and blue and broken beyond repair, no longer covered by a sheet. The reporter has his sleeves rolled up, indicating he's had a long day at work. He speaks for a bit, talking about me.

"And Jack Hunter, of course, was arrested after murdering eleven prostitutes, isn't that right, Dan?" the anchorwoman asks, the feed going back to her, her serious face on display.

"Sure is, Kim. Of course that's only eleven prostitutes that he admitted to."

"Has there been any speculation that Edward Hunter may have been involved?" Anchorwoman Kim says.

"At this stage the police aren't commenting on that, however from what I've learned it does seem unlikely. I think for Edward and Jodie Hunter, and for the rest of these people, it was a case of wrong place at the wrong time. As soon as we know more down here in Christchurch, we'll let you know."

Kim flashes her second expression at the screen, and then the image taken twenty years ago appears, of me in my school uniform by my father's side. I almost throw the remote at the TV. The story gets to the climax—or, in this case, a punch line. The van was found. It had been stolen. No trace of the money. No trace of the people in it. The six men scattered into the city.

I turn off the TV and sit in the darkness, wide awake, angry, hurting, and alone.

chapter nine

A man walking his dog called it in. He saw the smoke and called the fire department who rushed out before the blaze could spread out of control, latching onto trees and then maybe houses in the area, but not before the van could be destroyed. The twisted and charred skeleton is still smoldering, and Schroder knows any evidence inside is gone. There's still forensic evidence, but that'll take weeks—and even then it may lead to nothing.

The road is hard-packed dirt leading into a pine forest. The sides of the road are breaking up in areas from tree roots, patches of it blanketed in pine needles. About two kilometers from here in one direction people go mountain biking and jogging and horse riding, and two kilometers in another direction is the ocean, but right here the world is abandoned, and the men who came here knew that. The ground hasn't given way to any impressions from feet, or from another vehicle. The man with the dog doesn't remember seeing any other cars coming or leaving, and there isn't anybody else to ask. He can smell oil and gas and the branches that have blistered in the heat. Halogen lights have been set up, pointing at the van, lighting up the nearby trees and creating hundreds of shadows among them. There is no breeze at all, and every thirty seconds or so he has to swat away an insect about half the size of a fly.

Schroder can't stop thinking about Edward Hunter. He thinks about the dad, just your normal everyday average family man. All through the trial Jack Hunter with his smiles, his neat but cheap suits, never once appearing cocky or arrogant and certainly nothing like the insane person his lawyers wanted him to be. The defense told the jury that the dad heard voices, that he suffered from paranoid schizophrenia, that he could barely control what he was doing, let alone remember it. They said the voices took over, and when they did there was no Jack Hunter, but something else, something inside of him that was sick and twisted and had gone undiagnosed for years. The jury didn't buy it. The jury liked the prosecution's story better. That story went like this: Jack Hunter loved to kill prostitutes and he hated to be caught. Jack Hunter wasn't insane, because he got away with it for too many years. An insane man with no control over his actions would have been caught sooner. An insane man could not have covered up the crimes the way he did and lived the way he lived. The jury bought that story and Jack Hunter got life in jail. End of story.

He can remember the image of Edward hugging his dad on the morning. Since reaching into the bathtub checking for Edward's mother's pulse a year later, he hasn't really thought much about Edward. He remembered him again a few years later when he heard the sister had overdosed on heroin, but not since.

For the last few hours he's been talking to witnesses and reviewing the security footage from the bank. The footage is video without audio, and it's clear but not clear enough to zoom in on any of the bank robbers' features. They can tell height and sometimes weight, but nothing more. However, not just anybody can successfully rob a bank, and certainly there must be some experience in the team that pulled this job off. At a minimum, half of them will have a criminal record for armed assault—and in all likelihood all of them will have a record for something.

The next step is to talk to people in that world. Somebody somewhere has to know something—there's no way these men won't answer for what they did.

He watches the smoke spiral into the night for a while longer before getting into his car and driving back to the bank.

chapter ten

The funeral is on Monday. Jodie's body was rushed through the backlog of bodies that were rolled in on Friday. They didn't need to do much to her except take a hundred photos and go hunting around inside of her with a pair of tweezers searching for the shotgun pellets. Maybe they got it wrapped up since Christmas was coming. Maybe the funeral director freed up a spot so soon in his schedule because he's heading to the Gold Coast for the holidays. Whatever the reason for the rush, I'm glad for it. The idea of Jodie lying in the ground isn't what I'd call warming, but it's certainly better than having her sliced up and exposed on a cold metal gurney in the bowels of the hospital morgue.

For everybody else, it's a normal Monday. Others are off to work and the school holidays have kicked in, leaving thousands of unsupervised teenagers to drink beer and break into houses and steal big-screen TVs and game consoles. It's summer and the world is moving on and Christmas shopping is in full swing with mall parking lots jammed full and parents fighting in line for the next best thing. It's a stunning, bright sunny day, the kind of day I'm sure Jodie would have enjoyed, and if the choice was hers perhaps even the kind of day she'd like to be buried on. My bruises have faded. It's been three days since the bank robbery, and all six men are still on the loose. The city is understaffed by police and overstaffed with criminals—the balance is out of whack and nobody seems able to correct it. Wednesday was to be my last day at work for two weeks, the same for Jodie. Instead she's spending Christmas in a dirt plot and I'll be spending it God knows where.

I had to choose a dress for Jodie, and a coffin. Coffin shopping is something I never want to have to do again—different models have different specifications, the funeral director doing his best to guilt me into upgrading, as if a cheaper coffin would suggest to the world I hated my wife. Jodie's parents took care of the flowers, the priest, the music, and the church, and everything else. There are probably a thousand things going on around me to make this happen and I wouldn't know.

The cemetery is on the outskirts of town in a neighborhood where there are lots of trees and not so many houses and currently a large flock of seagulls circling above. There's a church off to one side of the graveyard which has been abandoned since the priest was murdered there almost six months ago, but reopened in time for Christmas with the arrival of a new priest, Father Jacob. The church has one of those rare histories that few churches have, the history where nobody died in its construction. Love or hate religion, one thing is sure—it's certainly leading the way in deaths. Religion takes more lives than cancer and coronaries and car crashes combined. A belt of trees form a barrier between the church and the closest of the graves; a couple of them have been cut down, fresh stumps surrounded by sawdust and bark jutting out of the ground, sun streaming between the gaps and hitting the stained-glass windows. A six-foot fence made up of iron bars with cobwebs and flaky paint stretches the distance between the cemetery and the road. Parked out front are a dozen media vans, nobody in them.

Father Jacob has a deep voice that sounds somber, the acoustics of the church helping him convey the depths of his words—which to me all sound hollow. He stands up at a podium a few meters from my wife, looking more like a wizard than a priest, his white hair in need of a trim, an outfit one might wear to a fancy dress party. He tells us about God, and Heaven, and I'm not real sure where I stand on those concepts right now. My grandparents raised me to believe in God, but these were the same people who raised my dad, and look how he turned out. I want to believe in something; it would mean Jodie is somewhere better than this world—and she is certainly somewhere better than Christchurch. And I want to believe in something to make it easier on Sam. I've thought about it a lot over the last few days, and I think it comes down to this—I want to believe in God, but right now I'm too damn angry with Him to do so.

It's almost thirty-five degrees outside, but it's cool in the church, and it's obvious I'm not the only one who feels it. There is something bad inside this place, maybe the same bad thing that got the previous priest murdered, or perhaps it's the ghost of that priest himself, still here, watching over us. I wonder if Father Jacob senses it, whether he wonders if he'll be the next priest to come to a dark end.

A lot of people show up—I never knew that I knew that many people. They show up from the firm I work at. There are plenty from Jodie's firm too, and of course it's not like we were social lepers, which means all our friends and family are here too. There are people I don't recognize, others I haven't seen in a long, long time. No one really knows what to say—except for John Morgan, who shakes my hand and reminds me, when I get the chance, to head in tomorrow and Wednesday to finish off the McClintoch file. I smile at him and think about putting him in a coffin of his own.

I don't have any family—my grandparents, who raised me and Belinda after Mum died, are both dead: a heart attack got my granddad; pneumonia and complications but mostly loneliness got my grandmother not long after. More than anybody, I wish Belinda was here. When we were young, before Dad got taken away, Belinda did her best to pretend I didn't exist, and when she couldn't pretend hard enough to make me disappear, she'd begrudgingly throw the occasional sentence my way. When we found out what Dad had done, she spoke to me more but her words were harsher. Then when we found Mum dead in the bathtub, she held my hand and stroked my hair while we waited for the police to arrive. She told me that day that she loved me, and that she would take care of me. Of course our grandparents ended up taking care of both of us, but it was a struggle for them. They were old and didn't really have the means to support us that well, but they did what they could to keep us from being put into foster care. Belinda always saw me as her responsibility. She was four years older than me, a big sister and mum all wrapped into one person, but at night she was neither of those—at night she used to sneak out of home and work the streets for money, and she'd come back crying with her pockets full of dirty banknotes and she'd hug me and tell me everything was going to be okay. Eventually it wasn't okay for her—she hated what she was doing, and the only way she could live with herself was to dull the pain, and that's when the drugs took hold of her. She moved out of our grandparents' house when she was sixteen but she came back every few days to see me. She always brought me something. Either a candy bar or a comic. She'd help me with my homework. She was always clean when she came visiting—or always looked clean—but sometimes she had the shakes, like she hadn't had a fix in a few days. My grandparents were in the wrong generation to notice what was happening, and I was too young to know what caused it.

Then one week she didn't come to visit. Then another week went by. Eventually the cops came. It was like that Wednesday morning all over again. They pulled into the street and knocked on the door and my life changed the same way it had every other time I saw them.

Sam is given a thousand hugs, almost all of them ending with the other person crying. Sam becomes numb to the tears. She's adorable in her little black dress and makes me want to cry every time I see her. She knows what's going on, but at the same time she doesn't know. She's been told Mummy has gone to Heaven, but a few times she's asked if Mummy will be coming home over

Christmas to visit. I wish I could cancel Christmas. I hate that the rest of the city gets something to enjoy.

Jodie's coffin is covered in flowers. Most of the church is. The accountant in me is wondering how much all of this is costing, and thinking how death must be the most profitable business in the world since we all get around to doing it sooner or later. The father inside of me holds Sam's hand tightly the entire time, drawing strength from her. The man inside me hurts, he's screaming inside, he's dying inside, he's confused, and he doesn't know what his future holds. The service lasts an hour. People come out of it saying it was "nice," but it's not the word I'd use. I don't know what it is. Certainly not nice. "Devastating," might be better. "Confusing" would work too. "Nice" seems to trivialize it.

Six people carry Jodie's coffin outside. Her dad, her two brothers, and three friends. Their faces are strained but I don't think it's from the coffin being heavy. Her brothers had to fly in from different parts of the country and tomorrow will fly back out. I keep a firm grip on Sam's hand as we walk behind them. Sam keeps a tight grip on her teddy bear with the other hand. The coffin is shiny and new and sure won't be that way in a few hours from now. I wonder how heavy it is, what kind of percentage of the weight is from my wife.

We reach the hearse. It's shiny and black, while death is dull and black. The rear door is open, waiting for her, waiting for the men to slide my wife inside as if they were furniture movers. The door closes, then we all seem to stand around for a minute or two, not really sure what to do next until we all kind of figure it out, and the hearse leaves and we follow it. We all drive in a row, our headlights on, Jodie leading the way. It's about a kilometer of winding road between the church and Jodie's new home so the drive is short and I'm not sure why no one walked. We find the missing occupants of the media vans about thirty meters from the grave, some with cameras set up on tripods, others on shoulder mounts. These people don't have any respect for Jodie, or for Sam or for myself, and none at all for the situation. They don't care about our loss, they care only about ratings, and the thing I know for certain in this world is that one day these people will become victims to their own stories. One day somebody, maybe some other son of a serial killer, will pick these vultures off one by one. But that day is in the future, and today Sam is the granddaughter of a serial killer, daughter of a murder victim, and the media are already speculating about her too. They call her cute and adorable, they call her loss a tragic one, and they wonder what kind of woman she will turn into—her life has this dark blemish now, and combined with her genes . . . they want to know what she will become.

The same men who loaded Jodie in the hearse go about unloading her. My wife has become cargo, her final voyage about to begin. They carry her from the hearse to the grave, lowering her onto some weird scaffolding erected over the top of it. Father Jacob thinks of more he wants to add, then, at exactly 3:27 on a Monday afternoon, the scaffolding moves and my wife is lowered into the ground, the six men who carried her standing silent among the crowd, hurting, while the six men who did this to her spend their money in the streets of Christchurch, enjoying the beautiful summer's day.

chapter eleven

The bank manager is buried on the same day at a different cemetery. We don't combine the events and hold one giant two-for-one funeral party to save money, or to make it easier on the media so they can save gas.

We pick up handfuls of dirt and throw it onto the coffin. It's a tradition I've never really understood. I've done it four times in the past: my mother, my sister, both my grandparents. Now my wife. I don't ever want to have to do it again.

The rest of the dirt is underneath a grass-colored piece of canvas, hidden away, and it's another tradition I don't understand. Are they worried the dirt will cement the reality that my blood-covered wife, funeral arrangements, and coffin could not? I don't know. Maybe it's the traditions that get people through the day.

Sam picks up a small handful of dirt and sprinkles it onto the coffin. She doesn't ask why. In fact she hasn't asked anything at all today—she's done what she's been told, quietly following me since we woke up this morning.

After the funeral we all drive to Jodie's parents' house. I look at the streets and the people and I want to leave this city and wish I'd done it years ago. The Christmas traffic slows us down—even at four o'clock on a Monday afternoon. Soccer mums are driving their kids around the city in SUVs and heading to the malls.

There are about thirty cars parked in my in-laws' street, and only two media vans. I have to park two blocks away. The distraction thing happens while I drive—I'll see a car getting ready to run a red light and I'll brake, I'll avoid him, the moment passes, and then Jodie hits my thoughts with such brutality I almost burst into tears. My days are made up like that—the memory of her loss impacting on me over and over, trying to break me. Or maybe no longer trying—maybe succeeding.

The weird food/funeral thing is taking place. It's another of the traditions. It was the same when my mum and sister died, my grandparents cooking a thousand sausage rolls for the guests, cracking open bottles of lemonade and grape juice, swallowing down food and sorrow and sharing stories. The house is almost standing room only with the amount of people here, but they part for me and Sam, and I lead her through the living room and out onto the porch into the sun. I tell her to go and play in her playhouse but she doesn't want to. She wants to keep holding my hand, and that's okay with me. On and off during the afternoon she'll smile at me like she's in on some secret that I don't know about. She thinks her mum is returning.

"*Mummy's a ghost,*" she said as Jodie hid under the sheets from her on the day she died.

One by one the guests fade away. I'm given handshakes and hugs and words of condolence, and none of them help. I'd put any one of these people into the ground if it would bring Jodie back.

In the end there's only family—and none of it is mine, except my daughter. It's Jodie's family, and as much as I want to leave and never see them again, I can't. None of this is their fault. None of it is my fault. I guess it's just one of those things. That's what murder is these days—just one of those things that happens, get used to it, deal with it, move on.

Sam is finally out in the playhouse Nat built for her a couple of years ago. Nat spent twenty years as a builder and the last ten years running a hardware shop. I'm sitting out on the porch watching her when he comes out and hands me a beer. His suit jacket is gone, his sleeves are rolled up, and his tie is askew. He has big forearms with long white hairs, and big hands that he uses to pry the top off his beer. I suddenly realize for the first time that as hard as it is for me, it's perhaps even harder for him.

"Hell of a day," he says, and he sits next to me at the outdoor table he built.

"Yeah."

"Hell of a service. They did . . . a great job," he says, maybe recognizing how hollow his words sound. "Notice how people came out of there saying the service was nice? I don't know what the hell they mean by that," he says. "I mean, I think I know what they mean, and I've probably said the same thing at other funerals. But the word doesn't fit. Does that make sense?"

"Yeah."

"I figure there's no alternative, right? I mean, what the hell else are people going to come out saying? That it was a bloody awful service? That they had a bad time? That they had a great time? I guess it's all you can say."

"I guess it is."

He lifts the bottle up to his lips and takes a long swallow. "They're going to catch those bastards," he says. "I wish to hell they'd put me in a room with them one at a time. I wish . . . ah hell," he says, and then, "I keep thinking I'm dreaming."

"I know."

Sam waves at us, then goes back to her world, talking to her teddy bears, maybe telling them about how nice the service was. *Mummy's a ghost.* Yeah, maybe she's talking to Jodie too.

"You have to feel the same way, right? If you could get your hands on those people?"

I'd love it. The words don't come out, thankfully, and they're not even my words. I'm not sure whose they are. "I'd kill them," I say, knowing that's what he wants to hear, wondering if it's actually something he thinks I'm capable of. Maybe he's hoping I am.

"It's going to be hard, taking care of her yourself."

"I know."

"But you're a good kid," he says. "You'll do great. I know it. And, well, we're always here for you."

I open up my beer and take a long sip so I don't have to speak.

"I know that you've always thought we didn't think much of you. And I know why you think that. And I admit, in the beginning, it worried me when Jodie told us she was dating you and who your dad was. Shit, don't think for a moment that we didn't know it was unfair to think like that, I mean, we're good people, we don't have prejudices against anybody. Doesn't matter who you are, you're good to us, we like you. Could be anybody—hell, even gay people. But, well, you don't imagine your daughter growing up and being with somebody whose father is a serial killer. And before you judge me on—"

"I don't judge you. I understand. I've lived with it my entire life."

"I know you have, son, and you don't deserve it. But it is what it is, and you'll go through it in ten years or more when Sam is old enough to date. Truth be told, I think we would have been fearful no matter who Jodie brought home. It took some getting used to, with your dad's past and everything, but I want you to know how proud we are of you, and we love you and we know how happy you made Jodie, and we have a granddaughter who means the world to us. We wouldn't have that precious little girl if you'd never met our Jodie."

I take another sip of beer, following his thought process, wondering if he chose those words specifically and hoping he didn't. He's saying they wouldn't have Sam if it wasn't for me. But he's also saying they'd still have Jodie.

"I wanted to let you know how much we believe in you," he says. "And that, well, we don't blame you for what happened. We know how, how you called out, how you tried to stop them from shooting that woman."

"Jodie would still be alive if I hadn't."

He doesn't answer for about twenty seconds. Just keeps working away at his beer. He wipes at his mouth and turns toward me. "I know," he says. "Don't think that I don't know that. And part of me, part of me is angry at you for that. Part of me thinks if you'd kept your mouth shut, none of this would be happening."

"I–"

"Let me finish," he says.

"But–"

"Please," he says, and holds his hand up. "You were doing the right thing. Me, in that situation, I don't know what I'd have done. Maybe nothing. I'd have been a coward and let that woman get shot, most probably. But you stood up. You didn't know you were risking Jodie—all you knew was you were risking yourself. You did a good thing, but part of me is always going to hate you for that, Eddie, and I can't help that."

"I get it. A big part me—hell, all of me hates me too for doing it."

"I know that. Weigh it all up, spread out the blame, and shit, Eddie, it wasn't your fault. It was the men who came into that bank. They're the ones responsible. Not you. And we want to let you know how much we're relying on you now. It's your job to take care of that little girl. You have to give up everything you can to make sure she's raised right. And no matter what, we're always going to be here for her. And for you. Remember that, Eddie. Remember that and you'll do okay."

He puts his hand on my shoulder. It's warm and comforting. For the briefest second I believe him that everything is going to be okay. I take another drink of the beer.

It's in your blood.

"Sorry?" I say.

"I said you'll do okay."

"No, after that. You said something after that."

"No, I'm pretty sure I didn't."

Suddenly I'm also sure he didn't. *It's in your blood.* It was the same voice I heard earlier, the one that told me I'd be hearing from it soon, and now I recognize it. It's been almost twenty years, but it's the voice from when I was a kid and the neighbor's dog wouldn't stop barking. It's my dad's monster—it found me twice when I was nine, and now it's found me again.

70

chapter twelve

It's dark by the time we get home. It's a three-quarter moon. It throws white light over the house and reflects off the front windows and makes the house look very empty. I park the car in the driveway and can't be bothered putting it in the garage. Jodie's car is still parked in town near her work and can stay there a while longer yet. I grab the mail and take Sam inside. One of the things about the new house we were going to get was it had an adjoining garage. It was something we both wanted, because of the brutal Christchurch winters.

Jodie doesn't have to worry about that anymore, now, does she . . .

"Shut up," I whisper.

"What, Daddy?" Sam asks, her voice sleepy, her eyes half closed.

"Nothing, honey," I say, and I carry her inside.

The house has gotten tidier over the last couple of days mainly because I found myself wandering through the rooms, never really sure what to do. Sometimes I'd spend hours in front of the TV, watching the news and staring at whatever else was on. Other times I'd surf the net, looking for updates on the case. Most of the time people would show up to spend time with us. Sam kept mostly to herself. Mogo would show up for food and nothing else. I'd clean the house sporadically, sometimes cleaning the same room only an hour after I'd last done it. I'd play with Sam. We'd watch TV together. We'd sit outside together. It was tough.

I carry Sam down to her bedroom. I keep searching for a glimpse of my wife, a shadow, a movement somewhere, something to let me know in some way she is still here. I lay Sam on her bed—Disney characters scattered in the pattern of the bedspread. She's asleep again. I get her into her pajamas. She wakes a little but is too tired to help.

I grab a beer from the fridge. I never bought any, but since Saturday friends have been showing up to share their sorrow with me, the women bringing wine, the men, beer, and in the beginning I thought I had enough to last me a lifetime, but now I'm not so sure. Now I think there might only be enough here for a few days. I settle in front of the TV and wait for the news to come on. The bank robbery, the funerals, they don't even lead the news anymore. The lead story is about a seventy-five-year-old woman who, in the parking lot of a shopping mall, mistook her car for an identical-colored and almost identical-shaped vehicle parked next to it. The owner, seeing her putting her key into his lock, rushed over and shoved her so hard she fell over, hit her head on the sidewalk, and was pronounced dead at the scene. The second story is about a turned-over truck that allowed a few dozen sheep to escape on a notorious stretch of highway in the North Island. Nobody was killed. Then come the funerals, snippets from them both in a montage with slow classical music playing over the top of it, like it's a movie preview. The coffins are different colors and styles, and everybody is dressed smartly. My daughter gets a lot of attention—it shows us following the coffin. Another daughter—three times Sam's age—follows the other coffin. Then at the end of the story a brief report saying the men haven't been captured, and that any member of the public with information is asked to call the hotline listed below.

I finish the beer and grab another. I open up the mail. There are two letters from the bank. The first one is brief.

DEAR MR. HUNTER,

IN WHAT MUST BE A VERY DIFFICULT TIME FOR YOU AND YOUR FAMILY, WE AT SOUTH PACIFIC BANK WOULD LIKE TO OFFER OUR SINCEREST CONDOLENCES FOR THE LOSS OF YOUR WIFE.

THE TRAGIC INCIDENT THAT HAPPENED OUTSIDE THE BANK HAS TOUCHED THE ENTIRE STAFF AND, NEEDLESS TO SAY, YOU AND YOUR FAMILY REMAIN IN OUR THOUGHTS AND OUR PRAYERS.

SINCERELY,

DEAN WELLINGTON

I read the letter a couple of times, looking at the words Dean Wellington used. He managed to sum the entire murder of my wife as an "incident" and convey his horror at it all in two paragraphs. I wonder if he used the words "outside the bank" specifically, hoping it will absolve any responsibility the branch has toward what happened.

The second letter isn't as brief. It's obviously a form letter with a brief scrawl of a signature at the bottom. It's been overnighted down from Auckland, meaning they must have gotten to work on our loan application within hours of Jodie dying.

MR. EDWARD HUNTER,

UNFORTUNATELY, AS YOU KNOW, THE PROPERTY MARKET AT THIS CURRENT TIME IS EXTREMELY VOLATILE, WHICH REQUIRES US TO TIGHTEN THE CRITERIA ON WHICH WE BASE OUR HOME LOANS.

BASED ON THESE CRITERIA, WE ARE UNABLE TO APPROVE YOUR APPLICATION AT THIS TIME.

I read on. The letter goes on for another page, listing some of the criteria that I no longer fit. In the end I skim over the details and go right to the end.

AS THE MARKET IS IN A CONSTANT STATE OF CHANGE, WE WOULD BE HAPPY TO REVIEW THIS DECISION AT A LATER DATE. IN THE MEANTIME, WE HOPE THAT WE CAN CONTINUE TO ASSIST YOU WITH ALL YOUR BANKING NEEDS.

YOURS SINCERELY,

KATIE HUGHES

I read the letter a second time, finishing off my second beer, the anger burning inside me, and yet I feel no disbelief at all. Katie Hughes must have typed this letter up pretty damn fast. I check the postmark and see it got posted on Saturday. I wonder if Hughes or Wellington spent an expensive Friday afternoon with lawyers to see where they stood on the whole "incident." I finish a third beer while flicking through the phone book.

I'm not sure why I do it, but I look Dean Wellington up and write down his address before finishing off a third beer and deciding it might be about time to head off to bed.

chapter thirteen

I wake up and everything is as it should be. My wife is alive. We've bought the new house. Sam is Sam and Mogo is being Mogo. Then those thoughts become blurred, my bedroom comes into focus, and Jodie isn't in bed next to me. I reach over and her side is cold, untouched, and then it all comes racing back, as it did yesterday morning, and every morning since the . . . for some reason I think *accident* but that's the wrong word. Since the *what?*

The execution the voice says, and I agree, though Dean Wellington would say "incident."

It's after eight already. Normally Sam would be up watching cartoons and making a mess, but this morning she's still asleep, the last few days . . .

Since the execution . . .

The last few days since the execution she's been sleeping later.

I sit on the porch and eat cereal directly out of the packet. The Tuesday-morning sun is slowly climbing into the sky. There's a truck and a cherry picker out in the street about half a block away, motors and chainsaws making plenty of noise as they trim tops of trees away from the power lines. My head is slightly fuzzy and my mouth feels like I spent time last night licking the carpet. The cereal is dry and sticks to the roof of it. I think about work and the file I should be working on, and whether not going in today and no longer giving a damn about it means I no longer have a job. I wonder what kind of letter Dean Wellington would send if he knew I was dropping from one income down to none.

The phone rings and I head inside for it, wanting to stop it from waking Sam.

"Jack?"

The voice is familiar in the way you can flick on the radio and hear a song you haven't heard in twenty years and know how it goes. When you hear that song, your mind starts scrambling, taking you back to a time when you heard it last. Good memory or bad, you're in that moment again, the smells, the sounds, the sights, they're all there.

"Who is this?" I ask, and I remember the handcuffs, the police, the smile on his face when he watched me from the back of the police car. I remember the dog, I remember the weight of the piece of steak in the plastic bag. I can feel the cold sunlight, my school uniform, my mother holding my hand and holding Belinda's hand. I can remember the neighbors pouring out of their houses, the women with their hands over their mouths in shock, the men shaking their heads, the long line of police cars, dozens of cops, all showing up in force as if to arrest a small army. I remember the media vans, the photographers.

"Jack, it's me. It's your father."

I don't say anything. The kitchen disappears, the world disappears, all fading away as the front door of my childhood home appears, the policemen, the disgust on their faces. Of course that childhood home is gone now. About three months after Mum died, when I was living with Belinda at my grandparents', somebody went along and set fire to that house. Nobody was ever caught. I always thought maybe Belinda did it, but it could have been anybody. Dad hurt a lot of people.

"I'm calling to—"

"I don't care why you're calling," I say, and I tighten my hand on the phone and for some reason, for some freaky-shit-get-the-hell-out-of-here kinda reason, I don't hang up.

"I'm calling to tell you how sorry I am."

I let his sentence hang and he waits patiently. I guess my father is used to being patient.

"You've had twenty years to apologize," I say. "Anyway, you're saying it to the wrong person, and you picked the worst damn time to do it."

"Not . . . not about the past, Jack. I'm ringing to tell you how sorry I am about Jodie. I wish things had been different. For her. For you. For everybody."

"How the hell do you know about Jodie?" I ask. "How do you know a damn thing about me or Jodie?"

"This isn't the moon they're keeping us locked away on, Jack."

"Don't call me that."

"What?"

"Jack. Don't call me Jack."

"Oh? What am I supposed to call you?"

"Don't call me anything. What the hell do you want? You ringing to tell me you know what it's like to lose somebody? Like the way you lost Mum and Belinda?"

"I know you're angry at me."

"No. How could I possibly be angry at you? You've really been there for me, a real role model."

"Jack . . ."

"What do you want, Dad?" I ask, immediately nauseous at how comfortable the word "Dad" feels in my mouth. I'm nine years old all over again. The photo that told the world I was the son of a serial killer flashes into my mind. The memory turns as black and white as the picture. I'm holding on to my father, the police are taking him away, and my mum is trying to separate us, black-and-white tears spilling down my black-and-white face. The policemen weren't friendly toward any of us. None of them wanted to touch me or push me away, as if they feared the killer gene they were so sure I would inherit could contaminate them, that it would jump from me and land on their hands and burrow under their skin. It would tell them bad things and make them suck on the end of a pistol at the end of a long tiring day. They looked at my mother and my sister and me with open hatred, so sure all of us had been in on the action, that Dad had brought the hookers home for the holidays, that we'd taken turns at draining the life out of them, raping them, a good-ol'-splasharoo in blood, the son and daughter committing the sins of the mother and father.

"I want to see you," my dad says, snapping me out of the memory, and my skin crawls, not at his request, but in the undeniable knowledge that yes indeed I'm going to go and see him.

"I can't."

"You can."

"I'm busy."

"It's important."

"Being a father is important. Not killing eleven women is important. You staying locked up is important."

"I'm still your father. You can deny it as much as you want, but—"

"I do deny it."

"I'm sorry the way it worked out."

"You make it sound like you had a different plan. How many more would have died, Dad? Another dozen?"

"We'll talk about it when you get here."

"Go to hell," I say.

"I'm already there," he says. "Please, son, it's important I see you," he says, and he hangs up, and I'm angry at his arrogance as he leaves me holding the phone. I'm scared at the prospect of seeing him, yet curious too, and perhaps, yes, just a spark of this—perhaps a little excited.

"Who was on the phone, Daddy?" Sam asks.

I didn't even know she was in the kitchen. I turn toward her. She's still wearing her pajamas, the teddy bear clutched under her arm, and for the first time I realize that she's hardly put that teddy bear down since her mother died. The bear's name is Mr. Fluff 'n' Stuff, and I bought him for Sam's first birthday. The bear has fared rather well over the five and a half years since then, but he's tattered around the edges and grubby in places, and if you asked the bear he'd probably tell you he was ready for retirement.

"It was nobody," I say.

"You called him Dad."

"You must have misheard," I say, and it's a small lie but it hurts like a big one.

"You did. I heard you."

"I'm sorry, baby, you're right. I did say Dad."

"Am I going to live with them?"

"What?"

"Daddy-Nat and Gramma," she says, and she thinks that's who I was talking to.

"Why do you say that?"

"I don't know. Mummy's gone and I thought you might want a new family now."

"Is that what somebody told you?" I say, immediately . . .

Make them suffer!

. . . angry at my in-laws for poisoning her mind like that. I keep my voice low and calm and friendly, a singsong voice, like when the cat sits at the door and I'm trying to convince him to come in.

"No, nobody told me. But on TV sometimes that's what happens. Is that why Mummy left? Because she didn't want to be with me anymore?"

"Of course not, baby," I say, and I crouch down in front of her. "Mummy loves you very much, I know that—"

"You smell like the art teacher," Sam says, interrupting me.

"Huh?"

"After lunch sometimes when we have art. He has the same aftershave."

I smile. No more beer for Daddy. "Give Daddy a big hug, then eat some breakfast. I'm going to drop you off at Daddy-Nat's and Grandma's house for a bit. I have somebody I have to see, but I promise I won't be long. I love you, sweetie."

"I don't want cereal," she says.

"You can have what you want," I tell her, which is a mistake, because thirty minutes later we're sitting in a McDonald's, the day heating up, and all I can think about is my father and what it is he wants to tell me.

chapter fourteen

The media called my dad "Jack the Hunter." They played the angle up and seemed real excited about the symmetry it suggested. He was a modern-day Jack the Ripper with almost a perfect name for it, the best, in fact, unless of course in the late nineteenth century the real killer's name was Jack Ripper.

Before he was caught, there was no name for him. There wasn't really much of an interest. A prostitute would go missing and nobody would care. Another would go missing two or three or four years later and nobody searched for a connection. Then some of them showed up. Somebody somewhere figured out that prostitutes over a twenty-five-year period were dying in bad and similar ways. The media told the country about it, but they had no catchy title. They called him the "Prostitute Killer," and the articles were small and easy to miss. Then came the arrest, then came the statistics, then came the connection to a name in history from the opposite side of the world and my dad became the worst kind of celebrity.

I've never visited my dad. We may share the same name and DNA but that's all. I spent nine years of my life being Jack Jr. before going by my middle name. Sometimes when I was in trouble at home, Mum would call me Jack-son. She would save that name for when she wanted my dad to deal with me. I was his son and his responsibility, like when I failed a subject at school or cut the hair off my sister's favorite doll. Belinda would call me Jacky in the times before our lives changed, and kept telling me I looked like a girl.

My last memory of Dad is that shy, humble smile of his, flashed at me from the back of a police car, his head twisted toward us, not a hint of shame in his features, almost a look of relief in some ways, as if he didn't have to hide his true self anymore.

I've seen him a few times since, but only on TV and in the papers. Nobody has taken a photo of him in about eighteen years, not since he got snapped dozens of times being led from the back of a van to the back steps of the courthouse. Only reason I knew he was still alive was because nobody has ever rung to tell me otherwise.

I don't know whether you have to phone ahead or simply show up, but once I drop Sam off I use my cell phone and call directory and ask for the number. A minute later I'm on the phone to the visitation department. I ask for directions and compare them to a map that's about ten years out of date but does the job.

It's a thirty-minute drive from my in-laws' place. I take a shortcut out behind the airport where the roads are narrower but have a higher speed limit. There are cars parked up off the sides, the front windscreens facing the runways on the other side of the chain-link fences, people inside them watching for hours on end the planes come and go. I head down a highway enclosed by pastures, the road edged with fir trees and wildflowers. There are large transmission towers growing out of the fields and shrinking off into the distance. The road markings are all faded from the sun and worn from constant traffic. Mailboxes stand to attention every kilometer or so where gravel roads twist off from the highway between fields of gorse, winding their way toward large farmhouses built to capture the sun.

The prison is hidden out of sight beyond fields of trees, well away from homes that escapees would visit within minutes of being on the run. The complex is a mixture of several buildings, several wings, all made up of concrete blocks and interconnected with more concrete blocks, the whole place with an industrial feel, as if inside are not the condemned, but men welding steel and creating the machinery that runs this city. Just concrete and steel everywhere, and wire too—plenty of razor-sharp wire tying the look together. A couple of guard towers up in the corners, unarmed men up in them staring down, ready to sound the alarm at the first sign of trouble. Behind it all the tall skeletons of cranes at work, dust in the air kicked up by heavy equipment, engine noise from the bulldozers and cement mixers carrying for miles. There's a long wing with scaffolding erected near the end and workmen busy on extending it, big burly men covered in grease and sweat who all possibly live within the walls they're creating.

The visitors' entrance is far more modern, like the entrance to a three-star hotel. There are large glass doors that seem as though they could be opening into a well-furnished foyer. The entire thing has the fresh look of renovations, and I wonder about the reasoning behind it. I'm not sure how it looked in the past, but the last few years have seen plenty of add-ons and updates to accommodate the new and the aspiring criminals this city is producing. Already some of the large open grounds out here have been zoned for more buildings, more cells, more inmates, and the grounds immediately nearby are already being converted. There have been editorials in the papers lately suggesting they build the concrete walls around Christchurch City and save some time; some even think we should take the biblical route and fill those walls up with water. I never believed them. I never knew Christchurch was really this bad—but now I know it's worse.

There is a landscaped garden with a lush lawn heading toward the glass doors. I'm not sure what image they're trying to sell here, but the whole thing seems very corporate. The doors open and it's air-conditioned inside, which is a relief, because the parking lot with the asphalt has to be over forty degrees. A woman watches me from behind a reception counter with Plexiglas separating her from me.

There are two men back there with her also. Three video surveillance cameras stare down at me from different angles within the room.

"Can I help you, sir?"

It's like a bank in here, large potted plants, chairs everywhere, the counter with the smiling woman. If six armed men burst into this room I don't think they'd get far. For the hundredth time today I wonder where those men are, and know they're about as far away from this prison as you can get.

"Sir?"

The visitor's entrance may be fresh and friendly, but the woman behind the desk is not. She's in her forties with the kind of steely look that could scare half of the inmates straight. "Ah, yeah, I'm here to visit somebody."

"Name?"

"Mine or his?"

"Both."

"Ah, I'm Jack Hunter," I say, hating the sound of the name, and saying it because that's the name my dad will have given them. "My dad is . . ."

"Jack the Hunter," she says, and she flinches away from me, just a little, but enough to notice. "Hang on a moment," she says, and she buzzes for one of the guards. "Take a seat." I do as she says in case she stands up and throws me into one.

It takes a couple of minutes for the guard to appear. He's older than me and a lot bigger and looks as if he can't wait for me to say the wrong thing.

"This way," he says, and I follow him.

"No touching," he says. "No yelling. No passing any objects. That's pretty much all you got to know, but you break any of those rules and you're out of here. You get me?"

"No touching, no yelling, no handing over anything. I get it," and I wonder if the rules are the same for everybody.

The corporate image disappears. We head down a concrete hallway to a heavy metal door, passing an office on the way full of video monitors showing images from the prison. There are a few guards there, and one of them comes out and pats me down and passes a metal detector over me. It beeps a few times and I have to leave my keys and wallet in a tray. The original guard leads me toward another door. It's buzzed open, and then we're in another corridor. Another metal door. Another buzzing sound. The guard opens the door and takes a step back. "In there," he says, and then he follows me inside.

I was expecting a row of phones with a thick piece of Plexiglas between them, covered in palm prints and scratches. Failing that, it'd be an interrogation room, my dad handcuffed and shackled to a chair. Instead it's a large room with about a dozen tables. There are plenty of other prisoners in their orange jumpsuits talking to family members. One of them I recognize, a man very much like my father. I've seen him scattered over the pages of the papers, his face always on TV. He's sitting opposite a woman and a man in their midsixties—perhaps his parents, because the woman is an older, female version of him. The man is the Christchurch Carver, and the media made the connection quicker with him and hyped him up as the city's most infamous serial killer—even though he has maintained his innocence. The Carver looks up at me. He's got a scar running down the side of his face and an eyelid that's all twisted and doesn't seem to fit right. He smiles and his broken eyelid droops.

A door at the opposite end of the room opens, and my dad comes through, a guard right behind him. For a second I'm back in time, watching his smile, then I'm further back, Dad throwing a ball with me, hugging me at night, putting a Band-Aid on my knee or removing a splinter, and back then Dad was the best dad in the world. When I was eight years old I even bought him a coffee mug that said the same thing. The mug lied. The memories lied too. He walks over toward me, but before he can reach out the guard following him reminds us of the no-touching rule—which is perfectly fine with me.

"Hello, son," he says, and I wonder if he rehearsed what his first words would be to me. I don't answer him. I don't know how. "I can't believe how much you've grown," my dad says, and he sits down and I keep standing.

"You thought I'd still be a kid?" I ask.

"No. Not at all. Take a seat, Jack."

"It's Edward these days."

"Not to me."

The thing that strikes me the most is how much Dad has changed, but at the same time how much he is exactly the same. He has to be in his midsixties at least, though I'm not sure of his exact age. He could almost be seventy. He looks seventy, if that's anything to go by. He was as large as life when I was kid—perhaps that's because he was out there taking everybody else's. He was a bigger man, certainly, but in jail the weight has slipped away from him, and my memories are old, and the combination of them means the man sitting ahead of me is not the man who raised me for the first third of my life. The time here has not only taken his weight, but also his hair. He's bald on top with a ring of grey hair around the edges, and sideburns that don't seem to match. He hasn't stopped smiling since the moment he saw me, his lips peeled back, showing teeth that are slightly crooked that I don't remember being crooked. His jaw is covered in stubble, his eyebrows longer now, hair sprouting from his ears and nose. But his eyes, his eyes are the same. Warm, friendly, smiling blue eyes that look at me with tenderness, and the wrinkles to the sides of them, the small wrinkles that appear when he smiles are the same, and Dad could be a hundred and ten years old and you'd still know him by his eyes. Is this me in the future? Is this the face I will one day have?

"It's been a while," I say, finally coming up with something. I sit down and the guard takes a few steps back and tries to pretend he isn't listening to what we're saying while Dad's guard wanders off to the other side of the room.

"You got no argument from me," Dad answers. "It'll be twenty-one years next winter. That sure does count as a long time."

Fact is, it's the longest time anybody has served in this prison. Your run-of-the-mill murders get you ten to twelve years with parole. Less if you find Jesus. But Dad strung himself together a collection of ladies that was too long not to go answered for, so the wheels of justice ground in a new direction for him and he became the first person ever to be given "life" where "life" actually meant he'd never step outside of these walls again.

"I have a granddaughter," he says. "Did you bring a picture?"

"No," I answer, even though there is one in my wallet. I don't want this man seeing her. I don't want this man being part of her life, and by the time she ever has to learn of him he will hopefully be dead.

We stare at each other and I offer nothing else. I hardly know what to say. I always thought I would. I thought I'd scream at him, and suddenly I'm finding there's something to be said about being with your dad again after all this time. Maybe I didn't stop loving him at all way back then.

"I'm sorry how it turned out," he says, and he spreads his hands magician style, as if he thinks his words carry more weight if he can prove he's not hiding anything up his sleeves. "With your mum. And especially with Belinda. I loved that little girl. It almost killed me what happened to her."

"You talk about her as if she was somebody you met," I say. "She was your daughter. My sister. And you were out there taking away other parents' little girls who were doing the same thing."

"True," he says. "Very true. But I still cry at night. I cry for the little girl I lost. I cry for the woman she never got to become."

"You never got to see who she did become. She gave up everything for me. She did your job and she did Mum's job and in the end it killed her. She's dead because of you. Mum's dead because of you."

"I know."

"You know? That's it? When you cry, is it from remorse or from guilt?"

"Always from both," he says. "Always."

"I doubt that. I think you cry because you got caught. What do you want?"

"I wanted to see you. I've always wanted to know how you are. I try to keep track as much as I can, which isn't much. If it hadn't been for Jodie, I'd never even know you were . . ."

"What?"

"Married," he finishes.

"What do you mean about Jodie?"

"She told me she'd never tell you, but she came to visit me. Twice."

"Don't you dare lie to me, Dad. You start lying and I'm out of here."

"It was eight years ago—the year before you got married. I think twenty-two is pretty young to get married, to be honest, but she didn't come to see me about marriage advice."

"And I don't need marriage advice from you," I say. *Especially now*, I think. "Why did she come to see you?" I ask, my stomach twisting into knots.

"The first time was to meet me. To see what I was like, maybe to see how life could have gone for you if you hadn't met somebody like her to keep you happy."

"What the hell is that supposed to mean? Mum couldn't make you happy? You make it sound like it was her fault you killed those people, that if she'd been a better wife then . . ."

"That's not what I mean at all," he says, holding up his hand to stop me.

"Then what?"

"It was a poor choice of words. Son, I never meant any of this to happen."

"You didn't? Thanks, Dad. That's wonderful to hear. I wish I could repay you for those kind words. Maybe if you ever get out of here we can hang out together, maybe go bowling."

"The second time," he says, ignoring me, "she was pregnant."

My stomach tightens. I hate the idea of her sitting out here, facing my father, exposing her deep-down fears, telling him she was scared that the things he did would run in the family. I hate the idea she exposed Sam to this kind of evil. I'm immediately angry at her for that. Angry at her for coming here, angry at her for dying.

"She was a real nice kid, and I didn't hold it against her for hating me. I'm not kidding myself, I've got no friends in this world, and I've done nothing to deserve any, and anything she had to say to me I'd heard before."

"What's your point, Dad?"

"Dad. I like the way that sounds."

"Enjoy it over the next two minutes. You're never going to hear it again."

"I want to meet my granddaughter."

"Out of the question. Why did Jodie come to see you the second time?"

"I have a right to see her. She's blood."

"No. She's nothing like you and she's nothing to you. Why did Jodie come back?"

"She came to tell me you were a good man and I didn't deserve to have you as a son. She told me I would be a grandfather and would never meet my grandchildren. She told me I had ruined a lot of lives, but yours wasn't one of them. She said she was fixing the damage inside of you that I'd done. She wanted me to know you were a good man and were going to make a great father. That was her gift to me, Jack. You were one lucky man meeting her, and you did the right thing by getting a ring on her finger as early as you did." He leans forward. "But you are different. You're my son, and she sensed it in you."

"Shut up."

"I really am sorry about what happened to her, son. A waste, such a waste. I have some idea what you're going through, and it's hard, son, it really is hard, and no matter how hollow it sounds, it's true when people tell you that time does help. It doesn't heal, but it helps. You will move on, and you have Sam, and if she's anything like Jodie then you've got a beautiful little girl to look after."

"I know, I know," I say. "If it weren't for her . . ."

I trail off, and neither of us fills the silence for a few more seconds until Dad leans forward and looks me right in the eye. "Have you heard it yet?" he asks.

"What are you talking about?" I ask, leaning back.

My dad leans back too, imitating me, but then he crosses one leg over the other and taps his fingers on his knee.

"When you were a kid I used to take you and Belinda to the park. You remember? There was a fort there you'd always play on. Had a tire with chains on it that had been turned into a swing. There was a pole you could slide down. There was bark everywhere, and bars you could climb, ropes and chains you could hang from."

"This going anywhere?"

"There was a merry-go-round there too. You two used to play on that thing so fast that when you came to a stop and stood up, you'd fall over, dizzy as hell, clutching onto the ground as if it were moving, trying to keep it still."

"What is this? Some kind of father–son moment that you saw on TV and are trying to emulate?"

"One day, when you were eight," he says, "when we were there, there was a man there too, walking his dog. It got off its leash and ran over to the fort where you and Belinda were riding the merry-go-round. You came to a stop and spilled off it, and the dog, it was all excited and tried sniffing Belinda. She got scared and she ran."

"I don't remember."

"It ran after her and tried to bite her, and she kept running and trying to watch the dog all at the same time, and she got off balance. She ran right into a tree and knocked herself out. Got her forehead grazed up. You remember what you said when we were carrying her back to the car?"

"Not really."

My dad leans forward, and in a lower voice, he tells me. "You said you would kill it."

"No I didn't."

"Six months after that, the dog a few houses down from us that always used to bark, you remember that dog . . . ?"

"Not really."

"It was the same dog from the park. This big black dog with a lot of bark. That dog got itself killed."

"I don't remember."

"That's a long time to be angry at an animal," Dad says.

"What the hell are you talking about?"

"You don't think I noticed the steak was missing?" he asks, his voice low now, and I hadn't noticed but I've leaned in close to him. "I told your mother I'd taken it. She never knew it was you who killed that dog. But I knew. Is that when you first heard it?"

"You're delusional."

"I think it probably was. You might have heard it earlier but didn't know what it was. It would have taken a while to build up the courage. I first heard it when I was the same age," he says. "This voice that was different from me, these thoughts that weren't mine. They told me to do things that I didn't want to do. I refused—in the beginning. Then I gave in, hoping it would shut the voice up. Soon the voice was the same as my own, and in the end I couldn't even tell the difference."

"You're sick," I say.

"I know. That's what I said twenty years ago. Hell, I'm not so unreasonable that I know hearing a voice isn't right. But right or wrong, I heard it. I don't blame you for never coming to ask me about it, but . . ."

"I should never have come here."

"When you killed that dog, it was because you were hearing a voice of your own."

"I didn't kill any dog."

"What happened after that?" he asks. "Did you keep hearing the voice, or did it disappear? Have you been giving in to it all these years? Are there graves out there waiting to be found?"

"I'm nothing like you." I begin to stand. He reaches across and grabs me, and before the guard can say anything he lets go. I sit back down.

"The darkness. That's what I called it," he says. "I know you're listening to it, but you also have to control it. If you can't, it will take you to places before you're ready. It doesn't care if you get caught—it just wants to see blood. You have to rein that voice in, need to come to an understanding with it and, if you're hearing it now, and I'm sure you are, then you have to find a way to stop it from overtaking you."

"I have no darkness."

"It never goes away," he says. "At night I can hear it whispering, but I have no outlet for it here. It's faded some over the years, sure, but it's still there, no denying that."

"Why are you telling me this?"

"To protect you," he says, "from the same thing that happened to me. Please, son, let me help you."

"I call it the monster," I say, the words out of my mouth before I can stop them, and Dad slowly nods, and for an awful moment I think my dad is going to smile, and say something sickening, perhaps a *that's my boy*, but he doesn't. The warmth goes out of his eyes and he stops nodding.

"That's a shame, son. It really is."

"I never knew what else to call it. I figured you had a monster, and when you went to jail, it came to live with me. Came to live inside me."

"Not my monster," he says. "You proved that by killing the dog before I went to jail. You have your own darkness. I wish I could help you more, and I would, if I was out there with you. Son, word around here is that the cops have no idea who killed Jodie."

I stare at him blankly.

"She didn't like me much, but I could see she was a good person. She was a good wife, I bet, and certainly a great mother, and I owe her for what she did for you. What happened to her—that's a shitty thing. A real shitty thing. Yet if you ask me, the fact the cops haven't caught anybody, that's a good thing."

"What?"

"It's a good thing, son. Think about it."

"What are you on about? How the hell can you say that? What are you? What in the hell are you?"

My dad leans forward in his chair then slowly pushes himself up. Both guards come over. "It was good talking to you, son." He starts to walk away.

"Fuck you!"

"No yelling," the guard says, and puts a hand on my shoulder and I shrug it off. The Christchurch Carver looks over and watches.

Dad turns back. "Go home and think about what happened to your wife," he says. "And take some advice from your old man . . ."

"Save it," I say.

"It's okay to listen to the voice," he says, then he disappears through the doorway.

chapter fifteen

Suction Cup Guy had a real name and Suction Cup Guy was murdered. His name was Arnold Langham and his friends called him Arnie. He was a husband and a dad and his forty-two years on this earth all ended when he was tossed from the apartment building. The suction cups were attached to him, he was stripped and dressed in a trench coat, one of his fingernails found buried in the roof as he tried to fight for survival, the reason for the staging still unknown. Langham no longer lived with his wife—hadn't lived with her since he'd beaten her up badly enough to spend three years in jail for it. The wife wasn't a suspect because she'd taken their son and moved north and west enough to hit the next country in line with New Zealand. Other than beating up his wife, Langham doesn't have any other criminal record—no assaults, no rapes, no breaking and entering. A couple of speeding tickets but that's all. He worked full time on an assembly line making control boards for motorized wheelchairs. It was an active case, but the urgency had dissipated—it's the way it was when one case you were working dealt with a wife-beater, and there was another case dealing with a group of bank robbers who killed two people while stealing what turned out to be 2.8 million in cash. It was about priorities—and at the moment the bank robbery was everybody's priority. Suction Cup Guy would have to wait. It was a shame that for the hundreds of man-hours invested so far, all they had were transcripts of pointless interviews and a burned-out van. They didn't even have the dye-pack-damaged money. He'd have thought any ruined money would have been dumped with the van and set on fire, but forensics—at least so far—had found no traces of it. No currency—no red ink. All he has are a lot of unanswered questions, two bodies in the ground who deserve to be put to rest, and a wife who was cold to him most of the weekend. The job was interfering with his family life. The last weekend before Christmas and he should have been spending it with his wife and daughter and their new baby boy, and at the rate the investigation is going his son will be in school and his wife will have left him before it's over. He's been lucky so far in that he hasn't missed any Christmases, but he's certainly missed plenty of other occasions; each one his wife remembers and, in times of arguments, reminds him of. Sometimes she reminds him he's the reason they're having children so late, and that he's the reason they're going to be in their sixties before the kids are old enough to move out of home.

There are plenty of criminals on the street who occasionally do a favor for the cops in return for some minor charges being overlooked. But this time there's nothing. The men responsible have involved nobody else. The cash, if not damaged, hasn't been circulating anywhere. Whoever did this knew what they were doing. They got out of the bank almost two minutes before the police arrived. Reading criminal records has led to hundreds of possibilities, but linking enough names together to form the gang that robbed the bank has been impossible. They've conducted almost two hundred interviews already and he wonders if any of the men who actually stormed into the bank have been spoken to. Probably. Hard to know.

Schroder is sipping at a cup of cooling coffee and has just hung up from a phone call from the prison. Turns out Edward Hunter went to see his father today. He wonders what would prompt him to do that after all these years.

There's a knock at his office door. "Somebody here to see you," an officer says.

"Who?"

"He says he has some information about the robbery."

"Another psychic?" Schroder asks. Whenever there is enough media coverage of a tragic event, the psychics come out of the woodwork. Jonas Jones, an ex-used-car dealer turned "renowned" psychic investigator who appears on TV giving "serious criminal insights" to cases the police have been unable to get a handle on, has already left over a dozen messages and has been banned from going any farther than the foyer in the police station.

"Worse. A shrink."

"Jesus."

"You want me to send him in?"

The thing about shrinks is that sometimes they can be worse than psychics. At least the psychics will put on a show. They'll light a few candles and pretend they're talking to the spirit world or tuning in to some kind of vision.

"Not really, but go ahead."

Benson Barlow is mostly bald with a serious comb-over, and Schroder wonders what other psychiatrists would say about it. In his midfifties and with a beard, the only thing missing from the shrink are elbow patches on his jacket and a pipe—but maybe that stuff he leaves in the office. After shaking hands, Schroder offers him a seat.

"The officer said you have some information about the robbery?"

"Well, in a way."

"What exactly does 'in a way' mean?"

"It means I don't actually know anything about the robbery itself, not in those kind of terms."

Schroder wonders if everybody who has a first and last name

starting with the same letter is going to be a thorn in his side. Benson Barlow. Jonas Jones. Theodore Tate. "Then why are you here? To offer a profile?"

"Not exactly," Barlow says, leaning forward. "Twenty years ago I was the psychiatrist who examined Jack Hunter."

"Which one?"

"Well, both, actually."

"And which one are you here to talk to me about? Jack Jr.?"

"Mostly, though he's Edward now. It was one of the first things he did when he was eighteen—legally change his name, though since the age of nine he wouldn't answer to anything other than Edward. Jack Sr. suffered from paranoid schizophrenia. He heard voices and he believed he was being controlled by them. Or it. It was only the one voice, and he called it the darkness."

"Come on, that was a line of BS they tried feeding to the jury. Nobody bought it."

"It wasn't bullshit, Detective. It's a real mental illness that people genuinely suffer from. It makes them think delusional thoughts. It can make you think you're being followed, chosen by God for a quest, it can make you think you're being watched by your neighbor or by the media. It can make you believe you're being controlled by an external source."

"And Jack Hunter thought he was on a quest for God?"

"Well, no. He thought there was a real darkness living inside him that needed to see blood to stay happy."

"Then he thought right. I don't see what this has to do with the robbery."

"Paranoid schizophrenia is a hereditary condition, Detective. What Jack Sr. has, there's a chance that Edward might be struggling with the same illness—perhaps only to a minor degree, something that can be treated with medication. But considering the numerous traumas the boy went through at an early age, his current loss may compound the situation into something more serious. All those years ago when he was my patient, he told me things—things that make me worry about him. I fear for him, and for what he's capable of."

"What kind of things?"

"I can't tell you what he said. Those sessions were private."

"So you've come here to tell me you can't tell me anything?"

"No. I've come here to tell you that Edward Hunter is potentially a danger to himself, possibly to others. Genetically, he's like his dad. Emotionally, I think they're the same. Edward stopped being my patient when he turned eighteen and I haven't seen him since, but from what I've learned over the last few days it's obvious he was living a very stable life in an environment he was comfortable with. But now things have changed. The death of his wife is a trigger, Detective. It's a huge red flag and I'm telling you, there's serious potential there for him to be a dangerous man, perhaps even as dangerous as his father."

Schroder picks up a pencil and rolls it between his fingers. "So what is it you want me to do? I can't go and lock him up to satisfy your suspicion of him. Why don't you get him in for some sessions?"

"I've tried. I've been leaving messages but he won't return them."

Schroder doesn't blame him. He wouldn't return the messages either. "So what do you want?"

Barlow shrugs. "Ideally, I want Edward to get help. There are medications that can keep him under control."

"You're assuming he has what his dad has—and even that's assuming his dad had anything other than a taste for blood."

"Even so," Barlow says, dismissing him and standing up as Schroder's office phone starts ringing. "I've done my professional duty. Ethically and legally I have to warn the police if I have a patient who I believe to be a danger to others or themselves, and that's what this is—it's a warning."

chapter sixteen

I listen to the lunchtime news on the way home. The guy who shoved and killed the woman in the parking lot is claiming he was on "P," the fashionable drug with the fashionable defense for murder—meaning he'll either get six months in jail or nine months in rehab since it really wasn't his fault, but the drug's fault, or the addiction's fault, or everybody else's fault for not reaching out and helping him sooner. Most of the sheep have been caught but four are still on the run. Maybe they'll team up and make more sheep between them and go about robbing farms. There is more news: a security guard was killed last night and found naked in town, a primary school was burned down but nobody was hurt, then there's sport and weather and nobody mentions the bank robbery anymore.

I get caught behind a slow-moving truck, adding about twenty minutes to my drive, the amount of exhaust fumes coming from the back of it bringing global warming twenty minutes closer to a final conclusion. I'm still angry when I get home. Angry at the news, at the police, at the monster inside me, at the world for moving on when it should be pausing, when it should be taking a time-out to mourn my wife and to ask the big question, "Why?" over and over, why did this have to happen, why is society the way it is, why isn't anybody doing anything about it?

I'm still angry at my dad. With twenty years between the last time I saw him and this time there should have been more to say. And why did he get me out there only to tell me it's a good thing that the police haven't caught the men who did this?

Don't kid yourself, you know exactly why.

"No," I say, and I grab a beer from the fridge.

Mostly I'm angry at myself. I didn't go out there to share anything with him. I don't really know why I went—certainly it wasn't to tell him about the monster, but those words came out as if they had a life of their own. And in a way I guess that's exactly what the monster is—a life of its own. I've kept hearing it over the last twenty years, small suggestions whispered to me that I've ignored, ideas on how to get rid of animals or people that I don't like.

My wife has been dead four days and in the ground for less than twenty-four hours and I'm losing my mind. I sit outside and let the sun burn my face and eyes before turning away, the bright shadows and shapes moving across my vision. I go through my wallet for the business card I slid in there on Friday, and when I find it I can't read the number on it and have to wait for a minute for my vision to settle.

"Detective Schroder," the detective says, answering his phone.

"Hi. It's, ah, Edward Hunter. I'm, ah, ringing to see—"

"I was just about to call you," he says.

"Yeah? You have something?" I ask, walking outside with the phone. "You've caught the men who killed Jodie?"

"No. Not yet, but trust me, Edward, we're following up some strong leads," he says, but he doesn't even sound like he could convince himself. "You have to be patient."

"I have been patient."

"I promise you, it's still my top priority."

"In three days it will have been a week," I point out.

"I understand your frustration," he says.

"I'm not so sure you do. How much did they get?"

"What?"

"How much money did they take from the bank?"

"I can't discuss that with you."

"Jodie was killed because of that money. Give me a break, Detective, I think I have more than a right to know how much my wife's life was worth."

"It doesn't work that way."

"Yeah, yeah, I know, because two people died," I say, and the accountant in me is doing the arithmetic, "so divide that number by two and that's how much she was worth. I want to know if she died for more or less than the price of a new car, more or less than the price of a house? Of course it depends on the house, on the car, but—"

"Look, Edward, I promise you we're doing our best. We really are. We have everybody we can spare searching for those men."

"Searching, not chasing," I say. "Maybe I should do your job for you," I say, and the words are out of my mouth before I can stop them, having come from nowhere, certainly not from me, and I realize they're not my words at all, but somebody else's. No, not somebody—something.

"What does that mean?" Schroder asks.

"It doesn't mean anything," I say. "I'm angry, that's all."

"I hear you went to visit your father today."

"What?"

"First time since he got put away. Why'd you do that?"

I slow down and think about his question, aware he's talking to me now in a different capacity—he's talking to me the way a cop talks to a suspect. He's fishing for information. "He rang me. Told me he wanted to see me."

"And you dropped everything to go."

"He's my father. He wanted to share his condolences. He wanted to know what the police were doing to get the men who killed my wife."

"Is that all?"

"Of course that's all. My wife got murdered, Detective. What father wouldn't want to try to console his son?"

"Have you been seeing anybody since the shooting? For help? A counselor, or a psychiatrist?"

"Why would I do that?" One of my neighbors starts up a lawn mower and I head back inside so I can hear Schroder clearly.

"To help you come to terms with what happened."

"I can come to terms in my own way."

"I hope that doesn't involve doing anything stupid."

"Like what?"

"Like trying to do my job."

"One of us has to try," I say, "because it seems to me nothing is getting done."

"A word of caution, Edward. Leave everything to us. We know what we're doing."

"Then prove it."

I hang up, finish my beer, grab out another one, but don't open it. I leave it on the kitchen counter and fire up the computer.

I go online and find all the newspaper reports from the last week that dealt with the robbery. There's enough of them that by the time I print them out I have a stack of paper a centimeter thick. I take them outside and sit in the sun, reading through them. Surveillance from the bank puts the entry of the six men at 1:13 p.m. They were in the bank for less than four minutes, though it sure felt longer. The police were called by several witnesses outside who saw the men enter, as well as people who first heard the shotgun blast, but they were first alerted by a silent alarm. I close my eyes and try to remember as best I can. The men had been in the bank for almost a minute before the bank manager was killed. The newspaper says it took six minutes for the police to arrive at the scene. The men had been gone for two minutes by that point. The newspaper doesn't say how much money was taken.

The accountant studies the figures. Four minutes. Six minutes. Six men. Two victims. Two fatal gunshots. An unnamed amount of money. The figures swirl around inside my head, I rest them against everything the newspapers say, try forcing them to fit against what I know, against my memories, but nothing sticks out, nothing shifts into such a focus as to tell me where to look next. The numbers mean nothing.

I pick up the sheaf of papers and throw them out into the yard. Most of them stay together, but the ones on the top and bottom slide away, the small breeze picking them up and pinning them into the corners of the yard. The answers are in the wind too, and though Schroder didn't say it, I know that the bank robbery is already history, the death of my wife and the bank manager pushed aside as the Christchurch Crime Rate keeps rolling on, gathering momentum, leading to what, God only knows.

I end up drinking the beer and falling asleep, not heavily, but enough for about an hour to slip by mostly unnoticed, and when I wake up the lawn mower has stopped and my face is tight, and when I reach up to touch it, it's tender from sunburn. When I stand up I realize that the few beers I've had, combined with the lack of food, have made me light-headed. I phone Nat and ask if they can take care of Sam tonight, and they tell me they can. In fact they sound more than happy to. I talk to Sam for a bit and she tells me she wants to come home and I tell her that she can't, not today, that Daddy has some things he has to take care of.

"But you promised," she says.

"I know. I'm sorry."

She finally accepts things can't be changed and hands the phone back to Nat, grumpy.

"She'll be okay," he says. "You know how kids can be."

"How's she doing?"

"You know how it is," he says, and he's right. I do know. He means that Sam's the same since the day we told her about her mum. Part shock and part disbelief and part simply not understanding. I'm the same way. We all are.

"Take care of yourself, Eddie," he says, and something in the way he says that makes me think that he thinks he won't be seeing me for a while. It's the kind of thing you'd say to a friend leaving for jail or war.

I watch the sun peak in the sky. It disappears behind the tip of a giant fir tree next door for ten minutes before coming back into view, and then it slides back down. I drink another beer and then another, then head out front and grab the mail. There's a letter from my insurance company. Both Jodie and myself have life insurance—but in a letter less than half a page long, our insurance company is holding back any decision to pay out because Jodie was killed in the commission of a crime. Life insurance is specifically there to cover accidents and illness—and does not cover murder, so the letter says, and they apologize for any inconvenience. I wonder why they got onto the case so quick—I hadn't even contacted them—and I figure they wanted to rush through the bad news before Christmas.

The sun gets lower and evening arrives. I play the "what-if" game, the one where what if we'd gone to the bank ten minutes later, or what if I'd kept my mouth shut, or what if I'd fought the men off. There are a lot of what-ifs. A thousand of them—of course it's a pointless game to play and I could spend the rest of my life out here under the sun, drinking beer, thinking about the could-have-beens and should-have-beens, the entire time the reality never forgotten—I'm the reason Jodie got killed.

More and more, the what-ifs begin to focus on the bank. I think about the security guard. I think about him a lot, and I imagine him acting.

But he didn't, did he. He just stood there and did nothing.

Nothing! the monster says, and I guess the first part in the road to recovery, like being an alcoholic, is admitting you have a problem. So yeah, I admit, I have a monster.

And it's nice to be here, it says, *nice to be welcomed again after all this time.*

The security guard, trained to help, there to defend, there to stop the innocent from being hurt, he did nothing. Not a goddamn thing.

I open up another beer.

Choosing to do nothing was the same as doing something. Doing nothing is what got everybody killed. You calling out—that didn't get Jodie all shot up. The security guard—it's his fault. He didn't do his job.

"Damn straight," I say.

I replay that moment over and over, and I'm not sure how it happens, but things shift a little and the truth appears, so obvious now, and it explains a lot. The first time I run things through, the security guard does nothing as the security tapes and history books state. But I slow down the action in my head, and then I notice something the cameras didn't have the angle or the emotion to notice—this time the security guard smiles as the men come in, he smiles before he is smashed in the face with the butt of a shotgun. Then I slow it down even more, and there is more than a smile, but a wink and a nod of the head.

The security guard was in on it!

I slow it down again, the men rush in, the first one approaches the guard, and this time there's the smile, the wink, the nod, and this time the guard puts his hand out and the bad guy takes it, they shake hands, there's another nod, and *bang*, the guard is smashed in the head.

Once more. The men come in. One approaches the guard. The wink. The nod. The grin. The handshake. They embrace. They part and then they share a small joke. The bad guy pushes his gun forward but this time the stock doesn't connect with the guard's jaw, but he falls anyway, he falls in a heap and when he lies on the ground the smile is still there.

Another grin. Another wink. Another shared joke, and the men spill deeper into the bank and steal and kill; the entire time the guard watches them.

I go through one last time. This time when they take my wife, the security guard sits up and begins to clap.

I put down the empty beer bottle. There's a row of them now, and thank God my friends, the ones with the platitude of "things will get better," the ones who don't know what to say, thank God they had the decency to bring lots of beer. Sure—they didn't have the decency to be there to save my wife, and they can't really help now, and since bringing beer is the best they can do then thank God for beer, thank God for people who think beer can heal the world.

I grab another one. It's cold and doesn't taste great but it goes down pretty quick. I head out into the backyard, stumbling—stupid yard—and go through the pages I threw out here earlier. I find some of the articles about the security guard. He was rushed to hospital with a serious concussion, which is a load of shit. The journalists—bless whatever it is they have that passes for hearts—have listed first and last names of everybody involved on the day—except, of course, for the six men who were more involved than anybody. I carry one of the stories about the guard back inside and fire up the computer. I search for the guard. Everybody in first-world countries these days is online somewhere, a member of some online community somewhere or whatever the hell is in fashion these days—people sharing their lives with strangers and credit-card thieves and . . .

Monsters . . .

. . . identity stealers and serial killers. The computer takes too long to load, which annoys me, but I kill time by grabbing another beer. The beer is calming me, I'm so full of serenity right now I could write a fucking musical.

I get online and Google the bastard and it's hard to type because the keyboard seems smaller. When I get his name entered plenty of stories from the last four days pop up. I don't bother reading them. Instead I go straight to the White Pages and let my fingers do the walking. Within twenty seconds I have his address. Telecom is my friend.

Our accomplice.

"I think it's time we go visit him," I say.

I can't wait, the monster says.

"One more beer for the road," I suggest.

Hell, have two—you deserve it, the monster says, and I get changed and then we go for a drive.

chapter seventeen

My car is a four-door sedan family vehicle, but I guess I can get rid of two of the doors since I won't be using them anymore. Maybe trade it in for a sports car—maybe let Sam choose the color. We walk out to it, my monster and me, stumbling down the driveway, almost—but thank-God-not-quite—dropping my beer. I can't get the door open but then figure out it's still locked, so I unlock it and things work out great. I get behind the wheel and at first I think somebody has shifted the ignition, so I have to play around with the key, but it gets there in the end, scraping over the edges in the beginning before slotting home.

The mailbox almost becomes the first casualty of the evening, and then the neighbor's cat, but things straighten out and the road points ahead and we follow it. Between us one of us reads the map while the other drives, the roads and intersections and other cars passing by in a blur of color and sound.

Christchurch is a better-looking city the later it gets in the day because the darkness helps hide the infection. I see it all around now—I was ignorant of it until four days ago. In the morning the sun will come up and tear that scab right off, the criminals will spew forth from their hovels, holes, and dens, merrily stealing and raping and killing their way through the twelve days of Christmas. The evening is still warm, and there are a few people out enjoying it, some of them walking hand in hand, or towing a dog on a leash, others on mountain bikes. It's after nine o'clock, the sun has gone but it's still light, the time of day approaching when it can go from light to dark in a matter of minutes. I drive past a park where a father and son are pointing up at a kite caught in a tall tree, stranded and pierced by branches. In the same park a group of teenagers are kicking a rugby ball back and forth, spiraling it high into the air before it gets too dark. There's a fort and a merry-go-round and it reminds me of the story Dad told me earlier.

The Security Guard—one Mr. "let me laugh my ass off while your wife is getting gunned down" Gerald Painter, lives in a quiet street with lots of trees and gardens and homes that all seem the same, and I figure Mr. Gerald Painter should have become a painter and not a guard and if he'd done that, taken that one little path his destiny and last name were trying to point him toward, then this Tuesday night three days from Christmas would be a very different Tuesday night than it will be for him now. It's darker by the time I get there and I have my headlights burning. Painter's white-trash car with the big-block million-decibel engine and fiery paint job he must surely own isn't parked out on the street or up the driveway. Instead there's a four-door sedan, a Toyota I think, a white one, with a FOR SALE sign in the window.

We drive past the house, head down to the end of the street, turn around, and drive back. We slow down, taking another look. Painter is in there, counting his money, wanting to spend it but having to wait. We drive past and pull over, the house on the same side of the road as us. I shut off the engine and turn off the lights and we sit in silence for a bit, thinking, thinking.

Everything is packed into Sam's schoolbag. It was the only thing I could find. They fit in there easily enough, this bright red bag with a weird cartoon character of a dinosaur on it that is loved by children everywhere, but if it caught a flight into the country it wouldn't get past customs. I wasn't sure what I was going to need, but we figured it out in the end. Rope. A knife. Actually a couple of knives. Duct tape. Gloves. I don't have any balaclavas, and the best I could come up with was a baseball cap. The beer I was carrying has fallen over during the drive and neither of us thought to bring a fresh one, which means there's still much to learn.

I turn off the interior dome light, then open the door. There are Christmas lights up on some of the houses, and in most of the windows you can see bright lights coming from make-believe trees. I lean against the car, then pull away from it when it sways behind me. I move around to the passenger door and open it and grab out Sam's bag. I carry it by the strap, walk across the grass out the front of the neighboring house, then the strap on the bag unthreads because I'm holding the wrong one, the bag opens, and everything spills out onto the lawn, jangling and clanging against each other.

"Shit."

Shit.

I crouch down and pack everything into the bag, careful not to get cut. I keep looking around for anybody watching, but nobody is, at least not that I can see. Everything goes back in okay, even the hat, which for some reason I've forgotten to put on. I grab it out and prick my finger on the knife.

"Aw, Jesus," I say, shaking my hand, then sucking the cut on my thumb. It's not much, but it hurts. I stand up and take a few more steps forward. I stare at the house, wondering why it's different from when we drove past two minutes earlier, then realize I'm standing in front of the wrong one. I've led us the opposite way.

We turn around and head past my car toward the correct house. I don't know what the next step is, I wait for my companion to fill in the blanks, and he does, because my monster is a real team player. He takes over and leads us up the path to the front door. I lean against the house while he puts his finger out and rings the bell.

chapter eighteen

Nice house. Nice street. A family street. Not a white-trash, let's-rob-a-bank kind of street, but I guess those bastards can afford to live where they want.

The house is a single-storey dwelling painted one of those Latin-sounding coffee-color names. The yard smells of freshly mown lawn, small different-colored flax bushes have been evenly spaced out around the house, so even I bet they were measured out, some with red leaves, others with green. They're surrounded by yellowy white limestone instead of dirt or bark, a tidy low-maintenance garden planted on layers of weedmat I imagine, the kind of garden Jodie wanted and the kind of garden we were going to have until Gerald Painter took all that away from us. There's a silver birch tree out front with the roots climbing out of the ground and cracking the sidewalk.

It's a brick home, a nice solid home, with a nice solid front door with thin pieces of glass striped down one third in from the left-hand side and one third in from the right-hand side, with a big matte-silver door handle on the right. The bell is a small black box with a white button that buzzes for as long as you hold it. I can hear it buzzing as the monster holds it down. He doesn't let it go until we can see a shadowed image moving down the hallway toward the door, slowly and not quite in a straight line, all detail of the figure distorted in the strips of glass.

The door opens. It opens my future and this man's fate, this man with the bruises on his face and neck that resemble the bruises on mine. His nose has a small bandaged brace over it. He squints and presses his face forward to get a better look, and we want to shove the steak knife right into his head.

His eyes widen as he recognizes me—not us—just me—and for some reason he can't see the monster, because a smile, not the your-wife-is-dead-and-it's-my-fault-fuck-you smile, but a sad, sympathetic smile, stretches out beneath the bandaged brace.

"Come in," he says, before either of us say a word.

"Thank you," we say, and he closes the door behind us.

"I kind of thought you might show up," he says. He walks ahead of us, he's limping slightly, and he veers toward the left and has to keep correcting himself. As far as hallways go, it seems okay. Photos that seem fuzzy to me, a bookcase, a houseplant, all boring shit unless you lived here. He leads me into the dining room which is tidy and doesn't have any beer bottles anywhere even though he seems drunker than me. "Take a seat," he says, and there are seats at a breakfast bar of the kitchen, and we take one. It's a few degrees warmer inside than out and a set of French doors are wide open, the dining room flowing out onto a deck where there's outdoor lighting and a gas barbecue and a picnic table that's turned silver in the sun. There's a Christmas tree in the living room tall enough to touch the ceiling and thick enough to hold what must be about five hundred decorations.

"You . . . ah, you thought I might, might show up?" I ask, trying really hard not to slur my words.

"Can I get you something to drink? I don't have anything alcoholic," he says. "I did, until my wife poured it all down the sink. Doctor's orders of course. Not that it stopped me from trying. I've got Coke or Sprite but it's not the same. Want something?"

"Why'd, why'd you think, that, ah, that I was going to"—I suck in a deep breath and exhale loudly—"to, ah, show up?"

He shrugs. "I don't know."

Painter is taking on a slightly blurry complexion. It's as though he's standing with his identical ghost, his ghost living almost exactly in the same place but off by a few millimeters, so it looks like it's trying to peel itself away. When I rub at my eyes the ghost disappears.

"Yes you do. You wouldn't"—I take another deep breath and can taste beer, and suddenly I really have to take a leak—"wouldn't have said anything otherwise."

Painter is a man in his mid to late forties with a shaved head and dark eyes that don't seem to focus well. He takes a seat at the kitchen bar, sitting slowly, exhaling heavily, and holding on to the bench at the same time. There's a microwave in view behind him with a clock that doesn't match my inner perception of time because it's telling me I've already been here five minutes and I'm sure only one has passed.

"Since the . . . robbery, I've had problems," he says. "Something in here," he says, and he taps his head, and I realize the shaved head is fresh, "got broken. I mean, the doctors had bigger words for it, but if you ground those words up and put them in their simplest form, that's what they'd say. I can't walk straight. I reach for something and I miss. I take a piss and it goes all over the floor. I've got this ringing in my ears that won't stop, and sometimes for no good reason I'll just start to cry. It's permanent too. They had big words for that also, but it didn't matter how they tried to tie a goddamn bow on it, the gift was the same either way. Got this for life," he says. "Can't ever work again. Can't drive. Can hardly ever go into public. Don't know what I'll do. I'll lose my house, that's for sure. I got insurance for what happened to me, but it doesn't cover shit. But hey, look at me, bitching about what happened to me, what happened to me ain't worth a damn considering what happened to you. To your wife and the bank manager."

I put the bag up on the counter.

Open it, open it, open it.

We open it. My bladder is going to explode.

"You gonna say anything?" he asks.

"What do, do you . . . want to hear from us?"

"Us?"

Us? Did I say us? No. I didn't. "I said me."

"You said us."

"It was a, a mistake. Tell me. What do you want to hear?"

"I don't know."

"You said you were expecting me," I say, focusing really hard on the words.

"Not really expecting. Hoping, I guess, is the word."

"Hoping? Why?"

"I don't know why, not really."

"Tell me."

He spends a few seconds exhaling, grimacing at the same time. He can't keep his hands still. "I can hardly sleep," he says, "and when I do, there are always dreams. I didn't see anybody die, but I know they did. I saw them after, you know, after they were shot. I saw your wife, I mean, I didn't see her die, and I was still unconscious when they took me away, but I see her dying anyway. The reason I didn't see it for real was I messed up and let them get me without a fight. I mean, they could have killed me instead, right? I'd rather have died trying than . . . than this. I dream about them, you know. About the men who did this. I dream about the ones who died. Your wife comes to me at night, in my dreams."

"What does she say?" I ask, genuinely curious. She hasn't come to see me yet.

"She tells me there was nothing I could have done."

"You believe her?"

"No."

"You're pathetic," I say, but the words aren't mine. "Fucking pathetic."

"I know," he says, and tries to fight back tears.

"Stop crying."

"I'm not crying," he says, choking on the words.

"Jesus," I say, slowly shaking my head, but I'm sober now, no longer in danger of throwing up. "You could have stopped them," I say, my words forceful now, clear.

"You think I didn't want to? Ah shit, it's not fair, I mean, six of them, all with guns, and what the hell do I have?" he says, wiping at his eyes before the tears can fall. "Certainly no weapon of any sort. The bank gives me a uniform and that's it. I mean, that's not exactly a deterrent against professional bank robbers. Shit, I can't even keep the damn skateboarders off the front sidewalk. I wanted to do more, I wish I could have done more, but . . . ah shit . . . ," he says. "Are you . . . are you here to kill me?"

"Is that what you want?"

"I . . . I think so." His hands are clenched and shaking. Tears are running down his face. "I . . . I don't have the courage to do it myself."

All those memories earlier today that weren't memories, but more like reels of film of different scenarios that rolled through my head, they play out again, and in each one there is nothing this man could have done. One unarmed man against six men with shotguns. Each time he tried to protect us, one or more of the guns would put him in his place, his chest and head exploding into a ball of blood. "You could have saved my wife," I hear myself saying, even though I know it isn't true.

I reach into the bag and pull out a serrated steak knife. He doesn't seem as thrilled about dying as he did five seconds ago, but he doesn't move or try to fight me.

He cries harder. "I'm so sorry," he says. "It should've been me, it should've been me who died."

"You're right. It should have been."

"I . . . I wanted to do it myself," he says, when we stand up and move closer to him. "But I couldn't. I was too scared. I heard who you are and I wondered if you might come, if you were anything like your dad."

"Edward the Hunter," I say. I thought my hand would be shaking, but it isn't, it's firm and we hold the knife firmly and our nerves are steady. "I can't fight my destiny," I say.

"Please, just make it quick."

"We will."

"Thank you," he says, but I'm not so sure he means it.

chapter nineteen

I head for outside, my hands shaking, the bag in one hand, the knife tucked away inside it. In the end I didn't use any of the other supplies. Next time I'll travel lighter.

I'm still in the doorway when a car pulls into the driveway. It's similar to the one already parked there—same color, a bit smaller, equally as foreign. The passenger door opens and a little girl climbs out, and at first I can't make sense of it. The headlights have blinded me, it's dark out, so in that moment I think the little girl is Sam. No real reason for that—I'm at a stranger's house, Sam is at her grandparents', Sam will be in bed with Mr. Fluff 'n' Stuff, curled up and asleep and dreaming of her mother. But the thought comes anyway, this little girl runs up to me and yells, "Daddy," before she comes to a dead stop, staring up at me and then staring at the cartoon character bag in my hand.

The headlights turn off and the engine dies and the driver's door opens. A woman steps out—Painter's wife—and has noticed I'm standing here, but hasn't taken a good enough look to realize I'm not her husband.

"I thought maybe once we get her to bed, we might want to take a . . .," she says, approaching me, and then, like her daughter, she comes to a complete stop.

"Who are you?" she asks, her eyes narrowing.

"I was just leaving," I say.

"Oh my God," she says, and the recognition is there now. "Oh my God, is that blood on your shirt? What have you done to Gerald?"

I don't answer her.

She picks her daughter up and cradles her. I take a few steps toward the driveway and she backs toward the car.

"Gerald!" she yells.

He doesn't answer.

"What have you done with my husband?"

"Nothing," I say.

"What did you do to him?" she repeats. Her body pushes against the car and she jumps as if she forgot it was there.

I circle around her and she turns, watching me the entire time. The night is cooling off and clouding over. "Nothing," I repeat.

"It's okay, honey," Gerald says, coming to the door. "He didn't do anything to me."

"Are you okay?" she asks.

"Yeah. About as okay as I'll ever be."

"Are you crying?" she asks him, then she turns to me. "The blood on your clothes . . .," she says, and trails off.

"It's my wife's blood," I say and slowly begin negotiating a path toward my car.

"I know who you are," she says. "It wasn't his fault!"

"Honey, it's okay," Gerald says. "It's really okay."

"I know it wasn't," I say, and these words are mine now, clear and sober, they come from me, and when I get past the wife she puts her daughter on the ground, and the little girl runs over to her daddy and hugs him fiercely.

"Who's that strange man?" she asks.

"It's why I came here. To tell him I know it wasn't his fault," I say.

I turn toward Gerald who's holding his daughter tightly. "It wasn't. I know that now."

I turn back to the wife. Some of her anger drains away, but she says nothing. Gerald keeps crying. Sobbing heavily now, tearful, deep sobs that make me angry, remorseful, and a whole lot of wanting to leave. I tighten my grip on the bag and continue toward the street. I hold it tightly to make sure it isn't going to spill open like before.

The woman stays against the car but keeps watching me. "It wasn't his fault," she says.

"I know."

"You know that now," she says, "after being here," she says, her eyes going to the bag for a quick second. "But what about before you got here? Did you know that then?"

I don't answer.

"We're moving," she says. "The house goes on the market next week, but I don't think we can wait until it sells. My sister was murdered last year, she came home from the picture theater one night and this madman broke into her house and killed her. My sister spent her life in a goddamn wheelchair, and this city's version of karma gets her raped and killed. A colleague from work disappeared a few months ago and got found a month later, cut up into a dozen pieces by a lawn mower. We have to leave. What happened to Gerald, I thank God it wasn't worse. It was for you, I know that, but my husband, he's ruined now. I still love him and will always be with him, but what those men did, he's a victim too. They killed him and left him alive. My husband is a broken man."

"It's a broken city," I say, and I turn my back on her and walk away.

chapter twenty

You goddamn pussy!

"He had nothing to do with it."

He let your wife die.

"It wasn't his fault."

You know what—stop with the bullshit. You're nothing like your father.

"I don't want to be."

Well, you need to be if you want vengeance for Jodie. Or does that not matter anymore?

"Of course it does."

Then the voice is gone.

I walk straight in the beginning, my legs are solid, but then I stagger a little, then a little more, and by the time I get to the car I'm holding my stomach, the world swaying out of control. I drop to my knees and hold the ground in probably the same way my dad described when me and Belinda would finally climb off the merry-go-round. I don't think I ever threw up back then, but this time my stomach tightens, my throat catches, then hot vomit gushes from my mouth, frothy beer and bile splashing into a puddle next to my car door. I get back to my feet, this horrid, burning taste in my mouth, and I wipe a hand across my mouth, and then I realize two things at the same time—first of all, I don't know where my keys are, the second thing is I've dropped the bag again. The sobriety that the monster brought with him has just as quickly left with him too, abandoning me, and suddenly the world is spinning one way while my mind sways another, the mixture not good, and I feel very, very ill.

The bag is a few meters away. I head back and snatch it up. I pat down my pockets but my keys haven't appeared since I patted them down twenty seconds earlier. I reach the car and there's a black and white cat sitting on the hood, staring at me. It watches me peer inside the car in case the keys are hanging from the ignition, but they're not. I realize I've dropped the bag again. I move around the car and the keys are on the ground next to the puddle of vomit. I snatch them up, then fumble them then drop them right inside the bile-beer stew. Jesus. I pick them up and they drip, and when I try to wipe them on the grass I almost fall over and my hat falls off. I pick up the bag and the hat and spend too long unlocking the passenger door. The cat takes off and hides behind the closest bush it can find. I toss everything into the backseat.

The night has darkened considerably since I arrived, making the Christmas lights on the surrounding houses appear brighter. They're not bright enough to light me up as I stand against the side of my car finally relieving the pain from my bladder by emptying it on the lawn. It's either that or piss myself in the car. A half dozen plastic Santas stare down at me, mounted on roofs, all thinking the same thing—that they'd rather be somewhere else.

When I'm done I slouch in the driver's seat and discover there are two steering wheels ahead of me and two roads, but they merge into one when I put my left hand over my right eye. Small drops of rain appear on the windscreen. Gerald Painter is still inside his house with his family, and he's probably still crying. I put a hand on my chest to check my heartbeat, thinking that it ought to be racing, but it's not. I could have been a killer right now, and if the monster had his way, I would be. The question is, how long can I keep it quiet for? No, wait—the real question is, do I want it to be quiet?

I fold my arms onto the steering wheel and rest my head on them. I close my eyes for a few moments, and when I open them again it's to the sound of tapping on the driver's-side window and it's pouring with rain outside.

chapter twenty-one

"What the hell are you doing here, Edward?" he asks, and part of him, a small part, already knows. Or suspects. The warning Benson Barlow gave him has been stuck in his head all day, a warning that hasn't been easy to dismiss—especially since Edward visited his father today and now he's parked only two houses away from the security guard injured during the robbery.

"Who . . . who's that?" Edward asks, and he lifts his hand up to shield his eyes even though there's no real light.

"Come on, I'm giving you a lift home."

"What?"

"Get out and move into the passenger seat," he says, and opens the door for him. "And hurry up. I'm getting drenched out here."

Edward gets out. He gasps in a lungful of air which pains him, he doubles over, then he gets onto his hands and starts gagging. A puddle of vomit appears. The rain is coming down hard and from nowhere—certainly nobody in the weather forecasting world predicted it. The back of Edward's shirt is already soaked through. He waits a bit while Edward coughs, and when it seems like the man is never going to get back up, he reaches down and grabs his shoulder. "Come on, we have to go."

He helps Edward to his feet, careful not to step in any vomit. Edward twists his body so he can see up the street. There is a patrol car parked about twenty meters away. Schroder leads him around to the passenger side where there are more rain-washed puddles of vomit.

"What the hell are you doing here?" Schroder asks.

"I was sleeping."

"Are they the same clothes you were wearing at the bank?"

"Maybe."

"They're covered in your wife's blood."

"Are they?"

"Get in," Schroder says, unamused. Edward gets in the passenger side and Schroder races around and gets in behind the wheel. An hour ago all he had to do was move and he broke out in a sweat. Now he's shivering. The inside of the car fogs up and he turns on the air-conditioning to clear the windscreen. The car that brought him here follows. He turns on the wipers. Already the rain is easing up, and by the time he's driven a couple of blocks it's almost completely stopped.

"Look, Edward," he says, his tone softer now, "I know you want answers, but coming here isn't the place where you'll find them."

"I know."

"Then why'd you come?"

"I don't know."

"Uh-huh. Gerald Painter had nothing to do with the robbery. He's a victim as much as anybody."

"Not as much as Jodie," Edward answers, and Schroder knows it's a good point.

"Look, I know it's hard, and the situation is shit, but you gotta man up. You've got a little girl that's depending on you."

"I know that," Edward says. "People don't need to remind me. You think my wife getting killed makes me forget about Sam?"

"Of course not. Problem is you do need reminding. If you didn't, you wouldn't be here right now. You wouldn't be drunk and one step away from killing yourself in a car accident."

"Why'd you come here?" Edward asks.

"Gerald Painter's wife called us. She said you came to visit him tonight, and according to her it wasn't exactly a social call. Why'd you show up?"

"Why don't you ask her?"

"She doesn't know, and Gerald Painter isn't saying much, but I have to tell you, Edward, I don't like your being here. And you're drunk and you're wearing the clothes with your wife's blood on them. Mrs. Painter isn't the only one who called you in—another neighbor saw you stumbling to your car and pissing on the lawn. The constables in the patrol car back there, they came here to take you away. Me being here, this is a favor, Edward. I'm here to take you home and keep you out of jail for the night. I'm here to stop you from making any further mistakes."

"You want my thanks now? How about you earn it by finding the men who killed Jodie?"

"Why did you come here?" Schroder asks.

"I don't know."

"I think you know."

Edward shrugs.

"I think you blame Painter for not doing enough to save your wife. I think you wanted to make him hurt for what happened, and then you got here and found he already was hurting and that none of this was his fault. I think if you hadn't made that realization then right now I wouldn't be doing you any favors. We'd be having a very different conversation."

Edward says nothing, just stares out the window at the night. Schroder stays quiet for a bit, thinking about Benson Barlow and the shrink's warning.

"I have a friend," Schroder says, "that you remind me of in a way. He looked into something he shouldn't have, and it cost him. Same thing happened to him that's happening to you. He thought drinking was the answer, but it screwed him up, screwed with his judgment. He went out one night in his car and ran into a woman, almost killed her. That shit will happen to you if you don't get a grip on things. My friend, he was a cop once who knew better. You'll end up falling into an abyss right alongside him, and his abyss now has him in jail. He's locked away for six months for what he did. That what you want? To leave your little girl for six months?"

Edward doesn't answer him.

"Or it'll be worse. You'll head out driving and you'll have your daughter with you. You'll drag her into that abyss and get her killed."

Still nothing.

"Look, Edward, we'll get the men who did this. These people, they always get caught. Always."

"And you always let them go," Edward says. "Isn't that it? You'll find these guys and you'll find you've dealt with them before, locked them away before, and let them right out."

"It's not like that," he says.

"Isn't it? How about you explain it to me."

"We kept your father locked away."

"But he's the only one, right? Everybody else gets tossed back out onto the street to do whatever it is they want to do."

"You think I don't know that? You think it's easy being a cop in this city? What would . . .," he trails off. "Look, what's the alternative? That we don't try? You know how many cops we're losing every year because nobody wants to try anymore? The last year, Edward, the last year has been damn hard. With all that's happened—hell, even I have days where I want to give up. It's what this city does. It produces these people. It catches them, takes them into its prisons, then churns them back out harder and rougher than they were going in. But we're trying, Edward, and we're making progress. Things will change. We're doing the best we can with what we have, and I promise you, we'll get the men who killed your wife. And I promise you they will pay."

"People think I'm the same as him," I say.

"What?"

122

"My father. They think I'm the same as him. People recognize me from the news and think I'm going to be the next big serial killer."

"No one recognizes you from the news, Edward," he says, remembering what Barlow said. "That was twenty years ago. And you weren't to blame for anything then."

"People are ready to convict me, they want to send me away for life. They're frightened of me. But these men, why aren't we frightened of them enough to keep them locked away forever? When you find them, Detective, and lock them away, what then? How long until you have to find them again for killing somebody else's wife? Three years? Five?"

"I promise they'll pay, Edward," he says.

They reach the house and Schroder pulls into the driveway and they both climb out. The car following pulls up to the curb, its tires scraping against it. The wheels have splashed rain and dirt off the road onto the bottom half of the car.

They walk to the front door and Schroder unlocks it.

"What happened to your friend?" Edward asks.

"Huh?"

"The friend you were telling me about. He was looking into something. He ever sober up and find it?"

"Yeah. He found it, and people died because of it."

"He lose his family to bank robbers?"

"I'll keep these tonight," Schroder says, and he rattles the keys. "You can pick them up from the station in the morning. Where are the spares?"

"I don't have any."

"Everybody has spare keys."

"Not me 'cause I never lose them."

"Okay, Edward. Go and get some sleep," he says. "Don't do anything else stupid tonight. Don't make me regret helping you out." He closes the door and heads to the other car and drives away.

chapter twenty-two

I take a leak, find the spare keys, take another leak, grab a beer, grab a jacket, and within ten minutes of being dropped off home I'm back on the road, which is better than jail, which is where I thought Schroder was going to take me for what the monster had wanted me to do tonight. The spare keys have Jodie's car key too, and for a few seconds I can't figure out which one to jam into the ignition.

The car is harder to control than normal and there must be something wrong with it. I'm steering straight but the car keeps veering off to the left, and other times off to the right. It's not the time to have a faulty car—the road ahead of me isn't exactly laid out clearly because my vision is shot to hell. Everything is blurry, and when I squint I end up seeing double. I lose control of the car and hit the curb and come to a stop. I can see my house in the rear-vision mirror—I've only driven about thirty meters.

I give it another go, slower this time, more focused. There is even less traffic on the road now. A few people are out shopping since the malls are still open, Christmas extending the closing hours till midnight. Statistically, some of these people will go bankrupt over the Christmas season. Statistically, many of them will come home to find their homes have been burgled, or they'll walk out of a mall to find their cars have been stolen. Statistically, one of these people will show up dead on some grass verge in the morning and Schroder's caseload will become that much heavier for it.

I'm not familiar with the area and get lost on the way to the cemetery. I run a couple of red lights by accident, but I also end up sitting at a few green lights, which I figure balances the equation. I make it there safely and turn into the cemetery driveway. There is no detail in the church, only an absence of light, a dark shape somewhat darker than the night around it. I keep driving ahead and quickly become lost. I haven't been out here since Jodie was buried, and then I was following everybody else. Now it's a maze. The church disappears behind the line of trees, then it's graves and grass everywhere, broken up by more trees. Maybe this is why it's called the Garden City—the view is fucking fantastic when you're dead.

I drive around for about five minutes before deciding I can cover more ground on foot. I grab the beer and get out and lean against the car to open it, but slide right off the wet surface. I hit the ground and scrape my knees and drop the beer and it takes me a minute to find it. I walk among the plots searching for Jodie, even calling out to her after a few minutes. In the end I'm too tired to keep going. I sit down and lean against a grave that's not as old as the others. The grass is very wet and the water leaches into my pants. There are gaps in the cloud cover letting moonlight through but I can't see any moon. A light breeze pushes my wet clothes against my skin. I pop open the beer and it fizzes up from the earlier fall. What doesn't froth out keeps me warm as the night continues to cool around me. I talk to Jodie even though the person beneath me isn't Jodie, but someone who died a few months ago in his early twenties, according to the script on the stone, but it doesn't say anything else about him—maybe nobody cared enough, or maybe people were glad he died.

"I'm so sorry, Jodie," I say. "For everything. I'm sorry you died.

I'm sorry it was my fault. I'm sorry I smashed the plates against the kitchen wall."

Jodie and the guy beneath me ignore me. The cemetery is deathly quiet but scenic. The sky is clearing, the veil of cloud is pulled back revealing thousands of stars. They light up the night, silhouetting the trees, shining down on the grounds where Death and a few of the friends he's made over the years are buried all around me. The breeze becomes warm again and strong too, coming from the northwest over the Port Hills, which are lit up with street- and house lights, whipping across acres of tussock and grass and rock before sweeping down into the city. By the time it reaches the cemetery it's picking up leaves and petals and throwing them about, it blows dirt into my eyes and I have to turn my back to it. Pretty soon the stars dim and I can no longer taste beer. I wake up what ought to be only a few minutes later, but must be several hours since the moon has been replaced by the sun. The bright light hits my eyes so hard it almost knocks a hole in the back of my head. I roll onto my side to bury my head into my pillow but there's only grass and a cement marker. I rub my eyes and have no idea where I am for about two seconds, then it all rushes back to me. The breeze has died back down. I figure I'm one of many who have fallen asleep with a bottle of something out here with their loved ones cold in the ground. My clothes smell of sweat and vomit and Jodie's blood.

My body is aching as I stand up, the muscles stiff and sore. I'm not sure where my car is so I pick a direction and walk. Nothing is familiar as everything looks the same. I walk for twenty minutes in an expanding circle before finding it. The keys are still in the ignition. There are already a couple of mourners who throw me suspicious glances, probably because I look like I just crawled out of one of the graves here. The cemetery is in need of a caretaker—the lawns are too long and the gardens are being overrun by a crime wave of weeds. One side of the car is in bright sun, the other has wet leaves stuck to it.

I take the backstreets home instead of the main ones, figuring they'll be quicker, and figuring wrong. I pass a couple of people building fences, others mowing lawns, summertime activities that seem a world away from the world I live in now. When I finally make it, I race into the bathroom and take a leak doing my best to hit the bowl and not the floor and my feet. I'm pretty sure I'm draining off the only fluids I have in my body.

I stagger through to the kitchen and open the fridge. The milk has expired but it seems to taste okay and I drink half a glass of it before deciding milk is the absolute last thing I want right now. I look at the beer. Strike that—milk ain't that bad after all.

I lean against the kitchen bench, disoriented and lost, like I don't belong here, and that makes it harder for me to remember exactly what happened last night. Part of me doesn't even feel like I'm back home: I'm stuck somewhere, maybe in some purgatory where the milk is always expired and my mouth is dry and my tongue sticks to the roof of it. Even my teeth are sore from grinding them in my sleep. I hang the bloody bank clothes back up before taking a long shower. It revives me a bit, at least physically, but mentally I'm exhausted as the memories of last night trickle back in.

Mostly I'm ashamed by it all.

My heart quickens as I recall pulling the knife up short of cutting Painter. I want to throw up again. I have no idea why in the hell I even went to Gerald Painter's house. No idea what the plan was. If I'd killed Gerald Painter, would the monster have kept me sober, or abandoned me when that first splash of blood arced up onto the ceiling? What would have happened to his wife and daughter if they'd walked in on me?

I tidy the kitchen, opening up and draining the remaining beer and wine down the sink. I remember what else Schroder said last night, then more importantly I remember what I said to him, and those memories seem to collide in a nice little way that jumbles everything up, and suddenly what my dad said to me as he walked away makes sense—*It's okay to listen to the voice.*

I'm still a bit drunk, and I might be over the limit, but the world doesn't sway around much as I drive through it. I find a park near the police station. My keys are waiting for me in the foyer behind the reception desk. They don't ask me any questions about last night. All they do is ask for ID to make sure the keys belong to me. Schroder isn't around. He's probably at the beach somewhere or getting the last of his shopping done while Jodie lies cold in the ground. I realize I haven't got Sam anything yet either for Christmas—me and Jodie always left that kind of thing till the last few days. There's a guy out in front of the station with a sandwich board over his shoulders, he's holding up a Bible and preaching his views in an abusive tone and I wonder if he knows Henry the homeless guy.

I drive out to the prison, passing a couple of malls on the way where traffic is spilling out from the parking lot onto the road, Christmas shopping in full bloom now, people pushing carts full of groceries. There's a billboard twice the size of a bus staked into the ground on the edge of the city advertising a brand-new subdivision, calling it the suburb of the future. I wonder what that means. I wonder if the billboard means Christchurch is stuck in the past, or that the new subdivision will resemble something out of *The Jetsons*. There is smoke drifting up from the fields, farmers burning off waste. Large irrigation units are watering crops under the hot sun.

Sam's bag is still packed in the backseat, full of goodies of death that I have to return to their rightful place. If Curious Schroder had taken a peek, things might have turned out very different.

I don't phone ahead this time. I park the car in the same spot and the same woman I spoke to yesterday is here today, the same smile—a smile that could make beached whales roll back into the water—falters when she recognizes me.

"I'm here to see my father," I say, as if there could be any one of a hundred reasons.

"He's been waiting for you," she says.

"But . . . I didn't phone ahead."

"Must be a miracle," she says, but she's wrong. I don't know what to think about my dad figuring that I'd show back up. Mostly it pisses me off that he's arrogant enough to think it, and I suspect perhaps arrogance is the wrong word since he was right.

"You listened to the voice," he says, once the guard has escorted me down to the visitors' room. It was the same guard from yesterday and he gave me the same rules as yesterday, reinforcing the no-yelling one twice. There are fewer people in the visitors' room, which should make it seem bigger, but somehow it has the opposite effect. Fewer people makes it colder, stagnant, far more depressing, it makes it seem the walls are closing in and I can only imagine what the cells must be like. The Carver isn't anywhere to be seen. Nobody pays me any interest.

I sit opposite him. He's different from yesterday. Younger, if that's possible—as though all this is rejuvenating him.

"Let me ask you something," he says. "You think being an accountant gives you the credentials to know what the entire sum of a man is?"

"What?"

"See, twenty years in here, I have them. A man is made up of many parts," he says. "There are things within his core. They are shaped by his family, his friends, shaped by the blood that runs through him. Of course the events shape a man too. Those in the past, and those unfolding in front of him. I am the sum of many things," he says. "You, your sister, your mother, they were part of me, as well as my own family, growing up. But it wasn't enough to make me complete. I thought it might be, I mean, when I first met your mother and when our family began, I thought it might be enough. But it wasn't. You and me, we're made up from the same components."

"You're full of shit," I say.

"You're my son," he says. "You can't deny much of what is inside me is inside you too."

"You're wrong. I can deny that because it isn't true. You, me, we're nothing alike."

"Why'd you become an accountant?" he asks.

I lean back, unsure of his point. "I don't know," I say, shrugging.

"Want to know what I think?"

"No."

"Well, you're going to hear—after all, it's why you came out here."

"Then why ask," I say, shaking my head. "Just spit it out."

"It was to make me proud. You wanted to be an accountant like your dad."

"Wait . . ."

"What for? So you can deny it."

"Wait . . . you were an accountant?"

"You were nine years old when I was taken away. Don't try pretending you have no idea what I used to do for a living. You're just like your old man," he says.

I don't answer him. I don't even want to think about it.

"And the voice confirms it. My darkness and your monster—they're as similar as we are."

"This is crazy," I say. "You're crazy. I don't know why I came along. I hate myself for showing up yesterday. I'm going to go," I say, but don't make any motion.

"You came here to learn," he says, "not to dismiss everything I say."

"No. I came here because . . . ," I trail off, suddenly unsure.

"Because you want answers. Everything that's happened over the last week . . . You're hearing the voice, aren't you, Jack? It's come back."

My dad smiles. It's the same smile I remember when I was a kid, and part of me, one small part of what makes up the whole of who I am—at least according to my dad—wants to hug him, wants to cry against his chest and ask him to make everything better.

"You're here to ask for my help," he adds.

I lean forward and the guard seems about to say something, but stops when he sees I'm not leaning forward for a hug or punch. I lower my voice. "You said it was a good thing the cops had no idea who killed Jodie. What did you mean by that?"

My dad glances up at the guard, who is openly staring at us, then my dad leans in too, and suddenly we're pals, we're whispering secrets—let the good times roll.

"It means what you think it means."

"I think it means that you're insane. That you couldn't care less about what happened to my family. Or even to your family."

"No you don't," he says. "It means what it means."

"Which is?"

"It means those men are still out there, awaiting justice, and there isn't any reason it has to be police justice."

"Except for the law," I say.

"Did the law step in to save your wife?" he asks. "Does the law warm up the other side of your bed at night? Does it give your daughter somebody to look up to? Make her school lunches and tuck her in at night and tell her to have sweet dreams? Is the law there to hold your life together, is it there to hold your daughter's hand and tell her everything is going to be all right? Was it there to stop the blood dripping out of Jodie's body when she hit the road?"

"Shut up," I say. "I don't want you talking about her like that."

"Twenty years ago, son, you weren't ready to kill that dog, but the darkness, your monster, made you do it. You killed that dog and the police came sniffing around with their questions. The darkness tries to make you impulsive, son, and twenty years ago your darkness got me arrested."

"Huh? What are you talking about?"

"It was that damn dog. You killed it, and you invited the police into our neighborhood. Do you remember you wrapped the steak in a plastic bag? You did, and when you gave the steak to the dog you dropped the plastic bag. The bag was from home, son, and it had my fingerprints on it. They matched the prints found with the prostitutes. The police got warrants to search houses in the street because they knew a killer lived there. They came with their questions and then they came back with more. They searched the garage, son. They looked for the mix of sharp things you put into that steak, and they found them. But they found other things too. Other . . . mementos."

"You kept things from the victims?"

"Small things. Earrings, mostly. Sometimes a necklace. I couldn't help myself. They came looking for fishhooks and nails and they found souvenirs of my women."

"You were . . . wait, you were caught because of me?" I ask.

"It wasn't your fault," he says.

"Honestly, I don't know if I care whether it was my fault or not," I say. And it's true. Am I glad my father was caught and could no longer kill? Yes. Am I upset he was taken away? Absolutely. I think about what it means. On one hand I'm a hero. I saved future victims.

On the other hand I betrayed my family. If I hadn't listened to the voice, if I hadn't killed that dog, my sister, my mother, they'd still be alive. I killed them as surely as I killed that dog. Last week I sacrificed Jodie to save a bank teller. Twenty years ago I sacrificed my family to save other prostitutes. What does that make me? Does it make me a trader in death?

"Son, I'm not blaming you. You couldn't know, and you were too young to control the darkness. Since that dog you killed, how many times have you heard it?"

"Why are you telling me any of this?"

"The men who did this, they have something inside them too, not a voice like we have, but something that makes them different. Each of them must have some criminal history," he says. "Think about it, it's obvious."

I think about it. I think about what Schroder said last night, our nice friendly chat about people getting locked away and let right back out, our nice friendly chat about what a huge revolving door prison is these days.

"They've all spent time in jail," he carries on. "Had to have. I'm betting some of them, if not all of them, probably met in jail. That's what jail is, right? For me, it's my home. I'll never see outside of these walls again, but for these men it's a place to learn new skills, make new friends."

I stay silent, but continue to listen.

"Jail takes people in, it educates them in very, very dangerous ways, then it spits them back out into society. Most if not all of Jodie's killers have walked in and out of these doors for various crimes."

"And you know who these people are, right? It's why you're telling me. You want me to find these people to satisfy your darkness."

"I think we can help each other out," he says.

"No way. This is bullshit," I say. "I'm not helping you out."

"Would that be such a bad thing, son? Or would you rather let them go free? The voice can be a bad thing, son, but it can be a good thing too. You can use it to make the men who did this pay for what happened."

"To satisfy your darkness?"

"No. To keep you sane. If you can't control it the way I could, you're going to hurt good people."

"Hang on a second. Are you saying you controlled it all those years?"

"Of course. I gave in to it as well, in a way, but I controlled it. That's why I never killed anybody who mattered."

"You killed eleven prostitutes," I say. "How can you say they don't matter?"

"They don't."

"They do."

"Compared to what? Compared to my own family? My friends? Our neighbors? They didn't matter compared to anybody else I knew. Once you can control it, it'll keep you from hurting good people. It'll keep you from going off the rails and losing your daughter. The monster won't go away now, not if it's taking the steering wheel and making you do things. If you can't control it, you're going to be more like your old man than you ever thought possible. We're blood men," he says.

"What?"

"Other people, they're attracted to looks, or money, nice jobs, all the hollow things in this world. Other men are attracted to tits or ass, women are attracted to smiles and eyes. Your monster, my darkness, they're attracted to blood. It makes us blood men."

He stands up, and suddenly I realize that this meeting, if that's the word for it, is over. I stand up too. Dad reaches over and grabs my hands.

"No touching," the guard says, and when Dad doesn't let go, the guard comes over and separates us. "That's enough for today," the guard says, stamping his authority on us.

Dad walks away. "I love you, son," he says, but he doesn't turn back to say it. "No matter what happens now, remember that."

I don't know how to answer him, so I don't. I walk away too. And it's not until I'm in the parking lot that I look down at the folded piece of paper in my hand.

chapter twenty-three

I haven't seen my father's handwriting in twenty years. He used to help me with my homework. We'd lie down on the floor in the living room with the TV going but the volume mostly down, discussing why bees collected honey or how seven wouldn't divide into twelve. He'd write things down for me, he'd read over my assignments and jot down ideas in the margins, other times he'd take notes out of whatever books I was searching through for answers. He has this elegant printing style, where the letters don't bleed into each other, each one separate, easy to read, easy to recognize even after all this time. He always wanted me to be the best that I could at school. Those days come back to me, the smells of my mum baking something, or cooking dinner, the TV going, laughter, warm weather, a dog barking, school uniforms, life.

Another car pulls into the parking lot. It's a rundown Mercedes, the type that isn't old enough to be classic, but nowhere new enough to be cool. There's a long scratch running along the bottom of the passenger side. A guy, maybe around twenty, steps out of it, his dreadlocks bouncing.

"Hey, bro, what up?" he asks, tilting his head upward as he does so. I immediately hate him. His T-shirt is full of holes and has *I ATE AT THE BLEEDING BUDGIE* all in capital letters across the front of it. No picture, no further explanation, maybe there's a punch line on the back, but I don't look. He realizes his mistake in speaking to me because I ignore him. He shrugs and heads in through the glass doors.

The air in the car is so hot it almost curls the paper my dad gave me. I wind the windows down but it doesn't help. I read it over a couple of times and think about what it means.

LISTEN TO THE VOICE. SHANE KINGSLY. 23 STONEVIEW ROAD.

I drive home, but the only voice speaking comes from the radio. The news comes on but the announcer ignores the bank robbery and doesn't mention anything about the men being caught. I end up pulling in behind another slow-moving truck so I take a different way home, getting caught instead at a set of roadworks where the street has been ripped up and there's dust and dirt in the air. There are exposed pipes and wiring and machinery but nobody around, the workers off for the Christmas break, the roadworks now in limbo until sometime next month. Tiny bits of gravel shoot out from beneath the tires of the car ahead of me, hitting the windscreen but not chipping it. My cell phone rings. I recognize the number.

"You went to visit your dad again," Schroder says. "Want to tell me why?"

"He's my dad. I don't need a reason other than that. And I certainly don't need to give a reason to you."

"You sound different, Edward."

"Yeah?"

"Yeah. You sound like you've been thinking about things, and I'm pretty sure I wouldn't like the kind of things you've been thinking."

Somehow I think Schroder is the kind of guy who might like what I was thinking—problem is I can't share with him. "Are you ringing to tell me you've caught the men who killed my wife?"

"We're working on it."

"I thought so. So why are you calling, other than to bust my balls for visiting my dad?"

"To remind you not to get any bad ideas."

"I don't even know what that means."

"I think you do. I think you're so lost right now you're turning to your father for advice, and trust me, he's the last person you want to be turning to."

"I keep thinking if you spent less time worrying about my life, you'd spend more time on catching the people who ruined it."

"Don't do anything stupid, Edward."

"To who? Nobody knows who I could do anything stupid to anyway!" I say, and I hang up. He doesn't call back.

Back home I sit at the dinner table and smooth the piece of paper out, pressing it flat against the wood, pushing my fingertips and palms onto it as if ironing out the wrinkles. My house is still empty. No shadows, no presence, my wife even less here today than she was yesterday. I have a name and an address and I don't know what I'm supposed to do with it. Not once did I even think of giving that information to Schroder when I was on the phone, and weighing it up now I'm glad I didn't. It wasn't Schroder's wife who got killed. Does that mean I'm listening to the voice?

I listen for it now. There's nothing.

I can't go through what I went through last night. Can't drive to this man's house and . . . and what?

Let me help you.

And there it is.

"No," I say, and the word sounds empty in my empty home.

We can do this.

"No."

Then let me do this for you.

I go online and search for Shane Kingsly. He shows up pretty quick, he's made the news on and off his entire life. Nothing big—

not in the taking-a-life way of being big. He's done plenty of shitty things. Plenty of theft convictions. He has some assault charges, and a couple of drug possession charges. Not all the statistics are here to tell me how many years he's spent in jail on and off. His last sentence was for two years after he held up a service station with a shotgun. It doesn't say when he was released from jail, but it must have been early for being a model prisoner—which I guess is easy to do when there aren't any service stations or shotguns in prison. This man was one of the six, but he wasn't the one who planned it. Is this the man that killed Jodie? He may well be.

When the phone rings it's my father-in-law.

"When are you coming to pick Sam up?" he asks. "She misses you."

"I know. I'm sorry," I hear myself saying. I'm on automatic now. "I've been busy. I've been at the police station all morning."

"Do they have . . . any news?"

"Not yet."

"Are you okay, Edward? You sound weird."

"I'm fine. Can I talk to Sam?"

"Sure. Hang on a second."

"Daddy?"

"Hello, honey. Daddy-Nat and Gramma taking good care of you?"

"We've been putting up a Christmas tree," she says. "They let me help. It was so cool. Will Santa bring something for Mummy this year?"

I sit down, my legs weak. I suddenly realize that I have no idea where our cat is. I can't even remember the last time I saw him, and I'm not even sure if I've been feeding him or if he's even still alive. Jesus—the monster didn't get him when I was drunk, did it?

"Daddy?"

"Not this year, honey. I'm going to come and see you, okay? Tell Daddy-Nat and Gramma that I'm on my way."

"Okay, Daddy," she says, and hangs up without another word.

I pack some of her clothes. Jodie bought a bag for this a couple of years ago as occasionally Sam spends the night at her grandparents'.

I find a couple of toys, and I figure it ought to be enough. Everything else—pajamas, toothbrush, et cetera—are at Nat's house.

The sun is still blazing bright, the day isn't as hot as it was a few hours ago but I still drive with the window down. Christchurch weather has the ability to turn on a dime. There are bus stops full of people all waiting to go somewhere, tourists with backpacks half the size of them visiting the Garden City, mums with baby carriages and bags full of shopping. Every mailbox outside every house is jammed full of supermarket and store brochures. Kids on front lawns are running through and sitting on top of sprinklers. I pass hedgehogs flattened by cars and dogs walking freely along sidewalks, sniffing at fast-food bags dropped in the gutters. I'm in control the entire drive, and I'm in control when I pull up in the driveway and step out. Sam comes and hugs me, and leads me inside to show off the Christmas tree. It's the same tree they have every year. I smile at the tree and say how good it looks, but the truth is I'll probably never enjoy Christmas again.

"You look like hell," Nat says, and I guess he's right—I haven't really checked.

"Can I fix you something to eat?" Diana asks.

"Sure, thanks," I say. I don't think I've eaten anything since the boxed cereal yesterday.

I spend a couple hours at the house. I fit in well enough, but it's like I'm an outsider the entire time, and even though my in-laws try hard, I think this may be the last time I visit them—other than to drop Sam off or pick her up. I can't be here with them, and I don't know why. They don't blame me for what happened, but their pain and loss are written all over their faces. I don't need to see that, not now, perhaps never again. After dinner we sit out on the porch, me and Nat, him drinking a beer and wondering why I don't want one too.

"Listen, Nat, can you watch Sam again tonight? There's something I have to do."

He takes a long swallow of beer before answering. "You know, Eddie, I'm not kidding when I say you look like hell."

"I know."

"The only thing you ought to be doing right now is taking care of what family you have left."

"That is what I'm doing."

"Uh-huh. And how exactly are you doing that?"

"Can you take care of Sam or not?"

"Of course we can, Eddie, you know that. I'm just worried you're thinking of doing something stupid."

"Like what?"

"I don't know. Something. Stupid."

"I'm only helping the police with a few things."

"You've got a daughter who needs you. I'm not telling you to let go of what happened, but you have to let the police do their job. A man needs to know what his priorities are."

"I know. You're right. It's only for tonight," I say, "I promise."

"Okay, Edward. And don't worry, I won't hold you to your promise," he says, and finishes off his beer.

chapter twenty-four

I sit in my living room with the curtains closed and the stereo off and the TV off and the phones off. I'm sick of the world. Sick of my phone—sick of messages left by reporters and the psychiatrist I used to see years ago and by people wanting to check up on me. I stare at the TV as if it were on. In the beginning I can see my reflection, but the later the day becomes the harder it gets to see. I have nothing to do but wait for it to become dark. I stare at the Christmas tree and once again I think about taking it down, but once again I decide to leave it up for Sam. The sun comes in through one of the living room windows, it climbs up the walls as it sinks toward the horizon, reflecting off the shiny balls and bells on the tree. It moves over a photo of Sam, over a wedding photo of me and Jodie, it reflects across the room, orange light, weakening, and then it's gone.

I keep waiting.

Darkness settles in. An hour goes by. I switch on the TV and there's a New Zealand–made show about psychics on. They're trying to solve the crimes the police haven't been able to. A short time ago this kind of thing disgusted me. People were making money off the misery of victims—from the psychics themselves to anybody who had anything to do with the shooting of the show. Women were raped and murdered only to have their story re-enacted and retold by psychics trying to make a quick buck, and the TV-viewing public loved it—or at least enough of them did to keep making the show. But now I think of it differently. If the police can't do their job, maybe the psychics can. Before I can change channels, the front of the bank appears, then two side-by-side photos, one of my wife, one of the bank manager. Jonas Jones, the main psychic on the show, sits down at an office table that may or may not be inside the bank, closes his eyes, and, surrounded by burning candles, tells the public that the stolen money is still in Christchurch, hidden, somewhere near water, which is a great feat considering Christchurch is on the edge of an ocean. No wonder psychics aren't winning the lottery every week.

Midnight comes and goes.

I get changed at one o'clock. The shirt has dried out from last night and is stiff and scratches at me and smells the same as it did this morning. I drive through the early-Thursday-morning streets, most of them deserted until I get toward town, where there are sparks of life from the drunk and disorderly. In suburbia Christmas lights flash at me from windows and roofs and trees, the dark air illuminated by the reds and yellows as well as the pale light from the moon. If Jodie were alive it would all look fantastic. Instead it's gaudy and cheap, the decorations coming from sweatshop factories in third-world countries. It makes the people in these houses seem desperate to cling to happiness.

If map reading was one of Darwin's tests for survival of the fittest, I'd have been screwed long ago. It takes me a while, but I manage to find the address. Draw a straight line on a map and plot the neighborhoods on it, and they go steadily downhill, nice homes near town, okay homes further away, homes that can only be improved with the introduction of a Molotov cocktail further out again. This is where the map takes me, into a neighborhood you'd normally see on the news where the insurgents are fighting off an invading army.

I keep a steady pace, not wanting to risk slowing down. I pass beaten-up cars, old washing machines parked on the sidewalk, random pieces of timber, split-open rubbish bags with waste spilling out. The street I want isn't any better. Every yard is covered in brown grass and dog crap. Half of the streetlights don't work. Only a few of the homes have fences, and those that do have about a quarter of a fence at most, every third or fourth paling stolen or used as firewood. A few years ago a neighborhood like this wouldn't have existed. There were bad areas but not to this extent. Study the line I plotted on the map, and you'd see this neighborhood is spreading, it's like a virus, touching other suburbs, infecting them, finally consuming them before moving further on. Gerald Painter's wife is right to move her family away. They live maybe five kilometers from here in a nice street with nice cars and nice trees, but it's only a matter of time before the virus parks up outside their house and moves in.

I drive past the house I want, my heart racing, my palms sweaty, but all I've come to do is see the house, maybe catch a glimpse of Shane Kingsly, then drive home and . . .

Well, drive home and do something. I don't know what. Maybe phone the police. Maybe go to bed. Maybe write his name down next to Dean Wellington and the life insurance guy.

Then why is Sam's bag still in the backseat?

"I forgot to take it out," I say. The killing kit is still stuffed inside.

Then why'd you get changed?

"How about shutting up?"

I park a few houses down under a busted light, this time on the opposite side of the road, this time with the house ahead of me so I can keep watch. That's the plan. Sit for a while. Watch for a while. Then leave.

Yeah right.

Immediately I realize the problem. This isn't the kind of place I can sit for a while. I stand out here. Soon one of the neighbors will come to mug me, or kill me. I've seen all that I can safely see, and now it's time to leave.

Like hell it is. Let me help you.

"No."

Fine. Have it your way. Let the men who did this to Jodie go free. Go back to your life and move on. It's not long until you hear that from everybody you know. Move on.

"What do you need me to do?" I ask.

We climb out of the car. I turn a three-sixty looking for somebody, anybody, but there is nobody. I grab Sam's bag and carry it tightly.

We move onto the edge of the property. The dry grass crunches underfoot. I hunker down and pull on the hat and the gardening gloves and take a knife out, then move closer to the house. There are no lights on inside. None of the houses in the street have any Christmas lights. Santa doesn't even know this place exists. Kingsly's house is government subsidized, maybe sixty years old, made from wood siding that hasn't seen fresh paint in all that time. The guttering is covered in dark mould and sags in places where it's all cracked and busted. There are clumps of grass growing out of it. There is a run-down car parked up the driveway, another one on the lawn, and if you combined all the bits that worked you'd have a car that probably wouldn't get you anywhere. I slowly approach the house and try to peer in through the windows. I can't see a damn thing.

I head easily around the side of the house, walking slowly, careful in case there are dogs here, but so far nothing has barked at me. I thought a neighborhood like this would have a thousand dogs. Maybe the virus got them.

I look through the back windows and get the same result. The back door is locked. I don't know how to get inside. I guess knocking on the door is the way to go.

No it's not. We don't know how many people are inside. We don't know who will answer. It's easier than that. Just follow my lead.

There aren't many places in the backyard to hide, but I find a gap in a mangle of hedge that's overgrown in the corner. We move toward it, searching the ground for something to throw. I take aim and fire a stone hard up onto the roof. It thumps heavily, and I duck in behind the hedge, the branches scratching at me and snagging my clothes. I stay absolutely still. Nothing happens. I throw a second stone twenty seconds later.

A light comes on inside the house. Just one light in a bedroom.

Could mean the other bedrooms are empty. Could mean the others are better sleepers. A few moments later I can hear the front door open. Twenty seconds after that it closes, and not long after that the back door opens. A man, silhouetted by the hallway light, steps into the backyard. He's wearing pajama bottoms and nothing on top. Tattoos that probably have violent stories behind them climb up his body from under the waistband. He's skinny and tall and looks like he's spent too many years in jail and the rest of them on drugs. He takes a customary glance over the backyard, shrugs for his own benefit, then goes back inside. I wait until the lights go off, then I wait another few minutes, then I throw a third stone, same speed, same place, same kind of sound.

The light comes on much quicker this time. Still just the one light. Front door. Nothing. Then back door. He walks out into the yard.

"Fuck is out there?" he asks, and he probably asked the same thing out the front and got the same answer, but he's probably thinking he's talking to a cat or a possum.

We don't answer him. He doesn't walk far, stays near the door, wondering if the sound was an animal, or a pinecone falling from somewhere. Only difference between this time and the last time is this time he's carrying a flashlight. He's not using it as a flashlight, though, he's using it as a weapon. It's not even switched on. It's black and steel and about the length of his forearm and I figure if he had a better weapon he would have brought it out here. Nobody brings a flashlight to a gunfight. He heads back inside. The light goes off. Silence.

We give it ten minutes this time. Long enough for him to think the sound isn't coming back. Long enough that he might be falling asleep again.

This time the lights don't come on. The front door doesn't open. Only the back door, and it's fired open quickly and he storms outside, the meat of the flashlight slapping into the palm of his hand. He's dressed this time, black jeans, black top, black everything.

"Who's out there?" he yells. "That you, Reece? This ain't funny."

He moves deeper into the yard. He switches on the flashlight and spotlights random areas. He passes it over the hedge but he doesn't squat down or move branches aside or come any closer. He doesn't circle behind it. He thinks whatever is being thrown on his roof is either some random event or it's being thrown from outside his yard. He walks one way, then the other way, and he comes back to the doorway and he stares out toward us awhile without seeing us, then he closes the door. His bedroom light turns on and off, but he's not in there, he's waiting inside the doorway, waiting for the next sound, ready to burst out at a second's notice.

I move away from the hedge, slowly, confident slow movement will be less likely to draw his attention in case he's watching from the window. I put more distance between the house and us, backing into the neighboring property, a similar house in similar disrepair, same warped wood siding, same dirt-packed yard, probably the same kind of person living inside. I keep the hedge between me and Kingsly. I head slowly down the side of the next-door house and make it back out to the road. My car is still where I left it. All the wheels are still on it. I figure it's like winning the lottery out here. I move to the front of Kingsly's house and walk up the pathway, staying low, moving slow. I stick the bag on the path halfway between the house and the road. I reach the front door and squat down and take a few moments to calm down, drawing strength from the monster.

I knock. Twice. Two loud, heavy knocks. Footsteps pound down the hallway. I run, staying low, back to the side of the house before he gets the door open. I can hear him saying something but I'm not sure what, something that sounds like "what the fuck." I reach the back of the house and put my hand on the door handle and trust in Kingsly's desperation to get outside as fast as he could. Sure enough, the handle turns and the door opens. I can't see a thing inside. The hallway has a bend in it, so I can't see Kingsly either. He's outside. I can hear him walking around out there, asking who's out there, when he should be asking an entirely different question. He should be asking who's in here. I close the door. I head into the bedroom where the light was turning on and off before, using my hands to lead the way, almost tripping on rope lining the floor. Kingsly stays outside for another minute before returning to the hallway. The front door closes.

We wait in the dark for him to come into the bedroom.

chapter twenty-five

Kingsly heads out to the backyard. He moves around out there for a minute, swearing loudly, unsure of what he's looking for. He knows he's not dealing with pinecones anymore. He finally comes back in. He walks up and down the hallway a few times with the lights off. I'm not sure why, but as he does, it comes to me that I've already made my first mistake. The knife won't make him talk. He isn't going to come in here and see the steak knife in my hand, then start talking.

I can't see anything, but I can hear him. All I can see are the numbers from the clock radio and a small glow coming from the power button of a stereo. Kingsly knows the layout of his own house, knows where to walk without banging into anything. He has the flashlight on which helps him, I guess, but helps me too.

The flashlight beam comes into the room from the hallway, lighting up part of the bed from the angle he's on. The light grows in size the closer he gets. I squat down and wait for him, the knife out ahead of me. As he comes into the room, he twists the flashlight toward the light switch and reaches for it.

He switches it on at the exact time I move forward. I can't kill him. I need him. I need names and addresses and information that he can't provide if I stick the knife into his throat. So I aim for his shoulder. He hears me coming and turns and lifts his arm. It throws off my aim. The knife bites into his hand and pushes it back to the wall, but the knife goes into the wall too, right through the drywall, the blade burying down to the hilt, extending all the way into the wall and ripping into the wiring behind the light switch.

Every single muscle in my body tightens, my head crashes up into his chin, my right arm numb and in pain. I can't let go of the knife. Every muscle in Kingsly goes tight too, his arm with the flashlight swings up randomly, the metal casing hits me hard in the shoulder and pushes me back. My hand comes off the knife and I fall down and quickly back away, hitting the bed and pushing the mattress askew.

Then nothing.

Kingsly stands almost still. There are veins standing out in his neck and forehead. He's still holding the flashlight, his arm straight up in the air like he's asking a question. He isn't screaming. Isn't trying to pull the knife away. I can hear a low hum, and a couple of sparks fly from the wall from behind his hand, but nothing else. No crackle of electricity. Almost perfect silence—except for the low hum.

Then I realize he actually is moving. Small, shallow movements, almost every part of him swaying minutely back and forth, convulsing almost, as if he's having an epileptic fit but doesn't have the energy to give it his all. He can't break the contact, all he can do is this death dance as the power flows through him. His feet seem bolted to the floor. The lights in the bedroom fade, then come on real bright, then fade again. One of them blows, the other one brightens, dims, brightens.

Kingsly's face is in a tight grimace, his lips are pulled back and his teeth have clenched tight on his protruded tongue. The tip of it, a slug-sized piece, sticks out between them. His body keeps shaking, harder now, spasms rolling up and down his tall frame, blood splashing up onto his nose and face and down his chin. The tip of his tongue comes away, the bloody side of it hits the wall and grips a little, sliding down the wall like a pickle on a window at McDonald's. It hits the floor. The front of his pants darken. I can smell shit. I can smell barbecue. His eyes bulge from his face. No smoke anywhere.

A small flame jets out from the wall and equally as fast goes out. The humming comes to a stop. The light goes out. The flashlight hits the ground and stays going. Slowly, Kingsly slides down the wall, following his tongue. He slides as far as his pinned hand will allow, which is enough for his knees to bend and his face to press up against the doorjamb, his upper lip snagging on the latch and stretching out before tearing on the way. His head lolls over his shoulder, his eyes staring at me, no smoke coming from them. Other than the torn lip and bloody stump of a tongue, he's not in too bad a shape. Of course one look into his now-empty eyes is an immediate giveaway that things aren't good for the guy.

Something in his hand gives. I'm not sure what, exactly, but his hand forks open in a V as his body weight pulls it down past the blade, and then the rest of him slides down the wall and he tips onto the floor, covering the flashlight and blanketing me in darkness.

I can hear my own breathing. Ragged-sounding. Painful-sounding. Panicked.

I can't hear Kingsly. Can't see him. My arm hurts and so does my chest. There's a sharp pain right down in the base of my throat. My heart is thumping. I count off the seconds. One. Two. My entire body has broken out in a sweat. Three. I push myself further away from him, backing into the corner of the bed. Four. I can't figure out why the fuses didn't pop and cut the power. Five.

I take my cell phone out of my pocket and learn another lesson. Bringing a cell phone is a mistake unless it's turned off. If somebody had called while I was hiding behind the hedge, or in the bedroom, things would have gone very differently. I point the display away from me and it lights up the meter or so ahead. I can't see much except my own feet and the floor. I get to my knees and move closer to Kingsly. The power is out but I don't touch him. I kick him to roll him off the flashlight so I can see better.

I've killed a man.

And you liked it.

There's a long cut in the palm of my right hand; it's not too deep but it's very ragged. The knife has ripped right through the glove when I slid forward after stabbing him. It's also why I got electrocuted. If he hadn't hit me with the flashlight I could be lying right beside him now. I touch the side of his face and poke him. His head lolls to the side and doesn't loll back. His face is puffy and his lips pulled back and pieces of flesh from the bloody stump of his tongue are threaded through the small gaps in his teeth. The fuses should have popped. A circuit breaker should have kicked in somehow. The voltage shouldn't have done this to him.

I grab the flashlight. There is blood on the wall, on the floor, all over the knife and his arm, and some of his blood has mixed with the wound in my hand. I scoot myself back against the bed, roll onto my side, gag, open my mouth, and . . .

And nothing. Nothing happens. I stop gagging. I can taste vomit but none appears. I move off the floor and onto the bed, trailing blood with me. I put my own hands on the bed, bleeding into it, and I realize there is no way I can ever get away with any of this.

"You did this to me," I say.

You? I am you!

I keep staring at him, waiting for him to do something. He doesn't. I wait for somebody to appear. Nobody does. And nobody will.

I head into the hallway and find the fuse box almost immediately—the ropes I was stepping on earlier turn out to be power cables coming out of it and snaking across the floor. They're pinned up to the fuse box with alligator clips. The fuse box is one of those old ones that requires wire to be wound between the terminals, except in this case there is no wire between any of them, instead there are five-centimeter nails, wedged in where the fuses would slot. One of them has melted in the middle. A wire fuse would have broken in a tenth of a second. The nail took thirty seconds. I try the hallway lights and they come on. The only fuse to have blown is the one for the bedroom.

I follow the cables along the floor into another bedroom. The door is heavy to open and warm to touch. When it opens a thick piece of foam attached to the base of the door slides across the floor, and immediately orange light comes out, warming my face. The bedroom has been converted into a marijuana greenhouse. There are tables running from one wall to the other, full of beds of plants. There are heat lamps hanging from the ceiling over each of them. The room is more humid than it is bright. All the curtains are drawn, and in front of the curtains are large pieces of plywood, blocking any view from the outside world. I take a step inside; the air gets thicker. There are watering cans, bags of fertilizer, all the little knickknacks that old ladies with green fingers have. All of the plants stand about thirty centimeters high. I wonder how long they take to grow, how much money is invested here. I wonder what will happen to them now Kingsly is dead. I push some of them off the tables, they hit the floor and fall out of their trays, the roots exposed, the dirt exploding outward in every direction. I stomp on them, crushing the spines and leaves, destroying the drugs, hoping that I'm creating a reason for Kingsly to have been killed. The police aren't going to look beyond a drug connection.

I step back out of the room and close the door.

There's enough hallway light to see into the bedroom, and I use the flashlight for the rest. A brick of money is poking out from beneath the edge of the mattress I knocked out of place when I fell down and pushed myself back earlier. I tip it up the rest of the way. Bricks of cash, fresh, virgin money, all of the bricks made up from hundred dollar notes. Could be between a quarter and half a million dollars here. I reach out to touch it, wanting a tactile experience as to how that money feels, but pull my hand back. This is the reason my wife died. Or at least one-sixth of the reason. In some ways I'm owed this money. But in a much bigger way I can't even touch it, let alone take it. This is blood money. I drop the mattress back onto it.

A pile of porn magazines are stacked on an old wooden chair by the bed. The clock radio sits on top of them, it's big and ugly and could be worth a lot of money since it's probably the first one ever built. The bed is a double with sheets balled up, white and grey and covered in hair, the mattress sagging in the middle. I get the idea that if I pulled the top sheet away and exposed the surface of that mattress, I wouldn't eat for two weeks. The stereo that added to the glow of the room is brand new, the cardboard box right next to it, big brand letters stamped across it. It's the only thing in this room built in the last decade.

There's an old school desk with a shaving mirror on top of it, it has thin sprinkles of white powder and a razor blade on it. A supermarket cart next to the window is full of plastic bags packed with dried-out marijuana. A shelf hammered into the wall on a slight angle has tobacco papers, tobacco, scissors, and tinfoil all looking ready to slide onto the floor. Posters of muscle cars and naked women hang on the walls, along with a mirror with writing stenciled over it, telling me what alcohol Kingsly loves to drink.

Tying it all together is a dead man on the floor with his eyes wide open and his teeth clenched tightly on a bloody stump of tongue. The carpet is threadbare and has what might be grease stains on it, as if somebody rolled a hundred-piece KFC meal back and forth picking up the dust instead of a vacuum cleaner.

I find the bathroom and take off the ruined glove and run my hand under the tap and try to wash my blood away and Kingsly's blood away but more blood keeps appearing. I pull the glove back on and wrap a pillowcase from the bedroom around it, knowing the infection from this house, this neighborhood, is inside me now.

In the kitchen I go through the cupboards, finding bleach in the laundry. I twist off the top and head through the house, splashing bleach over all the places where I've dripped blood, ruining the DNA—at least that's what I hope is happening. It smells awful, a sharp acrid smell that burns my nostrils. I tug the knife out of the wall. It no longer has a serrated edge near the top, the metal has blackened and melted there. A gargling air bubble appears on Kingsly's lips. I watch it, waiting for it to pop, but it doesn't, it slowly deflates, as if he's sucking the air back in. I pour bleach over the knife and carry it into the kitchen, then wrap it in a dish towel. My daughter's bag is by the front door. It's been turned upside down and the contents spilled out. Did Kingsly know he was looking at a killing kit?

The smell of bleach makes me nauseous and I breathe into the crook of my elbow to try and cope. I make a more detailed search of the house, hunting for anything that might give me the other names but come up short. Jesus, I don't even know if Kingsly was involved. He may have been. I spend little time questioning how bad I feel about the accident, because that's what it was—him getting killed—it was an accident. I decide that I'm still undecided. That is until I think about his past, the drug convictions, the armed robberies, and the more I think about them the less I care about what happened.

They all going to be accidents?

Maybe. I don't know.

There is no computer. No address book. I go through every scrap of paper I can find, sure there has to be more names here, and the longer I can't find anything, the more despondent I become. And angry. This was my link to these men. And I've killed it. I also don't find a balaclava, but if he was one of the six men in the bank, he would have thrown it away by now.

You're new at this, but you're doing great. Think. Think. How would these men communicate with him?

"A cell phone," I say.

Taking care not to step in the blood, I crouch over Kingsly and pat down the sides of his jeans. There's a lump in his right pocket. I reach inside and find a cell phone and a set of car keys. I splash more bleach over him before heading out the back door, wiping down the handles on the way, my daughter's bag slung over my shoulder.

I check Kingsly's car. It's an old Holden that's almost twice as big as any modern sedan. I'm careful not to get blood or fingerprints over the door. There's a metal strip on the passenger seat, about the same size as a crowbar, but much thinner. It's one of those tools a thief uses to pop the lock in a car. I go through the glove box but it's as useful as going through the house. I check the trunk: there are some tools in there but nothing else.

I get back to my car and I'm all full of surprises—surprised my car is still there, surprised that it's almost four a.m., surprised that the monster inside me for the moment hasn't anything else to say. I swing by the cemetery on the way home and have the same amount of luck finding my wife's grave as I did the night before.

chapter twenty-six

It's their first serious lead.

Fifteen one-hundred-dollar notes are hanging from a line strung across the back of the laundry. A tray of water and bleach next to them. Most of the notes are stained in red ink, the bleach doing nothing to clean them up, but a few are okay, the serial numbers matching the notes taken from the bank. Others are damaged from the small explosion, perhaps too badly in some cases. These are from the blocks of cash that had the ink packs inserted next to them.

Shane Kingsly has a rap sheet going back almost twenty years. It began with shoplifting and ended with armed robbery, the years in between littered with burglary charges. In fact the few times Kingsly hasn't been in trouble were the times he's spent in jail.

Schroder already knows none of the neighbors have seen anything. He already knew before any of them were questioned. This isn't what he'd call a police-friendly neighborhood. Nobody here is opening their doors and offering information and coffee and kind helpful words.

The house is a death trap, and according to the ME, Kingsly would have survived the attack if not for the overload of electricity. Schroder imagines living in a place like this but doesn't imagine it for too long—the mere thought of it is enough to make him want to go and take a bath. Cables are running from the fuse box to the marijuana room where they were powering heat and light. The house smells of dirt and in one room the air is so dry he's worried it's going to ignite. In another room it's cold and damp even though it's over thirty degrees outside. Nearly every wall in the house has mold growing on it, and every light fitting is covered in cobwebs.

"What do you think?" Landry asks. "A drug thing?"

Landry looks tired, with dark bags beneath his eyes. He looks in need of this Christmas break more than anybody.

"Unlikely. They'd have taken the drugs. If Kingsly was part of the robbery, then whoever killed him took his share of the cash, assuming it was here to begin with. So either it's one of his own crew, or somebody else."

"You think Hunter?"

"I don't want it to be him, but there's something else." He leads Landry down the hall to the back door. Outside, next to the step, is a solid-aluminium box with walls an inch thick, big enough to fit a soccer ball.

"What is it?" Landry asks. "Some kind of safe?"

"There's no lock on it. Doesn't even have a door. Just a lid. Open it up."

Landry lifts the top. "Jesus, is that blood?" he asks.

"Dye."

"Dye? From the exploding dye pack?"

"Yep."

"So the bank robbers isolated the bundles with the dye packs to protect the rest of the cash," Landry says.

"They came prepared. They must have had the box inside the van, and they knew they had only a couple of minutes to transfer the dangerous cash into it."

"They really knew their stuff," Landry says.

"Only it doesn't make sense," Schroder says. "Why not throw the cash out the window? Why go to the effort to keep it, and even then, why not leave the metal box with the van? Why bring it here?"

"Maybe they're planning on using it again?"

"Maybe, but I don't think that's it," Schroder answers. "There were hundreds of bricks of cash thrown into those bags, how do you think they knew which ones had the dye unit in it?"

"Maybe they used some kind of metal detector?"

"Yeah, and if they did, why hide it?"

"I'm not following . . ."

"I think they had inside help."

"What?"

"Think about it. When the four people went back to the vault, they all knew the dye packs had to be inserted. If somebody forgot, they'd look suspicious. But what if somebody loaded them into a specific place? Laid them on top, maybe marked them somehow? The bank crew get the bags back into the car and take out the marked notes and contain them immediately in the metal box. They can't throw them out the window because then we'd wonder how they found the dye packs among all that other cash. They couldn't leave the box with the van because we'd think the same thing."

"Jesus, you think somebody from the bank was in on it?"

"It makes sense," Schroder answers.

"You think this is the person who killed Kingsly?"

"They'd have taken the box."

"Maybe they didn't see it," Landry says.

"Maybe. Other possibility is this person, whoever they are, might be after the others. Next step is to run down Kingsly's known accomplices. See if we can find a link between somebody and the bank."

"So you think Hunter is capable of this?" Landry asks, nodding toward Shane Kingsly as he's carried from the house in a body bag on a stretcher.

"I don't know." Schroder thinks about Benson Barlow and his warning. "I hope not," he says, "but let's go find out."

chapter twenty-seven

The knocking wakes me. I unplugged the alarm clock last night since time doesn't really matter much these days. I get to my feet and pull back the curtain and the Christmas Eve sun is high enough to suggest it's sometime around noon. I knew the knocking would come today, I just didn't know when. The clothes I wore last night are gone. As is the murder weapon—or accident weapon, to be accurate. I've cleaned my hand up, put a fresh bandage on it, it hurts but that's the price you have to pay, I guess. First thing the monster made me do when I got home last night was drop a glass on the kitchen floor when I was trying to take painkillers.

I pull on some jeans and a shirt. My shoulder hurts and I rub at it. My body is stiff and sore. The knocking comes again.

I reach the door in bare feet. The house is closed up and the air is warm and stale. I open the front door and bright light floods in, the windscreen of the car parked out front reflecting a load of it into my eyes. I hold my hand up to shield them, squinting, exposing the bandage to the men standing outside.

"We have some developments," Detective Schroder says.

"What kind of developments?" I ask, and I realize that I haven't actually spoken out loud since leaving Sam last night at her grandparents." My voice catches and my mouth is dry and the words are croaky, and I have to repeat the sentence.

"Mind if we come in? This is Detective Landry," he says, and Detective Landry looks too small for his clothes and a little too tired to be working. I lead them inside and we sit in the living room. At least I do, and Landry does, but Schroder stays standing near the Christmas tree, which pisses me off. I don't offer them a drink. It's not a social call.

"You've found the men who murdered my wife?" I ask.

"We recovered some of the money at a homicide this morning," Landry says. "Drug dealer went and got himself murdered."

"So somebody bought drugs from him with the stolen cash?"

"That's quick thinking," Schroder says.

"I like that," Landry adds. "A quick thinker."

"But no. That's not what we're saying," Schroder says. "The cash we found was from the bank. It was stained with dye and damaged."

"I don't follow," I say.

Schroder explains to me what a dye pack is and it makes enough sense. The whole time I keep thinking there's something he's not telling me. Maybe they found something of mine at the scene. Could be a neighbor saw me—it doesn't seem likely, it was too dark. And why isn't he mentioning the rest of the money? The bricks of cash under the mattress weren't ruined with dye.

"How much of the money did you find?" I ask.

"Can't tell you that," Schroder says.

"Was this the man that killed Jodie?"

"No," Landry says.

"He was one of the six?" I ask.

"One of the seven," Schroder says.

"What?"

"Six men came into the bank," Schroder says, "but another man sat out in the car."

"A getaway driver?"

"A wheelman," Landry says.

"So one of them killed him?"

"Maybe."

"Who found him?" I ask.

"Now, why would you ask that?" he asks.

"If this is somebody who was in the gang that killed my wife, maybe whoever found him is part of it."

"They wouldn't have phoned it in," Schroder says. "It was his probation officer. The victim didn't show up this morning, and his probation officer came looking for him."

"So what are you saying? Who killed him?"

"We don't know," Landry says. "Doesn't make sense that somebody would kill him, and leave all those drugs behind."

And the money.

"Unless he was killed for a different reason," Schroder says.

"Something more personal," Landry says.

"Like revenge," Schroder says, the two cops bouncing off each other now.

"But you must know his accomplices, right?" I ask. "He would have worked with these men before?"

"We're looking into it," Schroder says.

"I don't understand, why have you come here to tell me this?"

"We thought it was important to keep you updated," Schroder says.

I don't think that's it at all. And he knows I don't believe him.

"You haven't exactly told me anything, except somebody who could have been part of the robbery got killed. How do you know he was the wheelman and not one of the six in the bank?"

"Height."

"What?"

"He was a tall man. None of the six in the bank were as tall as him. The bank crew were all average, this guy was over six foot."

"Still doesn't mean he drove the van," I say.

"He drove the van," Schroder says. "And he was part of the robbery."

"So now what? It means you'll have the others soon, right?"

"We have some leads," Schroder says, and the way he says it makes me think that they have some leads on who killed Kingsly, not who robbed the bank. "What happened to your hand?"

"I dropped a glass last night," I say, glancing over at the kitchen where I dropped the glass last night ready for this question. "I cut myself picking up the pieces. I should have gotten stitches."

"Uh-huh. And your daughter? Where's Sam?"

"At her grandparents'."

"So you were here alone last night?"

"Sounds like you have something to ask me." I say.

Schroder's cell phone goes off. He flips it open and walks off a few meters, keeping his voice low.

"Yeah. We want to know how you can be in two places at once," Landry says.

"What?"

"You're going to tell us you were at home alone last night, right?"

"I was."

"We got a description of you and your car seen outside our vic's house last night. In fact we're planning on having a lineup later on which you'll be coming along to."

"I wasn't there," I say, doing my best not to break out in a sweat.

"We can prove you were."

"No. You can't. Because I wasn't. My wife is killed, and you come here and treat me this way? Screw you, Detective," I say, my heart racing. "But you know what? I'm glad he's dead. Maybe you can find whoever's responsible and ask him to get the other six."

"Interesting you'd put it that way," Landry says. "See, when you say other six and not other five, that suggests you don't think the killer was one of the gang."

I don't answer him. Before he can start back at me, Schroder snaps his phone closed. "There's been a development," he says, looking uncomfortable. "I mean, an incident."

"What kind of incident?"

"It's your father," he says, and he stares at the ground for a few seconds before looking back up at me, and without him telling me, I already know what's happened. "You're going to need to come with us."

chapter twenty-eight

The back of the car is hot even with the air-conditioning going. The only other sound is the tires traveling over the road, neither detective seemingly in a talkative mood—not like twenty minutes ago. They probably don't know what to say. It's an unmarked sedan, so it doesn't look like I've been arrested, but it feels that way, sitting in the backseat, only the handcuffs are missing. I watch the landscape change as we head through different neighborhoods into the city, the sun beating down hard on all of it, nice areas, not-so-nice areas, other areas you'd kill yourself to avoid. We're delayed in the beginning, a minor car accident outside the Hagley Park golf course in town bringing cars to a crawl, a golf ball sliced out of bounds and into the windscreen of a car, sending the driver into a spiral. Other people are jogging the park circuit, cherry blossom trees lining the route. I think about the cell phone I took from Kingsly last night. It was blank. No records of any incoming or outgoing calls. No text messages. It was a new phone. A disposable phone.

We park around the back of the building next to a patrol car, audience to a family of ducklings on a nearby grass shoulder who seem to have lost their mother. We take a rear entrance and enter a cold corridor with linoleum flooring and plaster walls, a few Christmas decorations hurriedly stuck up on the walls with bits of tape. None of us say anything. We walk in single file, one cop ahead of me, one behind.

A nurse with bright blue eyes greets us and frowns at me before talking to Schroder. She gives him directions to the ward and I tune out the conversation. I can't stop looking at the patients scattered about the ground floor, people hooked up to IV drips on bags going for walks, some of them heading outside to puff on a cigarette, and I can't see a single person in this hospital that doesn't seem bored, this day stretching out into many others. If the hospital has air-conditioning, it must be buried somewhere, maybe in the nurses' lounge, because it's about forty degrees in here.

We go up a few flights, taking the elevator. The doors open into a corridor branching into different wards. Two police officers are standing outside one of the rooms. The larger of the two comes over and he must know Schroder because he nods at him and doesn't ask who any of us are. Landry holds back and makes a phone call. I'm left to stare at my feet.

"In the corner with the curtain drawn around him," the officer says.

There are six beds in the room, all spaced an equal distance apart, three on each side of the room. Christchurch Hospital isn't exactly the hub for medical advancement, but it makes do with what it has, even if most of what it has looks like it got ordered from a 1980s "Good Guide to Living" brochure. All the beds are full, but only one of them has a curtain pulled around it. There's a gap big enough between the curtain and floor to see the feet of a doctor, and as we approach, he pulls the curtain away—ta-da!—revealing my dad. For the briefest second I'm sure he's not going to be there, but of course he is, held down in his bed by tubes and a set of handcuffs connecting his right arm to the right rail.

Dad's eyes are closed, all warmth and color gone from his face.

His features have sunken, as if the near-death experience triggered an internal collapse in which his body began falling in on itself. This man is a cold-blooded killer, but he's also my dad, and seeing him this way—well, I don't know what I feel. He's in jail because I killed a dog twenty years ago.

"It's not as bad as it seems at first," the doctor says, after Schroder tells him who we are. "One wound with a sharp object into the chest from the side. Not real close to puncturing the left lung, but if the weapon had been longer, who knows? Sounds bad—and believe me, it is bad—but it could have been a whole lot worse. The operation went about as well as it could. He's heavily sedated still, won't be waking up till this evening."

"He'll be okay?" I ask. "He'll make a full recovery?"

"Should do," the doctor says, nodding toward my dad. "We'll keep him for a couple of days, and we'll check him every few days or so after that, but yes, your dad still has the rest of his life to look forward to. Of course we'll know more this evening once he's woken up. The only thing to worry about at this point is infection. We'll keep you updated," he says, then walks off to the next patient.

"Who did this?" I ask, turning to Schroder.

"Nobody knows. A fight broke out during lunch. Inmates swarmed each other, and when they were pulled apart the guards found him," Schroder says. "He was stabbed with a toothbrush, easy to file down, effective to use," he says, and he sounds like he's rattling off a sales pitch, like he makes a dollar for every filed-down toothbrush jammed into a convict. "Question is, why would somebody want him dead?"

"He killed a lot of women," I say.

"And people have had twenty years to try and kill him in jail. Why now? Why the day after you visit him for the second time?"

I shrug.

"See, the timing is pretty suggestive, Edward. Your dad knows as much as anybody that prisons are good places for bad people to meet. I think your dad figured he could do some detective work of his own. We checked criminal records and came up with names and we're still working that angle, and the ball's rolling now and we've got some real good leads, but your dad worked it quicker from the inside. Who was he working for? Does he want those names to give to you? Or to us?"

"I have no—"

"See, Edward, it gets me thinking. It makes me think he gave you a name. And our victim last night had a stab wound in his hand, a big dirty wound similar to the one that's on yours."

"The only person who knows what my father was doing is my father," I say. "And he stopped being my father twenty years ago."

"For you, maybe. Not for him."

"Well, maybe you can ask him when he wakes up."

"Don't worry, we will. First we'll go through his cell."

"Well, until then, if you don't mind, I'd like to spend a minute with him. Alone."

The detectives step away. I draw the curtain behind me for some privacy and then face my dad. It's the third time in three days. My wife murdered last week, my father almost killed this week—what will happen next week? People say that things happen in threes. The accountant in me has always known that's bullshit—but what if it's true?

I try to imagine how I'd be feeling if the knife had gone in differently, ten millimeters deeper or to the left, hitting whatever it is that it missed—whether I'd be happy or sad or indifferent. I reach for my father's hand but don't quite make it there. I don't want to touch him. This man isn't even my father. He used to be, once. Then he became something else. I may have called him "Dad" over the last few days, but he wasn't really that, not anymore. I don't really know what he is. All those years—add up the sum of a man, and his total, a serial killer. A demon. There isn't a single one of us who doesn't think he got what he deserved. Including me.

chapter twenty-nine

There are two things separating my dad from the morgue. The first is two hospital floors of concrete and steel. The second is ten millimeters of good luck. Schroder and Landry take me down into the basement of the hospital and I don't question it. I go along for the ride—which is a straight drop in an elevator that opens up into a corridor about a quarter of the temperature of the ones upstairs. We walk in the same order as before, with me in the middle. The corridor reminds me of the prison, concrete block with no Christmas fanfare, a painted line on the floor to follow. There's an office door and then there's a large set of double doors. We go through the double doors and the air gets even colder.

I've never been to the morgue before. Never seen for real what I've seen in dozens of variations of crime shows and movies over the years, the stark white tiles and dull-bladed instruments, saws with archaic designs even though they're modern, sharp edges with only one purpose in mind. Then you have to factor in the morgue guys—people sympathetic, people who seem to take each death personally, people making jokes while munching through sandwiches and pointing out the "this and that" of anatomy.

A man in his early to mid fifties walks over, his hands thrust deep in his pockets. He sighs deeply. "Been a long day," he says, and I can't help but glance at my watch and note that it's not even two o'clock yet. "You here to see our newest entry?"

"That him over there?" Schroder asks, and he nods toward a body on a gurney, naked and grey and looking nothing like I remember him looking last night.

"That's him. Haven't got to him yet. I'm running behind, what with all the Christmas suicides beginning earlier every year. I swear as soon as malls put up their trees and tinsel, people start jumping from bridges."

"'Tis the season," Landry says.

"We'll only be a few minutes," Schroder says.

"Take your time," he answers, then wanders off to an office, slowly shaking his head.

We walk over to the body. For a few moments it's hard to believe it's the same man. The tattoos seem diluted against his skin. His eyes are closed and the wound in his hand is open. It's ugly and raw and runs from the center of his palm right out the side. It would have hurt a hell of a lot if he'd lived. The edges of it have blackened.

"Is this the man you think I killed?" I ask.

"Nobody said we think you killed him," Landry says.

"You can cut the bullshit," I say. "So why are we here?"

"We were in the neighborhood," Schroder answers. "And I thought it would be good for you."

"In what way?"

"This could as easily have been you," he says.

"No. It couldn't have been. I didn't do this to him."

"I thought we were cutting the bullshit," he says. "Look, Eddie, you have to know you're messing with the wrong people here. I don't mean the cops, I mean these people," he says, and he points down at Kingsly. "This man is lying here today, but tomorrow or the next day, this is going to be you. Is that what you want?"

"Of course not."

"Then it's time you were straight and tell us what happened."

"I didn't kill him," I say.

"You sure of that?" Schroder asks.

They lead me back upstairs and out into the sun. We drive about two hundred meters until they turn in the opposite direction to my house. After a few more minutes it becomes pretty evident where we're heading. I don't complain. It's like we're taking a day trip, just driving around the city. The car ride to the prison is about the same as the ride to the hospital. Same amount of silent conversation, same amount of heat being thrown about by the air-conditioning. About the only thing different is the scenery. Farms with burned-off grass. Large fields full of dull animals burning in the sun, each of them with bad futures, slaughterhouses and dinner tables the only thing on their horizon. I can't imagine driving a tractor around, plowing fields, milking cows, getting up early and going to bed early, working the land, the soil under your nails, backbreaking work—but maybe if I could have imagined it five years ago I would have lived on a farm with Jodie, away from the city, away from banks and bank robbers.

These are the same sights convicts see if they manage to run free— but people don't really have to escape from jail when they're getting released so soon anyway, the big revolving-door policy kicking prisoners back into the public because there's no room for them, or no real desire to buck the system and say enough is enough.

We pull up further past the visitors' entrance and walk across the hot asphalt to a back door. The pavement between us and the work crews and cranes shimmers—it looks like a layer of water has pooled across it.

"Hope you don't mind," Schroder says.

"Why? You think coming out here is good for me too?"

We're given an escort through the maze of concrete corridors that have to be almost ten degrees cooler than the outside world. We make our way to general population where the temperature heats back up to hospital temperatures. I can smell the sweat and the hate and the blood and the evil of the inmates as we walk past their cells. The cells mostly have concrete-block fronts with heavy metal doors in the middle, all of them ovens in this heat. There are narrow gaps at head height to look through, and at the moment many of those gaps are full of eyes staring out at me.

From behind the doors prisoners yell at us, some ignore us, others ask for cigarettes; the lucky ones have probably passed out from the heat. We reach my father's cell. It's the same as any of the others we've passed. It's kind of surreal to see what my dad has called his home for the last twenty years. A concrete bunker with a metal door, a single metal bed bolted to the floor with an old mattress on top, a couple of posters taped up on the wall to add color, some books piled on the floor, everything neat and tidy, a stainless-steel toilet in the corner. I stand outside with four prison guards as Schroder and Landry begin tossing it over, turning everything upside down and pulling it apart. They take their time about it even though there aren't many places to search, letting me wait in the corridor, the inmates in my local proximity all talking to me. One of them calls me Eddie, then he tells the others who I am and they all start saying the same thing. They're all telling me they're going to be seeing me soon. One of them eventually gets around to wolf-whistling at me, and the others laugh. All I can see are their eyes staring out at me, and occasionally some fingers come out from the gaps too. This is why Schroder brought me here—to give me the other preview of my future. He's telling me I'm either going to end up in the morgue or in prison. I imagine spending twenty minutes inside one of those cells and the idea isn't pleasant. I wonder how my dad survived. I wonder what kept him alive, what kept him from tying his bedsheet into a noose.

The warden shows up. He's in a suit that probably cost all of a hundred bucks, and he has a neutral sick-of-the-same-shit look about him—like my dad almost getting murdered can't muster up a single ounce of excitement in him. He's in his midfifties and uses the facial expressions he's learned over all those years to look at me with complete contempt. Without saying a word to me, he heads into the cell and directs his wrath at Schroder.

168

"Who the hell said you could bring a civilian in here?" he asks, loud enough for most of the prisoners in the wing to hear. "Are you insane? This is an absolute breach of policy and will cost you your badge."

I don't hear Schroder's response—his voice is low and forceful, and when the warden responds his voice is low and forceful too. I try my best to listen in to what they're saying, but can't pick up much except a couple of names, one of which I've heard before. Their quiet argument goes on for a few minutes, and when the warden reemerges from the cell, he's no happier as he storms past me, followed by the two prison guards he brought with him, cheered along the way by some of the prisoners.

The two detectives keep searching my father's cell as if there could be a dozen hidden compartments, and after thirty minutes they come up with nothing. In the end they walk out dejected, like they were hoping for a reason to arrest my dad all over again. We're escorted back out the same way we came in.

In the car Schroder lays out the facts. There are no suspects in my father's case—except for the fifty men who piled on top of him. It seems unlikely that figure will be narrowed down, and even more unlikely they'll try to narrow it down. When my dad wakes up he may be able to help—but until then there's not much they can do.

I remember what my dad said yesterday when he gave me that name. He knew he was putting himself in danger. I think after twenty years he'd had enough of this place, he'd seen his son again, he'd seen an opportunity to be a father, and that was the best he was ever going to get.

We pass a couple of media vans going the other way, racing out toward the prison; news of my dad has already hit the city. It'll be on the news tonight, the prison as a backdrop, and I'll be on the news tonight and in the papers tomorrow too. They'll probably accuse me again of killing my wife. Of course that's just journalists being journalists, not caring if they turn my life upside down for the chance of a story. Each year the competition gets edgier and edgier, compelling them to give up their ethics—and tonight they'll be speculating on how far the apple really fell from the serial-killer family tree.

We reach my street and there are no media vans parked anywhere. They'll arrive though, with their cameras and lights and makeup kits. Landry is driving. He pulls up outside of the house and I climb out.

"Hang on a sec, Bill," Schroder says to Landry, then follows me out. "You can make our lives a lot easier, Edward, if you tell me what you and your father discussed. You probably don't see it, but it could go a long way toward catching the people who killed your wife."

"What makes you think that's what we were talking about?"

"Far as I can figure, there's plenty for you two to talk about—but with the timing the way it is, it's pretty obvious he was putting together a list of names. Look, Edward, you better think long and hard about what you want to do next," he says. "See, it doesn't look good for you. You go and see your father yesterday, and today one of the men who robbed that bank is dead. Then today your father gets a hit put out on him."

"I can't help that."

"I know you can't, Edward. But you're not seeing the big picture," he says.

"And what's that?"

"I'm not saying you killed our victim last night. We'll know soon—there was enough blood at the scene that somebody thought they could clean up with bleach, but they didn't get it all. We'll run it against your father's, check for DNA markers—that way we don't need a warrant for your DNA. So we'll know about you for sure, soon enough. The problem you've got is that I'm not the only one who thinks you were there. They tried to shut your dad up before he got more names. That means they're going to want to shut you up too. You're going to drown in the mess, Edward, unless you start helping us."

"You're wrong," I say, thinking about the small concrete cells, the other men inside them, and spending the next ten years there. "There's another alternative."

"Oh?"

"These people killed their own man for whatever reasons. Drugs, money, some weird gang-loyalty thing, whatever. They killed him, and that means they have no reason to come after me. They know I'm innocent."

"I certainly hope for your sake that's what happened," he says.

I open my mouth to answer, but am not sure how. I think about Sam and I think about the cells, and I think the best solution for everybody is if I take my daughter and leave. Today. Get the hell out of this city. Out of this country.

"The blood will tell us if you were there last night. You can save yourself a lot of pain by telling me the truth. You sure you want to play it this way?"

I don't answer him.

"Then you better watch your back," he says, then turns and heads to the car.

chapter thirty

I head inside. It's a beautiful day but I close the door on it. Nat and Diana were going to take Sam to the park today, so right now they're probably pushing her on a swing or making sure she doesn't fall off a slide. They don't have a cell phone. Well, they do, but they use it differently from the rest of the world—they only switch it on when they need to make a call, the rest of the time saving power, a habit I think most people in the retirement generation have. I try the cell phone now but it's switched off.

I try their home number on the chance they're home, but nobody answers and they don't have a machine. They're at the park or the pool or the mall. When she comes home, what do I do then? Tell Schroder the truth and live the next ten years of my life the way Dad has lived the last twenty? I can't do that, but I also can't take the chance of Sam becoming a target. I hate the idea of leaving my wife behind, but she'll understand. She'll want what's best for Sam—and what's best for Sam is somewhere like Australia or Europe. Last night was an accident, but Schroder will never believe that. There will be no more accidents, though. The police have a name, they have a starting place now, and they'll find the rest of the men who killed Jodie. Those men will be put away for eight or ten years and that's the best I can hope for. There will be future robberies, future victims, but there's nothing I can do about that.

Making the decision to leave is hard in some ways, easy in others—but once it's made there's no reason to delay. I know how guilty that's going to make me look. Damn it, I should've taken the money from Kingsly's house, to make this move a whole lot easier. I move around the living room but don't dwell on the fact that soon I'll never see this house again, my in-laws, this festering city that took my wife. With this in mind, my neighborhood is different—darker, everything gritty, it's now the kind of place where only one bad day separates it between suburbia and a war zone. I walk to the sidewalk and search up and down the road for the sedan I figure will be there. It's about fifty meters away, dark grey, two shapes behind the window, too far away to see their faces. They're going to babysit me, they're going to report every move I make to Schroder—which means I might make it to the airport but not on board a plane.

I drive up the street, watching the sedan in my mirror. It doesn't move, not until I reach the intersection, then it pulls out from the curb. I go around the corner. Twenty seconds later the car comes around the corner too. I've never been tailed before, and I don't know whether the driver is doing a good job or a bad one. Then I realize it all comes down to whether or not he cares about being seen. Schroder probably figures if I know the tail is there I'll be less of a problem for them. Fewer people will die.

I drive past an old miniature golf course that was brand new when my dad took me for the first and only time, when I was a kid. All the shine and color has drained from the signs over the years, the Wild West theme now just looks wild, as weeds and moss gradually pull the signs down into the earth. There are a couple of cars in front, but I can't see anybody playing through the wire-mesh fence. I still remember vividly Dad and me walking from one hole to the next, miniature water hazards and ramps all encompassed by a miniature ghost town, writing down our scores with miniature pencils. It was a simpler time back then, I guess. Smaller in a way.

I wonder what my dad would do if he were still free and knew he was being followed. This must have happened to him too, near the end, when the noose tightened. He probably wouldn't even have felt the pressure.

It takes fifteen minutes to get to my in-laws.' I pull up in the driveway and the sedan drives past. I get out and knock on the front door but nobody answers. I get my cell phone out and try calling again but still no answer. I walk around the house, through the side gate and into the backyard. I look through the windows for turned-over furniture and blood on the carpet, holding my breath as I move from one window to another, Schroder's warning coming to life in my imagination—but there's nothing out of place. I try the door. It's locked. I head to the garage and put my face against the window, and when I pull back I can see the reflection of the grey sedan pulling up. It sits there with the engine running. I turn toward it. The windows are up and the sun reflects off them so I can't see inside, not until the passenger-side window is wound down. A pale face with a sunburned nose looks at me from behind a pair of dark sunglasses.

"Eddie Hunter?" he says, and the way he asks it makes me nervous. If these were cops, they'd know who I was. They'd know where I've just led them. Reporters would know too.

"What do you want?" I ask.

"We know who killed your wife," he says, and my body instantly freezes. "For the right price we can tell you."

"What?"

"Nothing in this world is free," he says. "I got something here to show you, it'll prove what I'm saying," he says.

I take another step forward, a voice in my head yelling at me that this is a mistake, that I'm being lured closer. I take a step sideways, away from the car, and the barrel of a shotgun appears in the open window and fires.

chapter thirty-one

It's a matter of priorities. If one of the bank tellers was an inside man, they'll know soon enough. Schroder is confident a series of interviews will get them some answers before the day is out. Hell, maybe the whole thing will be over before Christmas Day even begins.

He drives back to Kingsly's house with Landry and drops him off. The plan is for Landry to get started on the interviews while Schroder goes back out to the prison. The trip there earlier didn't net them much. They found medication in Hunter's cell. The warden said he was given two pills to take every day. Adding up the pills they found suggests he stopped taking his meds the day of the robbery. Instead of flushing them, he was saving them. Maybe, Schroder thinks, Hunter was planning on building a stockpile to take the whole lot at once.

When he gets back to the prison, Theodore Tate is already waiting for him. Tate used to be a cop until a few years ago, when he turned private investigator, and after both those things he became a criminal. The visiting room is empty except for Schroder and Tate and one prison guard against the far wall, hardly paying any attention. It's been a few months since he last saw Tate. He hasn't changed much, except his hair is shorter and he's lost a bit of weight.

"Thanks for doing this, Tate," he says, sitting down opposite him.

"I was surprised you called," Tate says. "I mean, in the beginning I was. I thought you were calling to check up on me, to see how I was doing. It was a surprise, a nice one even. Then it turns out you wanted something."

"Look, Tate, I've been meaning to come and see you for some time now," he says, and even though he means it, he knows he would never actually have done it. There's nothing worse than seeing a fellow cop in jail—even if he isn't a fellow cop anymore. "I just, you know, didn't get around to it. You know how it is."

"Actually I don't. You could educate me. We could swap places and see how it goes."

"I understand why you're bitter, but it's not my fault you're in here."

"I realize that. Only sometimes it's easier if I can blame somebody else except myself. Hell, maybe it's even therapeutic," he says, smiling at that last bit. "So—what's new? How's Christchurch? Is it still broken?"

"It's not broken," Schroder says, and he really believes that. Really, absolutely, almost believes that.

"Yeah, well, I think it's broken no matter what side of the bars you're on. So what is it you want, Carl?"

"Your help. You heard about Hunter, right?"

"Everybody heard," Tate says.

"You heard anything more than that? Like who stabbed him?"

"Nothing. Why?"

"I think he was stabbed because he got hold of some names."

"What names?"

"I think he was putting together a list of the men who robbed the bank last week."

"And that got him stabbed?"

"Giving those names to his son got him stabbed," Schroder answers.

"And you think the son is going to go after these people?"

"I'm pretty sure he already has. One of the robbers was found dead this morning. The victim drove the van. Timing fits perfectly. Dad gives son a name, that guy shows up dead, the next day Dad gets stabbed. The scene this morning was pretty messy. He got killed by somebody who had no idea what they were doing. Whole thing could have been an accident, or a fluke, the way it played out."

"You think the son is capable of it?"

"You tell me," Schroder says. "You think it's possible for a man to kill in revenge for his family?"

"Depends on the man," Tate says.

"Well, this man has a father who's a serial killer. His shrink came to see me yesterday. He thinks Jack Hunter suffers from an illness that could be passed to the son. Paranoid schizophrenia—he says it can be hereditary. Says it's a medical thing. He told me Edward Hunter has the potential to be a real bad guy. I wasn't so sure, not then—but now I think so."

"So arrest him."

"We will, once we have more evidence. Landry tried to bluff him out saying we had a witness, but he didn't go for it. We have blood, though. That'll tell us."

"So where do I fit into this equation of yours?"

"Two different ways. You can find out who stabbed Hunter. That might lead us back to the bank crew. Or maybe you can get some names for us. Hunter managed it, so maybe you can manage it too."

"Nobody's going to talk to me."

"There's more of a chance they'll talk to you than to me."

"So why am I doing this for you? Why stick my neck out like that?"

"Because it's the right thing to do."

"For you, maybe. Not for me. My best chance of survival in here is to keep a low profile, which is damn hard to do when there are others in here I arrested back in the day."

"There's a girl in the equation. Edward Hunter has a daughter."

Tate slowly nods. "And you were waiting to lay that on me, figuring it would work."

"Did it?"

Tate stands up and Schroder follows suit. "I'll see what I can find."

chapter thirty-two

I drop down, the shotgun exploding, and I'm back at the bank all over again, the air-conditioning replaced by real air, the houseplants replaced by bushes and trees, the six men replaced by two men in a car. A hole appears in the garage door about the same time my knees crash into the concrete.

The car door starts to open. I have nowhere to run, I have no idea what to do. But then I realize I'm not alone, I have my monster with me and he knows what to do. We're already in action. I get up and run forward, the monster leading the way, the monster in full control and now I'm the one along for the ride. We get closer to the car. To me this seems the wrong way to be going, but I'm in no position to argue. A leg comes out of the car and touches the sidewalk: jeans and a black steel-capped boot. I drop down and ram the entire weight of my body into the door, leading with my shoulder, slamming it hard on the leg. The guy inside yells out and the shotgun drops somewhere inside the car, buying me a couple of seconds. I don't wait around. I run up the street, crossing behind the car, making it difficult for them to fire on me.

The car hits reverse. The transmission whines loudly as the gap closes. Words of anger spill out the window as the two men swear at each other, a miscommunication passing between them. Maybe the passenger wanted to get out and take another shot, or the driver wanted to hit me with the car in the beginning. I weave across to the opposite sidewalk. The car screeches to a halt. It fishtails so the front turns toward me. The doors fly open and the two men jump out, but the driver has forgotten he's still wearing his seat belt and he's pulled back in, his eyes wide in confusion.

The passenger runs around the side of the car and lines up another shot as I dive forward, getting behind a parked car and *bang*, metal is ripped out of the bodywork as I hit the ground. I get up and run, weaving between silver birch trees lining the street, waiting for the next shot, but there isn't one, only footsteps as they pound the ground behind me.

The houses in the street are all similar, around ten years old, in great condition but a little tired, none of them—thankfully—with any front fences. I race over the front yard and down the side of a house, hitting the side gate with my shoulder, busting the latch holding it closed. I get through and the gate swings back and the top section explodes in a cloud of splinters from the next gunshot. I go left, cutting across the backyard, over the deck and past the french doors and a small sandpit that has bright yellow toy trucks in it. I reach the corner of the house and go left again, back toward the road. This time there's a fence across, but no gate. I duck into the alcove by the back door. It's a glass laundry door that I ram my fist through, the bandage around my hand protecting me from any cuts. The glass shatters into a thousand tiny pieces. I reach inside and unlock the door and spill into the house, my feet slipping on the glass. I go left into a hallway as the men come into the house behind me. Nobody's home. I turn into a bedroom and shut the door behind me. I tip a chest of drawers across the doorway and a moment later it rattles as the men push against the door. The door wobbles in its frame as it's kicked. I try opening the windows, but they have security latches and only open far enough to fit my arm through. I grab the nearest thing, which is a clock radio, and yank it from the power socket and thrash it against the window. It cracks on the third hit, then smashes on the fourth. A shot roars from the hallway and a large hole appears in the door, then the entire thing folds in on itself with one more kick. I don't wait around to see the rest. I take a running jump where the window was and do my best to clear the glass, but end up dragging my right thigh along a shark tooth of glass jutting out from the frame.

I get straight to my feet and run toward the road, my shoe filling with blood. I hear tinkling glass as the man behind me breaks more of the glass out of the framework with the gun to make his jump easier. The front door of the house opens as I pass, and the man without the gun comes out, running hard at me. I put my head down and pump my arms and go as hard as I can, my feet pounding into the sidewalk, my foot splashing inside the shoe, creating a suction effect that squelches blood over the edge onto the ground. The only advantage I have is that these guys are wearing big heavy shoes and I'm not, and I figure my desire to survive is stronger than their desire to gun me down—though on that last part I'm not so sure. My legs are burning, my chest even more, every breath is like swallowing smoke.

I reach their car. Both doors are still open, the keys in the ignition, the motor running. I jump in and jam my foot on the clutch and accelerator and pop it into gear at the same time as he reaches me, pulling at my shoulder. I peel rubber, and as the car lurches forward the door slams hard on his fingers. He yelps, and as the car powers ahead, he falls forward too, dragged along beside the car. The window is still up but I can hear him screaming, can hear his knees scraping along the asphalt, his feet bouncing and kicking at it. I swerve left and right to shake him loose, the bones in his fingers breaking like gunfire. I take the car up to fifty. Then sixty. Still swerving, still trying to shake him loose.

No you're not. If you wanted him gone you'd pop the door open and watch him fall away. You're the one in control now.

I jam my foot hard on the brake and the car swerves. My passenger slingshots forward at the speed the car was doing two seconds before I jumped on the brakes. His hand bends all the way back on itself, the tops of his fingers against the back of his hand, then—*schrip*—a wet sound as the fingers come free—only they're not free at all, they're still in the door. Flesh tears from the base of his fingers and runs halfway up his forearm like an apple being peeled, muscle and tendons exposed, and then he's free, flying and then rolling past the car out on the street, his hand reduced to a piece of meat with only a pinkie and a thumb. He hits the ground hard, rolls a few times, and comes to a stop with his bloody hand cradled against his chest. He doesn't get up, just lies there, trying to figure out how things have gone so badly and why he's in so much pain.

The car comes to a complete stop sideways on the road. The guy with the shotgun is running toward me, getting bigger in the view from the passenger window. He's about two hundred meters away and could probably cover the distance in about nineteen seconds if he were an Olympic athlete and wearing running shoes, but he isn't, he's wearing jeans and heavy boots and carrying a shotgun and he's built big, and none of that is helping him right now. I figure I have thirty seconds until he reaches me, but he doesn't need to cover all that distance to put me back into range.

I gun the engine and the wheels spin up as I turn toward him, but I lose control; the car keeps turning and I end up facing away from him again. The engine stalls. The back windscreen explodes, a hailstorm of glass peppering the back of my seat and the dashboard as I hunker down. My hand finds the key and I twist it. A follow-up gunshot hits the rear wheel as the car comes back to life. I take off and the back of the car drops down as the tire shreds away. The ground vibrates through the rim and the chassis as I drive, pumping the blood out harder from my torn leg. There's a high-pitched squeal from the back of the car, making me wince. The steering wheel fights with me, but I keep forward and then the car jumps up—*boom dud*—and the front wheel goes over the legs of the guy with the missing fingers, and then—*schlock*—as the rim with no tire goes over him.

I can hear his screams over the sound of the car. In the mirror, I see him roll to one side, but his left leg doesn't move at all, it's still on the ground, severed. His right leg goes with him, blood jutting toward the sky like a fountain. He drags himself, and gets about half a meter between him and his severed leg before giving up.

His partner runs right past him and takes another shot, but it doesn't do any damage as I gun the engine, turn the wheel, and in a flurry of sparks, round the corner and leave them behind. I take the car up to sixty, race through a couple of intersections, take a hard right, and pull over.

I try calling Nat's cell phone again. I've got blood on my hands somehow and it smears the buttons on the phone. I keep hitting the wrong ones and have to lean back and take a couple of deep breaths before trying again. My hands are shaking so badly I have to hold the phone in both of them to get it to work. There's still no answer. Surely they're okay. If something happened to them it would have happened at the house, not in public.

Jodie was killed in public.

So where does that leave me?

It leaves you and anybody close to you in danger.

The media coverage was extensive, so the men who killed Jodie certainly know all about me and think I'm coming after them. These people, they know I killed their friend. They know my dad gave me a name, and they suspect he gave me more than one.

I pull away from the curb. I find myself heading toward home, then decide it's not the best place to go if I don't want to be found. Could be the guy with the shotgun has made one phone call and another pair of men are descending on my house right now.

I change direction. The way the car is handling, with the wheel rim squealing on the road and my forearms burning from trying to control it, I probably wouldn't have made it there anyway. Other cars slow down and people stare at me.

I pull over. I've put about two minutes between me and the shooter. When I open the door the three fingers that were jammed there are dislodged, all three connected by the back of the guy's hand and a long piece of skin resembling torn wallpaper. They hit the ground, the middle finger tapping louder than the other two because of a silver ring on it. The ring has been flattened and has a skull on it; maybe that's what kept his fingers from slipping out of the door. I climb out. My leg is covered in blood, my shoe so full of it now that it's leaking through the material. I feel woozy and grab on to the side of the car to stay balanced. I try calling Nat again but there's still no answer.

I get back into the car. There are dance-step footprints made up of blood on the ground where I was just standing. I start to feel dizzy, and then tired. I open the glove box and rummage through it. Tissues, a road map, a woman's sunglasses. There's a gym bag in the backseat covered in broken glass. It's open, and I can see a woman's clothes in there. Whoever this car belongs to, it sure as hell isn't either of the men who showed up in it.

I rest my head back. Even with my eyes closed the world keeps swaying. I hold my hands on my leg and the blood is warm, the world fades and it takes me with it.

chapter thirty-three

New tax regulations were being standardized, Inland Revenue was desperate to take more money from those who were poor, rich, and everybody in between. There were seminars being run by enthusiastic men in suits, the kind of men you see on TV late at night selling home gyms and futuristic kitchen equipment. The fun part about the seminars was we all had to pay to go along and learn new skills so we could stay in line with the new tax laws—and of course the seminars were run by Inland Revenue staff—which was another way of them making money.

I was in a room of around a hundred people—you could look down the row you were sitting in and see that each person had about the same amount of boredom pinned to their faces, like we were all watching a twelve-hour mime show. I looked down the row and at the same time a woman was looking back. I offered one of those "weird, huh?" kind of smiles, and she offered a "this is bullshit but what are you going to do?" response. There was that awkward social mingling afterward, where we all stood around drinking orange juice and not touching the half-cooked sausage rolls. I think the food was deliberately inedible so it could be offered at the next seminar and the one after that—all cost-cutting measures. I introduced myself to the woman I'd made eye contact with. Her name was Jodie.

I was shy around women. I hadn't really had much experience of them. I was afraid every woman I ever met was probably figuring I would try and cut them in half. Jodie didn't seem to know anybody else—and I thought perhaps in her own way she was a little socially awkward too. All I knew was she was supercute and alone and her earlier smile had made me feel good about myself in some weird way. Before I knew it, I'd asked her out for dinner.

Our first date I spent in some nervous daze where I could hardly look her in the eye. Our second date we caught a movie and then sat in a café for hours—and again I have no idea what we talked about. All I knew was there was something about this woman that made me look forward to having a future.

Part of me thinks it's happening right now—that first time I saw her, that first date, the first time we were in bed together. It's a memory and a dream and at the same time it's unwinding in front of me for the first time, all of it new and fresh and wonderful. Jodie is alive and in my world again and I want her to stay.

On our third date she's different, but I can't figure out how. Like when somebody wears glasses for the first time or gets their hair cut; it's something subtle until they tell you, and then it becomes obvious.

Our fourth date—this one a lunch date—and again there's a difference but I can't get a read on it. She seems lighter, somehow. Not in the sense that she's lost weight—but in another, hard-to-register kind of sense.

I'm reliving the fifth date when I realize what it is: she's paler, almost translucent around the edges. On our sixth date the skin is grey under her eyes and the tips of her fingers have turned blue. By the next date her hair is messed up and her clothes wrinkled, and the skin on the back of her hands is baggy, it's slipping, like she's had her hands in hot water for ages. There are dark shapes beneath the surface of her face, bruise shapes that aren't bruises, but something else. When we walk I put my hand on her back and it's damp with blood. Her strides are awkward, her muscles are cramped, it's as though she's walking on heels for the first time. Her arms move stiffly.

Then, on a dinner date, she struggles to get the food into her mouth, and when she does she finds it impossible to chew. When she takes a sip of wine, it runs out of her mouth and down her chin, it pools onto the tablecloth and blossoms outward. Her skin is even greyer, and in some areas it's coming away, revealing a darkness beneath. Dark spaghetti lines form in her features. We don't go out much anymore after that one. We hardly even look at each other. And every time I touch her she is colder than before.

Then on our last date, a lunch date on a hot Friday afternoon ahead of a bank appointment, I realize the woman I'm with is dead. The skin has pulled back around her face, making her eyeballs bigger, drying out and cracking her lips, her nose a loose blister, and she smells of earth and worms and rot.

"You need to be careful, Eddie," she says, and her mouth hardly moves when she speaks, her voice sounding like gravel has stuck in her throat. I can see her vocal cords moving behind the thin skin of her neck.

"What?"

"You have to choose what's best for you."

"I know."

"And Sam."

"I know."

"Don't let the monster choose for you."

"What monster?"

She reaches across the table. I'm certain she's trying to reach across from her world to my world, to come and get me. Her hand closes on mine, it's cold and clammy, a loose glove of skin slipping back and forth. Her smile slips too, it drags her face down, widening her eyes, and there is something moving beneath the surface of them, something wormlike. When her lips part to carry on the conversation another hand tightens on my shoulder, another voice enters the mix, and the restaurant disappears, the menus fade to nothing. My wife clings to the moment for a few more seconds, the strain obvious in her decaying features. She is silhouetted against a perfect white background, like a glowing movie theater screen. Then she too disappears, fading into the light in a second.

I open my eyes. I'm still sitting in the car. A woman with grey hair pulled into a tight ponytail and a crisp white shirt with sharp edges is kneeling next to me applying pressure to my leg. A man has his hands on my shoulders, then he hooks me beneath my armpits, his fingers digging into me. The world shifts strangely as I'm lifted onto a gurney. I can see the man's face and wonder if it's the same paramedic who tried to save Jodie. More pressure is applied to my leg, and when I try to look down at my body I find I can't. I can't even lift my head without the urge to be sick. I stare up at the sky. Blue sky, no clouds, a perfect day to . . . to what? To kill somebody? The two men who came after me certainly thought so.

I can feel the gurney moving but there's no reference point in the sky so I can't tell how fast we're going, and the sensation is like dropping through the air on a roller coaster. The ambulance comes into view and I'm hoisted inside. An IV is punctured into my arm and more pressure is applied to the wound and people go to work. I close my eyes. The ambulance doors close and the sirens don't come on.

Next time I open my eyes I'm in the hospital with the hallway lights whizzing by. There are two new faces above me. I'm wheeled into ER and stabbed a few times with needles and then my leg goes completely numb. My shoes are removed and my pants cut away. The blood is wiped off, revealing a deep gash, but the fact blood isn't spraying out hopefully means no major arteries have been cut.

"Not as bad as it looks," a doctor says, filling up a syringe. "We'll have you up and about in no time. You're not going to feel a thing," he says, but he's wrong. I mean, I can't feel the needle and sutures pushing through my flesh, but I feel anger and fear and . . . and something else.

Excitement.

No. I don't think it's that.

Yes it is. Stop lying to yourself. You're excited because you took down one more man. Only five to go now. Put your hand up and be proud.

"Proud of what?" I mutter.

"What?" the doctor asks.

"Nothing."

There's no time to be proud.

"What the hell do you think you're doing?" the doctor asks, when I try to get up.

"I have to get out of here."

"The hell you do," he says. "Mate, I haven't even begun sewing you back together here."

"I need to . . ."

"Lay back down or you're going to keep bleeding, and if you don't bleed out you'll get infected, and then you'll lose your leg. That what you want?"

It isn't what I want. He goes back to work, and is about halfway done when Schroder walks into the room.

chapter thirty-four

"You don't remember who loaded the dye pack?"

Because they weren't officially treating any of the bank staff as suspects, Landry and two other detectives were interviewing the other three people who went back to the vault, while Schroder dealt with the fourth—William Steiner. They were doing the interviews at the suspects' houses—this gave the detectives a better chance to get a sense of who they were talking to; whether or not they looked like they could use a few extra hundred grand. Maybe they'd spot a bag full of money somewhere too.

Steiner was a man in his midthirties with a pale complexion that helped highlight the acne scars around his neck. He didn't seem nervous, and before he could answer only the third question Schroder had time to ask—the one about who loaded the dye pack—Schroder's cell phone started ringing.

"Excuse me a moment," he said. He stood up from the living-room couch, stepped into the hallway, and opened the phone. He barely managed to get out two words before the information came racing in. Edward Hunter. A shoot-out. A dead man.

That had been ten minutes ago. The drive into town was quicker than the last few days, most people having finished their shopping by now.

"Quite some mess, Edward," he says, stepping around the doctor and looking down at the leg.

"It'll heal."

"I'm not talking about the leg. I'm talking about the scene you left behind."

Hunter is nervous. His hands are shaking and his eyes are big and he looks like he's wired on amphetamines. "I had to leave it behind," he answers. "If I hadn't got out of there I'd be dead right now."

Schroder nods. It's what he'd heard, and it's what the evidence supports. His next trip from here will be to the scene. "A lot of people watched you running for your life," he says. "A lot of witnesses."

"Any of them feel the urge to help?" Edward asks.

"What do you think?"

"I think you're here when you should be out there, looking for Jodie's killers."

Schroder ignores the remark. "I think you're lucky you're still alive," he says, "and that luck will run out if you don't tell me the truth."

"I want to see my daughter."

"Sure, Edward, no problem. As soon as you're done telling me what happened."

"I want to see her now."

"Where is she?"

"She's with her grandparents. I don't know where they are."

"Where are they supposed to be?" Schroder asks. Is there a chance the men who went after Edward would also go after his daughter? No . . . surely not . . .

"I don't know. At their house."

Schroder's stomach sinks. He tightens his features and tries to hide his concern. "And you haven't heard from them?"

"That's what I'm telling you."

He takes his cell phone out and heads a few meters away. While it rings, he watches the doctor, who so far has said nothing since he arrived, just kept on stitching. He's probably heard similar stories a hundred times already. Schroder passes the information about Sam on to the detectives at the scene then goes back to Edward.

"Okay, we're going to send somebody to bring her in here," he says, trying not to sound concerned. "In the meantime, tell me what happened."

Edward tells him what happened from the moment Schroder dropped him off to fleeing the scene in the stolen car, running over one of his attackers on the way.

"Okay, okay, that's good, Edward. What I really need you to do now is tell me what happened last night. Don't make me wait for the blood results. We don't have the luxury of time anymore, especially now that these people are coming for you."

"I don't know anything, except two men were trying to kill me. With all the people that called the cops, and the gunfire, and the blood and chaos, nobody got there in time to arrest the second guy, am I right?"

"Look, Edward, the car is going to show up all sorts of prints. The dead man wasn't wearing gloves, so the shooter probably wasn't either. Their plan would have been to wipe the car down or burn it. We'll find him, and that will lead to the others. All of them. What's the verdict?" he asks, turning toward the doctor.

"Nothing major. It's a deep laceration and he's lost some blood," the doctor says. "We'll bandage it up and keep him on a drip for a few more hours—but no reason we can't release him tonight. However, he'll have to stay off his feet for a couple of days."

"Come on, Edward," Schroder says as the doctor leaves them, "you're in some deep shit here. You absolutely have to tell me what happened last night with Greensly."

"You mean Kingsly," Edward finishes, and the look of horror at his mistake appears immediately.

Schroder slowly shakes his head back and forth a couple of times.

In some weird way he feels betrayed. He really wanted to believe Hunter was innocent.

"Kingsly," Schroder says, and he hangs on the word for a few seconds. "That's right, Edward. Not Greensly, but Kingsly. I never told you his name and the media don't know it yet. There's only one way you could have known that name, Edward, and that's if your father gave it to you."

"He gave me the name, but I never went there."

Schroder knows he did. He knows he went there and maybe he didn't intend to kill him, or maybe he did—either way the result was the same, and no matter how you look at it it's completely unfair. Right now Edward Hunter should be celebrating Christmas Eve with his wife and daughter. Easiest thing to do now is to get Hunter to confess, then take him into custody.

"Look, Edward," he says, keeping his voice low, "here's the thing—the last two years have been hell. Too many goddamn psychopaths running around. Two long years, and I'm tired, real tired of this shit. I look at this city and I want to believe it's a good city, and it is, it really is, there's still a lot of good here, Edward, a lot worth defending. So many people, they think this city has turned to shit, but it hasn't. It's my city, I love this city—but, like I keep telling you, it's on a precipice. Thing is, it doesn't have to fall. We can save this city, it can be returned to the way it was. Looking back, there are things I wish I'd done differently. Things that could have—expedited investigations. Things that could have saved lives. If I could do it all over, there are rules I would've broken. Sometimes the ends can justify the means, you know? Sometimes you have to do bad things for the greater good. Bad things to save the city.

"Killing Kingsly, that was a bad thing, but you helped defend the city by doing it. What you have to do is say he attacked you and you defended yourself. A jury isn't going to convict you on that, not when they know this son of a bitch helped kill your wife. Some scriptwriter will come along and ask to make a movie about it. And me—if it'd been my family that was hurt, I'd have done the same thing. You can't keep denying you were there, Edward, the blood will prove it. And these people after you, they'll keep coming. Let me take you into custody. Let me help you."

Edward turns his gaze from Schroder to the ceiling and stares at it for a long moment.

"Bring me my daughter first. I want to see her," Edward answers, "then we'll talk."

The curtain opens up and a nurse pushes forward a cart full of bandages and gauze pads. She smiles at Edward. "Looks nasty," she says, "but we'll get you up and about in no time. This won't take long," she adds.

"I'll leave you to it," Schroder says.

"Bring me Sam."

"I will. I promise," he answers, hoping it isn't already too late.

chapter thirty-five

It's another messy crime scene, the kind of scene where the killers had no real idea what they were doing. The house most of the action took place in belongs to a family with a couple of kids, who were lucky enough to be at the beach instead of at home. Schroder knows it easily could have been a whole lot different—knows the medical examiner could just as easily have been sending more than one station wagon. There's broken glass out the front and broken glass around the back and a busted-up door inside and blood in various places on the driveway and the sidewalk. There are holes in fences and in the side of a parked car from the shots fired.

The street has been closed off, limiting the view to only the neighbors. Even the reporters are being held back, their cameras in range but not much for them to see. The victim has been covered up, and the shape of the body shielded by patrol cars. It makes for a nice backdrop for the cameras, but nothing more. The car the two men stole and that Hunter escaped in has already been loaded onto the back of a flatbed truck and is on its way to the police station to be examined.

"So the shooter killed his partner," Schroder says, and Sheldon, the medical examiner, nods slowly, as if scared any quick movement will tear a muscle.

"One shot in the face," he says. "One shot in each hand."

"Confirms what witnesses said."

"Hell of a way to go," Sheldon says.

"We've seen much worse. Would he have survived the injuries from being run over?"

"Left leg completely severed, right leg half severed, half crushed. I'd have rated his chances as somewhere between extremely slim and none."

Unable to take his partner with him, and worried they could be identified, the shooter had taken steps to try and hide the identity of the dying man by blasting away his face and fingerprints. It didn't work: the forensics team have already emptied the victim's pockets, turning up some coins, a cigarette lighter, and a packet of smokes—all of which have clear fingerprints on them. They'll have a name within the next two hours. Plus they've got the car with another whole set of prints to narrow down. He looks over at the bump in the canvas sheet over the body where the severed leg is. The very bottom of it, with a shoe still attached, is sticking out from underneath, the canvas not big enough to hide the blood on the street. It looks like the guy was attacked by a bear.

"Jesus," Landry says, coming over as Sheldon leaves. "The Hunter family must really be cursed."

"Where are we on the interviews?"

"Still working on it. Surveillance from the vault doesn't suggest anything one way or the other. Just shows four panicked people stuffing money into bags," Landry says.

"Yeah, well, combined with the names we're going to get from this, I think by the end of the day we're going to know who all the players are. No sign of the in-laws and daughter?" Schroder asks.

"None. You really think these men have her?"

"Doubtful. I think they're somewhere completely unaware of

the danger they could be in. Anyway, I don't see any real reason for the robbers to go after Hunter's daughter. It gets them nothing—all it does is put them at risk."

"And Hunter?"

"He's freaked out, but he's doing okay."

"He give anything up about Kingsly?"

"Nothing," Schroder answers.

"You think he did it?"

"The bank robbers sure as hell think so. Both Hunters in one day. We have to find his daughter. Hunter said he'd talk once we got her safe."

"Every patrol car in the city has a description of them. We'll have her soon."

"I hope so," Schroder says, "for everybody's sake."

chapter thirty-six

They wheel me into another room when the stitches are done. Each stitch as it went in made me stronger. There are three other men in here in different states of pain and misery. One has both legs in casts, suspended above him. A man in his seventies is snoring, a bald patch with stitches on the side of his head. The third man is reading a magazine and coughing every fifteen seconds. There are two cops outside the door, either there to protect me or to stop me from fleeing. I think about my dad—he's in a different ward with cops of his own.

My leg hurts a lot. After an hour, a nurse comes in and holds up a chart with five "happy faces" on it. The first face is yellow and smiling. The last one is purple and has a large frown and an upside-down smile. The three faces between range in color from yellow to purple, their expressions from somewhat happy to pretty much unhappy.

"Point to the one that represents how you feel," she says.

I look for the happy face of the guy who had his wife murdered last week but he isn't on there. "Just give me some painkillers," I say, "and I'll be fine."

The nurse, who is overweight with breasts the size of bowling balls, gives me one more chance to get it right. "Point," she repeats.

I point to the smiley face. "Can I go now?"

"Soon," she says. "Now take these," and she hands me a small plastic cup with pills in it. I shake the two pills into my palm and she gives me a cup of water. "Drink," she says, as if I couldn't figure out the next step by myself. Then she takes my blood pressure and seems neither pleased nor concerned by the result. I don't understand the numbers.

"We've found your daughter," Schroder says, coming into the ward, and for the briefest of seconds I'm terrified, absolutely shit-scared because I don't know how he's going to finish that sentence. They found her at the park and she was playing on a swing with Mr. Fluff 'n' Stuff, or they found her covered in blood with her throat cut? Schroder's pause is so brief, so hardly noticeable, but for me it lasts a lifetime. "They'd gone to the movies. They're at home now."

"So . . . so they're okay?"

"They're okay. But they thought it might scare her too much to bring her down here to the hospital. We've got a man at their house to keep an eye on them until we get there."

"Just the one?"

"It's Christmas Eve," he says. "One's all we can spare, but it will be enough. You're the target, not them."

He tosses me a pair of pants that are old but are at least in better shape than mine. He also has a pair of sneakers that aren't full of blood, so I don't complain. The nurse with the bowling-ball breasts comes back and unhooks the IV from my arm.

"Ten minutes," Schroder says. "That's the deal. I give you ten minutes with your daughter, and then you're coming to the station to tell me everything."

The pain is instant when I stand; my leg throbs and I almost collapse. All the blood drains in one direction and I get light-headed. The nurse pushes me back toward the bed but I regain myself and straighten up. "See?" I say, pointing at my face. "A happy smile. I'm fine."

"You don't look fine."

"I will be."

It takes me longer than usual to get dressed, and instead of walking out of the hospital they push me out in a wheelchair. All the people that seemed to be around this afternoon have gone home for Christmas. We pass only two nurses on the way out and an orderly and nobody else, not even any visitors. Everything that was in my pockets is handed to me in a white paper bag. I don't bother opening it. At the hospital doors I leave the wheelchair behind. My leg is tight with all the new stitching.

Schroder is parked in one of the handicapped spots close to the door. The parking lot is empty except for two other cars. I think he's about to put me in the back of the car, but he lets me ride up front. He knows I've killed two people within the last twenty-four hours, and I'm sure he'll try to prove it once he gets me into an interrogation room. I have no idea how, but the day has stretched into night. I'm no longer wearing my watch—I don't even know if it's in the paper bag, or if I lost it in the excitement of the day, or maybe one of the paramedics stole it. It must be around 9:30.

There's a warm breeze. Clear sky. Perfect weather conditions for Santa, and if I were home with Sam, if I still had a family life, we'd watch TV together and watch Santa's approach to New Zealand, her excitement building at the presents to come. I still haven't got anything for her, but Nat and Diana took care of that, picking up and wrapping some gifts. The malls are closed and I'd like to have got her something myself. Jesus, I'm a bad father. How can I have not made an effort to pick her something up? Some toys, a doll, something to make her feel better. I'm focusing on revenge and not on the things that matter.

Revenge matters.

"You talk about defending the city like this is a war," I say, staring out the windows as we drive through town where drunk teenagers are roaming the streets.

200

"I could rant on about this city for the next five hours and it wouldn't be anything you didn't already know," he says. "There are thousands and thousands who live here, ignorant of the violence that is seething in the soul of this city, until one day it reaches out and pulls them down. You probably knew about it because of your dad. But it wasn't until last week that you really cared."

"I always cared. No matter what you think, I hate my father for what he did. I hate him for this inheritance he left me."

We reach my in-laws' street and approach the patch of ground where the man I ran over was shot and killed. There isn't any crime scene tape up anywhere. They probably had to roll it up as quick as they could and use it somewhere else. There would have been media and cops all over the place, but now they're gone, and there's nothing here to suggest what happened this afternoon. It's too dark to tell, but I'm sure the blood has been hosed away. I wonder if they picked the dead man up first, or his leg. I wonder how much a leg weighs.

From the paper bag, a cell phone rings.

Not my cell phone because I don't recognize the ringtone.

"You gonna get that?" Schroder asks.

I unfold the top of the bag and reach inside. The phone I took from Kingsly is lit up.

"Hello?" I say, my heart thumping.

"Listen carefully. You say one more word and I'm going to kill your little girl."

"Who . . ."

"Shut up," he says. "One more word and she's dead. I'm not kidding around. Now, tell me yes if you understand."

My mind goes completely blank, then everything rushes at me from the darkness, the bank robbery, the bodies, my daughter . . . my daughter what? "Yes," I say, the word hard to form through my dry mouth and I have to catch my breath. My hand is shaking and Schroder is too focused on driving to notice. He pulls in behind the cop car.

"Your girl, she's ours now. We own her. And unless you do exactly as I say, you'll never see her again. You get what I mean?"

"Yes," I say. I break out in a sweat.

"Good. Let me know when Schroder gets out of the car."

"Wait here while I have a quick word with the officer," Schroder says, mostly to himself because I'm not really listening to him. I nod.

"He's gone," I say.

"In a moment he's about to run into the house. I want you to go with him. When he reaches for his cell phone I want you to take it off him."

"You understand I'm in police custody."

"Of course we know, we've been watching you all afternoon," the voice says. "All the more incentive for you not to miss the right moment, Eddie. Don't mess it up. You'll get more instructions once you're inside. Now go!" He hangs up as Schroder runs back toward me.

chapter thirty-seven

Jesus, it's bad. Real bad. A dead officer out here and who knows how many dead people inside. Blood all over the inside of the patrol car. There should have been two cops watching tonight, hell, should have been four of them, but the budget didn't allow for the man-hours required, and nobody wanted to pull that shift on Christmas Eve, and damn it, goddamn it, he should have done more because this officer's blood is on his hands and so is the blood of anybody dead inside. His training tells him to wait for backup, but his instinct is to go inside, into the unknown. Either way, now he knows he has to as he sees Edward limping toward the front door.

"Get back in the car," Schroder yells, but Edward is ignoring him. He breaks into a run and grabs Edward at the front door.

"Get back in the car!" Schroder orders again. He tries to lift his cell phone to his ear while keeping Edward under control. He gets the phone about halfway up when Edward spins around and grabs it out of his hand.

"What the hell?" he says, but doesn't say anything else before the phone is snapped in half and tossed onto the ground. "Jesus, Eddie, what the hell?" he asks, and he shoves him against the side of the house.

"Sam isn't in there," Edward says.

"How do you know that? We haven't searched the house yet," Schroder asks as he presses Edward against the front door. "How would you know that?"

"They called me and told me. And they sounded impatient!"

"We need all the help we can get," Schroder says. Something isn't right, but he can see the fear in Edward's eyes and knows he's telling the truth.

He lets Edward go and opens the front door. All the lights are off. He goes inside and turns toward the living room. Edward follows him but there's nobody else here. He keeps flicking light switches and nothing appears out of place.

"The cop outside," Edward asks. "Where is he?"

"Dead," Schroder says. "Why'd you break the cell phone? Who called you?" he asks.

Edward doesn't answer. Schroder opens the hallway door. The only light on down there is coming from the bathroom. "Stay behind me," he says.

The bathtub is full of water. On the surface is a plastic tray, floating there, one corner nudged up against the side of the tub. On top of the tray is a brick of cash. Schroder steps into the bathroom and looks down at it, and he knows, he immediately knows he's made a mistake, a very costly one, and before he can try to rectify it he hears a shotgun being primed.

Schroder doesn't move. He keeps facing the bath and his face scrunches up, waiting for the gunshot. He wonders if he'll outlive that blast by a few seconds and will get to see the front of his chest spraying across the tile wall. When nothing happens, he slowly raises his hands and turns around. A solid man with tattoos on his hands and a thick black jersey covering the ones that probably continue up his arms is pointing a shotgun that covers both him and Edward.

"What do you want?" Schroder asks.

"Where's my daughter?" Edward asks.

"Where's the money?" the gunman asks.

"What?" Edward replies.

"The money you stole last night."

"What are you talking about?" Edward asks.

"I'm talking about the cash you took from Kingsly."

"What?" Edward asks, and he sounds genuinely confused.

"Don't bullshit me, boy. You answered the phone. Only way you could have got the phone was if you took it from Kingsly. So you took the money too. You return it, and we return your daughter."

"Wait, wait a moment," Schroder says. "The money, we took the money into evidence this morning. Edward didn't take it."

"No. What you took was a couple of thousand dollars. I'm talking about the four hundred thousand."

"Edward . . . ," Schroder says.

"I didn't take it," Edward says.

"Turn around and get on your knees."

"Why?" Edward asks.

"Not you. You, cop, get on your fucking knees and put your hands behind your head."

"Look, we can . . ."

"Now, asshole!"

It's the last thing Schroder wants to do, but he can't see an alternative. There's no way he can jump forward and battle for the shotgun. That's certain death. Turning around and putting his hands on his head suggests death, but at the moment it's all he has. He turns around and kneels down.

"Take his cuffs and use them on him."

Edward reaches into Schroder's pockets and finds the cuffs and latches them around Schroder's wrists.

"Drown him."

"What?" Edward says, and Schroder is thinking the same thing.

"Put his head in the bath and drown him."

"Wait," both Schroder and Edward say in unison.

"You heard me. Drown him or your daughter doesn't see tomorrow."

Schroder tries to get up but doesn't get far before his chest hits the edge of the bathtub. All of Edward's weight goes on top of him, pushing his face right down to the water.

"I can't," Edward says.

"Now. Do it. Do it now!" Tattoo Man says.

"I can't."

"You can if you want to save your daughter."

"Edward . . . ," Schroder says, but he doesn't know how to follow it up. There's nothing. He knows what's coming and he takes a deep breath.

"I'm sorry," Edward whispers before pushing his head into the water.

chapter thirty-eight

Schroder's cuffed arms make it impossible for him to fight his way out, though he seems to think differently. If I were any lighter he'd probably make it too. His head bangs against the bottom of the tub and the water turns a very pale shade of red. I pull more of his body from outside the tub and stuff it under the water. I hold him by the back of his neck, pushing hard, his muscles tightening—it's like holding down a mechanical bull. His feet thrash against the floor, the tips of his shoes draw black lines across the tiles. Water is splashing all up the walls and I'm already half soaked. The bandage on my hand is waterlogged and starts slipping off. I try to imagine that I'm drowning a dog, not a person—that mangy mutt from twenty years back—and imagining that actually helps, not much, but enough to stop me from letting him up. Schroder slows down. His feet stop hitting the floor. More of him slides into the tub.

"Keep holding him."

I keep holding him. A couple of bubbles break the surface.

Schroder's legs stop moving but he's still moving his head, still fighting, still desperate to survive. The seconds keep ticking away. Five more. Another five. The bubbles stop. There is one final shudder and then Schroder no longer struggles. I let go of him and he stays in the water, makes no effort to get up. I turn around. My hands are shaking and I drop to my knees and start to dry-retch.

"No time for this shit," the man says. "Get me the money."

I cough like I'm the one with lungs full of water. "Where, where are they? My, my daughter and in-laws?"

"The money," he says. "Then we talk."

"The money is here."

"Where?"

One more cough and I'm done. I slowly get to my feet, holding on to the side of the bath, careful not to touch Schroder. The guy with the gun isn't wearing a balaclava. He looks like he did this afternoon. He probably hasn't changed his clothes, or his gun. I doubt he's used it tonight because it's too noisy. I bet the policeman outside was killed a different way. I wonder how badly he wants to avoid using it.

"You'll kill me once you have it."

"You got this all wrong, boy. I am going to kill you. What you're doing now is you're buying your daughter's life."

"How do I know you'll let her go?"

"She doesn't know who we are. We got no reason to keep her. Now where's the goddamn money?"

"Living room," I say.

"Lead the way," he says, and he backs out of the bathroom.

I lead him down the hallway. We reach the living room. "At the end of the couch," I say, "against the wall."

"Grab it."

I reach down and grab the bag, trying to keep my injured leg as straight as I can. The bag is full of crayons and coloring pencils and some drawing books for Sam and is nowhere near big enough to hold all the money I saw last night. As usual it's open. I zip it closed, pick it up, and toss it at his feet.

"What the . . . ?" he says, and he looks down at it and . . .

Now. Now! Now!

We step forward, my monster and me, only this time I don't even need him, I'm so mad. I swing my arm upwards, entering Tattoo Man's line of sight from below, the pencil pointing straight up. He must see it coming, but he can't avoid it, can't even scream. He snaps his head upward as the pencil drives deep through his eye and, like a sneeze, thick, clear residue splashes all over my hand. He stands up as straight as a board. One hand releases the shotgun, which hangs by his other side for a moment before hitting the floor. He stays standing, staring at me, one eye bright and wide, the other a liquid mess with half a pencil behind it and half of that same pencil out in front. He doesn't fall while I wipe the eye juice and blood off my hand; he saves it until I crouch down and grab the shotgun. He falls the way a dead man falls, without a care in the world, without any conviction or fear, his face hitting the armrest of the couch and driving the pencil home before snapping it off. He ends up on his side, a jagged finger of wood in his eye, looking at me but not watching as I race toward the bathroom.

chapter thirty-nine

What are you doing?

I'm trying to save him.

Why?

I need him alive.

Why?

Shut up.

Only thing you should be doing right now is to enjoying the rush. God, that was a thing of beauty! Come on, Eddie, the way you drove that pencil home—sweet Jesus, that's a real winner of a memory—a real keeper—much better than Fido. Bet you a hundred to one that's the way your father felt when he took his knife and . . .

"I said shut up," I say, then breathe more air into Schroder. His chest rises when I breathe in and drops when I take my mouth away. There is no pulse. His body is limp and heavy. I figure he's been in the water three minutes tops.

I push at his chest. I'm not exactly sure what I'm doing. The last first-aid course I took was ten years ago and Schroder sure as hell feels a lot different from a dummy made of rubber and steel. I could be saving him, or I could be cracking his ribs and driving them into his lungs.

I breathe into him. Compress his chest ten times. Should it be ten? Twelve? Breathe into him again. How long do I give this? He's been dead close to four minutes. What's the cutoff before there's a serious risk of brain damage? Isn't it around four minutes? Only thing I can remember about the first-aid course was the instructor. She kept looking at me as though I were the reason the dummy wasn't breathing anymore.

Schroder convulses under me and a low roaring comes from his lungs. He begins coughing, his body almost doubling up. I roll him onto his side and he coughs out mouthful after mouthful of bathwater. Then he collapses onto his front, his forehead on his arm, breathing heavily into the floor, his body rising and falling seemingly more than need be as though he's putting on a show. Other than the show, he doesn't do anything else. Doesn't jump up to see if he's still in danger. Nothing. I've removed the handcuffs from one wrist, but they're still dangling from the other.

"Hessus," he mutters, but can't add anything else.

"I'm—"

"Hessus woo . . . ," he says, and raises a hand up to his face and cups his eyes. He coughs again, then tries to sit himself up and lean against the bath but can't make it.

"Come on," I say, and help him. He pulls his knees up against his chest and rests his head on them. The bandage on my hand is loose. I pull it off and dump it on the floor.

"Wash," he says, and doesn't elaborate for a few seconds, until "Wash hash," and then he begins coughing again.

"Wait here," I say, and I leave him.

I check the bedrooms. It's a three-bedroom house, built in the peak of the townhouse era and painted in showroom colors that are as boring as hell but managed to stay in style longer because of it. The first bedroom, the smallest of the three, has been set up for Sam. There's a single bed and kit-set furniture and toys and posters and nobody fought for their life in there. The next bedroom has been turned into an office, with a desk and computer against one wall and a treadmill adjacent to the other.

It leaves one room unchecked, and I walk into it praying that it'll be empty. I open the door. The air is warm and stale and feels like the room has been unearthed from the back of a very deep cave. Nat and Diana are both lying on the floor, their eyes wide open, staring right at me. I move over to them and crouch down and Nat lifts his head but can't do much more because he's been hog-tied, and so has Diana. I rush back down to the kitchen and grab a knife and a moment later they're free and rubbing their wrists.

"Jesus, Eddie, what's going on?" Nat asks. "Where's Sam?"

"I don't know. I think they have her."

"They have her? Who? Who has her?"

"I don't know. The men from the bank, I think."

"The ones who killed Jodie? Why the hell would they take Sam?"

"I don't know."

"You don't know?" he repeats, getting louder now. "You don't know? What the hell does that mean? You must know! You have to know!"

"I'm going to get her back."

"Oh, I know you will. For your sake. I'm pretty convinced you brought these men into our house. What have you done, Eddie?"

"I haven't done a goddamn thing," I say.

"They think you did," Diana is sobbing now. "And now they've taken our little Sam."

"If you've caused this, Eddie, if something happens to her," Nat says, "I swear I'll kill you. I will goddamn kill you."

I go back into the bathroom. Schroder doesn't have the strength to be angry or thankful. "You drowned me," he says.

"I saved you."

"You drowned me."

"I had no choice. If I hadn't, he'd have shot you. We'd both be dead. Now, listen, you—"

"You drowned me," he repeats.

With Nat's help, we get him to his feet, lead him into the dining room, and sit him down. My leg is bleeding and I try taking the weight off it as we walk. "You need to focus here," I say on the way. "This isn't about you. It's about my daughter."

"What?"

"You owe me, okay? You owe me your goddamn life. Tell me you understand that. Don't make me throw you back in the water. You owe me because if you'd done your job and caught the people responsible none of this would have happened. If you'd put more than one goddamn man on duty my daughter would still be here."

"Where is he? The man with the gun?"

"I took care of him."

"Same way you've been taking care of everybody else?"

"Not quite," I say. "The guy I ran over, that was an accident."

"Jesus, Eddie, what's going on?" Nat asks. "Do you know where Sam is?"

"And Kingsly?" Schroder asks. "Was he an accident too?"

"I was never there."

"He said you had Kingsly's cell phone. Plus you knew his name."

"There was a cell phone in the stolen car," I say, feeling nothing at how seamless the lies are coming now. "One of the paramedics must have thought it was mine and put it with my stuff. I didn't even know it was there."

He nods. "Okay, Edward, fine, we'll go with that for now."

"Maybe the man who tried killing us is the one who killed Kingsly."

"I'm not following any of this," Nat says. "Where's Sam?"

"Yeah, maybe. But he'd have taken the money with him, right?" Schroder answers.

"I don't have any money. If I did I'd have given it to him to get my daughter back."

"Now that I really do believe."

Nat helps me check through the rest of the house in case Sam's hidden here somewhere, in a cupboard or under a bed.

He takes one look at the dead guy on the floor and doesn't say a word. I check the playhouse outside—it's empty. It's what the men have been telling me—they have her, and I have to pay to get her back.

In the living room Diana is taking care of Schroder. She's brought him some dry clothes and probably offered to make him coffee in the way that anybody over sixty always has to offer something, no matter what the situation. Schroder's taken the other cuff off his wrist.

"We have to go," I say.

"We need to call for backup."

"We have to get the hell out of here first." I grab him by the collar and help him to his feet. "They have Sam. We have to do what it takes to get her back. Come on, you've got to help me."

"You all need to get out of here," Schroder says to my in-laws.

"To hell with what you want," Nat says, "we're helping you find Sam."

"No, no you're not," I say. "You'll only get in the way."

"Settle down," Schroder says. "Nobody is doing anything here except me. I'm calling for backup, and you're going to let the police take care of it."

"The same way you've taken care of finding the men who killed my daughter?" Diana asks.

"Look, we're doing—"

"What you can," Nat finishes. "To hell with that."

"So what, you and your wife are going to come along, is that what you think?"

"I'd like to," Nat says, "but I know my limitations. That's important in a man; and one thing we've learned since Jodie got shot is your limitations, Detective. This is why you're taking Eddie. He got us into this mess, and he knows what it takes to get us out of it. Like it or not, Detective, he's certainly done more to find these men than you ever have, and if he's responsible for what happened here, then I'll deal with him when this is over. But right now I have more faith in him finding my granddaughter than you. Call for backup. We'll deal with whoever you send here and help in any way we can, but right now you and Eddie need to get your asses out there and find Sam."

"You know he's right," I say, looking away from Nat to Schroder.

"Okay, okay, fine. Where's the man who did this?"

I lead him into the living room. A pool of blood has formed around the guy's head. He's ended up lying on top of the bag of pencils and crayons.

Nat and Diana stand in the doorway. "That's one of them," Nat says.

"And the other?" Schroder asks.

"The other one took Sam," Nat says. "Not much more I can tell you. I mean, he looked kind of like this one. Shaved head, tattoos—we can try to describe him. I'm pretty sure, if things had gone differently, he was going to kill us. I don't know why he hadn't already."

"We'll get some mug shots for you to go through," Schroder says. He steps closer to the body and I roll it so he can see it better. For a moment I wonder how many dead bodies this man has seen. Plenty, I guess. Certainly many more than my father ever saw.

"Oh my God," Diana says, when she sees the stub of the pencil. "Eddie . . . I didn't think you could, that you were . . . capable . . . ," her voice tails off.

"These bastards took my daughter!" I say, glaring at her. "You'd rather I let him shoot me? You'd rather have let him drown Schroder, then come down and shoot you and Nat? Let Sam die too?"

Nobody answers. Nat nods once, understanding, maybe for the first time seeing I'm doing what I can to get us through this alive. All of us.

"You recognize him?" I ask Schroder.

"No, I . . . wait." He crouches down over the body, then reaches for my hand when he wobbles. He coughs again, trace amounts of bathwater spattering on the dead guy. "He doesn't look familiar," he says when he's composed himself.

"He has to."

"He doesn't. I'll call it in. The fingerprints, we'll have a hit on them by now."

"Then what? You compile a list of names and spend a week making a case? We need to act tonight."

"I know, I know," he says. "Look, let me think, just give me a minute."

"We don't have time."

"Who phoned you?" he asks, "when we were outside?"

"They did."

"And they told you to take my phone off me."

"They said they'd hurt Sam if I didn't."

He looks down at the dead man.

"Call them back. Tell them you'll give it to them in exchange for Sam."

"What?"

"He was asking you for money you don't have. The rest of the crew are waiting for him to show up with it. But he's not going to. What value does your daughter have then?"

"And tell them what?"

"Tell them you have it."

It doesn't seem the best of ideas, but it's the only one. I go through the cell phone menu and find the recent calls. My fingers are shaking as I select the number then press CALL. It rings a couple of times, and then someone picks up.

chapter forty

"I have the money," I say, my grip tight on the phone.

"Where's my man?"

"He had an accident."

"So you think now you can buy your daughter back by dealing directly with me?"

"Yes."

"It's too late," he says. "Your daughter is about to have an accident too."

He hangs up. Nat is standing with his arm around Diana. They're both looking lost, like they don't recognize me, don't recognize the house. Schroder is changing his shirt. "What happened?" he asks.

I don't answer him. I stare at the phone as the rage inside me builds. I don't even know what I just heard.

"Eddie? What the hell did he say?" Nat asks.

"He . . . he said it was, was too late," I say.

Diana gasps and Nat tightens his grip on her. Without even being aware I'm about to do it, I kick the dead guy on the floor, over and over.

"Edward, calm down, just calm down a moment," Schroder says, putting his arms out in a consoling gesture, one arm threaded through a sleeve, the other one bare. "These men are professionals. They know what they're doing. They know if they kill her there's no money in it for them. Give them a minute. They'll call back."

"And if you're wrong?"

"Give it a minute," he says.

"A minute, maybe two," Nat says. "They'll call back. They always call back," he says, but Nat has no point of reference other than what he's seen on TV; he's trying to convince himself as much as the rest of us.

I kick the dead guy once more. His head rolls left and right, the pencil wedged in so tight it doesn't even wobble.

"I'm going to be sick," Diana says and rushes off to the bathroom. Nat stays in the living room for about five seconds before following her.

A minute goes by. Then another.

"You were wrong," I say.

"Give it time."

"I'm going to kill these people," I say, and that's true too. Schroder doesn't respond. He's probably thinking it's time to try and get some handcuffs on me. But he's also thinking that these guys tried to kill him, and he knows he owes me one.

"Look, Edward, you have to stop kidding yourself here. This isn't something you can deal with."

"I'm doing okay so far."

"Yeah? Tell that to your in-laws. Tell that to the dead officer outside. After everything you've said about being nothing like your father, you've got blood on your hands now."

We're blood men—that's what Dad said.

"I didn't do a damn thing," I say, but he's right. I got my wife killed by speaking out. The police officer outside is dead because of me. All this blood on my hands, some of it innocent, and I know I'm still not done.

The cell phone rings. My in-laws appear as if they'd been waiting around the corner. I answer it.

"I killed a cop for you," I say, before the caller has a chance to say a word. "I've killed two of your men already. This can all end. I'll bring you the money and you give me back my daughter."

There's a pause on the line. "She's still alive. For now," the man says. "An even trade. One hour. Come alone. If we see anybody else we'll kill her."

"Where?"

"I'll call you at the time. Don't want you having a chance to set something up."

He hangs up and I explain it to Schroder, who is about as happy as Nat and Diana—who look like the world has fallen apart around them.

"You can't do this alone, Edward. We need backup," Schroder says.

"They'll kill her if you make that call. I'm playing this safe, and that means paying for her. You owe me."

"He's right," Nat says to Schroder. "Give them the money and we get Sam back. It's like Eddie said, it's that simple."

"Except it's not that simple," I say, "because there is no money."

"What?"

"This money they're asking about, I don't have it. If I was there, if I had the money, I'd be using it to get my daughter back. Can the police department raise the cash?" I ask Schroder.

"The department wouldn't go for it," he says.

"Even if it meant saving Sam's life?"

"It doesn't work that way. If it did, people would be getting kidnapped all the time. We'd be throwing cash at every criminal in the city."

"What about the damn bank?" Nat asks. "This is all happening because of what happened there. Surely they'd give us the money. They have to! They owe us—they bloody well owe us!"

"I'll make a couple of calls and see what I can do."

"If Eddie doesn't have the money, then who does?" Nat asks.

"Maybe there wasn't any money," Schroder says, and I think of the bricks of cash lying on Kingsly's bed.

"There has to be," I say. "It's too much effort for them to go to if there wasn't."

"So who took it?" Schroder asks.

"What about the probation officer? You said he found the body, right?" I say.

"Yeah, he found the body, but you're making a dangerous assumption here. He's not a suspect in the killing. He has no motive to kill his client."

"That's my point. He wasn't a suspect, but he could have taken the money."

"No, the killer would have taken the money."

"Maybe Kingsly was killed for an entirely different reason. Maybe the killer didn't see the money."

"Something you want to share, Edward?"

"We can spend the next hour here making guesses," I say, "but at the moment the probation officer is the only thing we have." I reach down and pick up the dead man's shotgun. "Let's take a drive."

chapter forty-one

Schroder's chest is burning and it's tight and he swears there's still water in there. Still, all things considered, he's much better off now than he was twenty minutes ago. When he gets more time he'll think about those moments between when he stopped breathing and when he started up again. He's never been a religious person, but that hasn't stopped him from hoping there's something when all of this is over, maybe not a heaven in the traditional sense, but something close to it. If there is, he didn't get to see it, or even glimpse it. For him there was nothing. No memory—not even a memory of darkness. Or a memory of nothing. That's all there was. Drowning, and then not drowning anymore. Whoever said drowning was a peaceful death had no idea what they were talking about.

He follows Edward to the car. He can't stop coughing. He walks slightly off balance like a man with an inner-ear infection—or like a man who has been brought back from the dead.

Edward's car is still parked outside, and they take it since it doesn't resemble an unmarked police cruiser. But first Edward grabs the paper bag out of Schroder's car. Inside it are two sets of car keys and a wallet and another cell phone. They go past the patrol car with the dead officer inside. Partly it's his fault what happened; Edward was right about that—if he'd pressed those in charge to get more people watching Edward's daughter, maybe this could have been avoided. His notebook is wet but he's able to get the probation officer's name out of it, along with an address.

Edward drives because Schroder isn't up to it. The only thing he really wants to do is curl up in the backseat and fall asleep. Nat gave him his cell phone, and he uses it to call Landry. He explains as much of the situation as he feels like explaining—not telling him where they're heading—and listens as Landry updates him.

"Theodore Tate has been trying to get hold of you," Landry says. "Where's your cell?"

"Lost it. He leave a number?"

"He said he'd keep calling back every twenty minutes. Warden gave him permission to use the phone. He can reach you on the number you're calling from?"

"Okay. Text me the number for the warden's office and I'll call." He hangs up.

"You going to call the bank manager?" Edward asks.

"No."

"You said before that—"

"I know what I said, and that was only to keep your in-laws happy. There's no point in calling the bank. They won't play ball. If I thought there was any chance at all that they'd help—no matter how small—I'd call them. Shit, this is a goddamn mess," he says, more to himself than to Edward. "And I'm doing the wrong thing right now."

"You're doing the right thing," Edward says. "Anything else and my daughter is dead. We're doing what it takes to get her back."

"Within reason," he says.

Edward doesn't answer.

"They matched the prints from the car," Schroder says. "We got

222

two names—and I'm pretty sure they'll match the two dead men you've left behind."

"You know who they work with?"

"They've worked with lots of people. We're making progress. It's only a matter of time until we have more names."

"A matter of time. How much time? Five minutes? Five hours? Five days?"

The cell phone beeps. Landry's text has come through with the number for the warden's office. "Look, Edward, if I didn't get your point I wouldn't be here right now."

He dials the number and it rings a couple of times before it's answered by the warden. The warden doesn't seem thrilled by the fact he's still at the prison when he should be at home, but he doesn't give Schroder too much grief about it.

"He's here," the warden says, and Schroder can hear the phone being put down on the desk and then picked back up.

"Roger Harwick," Tate says, getting right to the point.

"Roger . . . Hardwick?"

"Harwick. No 'd.' "

"How do I know that name?"

"Everybody knows that name. You couldn't have missed it. He was all over the news this year. He was a small-time newspaper columnist convicted of molesting teenage boys."

"Oh yeah," he says, remembering how much joy it gave the media, ripping one of their own apart.

"He's served three months of a ten-year stretch. He's been nothing but a sperm bank for everybody around him since he got his teeth knocked out his first night in the joint. I think he got offered protection to kill Hunter."

"Any ideas who ordered the attempt?"

"I can keep asking around."

"Yeah. I appreciate it," he says, and hangs up.

"That was the prison you just rang, right?" Edward asks. "That about my father?"

"Yeah. We got a name."

"That Harwick guy?"

"Yeah."

"So you can spare resources to spend time at the jail, but you couldn't spare them to look after my daughter? Is that what you're telling me?"

"We're going to find her," Schroder says. "And no, we've got somebody on the inside working the angles."

"What, you mean your friend you were telling me about who got arrested for drinking and driving? The ex-cop?"

"He's reliable."

"Who is he?"

"It doesn't matter who he is," Schroder says, "what's important is what he learned."

"I heard you talking with the warden this afternoon. I heard you mention a name. Tate. I recognized it. And the detective you spoke to a few minutes ago, I heard him mention it. He's the guy you've been telling me about, right? Your buddy? Theodore Tate? The guy who got drunk and hurt somebody? Got people killed? He was in the news a lot last year. This the guy?"

"It doesn't matter who it is," Schroder says, dismissing the line of questioning.

"So why'd Harwick do it?"

"He was offered protection to do it. A murder like that this early on, Harwick would only get time served concurrently, maybe an extra year, but it increased his chances of living."

The probation officer's name is Austin Bracken. When they reach his house Schroder tells Edward to park up the driveway, but instead Edward pulls up two houses past.

"What the hell?"

"Just being cautious," Edward answers, grabbing the shotgun.

"You won't need that," Schroder says, thinking that Edward looks more hopeful than cautious.

"You don't know that."

"We don't know if he stole the money, and even if he did, this isn't somebody looking for you. We question him, see what he knows, and if he has the money we take it. Then we do things both your way and my way—you get to deliver the money, but we

224

call it in and get backup first—it's safer for both you and your daughter."

"He isn't going to give up the money if he has it. What the hell are you expecting? Knock on the door and he'll hand it over to you?"

"Something like that," Schroder says fully aware that he doesn't sound convincing. They'll talk to Bracken, and if he gets a bad vibe he'll call for backup. He's not taking any more chances tonight.

"He deals with scumbags every day of his life," Edward says. "You think you can break a person like that just by talking to him on his doorstep?"

"And you think pulling a shotgun on an innocent man will help? Let's get a read on him first and take it from there."

When they walk up to the front door, Schroder is still out of it, like he's walking through a world slightly out of sync. He knocks on the door and there's movement and voices and Schroder knocks again to hurry them up. A few seconds later a man answers the door, his shirt open and the large belt buckle on his pants hanging loose. He's around Schroder's age, but bigger. He has that slab look about him, the not-quite-fat-and-not-quite-muscle look. He has a handlebar mustache that's about a hundred years out of date.

"What the hell?" he asks, as soon as he sees them.

Schroder holds up his ID. The badge has dried out but the wallet is still wet. Bracken doesn't look at it, just stares at Schroder, and then at Edward, and Schroder is pretty sure he knows who each of them is.

"We have a couple of questions," Schroder says.

"At this time of night?"

"You're lucky we didn't show up at two in the morning."

"Questions about what?"

"Some routine stuff about Shane Kingsly."

"Like what?"

"Background."

"And you had to come to my house at this time of the night?"

"We're chasing some leads."

225

"With him?" he asks, and nods at Edward.

"Can we come in?" Schroder asks.

"I'm busy."

"It's important."

"It's Christmas Eve," he says. "I don't care if it's important or not."

"Actually . . . ," Schroder begins, but Edward interrupts him.

"Shit," Edward says. Both men look at him. "My phone," he says, patting down his pockets. "It's in the car. I know how to solve this."

"What?" Bracken says.

"Edward . . . ," Schroder says.

"Just a second," Edward says.

"Edward, wait," Schroder says.

"It's important," Edward answers, and Schroder watches him walk away for a few seconds before turning back to Bracken. His head is muggy and his thoughts are muddled, and he knows he's probably making a mistake right now but he can't seem to focus exactly on what that is. Edward saved his life before; and that aside, Schroder knows if he'd been better at his job, then Edward's daughter never would have been taken tonight. Whatever happens to her will be on his conscience. So yeah, maybe he does owe Hunter some slack. He knows he does—it's why he's here. It's why he hasn't turned on Edward and tried to handcuff him.

Question is, how much slack is he prepared to give him?

chapter forty-two

Austin Bracken lives in a neighborhood the virus hasn't hit yet. The houses are modern and well looked after and don't have front yards made up from rusting mechanical parts. The dashboard clock on the car says we're closing in on 10:30; it seems like the day has been about forty hours long. Most of the houses still have lights on inside them, people probably closing in on bedtime, watching the tail end of prime-time TV, waiting for the kids to have been asleep long enough so they can play Santa's role and put the presents under the tree. It's what I should be doing with Jodie. It's such a magical moment and I don't know if there'll ever be any more.

I could tell in two seconds Bracken had the money. I didn't even need the monster to help me out on that one. But Schroder couldn't even get his foot in the door. I grab the shotgun because we don't have time to play nice. We're meeting the people who have my daughter in about forty minutes and I have nothing to exchange for her. I carry the gun behind my back, nice and easy, the same way I'd hide a bouquet of flowers. I bring it into view and Bracken's eyes widen and Schroder sees his reaction and turns to face me, but he doesn't turn quick enough to avoid what happens. I crash the butt of the shotgun into Schroder's head, not as hard as the security guard got hit, but hard enough to make it count. His head rocks to the side and his eyes roll back and he drops real fast.

Bracken takes a few steps back as I take a few steps forward. Schroder stays slumped on the ground, doing what Schroder seems to be doing best lately.

"What do you want?" Bracken asks.

"The money."

"What?"

"The money you stole. I'm here for it."

"What the hell are you talking about?"

We get into the hallway and I kick back and close the door. It's a pretty nice house with a wide hall and modern furniture, and the outside looks nice, nice plants, nice paint job, garden gnomes in the garden and a policeman planted on the doorstep, not a Christmas decoration in sight. Bracken keeps moving down the hallway. I keep following.

"You stole money from Kingsly," I say. "Probably around four hundred thousand dollars," I say. "Maybe more, maybe less."

"No I didn't."

"Yes. You did."

"What are you on about? If he had money, why'd you think I'd take it? And how'd you even know what he had unless . . ." His expression changes, as if he's figuring it out, but it changes too much, as if it's an act. Something here isn't quite right but I don't know what.

"You killed him," he says, and something in the way he says it makes me think he already knew that. Not just thought it, or suspected it, but actually knew it, like he was there.

"The money," I say. "Take me to it."

"I don't have any money."

"The people that money belongs to have my daughter. They're going to kill her unless I get it back for them."

"Like I said, I don't have any money."

Listen to him—he's lying. If he was truly sorry he'd tell you where that money is. He'd act more sympathetic. He'd tell you that if he could help, he would.

"I think it's time you left," Bracken says.

"They're going to kill her."

"And I'm sorry about that, I truly am."

He truly isn't.

"Somebody else must have taken it," he carries on. "Somebody either before or after, I don't know, all I know is I don't have it."

He's lying.

"You're lying."

"It's the truth."

He's lying.

"Okay, then," I say. "Any ideas who?"

"What?"

"You were his probation officer. Who else did he work with?"

"I don't know. I'd have to check."

"The police didn't ask you this already?"

"I don't know. Yeah, I guess so."

"And?"

"And what? I gave them a bunch of names they already knew and it was a waste of time."

"Okay. Okay. Who else is here?"

"What?"

"In this house. Who else is here?"

"I don't know. Just some woman."

"Show me."

He leads me to a bedroom where a woman with large breasts and very big hair is finishing off getting dressed.

"I promise you this is the last goddamn time, you son of a bitch," she says, straightening up her skirt which is torn up the side. When Bracken doesn't answer, she looks up and sees first me and then the shotgun, and the anger washes out of her face, just like that, in about half a second, and gets replaced with a big amount of fear. Her eyes are puffy and mascara has run down her face, making her look like a Goth.

"What the . . . ," she says, but she runs out of words.

"Shut up," Bracken says to her, and then I make him do exactly that by banging him on the head with the gun as hard as I hit Schroder. He goes down about as hard and looks like he'll be staying down for about as long.

"Please, don't hurt me," the woman begs. "I didn't even want to be here."

She's wearing a really short skirt and high-heel shoes and must keep her yearly calorie intake at under a thousand. "You wanna earn some cash?" I ask.

She doesn't even think about it. "Does it involve hurting him?" she asks, and nods down at Bracken.

"That a problem for you?"

"You can save your cash, sugar," she says, the fear gone now. "This I'll do for free."

"Then we better get started," I say.

chapter forty-three

Torture is all about balance, and more often than not, proves to be an extremely ineffective way of getting information. It comes down to pain thresholds: inflict too much pain and the victim will end up saying anything to make it stop. Problem with that is it makes the information unreliable. Don't inflict enough pain and they'll continue to resist. Inflict way too much and the body shuts down. I think it comes down more to fear than pain. I have under thirty minutes to create as much fear in Bracken as I can before it's too late.

I don't know why I suddenly seem to know so much about torture. It's as if a section of my mind has been unlocked, a hidden vault of knowledge opening its contents up to me. The monster has something to do with it. I think to myself, this entire ordeal could be more Disney-oriented if I gave the monster a name—Mickey. Mickey is telling me how to torture a man. Mickey is begging me to kill him. But Mickey isn't in control here—not yet anyway.

Bracken is starting to come to, and he's noticing that his entire world has changed in the last few minutes. He's resuming transmission and finding himself naked and tied to a chair. He's shaking and he's cold and scared. On the dining table there are two tools: a steak tenderizer from his kitchen drawer that looks like a wooden mallet, and a very large chef's knife. The knife has a stained handle and is worn, the blade is chipped near the end but still very sharp.

I feel nothing.

Good. You're coming along nicely.

Detective Inspector Schroder hasn't resumed transmission yet, so maybe he took a harder knock—or it's an accumulative thing for him, having been drowned an hour ago. When he wakes up he'll find he's been dragged inside and propped up against the living-room wall with a clear view of the show, his hands cuffed behind him and his feet bound in front of him. There's a gag in his mouth because, truth is, I'm sick of hearing him talk.

The woman, who may or may not be a prostitute but who probably is, is also in the living room. Bracken blinks a few times, bringing his new world into focus. He sees the steak tenderizer and the knife and his imagination is conjuring up his future.

"Where's the money?"

His first impulse is anger. "Go to hell," he says, and I jam a dish towel in his mouth and swing the tenderizer as hard as I can into his knee. Something in there gives, and he lurches forward with so much force the chair jumps off the ground and nearly tips over. His leg can't kick forward because it's bound to the chair. His face turns red and then almost purple as tears stream from his eyes. He bites down so hard the dish towel is the only thing stopping his teeth from snapping off against each other. I give him two minutes to thrash around uselessly on the chair until he gets himself back under control.

The woman says nothing, just keeps on watching, all quiet now, maybe not so sure now about helping me out.

I pull the gag out.

"I've never figured out why they start with this kind of bullshit

232

in the movies," I say. "All this torture foreplay. I've always thought I could do better. Thing is, I've always been a simple man with simple pleasures. That's all. I had the most beautiful woman in the world as my wife, we have an amazing daughter together . . . and the things that made my dad who he was never touched me. But in those movies where guys like me torture guys like you, they never cross the line. They break bones and cut skin, and the guys they're torturing always seem to stand up to it. I figure there are two ways to make a man talk. You either go through his eyes or you go through his dick." I pick up the knife. "I'm gonna start with the latter, so you can still watch."

"Wait," he says.

"Too late," I say.

I move the knife to his groin. His red face suddenly goes pale. "My bedroom. In the closet," he says, the knife above his dick. "Under the manhole in the floor in the wardrobe. The money is in there. Take it. It's yours."

I put the gag back into his mouth before handing the knife and tenderizer to the woman, who looks at them as if they contain the Ebola virus. Then she takes them. She hefts them in her hands and gets a feel for the weight. "What am I supposed to do with these?"

"If he moves, then do what makes you happy."

"No problem," she says.

I head into Bracken's bedroom and open the wardrobe door. There aren't many clothes hanging in there, and most of what is there are all dark pieces, a size too big for me. I push them to one side, the hangers grating across the iron bar. There are shoes on the floor and a couple of cardboard boxes. I kick them out, exposing the floor. I get down on my knees. The stitches pull at the wound in my leg; I feel a couple of them pull through. I drag back the piece of carpet. There's a manhole cover with a hole drilled into it for me to hook my finger through. It leaves a gap one man could fit through, but not two.

I reach in and find a strap. I pull the bag up just as a muffled but unmistakable scream comes from the living room. I race out there. The woman has taken a few steps away from Bracken. She turns toward me and there's a line of blood, not very wide, arcing up her body from her midriff, across her chest and neck and over her face. Bracken's eyes are wide open and he's staring down at his body, which is exactly how it ought to be—except for about ten centimeters of steel coming out the bottom of his stomach. The other ten centimeters of the blade is nowhere to be seen, but it's obvious where it is.

"Shit," I whisper.

"He moved," she says.

"You didn't have to—"

"Didn't have to what?" she asks. "You said if he moves, then—"

"I know what I—"

"So that's what I did."

"Shit."

She reaches forward and grabs the handle.

"Wait," I say, dropping the bag, but it's too late. She pulls the knife out. She gives it a distasteful glance before offering it to me. Blood is overlapping the edges of the wound. Lots of blood.

She drops the knife on the carpet and moves against the wall. She has that look about her that people get when they think they had a really great idea but it hasn't turned out how they pictured; the thing she thought would make her happy is making her sick.

"He deserved it," she says. "He was a piece of—"

"I don't care," I say. I hunt around for something but I don't know what, then settle for the dish towel in his mouth.

"Oh God, oh God, oh Jesus," he says. "Oh Jesus."

I wad the dish towel up and push it against his stomach and he flinches back. I apply as much pressure as I can without jamming the dish towel right through his spine.

"Ah, ah fuck, ahhh!"

The blood keeps pouring out. He's scared and tired all at the same time, and a whole lot paler than when he answered his door earlier.

"I'm . . . I'm sorry I took it," Bracken says.

"I bet you are."

"The guy, the guy was . . . was. Dead. I figured . . . it wouldn't . . . Ah Jesus, hurt any . . . anybody."

"It hurt me. It got my daughter kidnapped. It got people killed. Almost got Detective Schroder here killed too. And it got you stuck with a knife."

"Oh Jesus, please, please, you have to help me."

"I'm trying."

"Call an ambulance."

"I want my money," the woman says, looking down at the bag.

"You said you were doing this for free."

"That was before all this . . . blood."

"Please, please, call an ambulance," Bracken says, quieter now.

"Five thousand," she says.

"You know who I am?" I ask her.

"What? Yeah, I guess. From the news."

"You know what my father did, then, right?"

She nods.

"People think that kind of thing is in the blood. You want to test if they're right?"

"Maybe I did say I'd do this for free."

"Maybe you did."

"Can I go now?"

"Make it quick."

Before she can get out of the room, Schroder makes a low moan. He's still casually leaning against the wall. He's had a long day. His eyes half open, nothing fixed in his view yet, and then there I am, holding a dish towel on a dying man. He tries to say something but can't.

"He did it," the woman says, pointing at me. "He did it," she repeats, and then she is gone.

The dish towel has soaked through with blood and I find another. It soaks through immediately too. I look at my watch. The hour is nearly up and I haven't heard back about the meeting.

"An ambulance," Bracken says, and his eyes are only half open now.

I take out the cell phone and start to call for help and then end the call. Instead I dial the number of the man who has my daughter. Bracken is suffering but it's his own fault and my daughter comes first. It begins to ring.

Only it sounds weird, like it's ringing in both ears, a continuous ringing.

It takes me another second to figure out why. I look at Bracken and he's got his eyes locked on all the blood. He's wishing he'd turned his cell phone off. Instead it's ringing from his pants pocket. I hang up and Bracken's phone stops. I dial it again and it starts back up. I hang up. Bracken's phone stops ringing, and I put the phone away, and any chance of calling an ambulance goes with it.

chapter forty-four

Bracken doesn't say a thing. Everything that seemed odd the moment I got here doesn't seem odd anymore. He watches as I take the cell phone out of his pants. There are a thousand things all fighting to be said, but in this moment not one of them can be heard. This man took my daughter and he has her somewhere. His eyes are open all the way again. Blood is still draining out of the wound.

"Please, please," he says, his words slurring slightly, "call am-am-bulance."

"Where's my daughter?"

"Please . . ."

"Is she here?"

"Help me and I'll tell you where she is."

I slap him across his face. Hard. "That's not how it works. You tell me where she is, then I help you."

He clenches his eyes shut, his mouth in an open grimace, his teeth tight against each other, revealing an overbite that I'll take the steak tenderizer to if he doesn't talk. His entire face has caved in somewhat, as if he's lost ten kilos in the last two minutes. Blood and now a mixture of urine too is pooling on the floor beneath him. It smells bad.

"Where is she?"

He doesn't answer, just keeps the grimace and the tight facial features of a man going through something very intense. It's pain and fear and maybe something spiritual too.

"Hey," I say, and I slap his face again.

He shakes his head and a moment later he doesn't seem to know where he is.

"Tell me where she is and I stop the bleeding. Schroder calls for an ambulance and you get fixed up. Quicker you talk, quicker I help you."

His eyes focus on me. "Take the, take . . ."—he sucks in a deep breath—"take the handcuffs off the cop first. You free him then I talk."

"You think he'll protect you?"

"He won't want to . . . but he has to." His face turns into a grimace again as he rides another wave of pain.

"Are you the son of a bitch who shot my wife?"

"No."

"Who, then? Give me a name. Is this the person who has my daughter?"

He doesn't answer. The pool of blood is still spreading, but not as quickly now.

"Answer me, damn it. How do I get her back?"

"Help me," he says, his voice low. His eyes focus on something above me before rolling into the back of his head. I slap his face and they roll back down and stare right at me.

"My daughter," I say.

"My daughter," he repeats, almost whispering now.

"Where's Sam?"

"Sam," he says, then he closes his eyes. I slap him but they don't open back up. I check him for a pulse but there's nothing.

"Wake up!" I slap him harder. "Please," I say, grabbing his shoulders, "tell me where she is."

The dead man doesn't answer. I look over at Schroder before sitting on the floor and resting my head in my hands with no idea at all what to do next. I think about what Dad said, about having to learn to control the monster otherwise it would make me do things I didn't want to do. Did the monster do this?

No. Of course not.

You knew she wanted to hurt him. Why leave her alone with him and a large knife? You knew it'd play out this way.

No. I didn't.

Yeah? How else you think it was going to go?

I lean forward and remove Schroder's gag.

"Listen to me, Edward," he says. "I know how it must have gone down. You snapped, and you certainly didn't mean to kill him. You were trying to get information, and you were right about Bracken, he knew where your daughter was. Let me help you."

"I didn't do it. It wasn't me that cut him."

"Then who? Who was that woman?"

"She was nobody."

"Come on, Edward, it's time to stop all of this. Too many people are getting hurt."

I put the gag back into his mouth. He doesn't struggle—he's resigned to the fact there's nothing he can do except wait things out. I get up and pace the living room, covering a few hundred meters over the same piece of carpet while I try and work it all out.

Bracken has two cell phones, it turns out. He has a normal one, with what appear to be work and family contacts. Then he has the second one, the one that rang earlier. There are only two numbers in the memory, with no name attached to either of them. One is for the phone I've been using. I scroll down to the other number and press CALL. It rings three times and then it's picked up.

"I'm still waiting," a man says.

"I have the money."

"Money?"

"Please, I can . . ."

The line goes dead. I call the number again but he's switched off the phone.

I keep pacing. Thinking about it.

"I know how it happened," I say to Schroder. "Bracken planned the whole thing, and when they split the money up they gave Kingsly his share. When Bracken found him this morning he took the money. Instead of breaking it evenly among his partners, he told them whoever killed Kingsly must have taken it. That way he could keep it all. There never was any plan to pay to get my daughter back. It was a charade. He stashed Sam somewhere with no intention of me paying to get her back, but as an act so the others would think I had the money. Bracken only guessed I'd killed Kingsly because the media kept speculating that I was capable of it. I don't even know if Sam's alive anymore. I have all this but nobody to trade it with," I say, and I open up the bag I found under the floor. It's full of identical bricks of cash that I found but didn't take last night. I don't even know the exact amount. It's all blood money that I don't want, but it may still be my only chance of finding Sam. Schroder doesn't nod or shake his head or offer anything useful. He's watching a man falling apart. "I bet Bracken was going to kill the guy who has Sam. It would tie up a loose end and give him more money. They were going to kill me too."

I go through the house. There's a bedroom that's been converted into an office, and I switch on the computer. While waiting for it to boot up, I go through the rest of the house. I check under the floor in the wardrobe where the money was hidden but there's nothing else down there. I check other wardrobes but find nothing. Every time I walk past Bracken's body I resist the urge to grab him by the shoulders and shake him.

I sit down in front of Bracken's computer and navigate around the desktop. It's a clean desktop with only a few icons, and I click one open to find a folder full of porn, maybe a hundred or so video clips. I don't watch any of them. I close the folder and go into his documents folder. Turns out Bracken is—or was—an aspiring novelist. There are a couple of manuscripts here that he's working on. I don't read any of them. There is a games folder, and a music folder, and then I go through the folders on the hard drive, looking for something, for anything related either to work or to robbing a bank. I go through his emails—and it turns out that Bracken doesn't have many friends. Even his address book is barren except for a half dozen people, half of whom share the same last name as him. I scan through the emails; mostly they're all bad jokes that have been circulated around the world millions of times already. There are no emails at all relating to work or to robbing a bank. There aren't any emails to or from Shane Kingsly. I spend fifteen minutes going through his computer—which is a long time when there's a corpse leaking blood all over the living-room floor—and in the end the only thing I've accomplished is to waste precious time.

Out in the living room, Schroder has disappeared. He's rolled himself out or got to his feet. I check the front door and it's open. I step outside but there's no sign of him. He could have jumped out fifteen minutes ago or only two, but either way the result is the same for me—the police are on their way.

I grab Bracken's pants and find his wallet, then head out to my car. I wonder what the statistics are now for Schroder—what percentage chance he has of bouncing along to a neighbor who will help him, or one that will try to cannibalize him.

I don't have the time to care.

chapter forty-five

It's no longer Christmas Eve—Christmas kicked in about two minutes ago and town is full of people celebrating. The homeless and the party animals mingle and mix and I can't help but hate all of them as they move through this world, ignorant to what some of us are going through to save our families.

The center of Christchurch is mapped around a bull's-eye of tourist markets and street performers and of course the Cathedral, a giant church over a hundred years old that's popular with tourists and God and graffiti artists—although these days the popular consensus is that God moved out of Christchurch, meaning that God is everywhere except here. It's all crammed into a location known as Cathedral Square. The Cathedral is packed with people celebrating Christmas Mass. The markets are gone, and the drunk, the homeless, and the glue sniffers have to share the Square with churchgoers as they sit on steps and huddle on park benches, living in perfect harmony.

The probation offices are only a few blocks away, in a part of town where the only clubs are strip joints, where the bouncers are bigger and the tattoos take up more real estate on their arms and necks than their counterparts at regular clubs. The building is six storeys, and probably houses other things too, maybe some law or accountancy firms. I got the address from a business card inside Bracken's wallet. The only windows on the ground floor are the automatic doors, which at this time of night are automatically impossible to open, unless I drive right into them. The rest of the building is tile and brick and has graffiti scrawled across it, showing off the creative talents of the city's youth.

There's an alleyway heading up the side of the building, and I pull the car in and swing around the back. My headlights wash over a guy leaning against a Dumpster with a woman kneeling in front of him. They both look at me. The guy has vomit down the front of his shirt and the woman doesn't look any better. They wave at my car as if trying to swat away a fly, before straightening their clothes and leaving.

At the back of the building, there are two doors about ten meters apart from each other. The accountant inside me works the numbers. The police are busy. It's been a long day for them, and even now they're at Bracken's house and at my in-laws' house and they're dealing with dead bodies, and Schroder is trying to round up the rest of the men who robbed the bank and find my daughter while the rest of the force are at home, taking the night off. That means if an alarm goes off I probably have a minute or two longer than usual. A place like this, it's more likely a patrol car will show up than a security firm. And in a city like this, maybe nobody will show up for an hour. Of course there's only one statistic that matters—my daughter. I will do whatever it takes to get her back.

Bracken's keys have a keycard hanging from them. One of the doors is the good old-fashioned lock and key, but the other door has a pad on the side of it. I swipe the card and there's a click; I try the door and it opens. I step inside and a fluorescent light blinks on overhead, blinding at first. There's a second door; this one with a numeric keypad. I lean back and kick near the handle. It takes five strong kicks because I have to use my left leg, and even then it jars through to my right, the door breaking at the same time as some of the stitches in my leg. An alarm beeps somewhere.

I'm in a corridor that has every fourth light going, which is enough to see by. It winds around to the front entrance where there's a foyer and two elevators and a flight of stairs. There's a directory by the lift: it turns out the probation offices are on the ground floor. I've left bloody footprints between the door I kicked down and the elevators. I press the elevator button and wait for the doors to open and step inside. I take off my shirt and wrap it over my foot while the elevator goes nowhere. Then I open the doors and step out. I press the button and send the elevator, empty, to the top floor.

I head to the probation office, no blood trail behind me, and use Bracken's swipe card to gain entry. The alarm keeps beeping, but still hasn't gone off. I enter a large waiting room with a series of offices scattered around the sides and back. None of the office doors have names on them. There's a giant reception desk in the middle of the room. I have no idea which office belongs to Bracken. The layout of the floor reminds me of my own office, which makes me think of a simple solution: I go into each office and look for family photos and drawings done by children, with the idea of eliminating the offices that do have them since Bracken doesn't; but the idea is a bust because there aren't any pictures anywhere. I guess probation offices aren't the kind of place where employees want to share their personal lives with the public. It's the type of place where one day they have a photo of their nine-year-old daughter up on the wall, and the next day they're taking that photo to Missing Persons. I try to think about what else could make Bracken's office stand out from any other.

Sixty seconds have passed since I entered the offices. A moment later a high-pitched scream shrieks from every corner of the building. I grab some Blu-Tack from the reception desk and ball it into my ears.

I take out Bracken's business card and the cell phone. There are three numbers on the card, an office line, his direct line, and his cell phone number. I dial the direct line but can't hear anything over the alarm. I head from office to office and barely manage to hear a phone ringing in the fourth one I try. There is a narrow angle of sight from the desk, past the reception area to a window leading outside. I glance at the view every few seconds, waiting for when it changes from parking meters and bike stands to patrol cars.

I switch on the computer which offers more light, then I go through the drawers. There are too many files to go through so I pile them onto the desk. The computer loads up and by the time a desktop appears I'm too nervous to hang around. I consider tearing the computer apart and taking the hard drive, but the files are probably on a server somewhere. The alarm is still shrieking and the Blu-Tack in my ears doesn't seem to be helping.

There's a gym bag behind the desk. I unzip it and dump the clothes on the floor. I'm packing everything I pulled out of the drawers into the bag when a patrol car pulls up outside.

As I reach the door to the foyer and elevators, the alarm goes quiet. The rest of the lights come on and I duck behind a desk. There are footsteps in the foyer, and voices. I can't quite hear what they're saying, but the words I'm looking for stick out from the rest—"blood," "elevator," and "top floor." The police out there know they have a lot of ground to cover, but they've noticed that the elevator with blood leading up to it has been sent to the top. A radio squawks, and one of them speaks into it. "Backup." The word is clear.

Another door opens, and then there are footsteps in the stairwell. Thirty seconds later the elevator doors open and close. The accountant and the monster think things through. We figure there are two cops here already and more coming soon, so I need to act now. We figure one of them is probably at the third or fourth floor now. He's laboring his way to the top floor while his partner rides up in comfort.

Another patrol car pulls up outside.

I untie the shirt from my foot and pull it back on. I open the door and run into the foyer, the gym bag in one hand, a stapler in the other, ready to hurl it hard in case somebody is still down here—but there's no one. I turn toward the main door. There are two police constables walking toward it, a man and a woman. They stop dead and stare at me and I do the same, me on one side of the door, them on the other, then they race forward and one of them grabs the door.

chapter forty-six

His head has cleared in the hour or so since he died, and he likes to think that the fuckups in that time were brought about by that experience, likes to think they're not the kind of mistakes he'd make on any other day.

Getting out of the house was easy. All Schroder had to do was caterpillar his way to the front door, get to his feet, twist his body so he could reach the door handle, and run like hell—or in this case bounce. It took him a couple of tiring minutes to reach a house that had lights on. He used his nose to ring the doorbell. It was a young couple whose kids had gone to bed; they were wrapping presents and had shared half a bottle of wine and seemed to look at Schroder with as much suspicion as anything, but he was thankful they took him in and cut the ties that held his feet. Nat's cell phone was still in his pocket, and he used it to phone the station, and then he phoned his wife. He told her he was running late, told her it was going to be a long night, told her he was sorry, and didn't tell her that a short time ago she was technically a widow. She told him she was disappointed but she understood, and he should get home when he could. It was the best-case scenario—and her first Christmas present to him.

By the time the first patrol car arrived, Edward was long gone. The responding officers removed Schroder's handcuffs.

"So where's he gone now?" Landry asks. They're standing in Bracken's living room, a photographer and a couple of other officers hanging out in the corner. Others are out canvassing the neighborhood, hoping to narrow down Hunter's destination.

"I don't know. But Jesus, Bill, everything that's happened—everything that Hunter did to Bracken, he was right in the end. Bracken was part of the robbery. He had somebody take Hunter's daughter, and now we've got nothing."

"Not nothing," Landry says. "We've got a couple of names. That gives us a bunch of known accomplices."

"Yeah, but in time to save Hunter's daughter?"

"He shouldn't have killed Bracken. He could have helped us."

"He says he didn't do it. Says the woman did it."

"You believe him?"

"I don't know."

"That's not much of an answer, Carl. Sounds more like you want to believe him but don't."

"Whether he did it or not, he's gone somewhere. Something here must have tipped him off."

"Maybe he found a name or an address."

"Yeah, and took it with him."

"Well, if we're lucky, maybe he'll succeed. Maybe he'll get his daughter back and take another couple of bad guys off the street."

"I don't see it working out that way," Schroder says.

"Sure. Would be good, though, right?"

A few more detectives arrive on the scene and join them in searching the house.

"It's official," Landry says, finishing up a phone call. "Our two victims today are also Bracken's cons."

"Like Kingsly."

"Yeah. That's three for three."

"So Bracken put the crew together," Schroder says. "I'll go to his office. Check his files. Maybe it's even where Hunter is heading."

"Maybe," Landry answers, and ten minutes later it turns out he's right.

chapter forty-seven

"Shit," the officer says, because the automatic doors are locked and don't open for him. He fumbles with the keys but I don't hang around to watch. I limp past the elevators, past the busted door and the footprints of blood toward the back entrance. I burst out behind the building into the alleyway. I reach my car, the shotgun still on the passenger seat. The woman cop is running down the alleyway toward me. I turn the shotgun toward her and she comes to a complete stop. She raises her hands the same way the bank manager did.

Kill her.

There's no need.

There's always a need. There always has been.

"Please," she says. She's a few years younger than me, and about as scared as I probably looked when six men came bursting through the bank doors. She takes a couple of steps away.

I prime the shotgun. She takes another step backward. Jodie was killed as a distraction and it worked. It commanded a huge police force and effort at the bank while they sped away. A shotgun blast here would do the same thing. It would give me more time to find my daughter.

Do it.

"Please, I have a family," she says.

"Move over there," I say, and I point the shotgun toward the door I just came out of. She reaches it and I move around to the driver's side of the car and climb in. I put the gun standing up from the footwell onto the passenger seat and the cop stays still. I reverse quickly back toward the road. A third patrol car shows up and covers the exit. I push hard on the accelerator and the back of my car hits the side of the patrol car right in the middle of the front wheel. The crash jolts me back and forward and the Blu-Tack falls out of my ears. The patrol car is pushed away from the side of the road. My car stalls and I restart it and jam my foot on the accelerator again and swerve out onto the road. The back of the car produces a rattling sound that gets louder the further I drive. The patrol car comes after me but manages all of five meters before taking a sharp right-hand turn, the axle probably broken. I slow down at the intersection, and when I push my foot back down the engine revs but doesn't grip and the car rolls without any acceleration. I try changing gears but it doesn't make a difference.

One of the other patrol cars comes away from the curb. I pull over and jump out, slinging bags over my shoulders, the money much heavier than the files. The patrol car is about a hundred and fifty meters away when I point the shotgun at the tattoo-covered bouncer at the strip club door and make my way inside.

The club is dark and there's cigarette smoke hanging in the air; it's like a fog rolled in, bringing with it the dregs of modern man. Girls in nothing but underwear, with breasts of all different sizes, are walking between the tables, some carrying drinks, others leading a patron by the hand toward a three-minute lap dance. The music is loud and aimed at the generation most of these girls seem to be in—one that's about ten years younger than mine. There are maybe fifteen or twenty patrons in the club, mostly men sitting by themselves, a group of six in front of the stage. I keep the shotgun by my side, pointing down, and nobody seems to notice it. Most of the lighting is aimed at the stage, where a girl in a nurse outfit who looks nothing like the nurse who showed me the happy face chart earlier today is spinning around a pole. The look on her face reminds me of the waitress on the day Jodie died, the look of the damned—it was a lifetime ago now.

I take a corridor that leads past the toilets to a fire-exit door. The police haven't hit the club yet. The toilets smell of disinfectant and the floor outside is wet. I hit the fire-exit door hard but the damn thing opens only about thirty centimeters, then bounces back, a chain flexing against the handles with a padlock securing it in place. I point the shotgun at the lock and people in the club scream when they hear it go off. The music keeps going and people are no longer watching the stage. The chain falls away and I take it with me outside. I jam the doors closed behind me and wrap the chain around the handles.

The alleyway is similar to the last one I was in, except this one runs at a different angle, along the back of clubs and shops instead of up between them. I turn right, passing more back entrances; from some come loud music, from others nothing. I stick with the direction and run for about sixty seconds, taking most of the weight on my left leg, hobbling more than running. I can hear sirens patrolling the streets. I climb a fence and drop into an open parking lot with bad lighting and about two cars. On the opposite side I take thirty seconds to catch my breath and begin to transfer the files out of the gym bag and stuff them in with the money. I tuck my arms through it and strap it onto my back and leave the empty bag behind and carry on moving.

The parking lot comes out a driveway on Manchester Street. There are cars that don't have sirens on them driving past, hookers standing on corners, run-of-the-mill people staggering down the street, some wearing Santa hats. I run across Manchester and head further from the central city, down Gloucester Street toward a one-way system where there is less lighting. A patrol car comes into the street and I duck in behind a row of bushes lining a tile shop and the car drives past. I move again, getting further away, the hookers becoming less frequent and harder-looking, like they'll do far more for far less. I cross Madras Street and keep heading east. The sirens aren't as loud now. I get another block before turning north, back toward home, slowing down as more blood runs out of my leg. I need somewhere I can read the files. Somewhere I can bandage myself back up.

I'm a good six or seven blocks away when the cell phone I took from Kingsly rings. I flip it open.

"Hello?"

"What the hell, Edward? You're making this a whole lot worse than it needs to be," Schroder says.

"I'm finding my daughter."

"No you're not. You're killing her. Look, we have some names, we're banging on some doors right now. We're going to find her."

"You can guarantee that?"

"I can guarantee we're doing our best."

"What about the person who visited Roger Harwick in jail?"

"Who?"

"Somebody had to visit Harwick before my dad got stabbed, right? Somebody from the outside."

"It's a good thought," he says, "except nobody came to see Harwick today, or yesterday. In fact nobody has been to see him since the bank robbery."

"That doesn't make any sense," I say. "Somebody had to talk to him."

"And somebody did. It means another inmate was visited and got told to pass the message along."

"Who?"

"We're looking into it. Problem is there are so many opportunities for Harwick to interact with another inmate. Could be there were other links in the chain. Somebody comes to see Inmate A, who speaks to Inmate B, who talks to Inmate C. Or maybe one of the guards organized it."

"So it's a dead end," I say.

"I'm doing what I can, Eddie."

"It's just never enough."

"Where are you?"

"I have to go."

"What did you find? Another name? An address? Edward, listen to me, if you know where your daughter is, you have to let me help you."

"I don't know where she is. Not yet."

"You're armed and running around the city, Edward. The word has come in—you're a threat. A SWAT team unit is coming for you. They see you with that shotgun, they're going to open fire. There won't be any dialogue. You hear what I'm saying?"

"I hear it," I say, and hang up, then I try calling Nat but the phone just rings and rings.

What I need is transport and somewhere to read over the files. I find somewhere secure to hide the shotgun before heading back onto the road to flag down a taxi. The first three go by, passengers already inside them; the fourth pulls over, the driver sees the blood on my leg, shakes his head, and drives off. Another taxi pulls up a few minutes later, and this time I keep the gym bag covering my leg. The blood on my shirt from where I wore it over my foot is all on the back, so the driver doesn't notice it. He just seems to be happy that I'm not carrying a shotgun, but struggles to express his gratitude in clear English. I tell him to take me back toward town, which doesn't please him because he was hoping for a bigger fare. There are a dozen patrol cars circling the streets, but their search patterns don't extend to taxis. They're out there dressed in black, carrying assault weapons and itching to take down Eddie the Hunter, the man they always knew would turn into a killer.

chapter forty-eight

There is blood leading from the kicked-in door to the elevators. It's how Hunter fooled the first two cops on the scene into thinking he'd gone upstairs. With all the mistakes Hunter has been making, Schroder knows there's at least something in that mind of his that's working. He wonders if he'd be doing the same thing if it was his daughter who'd been taken, and decides that he would. He'd do what it takes—which makes it hard to know the SWAT team is out there gunning for Hunter, ready to take him down.

Schroder has never had any reason to come down to the probation offices before, and he knows there's every chance after tonight he'll never come here again. The building is fairly nondescript and the offices inside about as impersonal as you can get, with rubber plants either side of the reception desk and a sunset picture hanging on the wall the only signs of excitement. He imagines it'd be hard to work in a place like this, getting to know people on a return basis as they're released every few years for the same crimes, addictions to drugs, taking other people's money, taking other people's lives, all in endless circles. At least, being a cop, your job is to put criminals away; these guys have to reintroduce criminals into the outside world, over and over and over again.

It's too early to tell if Edward had time to find anything here. After talking to him he got the impression Hunter was still winging it with no idea where to go next. That made him dangerous.

The IT woman, Geri Shepard, is currently going through Bracken's computer. Shepard—in her late twenties and with a body other women would kill for—is about as put out by being here as she is attractive.

"This couldn't wait?" she asks for the third time already. "You're real sure on that?"

"You found anything yet?" Schroder asks.

"Possibly. See here? We've got a list of files he accessed going back as far as you want. I still don't see why you can't tell me what you think Austin has done—it might make me be able to speed things up."

"Search for Shane Kingsly," he says, ignoring her. "When did Bracken access that file?"

She clicks away at the keyboard. "Today. The twenty-fourth. Though I guess it's the twenty-fifth now, right?"

Today would fall in line with what Bracken told them this morning. His client didn't show up, so he went to his house looking for him. Makes sense he'd have pulled the file.

"Is it standard practice for probation officers to immediately go to somebody's house if they've missed an appointment?"

"It depends on the probation officer, and it depends on the person who missed their appointment. It's not common, no, but it's not unheard of. Seems he accessed the guy's records yesterday too."

"Was there an appointment scheduled?"

"Hmm . . . that's weird. According to his planner, he wasn't due to see Kingsly for another week."

"What about Adam Sinclair?" Schroder asks. Sinclair is the man Edward hit with his car.

"Let me check. Um, November first."

"How often was he seeing Sinclair?"

"Ah . . . according to this, he wasn't."

"He wasn't?"

"No. Not according to this."

"Then why'd he pull his file?" he asks.

"I'm not sure. Maybe it was in relation to somebody else he was dealing with."

"Ryan Hann?" he says, Hann being the man Edward stabbed with a pencil.

"Um . . . same. November first. This is weird—Hann is also no longer under probation."

"Okay. Good. This is good. Can you find any other files he'd have no need to pull up that he accessed around that time period?"

"Hang on," she says, and works at the keyboard for another minute. "Here, we got five more names of people no longer under probation. Wait—make that four—one of these men just died," she says, and she twists the monitor so Schroder can take another look.

He scrolls down the list. It's a short list and it only takes a second for Arnold Langham's name to show up. Suction Cup Guy. "Jesus," he whispers. "He was part of it."

"What?"

Arnold Langham only had a criminal record for beating up his wife—but that in no way meant beating up his wife was the only criminal thing he had done. There were two possibilities he could see. Langham was involved with these other men, meaning there must be other things he was good at. He was recruited into the gang, then, leading up to the robbery, there must have been something about him the others didn't like or couldn't trust, and he became a liability. Shooting him or stabbing him could have brought the investigation closer to the bank robbers, but dressing him up like a pervert and throwing him off the top of a building, that pushed the investigation into a completely different direction.

The second possibility was Langham wasn't involved, but learned of the robbery and became a liability. Schroder is more inclined to go with the first possibility—it would suggest the gang was suddenly one man short, which would explain why Bracken chose Kingsly.

Either way, it still left Schroder with a list of four names, each belonging to a man whom Bracken recruited to steal $2.8 million in cash.

chapter forty-nine

When the taxi driver drops me off he smiles with relief, as he probably does every time he drops somebody off without getting stabbed. His English is perfect when he tells me how much the fare is, but not so good when figuring out the change. Gas price increases have pushed taxi fares up astronomically over the last few years—it's no wonder more and more people are drinking and driving. I tell him to keep the change.

I'm right next to the parking building where Jodie's car has been for the last week. My keys are still hanging in my car, but the spare keys have been in my pocket all day. I make my way upstairs. Jodie's car is a four-door Toyota about six years old. It starts on the first turn of the key and I let it warm up for thirty seconds. There's a modern stereo in the center console and a GPS on top of the dashboard that both seem to be defying the law of gravity, since they haven't fallen in some passerby's possession. I find Jodie's swipe card in the glove box and use it to exit the building.

I drive back the way I came and find the shotgun exactly where I'd left it. I try calling Nat and Diana again and get the same result. I drive a few minutes out of the city and pull over.

I stack up the files and go through them. The names and faces stare out at me, but none of them stand out. Twenty files, all of random people who have nothing to do with the case. After ten minutes it seems it's all been for nothing—whatever contact Bracken had with the men who killed my wife isn't to be found in these pages. There's no way I can make it back into the offices to check for more. I pack the files away and get moving.

There are even fewer cars in the hospital parking lot when I get there than there were earlier tonight—mine doubles the number; the other is a van with a bunch of guys a few years younger than me leaning against it drinking. I wrap the weapon in a jacket Jodie left in the back of her car.

Visiting hours are over and have been for probably six or seven hours. I walk in looking like somebody who knows where they're going and nobody says anything because there's nobody around. Not a single person in this part of the ground floor—everybody is either at home for Christmas or working in the emergency room. I make my way down the corridor to the elevators, not leaving any bloody footprints behind because my shoe has dried up. I go up to the fifth floor and step past a nurses' station that doesn't have any nurses. Only about half the lights are on that were on this afternoon and it's only about half the temperature. I reach the ward where my father is and there aren't any police officers outside like there were this afternoon—which the accountant in me puts down to simple supply and demand. Tonight the city is demanding the most from its guardians, and the police are supplying every man who's prepared to work overtime and ignore their family—which isn't many, it seems.

Still, this isn't going to be a walk in the park. There aren't any officers here, but there is a security guard sitting in a chair reading a magazine, doing what he can to stay awake. I help him out there by showing him the shotgun. He's in a similar situation to the one Gerald Painter was in last week—he's sitting here earning a minimum wage, armed with nothing useful. He doesn't even make it out of his chair. He wants to—he gets about halfway up before realizing there's no point in moving any further. He doesn't sit back down either—just stays suspended between the two actions.

"Don't say a word," I say.

"I won't."

"Stand up."

"Okay."

"Is there anybody else here?"

"Like who?"

"Police. Other security guards."

He shakes his head.

"Any nurses in there?" I ask, nodding toward the ward.

"There's one somewhere but I haven't seen her in about half an hour."

"Okay. You know who I am?"

He shrugs. "Am I supposed to?"

"That's my father in there you're looking after."

"Oh shit," he says. "Please, please, don't kill me."

"Then pay close attention."

I direct him into the ward. There are six men all sleeping in the room, a combination of snoring and farting coming from every corner: if somebody lit a match the air would ignite. The curtain is no longer pulled around my father's bed. He turns his head toward us.

"The curtain," he says, and nods toward it.

I reach up and pull the curtain around us. The security guard stands on the opposite side of the bed. My dad has his left arm free, but his right is still cuffed to the bed railing.

"I hear you've had a busy day, son," he says.

"They have Sam."

"What?" he asks, and his face looks pained.

"The men who killed Jodie. They took Sam tonight. They're going to kill her, Dad, they're going to kill her unless I can get her back."

The security guard doesn't seem sure what to do. He takes a small step back and ends up sitting down, most likely thinking he doesn't get paid enough for this.

"I had no idea," Dad says.

"I need names."

"I've given you a name."

"It didn't pan out. Dad, I wouldn't be here if there were any other choices. You must have something else."

"Hand me that water, son."

There's a glass of water on the stand next to the bed. I grab it for him. He takes a long slow sip before handing it back.

"Water tastes better here," he says. "In prison, by the time the water makes it to us about half a dozen guards have already spat in it. Or worse."

"Dad . . ."

"Kingsly was the driver, right?"

"Yes."

"So, minus the man you ran over, there are five more."

"Three more."

"Three?"

I give him the details. "The monster got them," I add.

"Okay, son. Well, I have another name that can help."

"Who?"

"Not so fast."

"What?"

"Twenty years is a long time," he says. "The air inside, it tastes different. It tastes stale, it tastes of desperation. At night, tough men who try to kill you during the day cry. In winter it's always so damn cold and in the summer it's so damn hot and . . . twenty years, son, twenty years is a long time."

"It's still better than what the women you killed got."

"Is it? Is it really?"

"I think if you could ask them, they'd agree."

"I'm not so sure," he says.

"The name?"

"I'm coming with you."

"What?"

"You want that name, you have to take me with you."

"They have Sam, Dad. Give me the goddamn name."

"I know they have Sam."

I point the shotgun at my father's chest. He flinches. "I'm not messing around, Dad."

"You going to shoot me?"

"If I have to."

"How's that going to help you?"

"It'll make me feel better."

"That's my boy," he says, and then smiles. "But you're not going to pull that trigger."

"Oh?"

"Too noisy. You won't make it out of here."

"Don't be so sure about that."

"And you'd be leaving without a name. You could look around, maybe try to find some drugs or tools to torture me, but the quickest and easiest option," he says, then rattles the handcuff against the frame, "is to take me with you."

"I can't."

"You can if you want to get your daughter back."

Take him with us. Things will go a lot quicker.

"Keys?" I ask, pointing the gun at the guard.

"I, ah . . . don't have them."

"Yeah you do," Dad says. "They have to in case they need to rush me back into surgery."

The guard stands up slowly and digs into his pocket.

"There was a time when there'd be more people guarding me," Dad says. "Back when I was younger, when I was somebody to be feared. Now, nobody knows who I am."

"That's funny," I say, "because everybody knows who I am."

The security guard leans in and unlocks the cuff, then pulls away fast, expecting my dad to try dragging a scalpel across his throat. Nothing happens. My dad lies in the same position and massages his wrist.

"I'm going to need a wheelchair," he says.

"You can't walk?"

"I got stabbed today, son, so no, I can't walk. At least not that well."

I point the shotgun at the guard again and give him a fresh set of instructions, and a few seconds later he's lying on the floor naked with one hand wrapped through the base of the bed frame and cuffed to his ankle. I take his phone and keys and step back to the other side of the curtain. The other five men still appear to be asleep. A nurse walks past the open doorway to the corridor but doesn't look in. She's probably so used to never seeing a security guard sitting outside the room that she doesn't notice him missing. I give her a few seconds' head start, then follow her out. She goes one way and I go the other, heading toward a row of wheelchairs I spotted earlier.

I get back to my father and half of me expects him to be gone and the other half expects him to have killed the guard, but nothing has changed—he's still lying on the bed. I slip the IV needle out of his wrist and help him into the security guard's clothes, which are a bit big but better than the hospital gown. He winces and breathes heavily, and does more of the same when I get him into the wheelchair. He holds his hands over the area where half a day ago surgeons were busy at work, and he keeps them snug against the wound as if trying to hold parts of himself inside.

"Stay quiet," I say to the guard. "Let us get out of here without having to shoot any nurses."

"Okay."

I have to put the gun in my father's lap so I can push the wheelchair. We reach the corridor. Dad's hands don't ever extend beyond the wound. We reach the elevators. I hide the shotgun behind my body when the doors open on the ground floor, then put it back in my father's lap when nobody shows up. I wheel him out of the hospital and out into the parking lot and past the same group of teenagers leaning against the van, who show interest in the shotgun by all becoming immensely quiet. I help Dad into the car and can't figure out how to fold the wheelchair into the boot, so leave it behind. I figure this entire thing should have been more difficult. I figure getting in to see my dad should have been hard enough, let alone getting him out. I figure a few years ago it would have been. A few years ago there were enough people left to care enough about paying one or two cops overtime or shifting some resources to have them sit beside him. If they can't pay them enough to protect my daughter, they sure won't pay them enough to guard an old man.

"Where to?" I ask.

"First I need some food."

"Dad . . ."

"I haven't had a real meal in twenty years, son."

"We don't have time."

"We'll make the time. I'm sure there'll be a McDonald's on the way."

"On the way to where?"

"On the way to the next name on the list," he says, and I pull away from the curb and follow my father's directions.

chapter fifty

Turns out the Serial Killer choice of food isn't a Happy Meal, but a Big Mac. Dad complains how it falls apart in his hands but still eats it as I drive, probably faster than any Big Mac has ever been eaten.

"I don't think your doctor would approve," I say.

"Probably not," he answers, following it with a Coke, "but he probably wouldn't have approved of me being stabbed either."

"Want to tell me about it?"

"Not much to tell," he says, then takes another bite.

I keep driving. Dad works away at the fries. When he's done, he balls up the wrappers and tosses everything out the window.

"Dad . . ."

"What?" he says. "People don't throw things out the window these days?"

"Where are we heading?"

"It all looks the same," he says. "Newer, maybe, but not much. A couple of apartment complexes, some new homes, other than that it's like I was here yesterday."

"Fascinating, Dad, it really is. Now, where are we heading?"

"You've killed four men starting with Shane Kingsly, is that right?"

"Something like that."

"So you've been listening to the monster, as you call it."

"Something like that."

"And now the rest of them have Sam and you're going to do what it takes to get her back."

"What's your point?"

"My point is that we're certainly alike."

"We're nothing alike."

"Whatever you say, Jack."

"Where to?"

"You know what, son, suddenly I don't feel so good," he says, and he grips his stomach.

I slow down. "I'll take you back to the hospital."

"No, no, it's not that. My stomach's bloated. Oh shit, I need to find a bathroom. This food, I haven't eaten food like this in twenty years, oh shit, oh shit, this is going to be bad."

"Just hold on," I say.

"That's great advice, son," he says, doubling over and holding an arm across his stomach.

I make a left and drive to a nearby service station, pulling up around the side where there's a bathroom door and Dad, hunched over, makes his way inside. I wait inside the car and five minutes later he comes back out, his skin even paler than when he went in.

"It's going to take a while getting used to the outside world," he says.

"Don't get too used to it. Once I get Sam back I'm taking you in."

"You don't mean that."

"Get in the car, Dad."

He gets in the car and we're back on the road. His skin is clammy and he doesn't look too good: I'm not sure whether it's the food or the stabbing he took earlier in the day. The roads are empty except for an occasional taxi taking the drunk home, or other killers out there looking for their daughters.

Dad gives me the address and I punch it into the GPS unit and it gives us the directions. Dad stares out the window watching the city, remembering it as best as he can. Occasionally we come across a new intersection that confuses him, but for the most part he knows his way around. I wonder if I'd be doing as good a job as him if I'd been inside for twenty years. I suspect there are plenty of other things my dad is still good at, other things that instinct and muscle memory would help him complete.

The neighborhood the GPS directs us into is another of the areas hit heavy by the virus—only this one has been hit by a rust epidemic too: the cars parked out front are all beaten up and gardens as dry as a bone. It's all out of date, as if the GPS has brought us to 1982 instead. Dad's still wobbly when I get him out of the car, but nowhere near as clammy as he was ten minutes ago.

"Tyler Layton," Dad says.

"He one of the guys?"

"He's why we're here."

I look at the street and the houses and the cars and I think, I've been here before, maybe not this exact location but certainly one just like it, certainly in a similar frame of mind to the one I'm in now, except instead of the monster in the passenger seat it's my father—a different type of monster but a monster nonetheless. Maybe we're all here, Dad's darkness and my monster riding in the backseat, chatting to each other, comparing stories and wagering on the outcome of the night. Schroder was wrong when he said the city is on a precipice. He's wrong in thinking it can still be saved. Just ask Jodie.

"Tell me about him," I say.

"There isn't much to tell."

"There has to be something."

"What do you want to hear, son? That he's a bad person who has whatever is coming to him coming to him?"

"Something like that."

"Let's go inside."

I follow Dad up to the front doorstep. We're only a couple of hours away until the dawn lights up this part of the world. It's becoming routine to me now. I knock on the door a couple of times and wait a minute before knocking again, and when the guy comes to the door I jam the shotgun into his face—and the rest is so familiar now I don't even need the monster.

Tyler Layton is exactly like the kind of person you'd expect to hold up a service station or a bank with a shotgun—except maybe a bit older than I'd expected. A shaved head with tattoos adorning his scalp, prison tear tattoos raining down his face, he's around ten years shy of Dad's age. He doesn't say a single word from the moment he sees the shotgun to the moment my dad finishes tying him up with cord he cuts from the venetian blinds. We don't get into any semantics about right and wrong and the ends justifying the means.

"Start talking," I say.

"About what?"

"About my daughter. Where is she?"

"This your son, Jack?" Tyler asks, watching my father.

"Answer the damn question," I say to Tyler.

"I don't know anything about your daughter," he says, keeping his eyes on Dad. "Been a long time, Jack. The security guard uniform doesn't suit you."

"Not that long," my dad says. "Not for me. Seems like it was only yesterday."

"It's been four years," Tyler says.

"Where's my daughter?" I ask.

"What's he talking about, Jack?" he asks my father.

"What the hell is going on here?" I ask.

"I knew your father real well," Tyler says, "if you catch my drift. Quite a few times if I remember correctly—though after the first few times I stopped remembering. Was it the same for you, Jack?"

"Tyler here was kind enough to introduce me to one of the darker elements of prison," my father says, but there is nothing kind-sounding about his voice at all. "He was there when I first got thrown in jail. My first night there and he broke four of my fingers and cracked two molars and shredded my asshole so hard I couldn't sit down for a month. I was barely fixed up before he went at it again. He was in

268

and out of jail over the years, but he always came looking for me."

"And now you've come looking for me," he says.

"What the hell, Dad? Does he have anything to do with Jodie or Sam?"

"No," Dad says.

"Then why are we here?"

"If we had more time," Dad says, talking to Tyler, "I'd cut you apart piece by piece."

Tyler doesn't answer him. For all his attempts to act as if he doesn't care, like this is just one more day in the life of one really tough bastard, there is a fear in his eyes identical to the look in that dog's eyes twenty years ago when it was chomping on a steak full of nails. He tightens the muscles in his arms.

"I always knew prison was going to be tough," Dad says. "I always knew it was going to be one of those places that turns out exactly as awful as you figured it would be before you ever set foot in the place. Thing is—" he says, and then I interrupt him.

"Dad, we don't have time for this. Sam is out there, we have to find her."

He looks at me, his eyes sharp, cutting into me. After a few seconds, he nods.

"You're right, son," he says. He puts his hands out. "The shotgun?"

"No," I say. "I didn't free you so you could kill people."

"Yes you did."

"Not people who have nothing to do with what happened."

"Give me the gun, son."

"Don't give it to him," Tyler says.

Give it to him. Let him take control for a bit. We'll get over this speed bump and find Sam.

"He's a bad man, son. If we turn our back on him other people will suffer for it."

Give him the shotgun.

"Do you want to know how many people he's hurt? How many women he's raped? Women like Jodie? Teenagers like the kind of girl Sam will become?"

I hand him the shotgun.

chapter fifty-one

It's all happening so fast. The night is becoming absolute chaos. Jack Hunter has escaped—helped by Edward—and Schroder has to push that fact to the back of his mind right at this moment and deal with it soon. At this rate he's doubting he'll make it home on Christmas Day for even five minutes. His wife will hate him, his daughter might too. Thankfully his son is only a few months old so at least somebody won't be pissed at him.

The SWAT team is running at about 50 percent, the other half having already left for the holidays or drunk already and not returning Schroder's calls, giving him a team short on manpower but a team nonetheless, still extremely capable. Schroder has already died once tonight and doesn't want that to be the start of a pattern. He has a better use for the team than he did half an hour ago, with them driving around looking for Hunter.

When his cell phone rings again, it's Anthony Watts, a detective who is currently with Edward Hunter's in-laws.

"They don't recognize any of the photos from the files," Watts says. "I mean, the only one they recognize is the victim lying dead on their living-room floor."

"Okay. Get back down to the probation offices. If Bracken scrambled to put all this together since finding Kingsly's body, then maybe this other person has a file he accessed today. It could give you a fresh set of mug shots."

Kelvin Johnson is on the top of the list of six names he printed out, predominantly because three of the other people are dead—including Ryan Hann, who died by pencil. Bracken wasn't on the list, giving Johnson a one-in-three chance of being the first. Incarcerated nine years ago for the robbery of a jewelry store in which a sales assistant permanently lost the use of one arm after he shot her, Johnson was released four years ago and upon his release had contact with his parole officer once a week for two years, then once a month for the following year. As of a year ago the justice system was satisfied that Kelvin Johnson was a model Christchurch citizen, having undergone the exact amount necessary of jail time and a probation period afterward.

Johnson lives in a government-subsidized house in an area of town that seems to attract violence the same way rotten food attracts flies. At the moment they're all parked four blocks away, a miniature command post set up.

"Two things," Schroder says, and the team of men listen intently. "First, we don't know for a fact Johnson was part of the robbery. Second thing is, even if he was, we don't know that he has anything to do with Sam Hunter being kidnapped, or if she is here. That means we need to be careful; we need to make sure there are no slipups, and that we get him in one piece. Any questions?"

There are always questions. They spend another ten minutes going over it. When they're ready, two vans pull in to the street where Johnson lives, one from each side. A drive-by three minutes earlier had confirmed there were no lights on inside the house, and no signs of life. A team of two people are parked on the street behind the house in case Johnson climbs the back fence in an attempt to get away.

The SWAT team members move quickly. They're all dressed in black and they hit the house hard and fast, busting in the door, and then there's thirty seconds of shouting and no gunfire. Schroder and Landry wait out on the street, and a minute later Johnson is led out in a pair of pajama bottoms and handcuffs.

"There's nobody else," Officer Liam Marshall, the man leading the unit, says. "No sign of any girl. The house is secure."

"Get him in the van," Landry says. "I'll try to convince him to talk while you check out the house."

"Maybe he doesn't know where she is."

"Maybe," Landry says, "but we'll know soon."

It takes Schroder three minutes to find the money. It's hidden above the manhole in the ceiling. Things are always hidden up there; he figures there isn't a burglar yet who hasn't considered hiding something in the roof.

He calls Landry and updates him. "He's definitely one of them, but there's nothing else in the house to suggest he had the girl here. If he'd taken her, he'd be with her now."

"Not if he's already killed her," Landry says.

"I know. I know," Schroder answers, and hangs up.

"One down and two to go," Marshall says, "and we're set for the next location."

"Let's go," Schroder says, and he gets in his car. He's about two minutes away from the second name on the list when the call comes in of a gunshot. The address doesn't match either of the other two addresses he still has to visit, and he wonders if the gunshot is random, or whether it means Hunter has found his daughter, or brought himself one step closer.

chapter fifty-two

Tyler's screams stop around the same time we reach the car. The gunshot tore through him and the seat of the chair and made it collapse into a splintery heap. His genitals and lower intestines are splashed out all over the floor. The arteries in his thighs are all torn up and coating the room in squirts of blood.

Could be this is the kind of neighborhood where nobody would even call the police, but we're not hanging about to take a poll. We reach the car and pick a direction and stick with it.

"Holy shit, Dad, you just killed an innocent man."

"No I didn't."

"What? You just—"

"You said innocent, Jack. Tyler was far from innocent. You could see that right off, right? It's why you gave me the gun."

"I gave you the gun to speed things along, that's all," I say. "Sam is out there somewhere, and you're turning all of this into you. You won't help me until I get you out of hospital. Then we go and see somebody who has nothing to do with what we're trying to do. All you're doing is proving we are absolutely nothing alike."

"He had it coming," Dad says. "And the darkness—it needed to be fed."

"To be fed? He said he hadn't seen you in four years. How'd you know where to go? No way you would have been keeping tabs on where he lived, not unless you were planning on making a visit. How'd you know you'd be getting the chance?"

"I didn't know," he says. "But before you showed up at the hospital, I was able to find out."

"How?"

"It doesn't matter."

"Why though? Why'd you want to find out?"

"You just sermonized about me making all of this about myself," he says, "now you're the one doing it. I thought you only cared about finding Sam."

"And it's obvious that's not your priority at all," I answer. "Because it all doesn't fit properly."

"You want my help or not?"

"That depends on whether you're going to actually start helping me, and I'm thinking you have no idea who to speak to next."

"Okay, okay," he says. "Bracken was the parole officer, right?"

"Right. But he took the money from Kingsly and didn't tell the others. Everybody thinks I have it."

"You do have it."

"Yeah, I have it now, but I didn't have it earlier, and now I don't know how to get hold of any of them."

"Maybe they know how to get hold of you? You took his phone, right?"

"Yeah—but nobody's called."

"He give you anything, anything at all?" Dad asks.

"Bracken? No. Nothing."

"You search his house?"

"Yeah. And his office. There was a cell number in his phone but it doesn't connect."

"You went to his office?"

"I didn't find much. Just some files that didn't lead anywhere."

"Where are they?"

I nod toward the backseat. Dad reaches over for the bag and grunts when he tries to lift it.

"They're on top," I say, and a moment later he has them in his hands.

"Who the hell are these people?" he asks, opening the first couple of folders.

"Nobody," I say. "Just files the probation officer had in his drawer."

"So they're clients he has. You went to his office and found his current work and nothing else."

"I didn't have time to keep looking."

"You should have made the time. These are useless," he says. "Some of these people don't even have a record for armed robbery. What have we got here," he says, thumbing through them, "we've got half a dozen armed holdups, an arson, a couple of rapists, a couple of drug traffickers, a kidnapper, a compulsive shoplifter—any of them could be part of this thing."

"I know, Dad, I already know. Two men took Sam tonight, one of them I killed, the other one has her. Nat and Diana, they saw the other guy."

"Have you showed the folders to them?"

"I can't. The police are with them. Schroder was going to get them to check out some mug shots."

"So maybe they have a name already. Maybe the police have already found Sam."

"And maybe they haven't."

"Call them."

"The police?"

"No, your in-laws. Maybe they've made an ID and can give us a name."

"I've been trying."

"Well, try again."

I pull over. After ten rings I'm about to hang up when suddenly it's picked up.

"Hello?"

"Nat?"

"Jesus, Eddie, where the hell are you?"

"I'm looking for Sam. Where the hell else would I be?"

"With your father? The police say you broke him out."

"He's helping."

"He's a monster."

"So is the man who took Sam. Were you able to make an ID?"

"Not at first. The cops know who the bank robbers are but none of them took Sam. The detective who showed them to us brought back a new batch of photos. We picked him out right away, Edward. The police know who took Sam."

"They have the name, but that's not the same as having Sam, is it?"

"Well, no."

"Then give me the name of the man who took her."

"I don't know, Eddie. I think the police are better equipped."

"The police, if they find her, will put the man who took her in jail for five or ten years and then let him go. That what you want? Remember when you said you wished you could have time alone with the people who killed Jodie?"

"We only want Sam back safely."

"Give me the name. I swear to you, Nat, I'm not going to do anything that puts her at risk."

"I don't know . . ."

"I deserve to know the name of the man who kidnapped my daughter, Nat. Jesus—she's my daughter. My daughter!"

"Oliver Church," he says, and I recognize the name. "That's all I know. I don't know any addresses or anything else."

"Thank you," I say, and I hang up.

"See, I knew they'd answer the phone," Dad says. "I'm your good-luck charm."

"Give me the folders."

He hands them over. The fourth one in belongs to Oliver Church. Out of the list of crimes in the files, Oliver Church is the only one who has kidnapping and manslaughter next to his name, but there are no details of the crimes.

"Address won't be current," Dad says, "so no point in going to his house, and even if it is current he sure as hell won't have taken Sam there."

"You ever hear of him?"

"Never. Can't your in-laws go online and find out about him?"

"They barely know what online means."

"Well, there has to somebody you can ask."

"Not really. What we need is a computer," I say, looking out the windows, knowing that nine out of every ten houses out there has one. I think about all my conversations with Schroder, about my dad in jail, about the stabbing, about the ex-cop working for Schroder trying to solve part of the case.

The ex-cop.

Because Christchurch is clinging to the past, it's still possible to pass an occasional phone booth, and I drive back toward town to find one. The Yellow Pages have been torn out, and so has the phone receiver, but the White Pages are still there and I use them to look up a name and address.

chapter fifty-three

All the lights are off inside the house, as they are in every other house in the street. The difference between this house and the others is the others all have a Christmasy look about them, lights and decorations in the window, oozing joy and peace to the world. This house is cold and certainly empty, and when I break a window and make my way inside it feels like my house, like something has been lost from this home the same way something was lost from mine.

I use the cell phone to create some light, then decide that it's so late in the night I'd have to be really unlucky if somebody saw the lights burning, so I flick them on. I open up the back door for Dad and he comes inside.

It's a three-bedroom home with one bedroom set up for a young girl, perhaps one similar to Sam's age. The room hasn't been slept in for a long time, and it's far tidier than any young girl would ever leave it. There's an office with not much in it, but it has a computer, and the remaining bedroom has a big bed with folded clothes lying on top.

"Who lives here?" Dad asks, looking at some of the photos. "You know this guy?"

"Not really," I say.

"He seems familiar."

"Maybe you've seen him around."

"Only place I've been around lately is jail," Dad says.

"And there's your answer."

The house belongs to Theodore Tate—the ex-police officer Schroder told me about a few times, the man in jail for drunk driving, the guy who figured out who stabbed my dad. There are other photos on the wall—a pretty woman and a young girl around Sam's age. I wonder what happened to Tate's family, and have a real bad feeling that somehow the virus got them the same way it got mine. Maybe Tate lost his wife and went seeking revenge in an attempt to save his daughter. Maybe when he gets out of jail he'll keep on searching.

I go online and quickly scan the latest news reports. The name of the man I ran over this afternoon has been released—Adam Sinclair. There are already many details: a year or so ago there wouldn't be any names released for at least a day, let alone facts, but these days you can see a dead body on the front page of the newspaper.

The reports spell out the events and are unusually accurate. They say two men tried to kill me; one of them was hit by a car when I fled the scene, and the second man then executed the first. The reports are unclear on why the men were after me—but hint at my involvement in the killing of Shane Kingsly. The phrase "revenge killing" shows up about five times—as my hypothetical reason for killing Shane Kingsly, and as their reason for trying to kill me. It's the first time in twenty years that the media has guessed correctly what I might be capable of.

Tonight's deaths are still too soon for there to be any details, plus it's Christmas, so most of the reporters are doing society a favor and taking the night off. There's only a vague outline with no names, stating that one of the two victims is a police officer. Bracken's death is still too early to even get a mention.

I type Oliver Church's name into the computer and a minute later we have his story.

Nine years ago Church kidnapped a six-year-old boy and tried to ransom him back to his parents, but he got busted when he went to pick up the money. Church took the child to an abandoned slaughterhouse north of the city. When he got caught, he wouldn't give up the location of the child. He tried to make a deal to cut back jail time for the safety of the child. Lawyers came to the party, but by the time they struck a deal the child had died—combination of cold and hunger and everything else that happens when you tie a kid up and leave them in a place like that. Poor kid probably died of fright. That's why it was manslaughter and not murder. Because of the deal he made, he only got six years. Didn't matter that the boy had died: the deal was for the boy's location, and since nothing specific was put in writing saying the boy had to be alive, nothing could be done to reverse the deal.

"You think he could kill a child deliberately?" I ask Dad.

"Make no mistake, son. That is what he did. He was in custody for three days without giving up the location. He knew that kid was going to die and he did nothing to stop it. That means he can do it again. It should only be about the money, but this guy—shit, look at these stories. The men who robbed the bank, maybe they're all killers, maybe just one or two of them, but if Bracken hired this guy it means none of that crew are capable of killing a child. Church is."

"Oh Jesus, Dad, what do we do? What the hell do we do?"

"He's not going to take Sam somewhere she can figure out how to lead the police back to. He'll have somewhere else. For now, it's about the money."

"But there is no money, don't you get that? There never was! Bracken knew I never had it, he was just playing the game so the others would believe."

"Then maybe Oliver Church believes it too," Dad says. "You better hope like hell that he does."

"It still doesn't tell us where she is."

"Criminals return to what they know best," Dad says. "That I know for a fact. The slaughterhouse has been abandoned a long time," he says. "Way back when I was a teenager. We used to call it the Laughterhouse."

"You think she's there?"

"At this stage we have nothing else."

It's a twenty-five minute drive which I cover in about twelve, at times hitting speeds that Santa would be impressed by. Christmas decorations pass us in a blur, turning into streaks of light. We don't see a single car on the road. I slow down at red lights before blowing right through them. Suburbia ends and the pastures start again like they do in every direction in this city—except for the east; only way you can keep going east in this city is if your car can float. I try the cell phone number from Bracken's phone again but there's no joy, which isn't fair because Christmas is supposed to be a time of joy.

When we reach the slaughterhouse we pull up short of the road leading up to it. I leave all three cell phones—my one, Kingsly's, and Bracken's—in the car, and we get out. The ground is cool and damp, as if the ghosts of thousands of animals have drained into the soil. I stash the bag of money in the boot and grab a flashlight from the emergency breakdown kit.

"This prostitute at the probation officer's house, you get a name?" Dad asks.

"What? Why?"

"Just curious."

"No. No name."

The road is ankle-breaking material, cracked and busted from the weight of trucks that once upon a time used to go up and down it, so we walk off to the side where the dirt is hard packed. We have to walk slower because of our wounds, Dad's and mine. I figure it's been a long day for him too.

Christmas doesn't quite reach out here. No tinsel or lights, just a bleak setting with shadows cast only by the moonlight and stars.

"What'd she look like, then?"

"What?"

"The prostitute. What'd she look like?"

"I don't know. The way they all look."

"They all look different, son. Trust me. It's only on the inside they look the same."

I don't ask him what he means by that and thankfully he doesn't elaborate. We keep walking.

"You're not really going to take me back after all this, are you, son?" he asks.

I don't answer him.

The slaughterhouse comes into view. It seems to grow out of the earth the closer we get, looming out of the darkness and bearing down on us. The words NORTH CITY SLAUGHTERHOUSE have been stenciled in letters a meter high, big enough to make out in the dark. The smell is still here, even decades after the place has shut down, hanging in the still air. Or maybe the smell is only in my imagination. There's certainly something here. I wonder how bad it smelled back then. The slaughterhouse was only up and running for two years or so before it was closed down, a victim of expanding suburbia that never did expand. The building was shut down before the road leading up to it could be repaved in thicker cement, the land sold, and then nothing, until somebody came along with a couple of tins of spray paint and blacked out the "S" on the word Slaughterhouse.

Fifteen years ago this building was the scene of a double homicide, and nine years ago it was used to hide a boy who died from fear while a man tried to shave some years off his sentence. Tonight it possibly holds my daughter.

A dark four-door sedan is parked in front of the building. We split up; Dad heads toward the back and I head toward the car. We work well together, not having to talk, only a minimum of hand gestures, as if we've done this before. I can tell my dad is enjoying it and I hate him for that. I reach the car and take a look inside before moving on.

The slaughterhouse walls are mostly made up of concrete blocks, with some sections of corrugated iron. The base of it is lined in mold that grows up the walls, darker near the bottom where it grows the thickest, and there are plenty of weeds growing up through the cracks in the sidewalk. I reach a window but can't see a damn thing inside. The side door leading into an office area is lying on the ground, the top hinge busted, the bottom hinge still attached but twisted ninety degrees. The temperature drops when I step through. I stand still and listen before turning on the flashlight. There's no furniture anywhere, nothing hanging on the walls, nothing on the concrete floor. The room has been completely stripped. The door to the corridor has been removed. I head through, and another empty doorway later and I'm in the slaughterhouse, a huge, cavernous room that smells of rot. The air is graveyard cold, and the darkness seems to suck at the back of my eyeballs. The flashlight doesn't even break the dark, just lights up a thin beam of it and is lost. I can sense large hooks hanging from the ceiling ahead of me somewhere, but can't see them. There's machinery left here to rust—the tools of the trade that started the animals down the path from living, breathing entities to supermarket specials and hamburgers. No wonder a young boy, tied up and left alone out here, died.

I turn back into the corridor. There's a bend in it, and once around it I can see a light coming from beneath a door not too far ahead—one of the few doors remaining. It's a heavy wooden door, the bottom of it lined with vertical scratches, probably from rats. I reach it and put my face against it and listen but can't hear a thing.

I suck in a couple of deep breaths, tighten my grip on the shotgun, and swing the door open.

chapter fifty-four

The second name on the list, Zach Everest, is a bust. The SWAT team ended up breaking into a house that Everest hadn't set foot in for about two years, and the new residents weren't thrilled at the intrusion—let alone the kids who, having heard the commotion, were horribly disappointed to see six men in black storming into their home instead of one man dressed in red. There are no other known addresses for Everest, but Schroder knows it's only a matter of time now—probably less than a day, he guesses—before they have him in custody.

Reports have already come in about the gunshot victim half an hour ago. Tyler Layton was tied to a chair and executed. Witnesses woken by the noise reported two men fleeing the scene in a four-door sedan that certainly doesn't belong to Edward Hunter, because Hunter's car got busted up in town, but which might have been his wife's. At this point there's nothing to connect Hunter and his dad to the killing, and nothing to connect Tyler Layton to any of the men responsible for the bank robbery or the abduction of Sam Hunter—but Schroder is confident there will be a link somewhere. Layton has a criminal record long enough to pretty much guarantee some interaction with Jack Hunter or the bank robbers—and the way the night is going, Jack Sr. seems to be the catalyst for all the violence around here.

At the moment Oliver Church is the far more urgent target. Church kidnapped and killed a boy, for which he only served six years. Schroder knows Church's involvement ups the danger factor for Sam Hunter. Bracken didn't choose somebody who would just stash the kid away for a few hours and free her somewhere, but somebody capable of ending the life of someone so young.

He redirects the assault team to Church's address, and twenty minutes later it's all for nothing. The address is current—there's mail inside addressed to Church, there's fresh food in the fridge and a half-empty packet of cigarettes on the table, but no sign of Church.

More detectives arrive, among them Detective Watts, who has Church's criminal record with him.

"A model prisoner," Watts says. "According to the file he made every meeting with his probation officer."

"There has to be another address."

"Only other thing listed here is his parents," Watts says.

"And we've already sent people there. He's probably somewhere with the girl, somewhere he's stashed her away with nobody else around."

"That could be any one of a thousand places," Watts says.

"That's not real helpful," Schroder snaps at him. "Look, there can't be too many possibilities. It's probably somewhere he knows, right?" He looks back down at the file. "Last time he took the kid to the North City Slaughterhouse."

"You think he's taken her there?"

"Only one way to find out," Schroder says. He needs coffee and he needs a break and he needs this all to be over and for Sam to be returned safely. "It's as good a place as any."

He calls Landry for an update. "Johnson knows nothing," Landry says. "He certainly robbed the bank, but he's not giving anything up. I think he knew Sam Hunter was going to be taken, but I don't think he knew who by, or where she's being held."

Liam Marshall comes over. "We're all ready to hit the next house."

"Let's go," Schroder says. On the way he makes a call to the station and asks for a patrol car to head out urgently to the North City Slaughterhouse to take a look around.

chapter fifty-five

Everything looks normal. Take away the fact that the man sitting down playing on a handheld games unit isn't anybody I've seen before. Take away the fact the floor is concrete and the windows are boarded up and the walls have graffiti on them. Ignore the damp air, ignore the smell that's etched into the walls like a stubborn stain, ignore the fact the mattress my daughter is lying on is a hundred years old, and it's all normal, just a night in at home.

The light coming from a battery lantern is pale blue and doesn't make the room any prettier. There's a couple of relics in here—an old rusted filing cabinet, a laminated table that must weigh close to fifty kilos, cables and wires hanging freely from the ceiling like spiderwebs. Church lowers the game unit. It keeps making animal fighting sounds. There's a cell phone on the table next to him and I wonder what he's waiting for.

"Oh Jesus, please don't kill me," he says, and it's taking all my willpower not to. He's as thin and as creepy-looking as he was in the photos in his file.

"You took my daughter."

"I know, I know, but it was just business."

"And so is this," I say, and I pump the shotgun.

"Wait, wait," he says, putting his hands up. "We can deal," he says.

"Deal?"

"I can give you a name."

"Yeah? What name? Austin Bracken?"

"Shit."

"Exactly."

"Wait, wait, there has to be something I can offer."

I move toward Sam, keeping the gun trained on Church. When I reach the mattress I squat down but decide not to wake her. My little princess is dreaming of much happier times, her little mouth wide open.

My father walks into the room. He's found a piece of rebar about half a meter long with a small chunk of concrete attached to the end. He looks at Church, then at me, then down at Sam, and he smiles at her, comes across, and crouches down. It's the first time he's ever seen her and the emotion gets to him. I've never seen it before—but my father starts to cry.

"So this is my granddaughter," he says. "She's beautiful."

"She's exactly like her mother," I say.

Mummy's a ghost.

I stroke her hair back. "He doesn't know anything useful," I say, nodding toward Church.

"You sure?" he asks, wiping at the tears.

"Please, guys, I can help you."

"I'm taking Sam out to the car," I say.

"I think that's best, son."

"You'll be okay here?"

"It's been twenty years, son. I have certain needs. Best you hurry up and get your little girl out of here. If he knows anything more, I'll find out. I promise."

I scoop Sam up. She tightens her arms around my neck without waking. "I'm done," I say to Dad, keeping my voice low, not wanting to wake Sam. "Whether you learn anything or not, I'm done now. The police can do the rest. Whatever this bastard has to say, we'll hand the information over."

"Okay, son. I understand. Leave me the shotgun, would you?"

"Come on, let me help you out here," Church says, "All I know is my old probation officer called me up and told me I had to help him out. He said if I didn't he'd make life hard for me. I don't know anything else. There's no need to do this, any of this. It was business, I swear, just business."

"Shut up," Dad says, then turns toward me. "The shotgun, son."

I think about Jodie and her parents, then I think about the cop parked outside their house and the bank manager and then I think about Gerald Painter. I hand Dad the shotgun and carry Sam outside.

chapter fifty-six

The dark sky is breaking on the horizon, a purple-colored light bruising the edge of the world. I carry Sam over my shoulder and she's chilly; I wonder if her blanket is still in Jodie's car. I walk quietly. I keep waiting for the gunshot that will send hundreds of birds into the sky and Sam jumping out of her skin. I buckle her into the backseat, tucking the blanket in around her and under her chin. I sit in the driver's seat and wonder what Dad is doing right now, but I don't go and check. I look at the cell phones, killing time while my father kills time in a different way. I've missed a couple of calls from Schroder but I don't phone him back. I turn them off. I don't care about anything else now except Sam.

After a couple of minutes an engine revs loudly, then headlights appear as a car races toward us, slightly out of control, as if driven by someone who hasn't driven a car in twenty years. It swerves past us, then it's gone, a dust cloud following it.

I turn the key but nothing happens. I try a couple more times but the result is the same. I pop the hood. Dad hasn't done any damage. All he's done is tug the leads off the spark plugs. It only takes me a minute to secure them back into place, but it's all the head start he needs. I pop the boot. The bag of money is gone. The taillights of Dad's new car have disappeared; he's getting further away, with a shotgun and a bag full of cash and his desires of the last twenty years no longer suppressed.

I don't bother chasing him because I'd never catch him, not unless I drove at speeds that would put my daughter's life at risk. What I said to Dad earlier still stands now—I'm done with it. The police can catch the rest of the men—they surely know by now who they're looking for. On the chance they haven't been caught, I can't go back home and can't go to my in-laws'. Driving into the police station is an unknown—too many reasons for them to arrest me. By now they want to put me away, if for nothing else than for freeing my father. They're out there searching for him too. Before I end up in jail I want to at least spend Christmas Day with my daughter.

My head is jumbled up with anger and hate and fear, and I'm so tired that, in the end, the easiest decision is to head to a motel. I find a place modern enough to have been built this year, with a sign out front saying VACANCY. I park outside the office and ring the bell and a couple of minutes later a sleepy man in his fifties appears and helps me out. I pay with cash.

The room is as modern as the surroundings would suggest, but I don't really take the time to check them out. I carry Sam and put her gently into bed, taking off only her shoes, then I collapse on top of my bed and fall asleep.

chapter fifty-seven

They're shooting one in four. They found Kelvin Johnson, but the other two bank robbers are in the wind, along with Oliver Church—though news of another body means Church may have been found. Dawn has come and gone and Schroder is dead on his feet. They all are. They all feel like zombies and look like zombies and it's nights like these that keep divorce lawyers rolling in cash.

The SWAT team is long gone now, having packed away its guns and headed for home, all of them still on standby if needed—all of them probably tempted to switch off their phones. Schroder knows that he is. They've busted into four houses and for all their efforts they've come away with one suspect.

The patrol officers sent to check the slaughterhouse have reported a body, the head of a male so badly damaged that identification was impossible. No sign of anybody else, but a couple of magazines, a small games unit, and a battery-powered lantern suggest whoever was out there had been there most of the night.

It's a twenty-five-minute drive to the slaughterhouse from his last location. He's too tired to drive fast, and has the window down so the air can whistle around his face to keep him awake. He makes a couple of calls to get the ball rolling, organizes the forensics techies to come out; long nights for everybody now turning into long mornings too.

The slaughterhouse is an imposing building in the early-morning light. It's mostly made up of concrete that could probably survive an atomic bomb. There's a police car parked outside with two officers sitting in it. The air is full of birdsong and the loudest sound is Schroder's feet across the ground. The officers lead him inside and he keeps yawning on the way. Assuming he ever makes it home, he's going to sleep for about twenty-four hours, he thinks; but at this stage it's an assumption he wouldn't bet his life on.

Oliver Church is surrounded in blood. He thinks it's Oliver Church. The clothes certainly suggest it's not Edward Hunter or his father, and he doesn't see too many other possibilities at this point. Church's head is twisted to the side with a large indentation in the side of it which has elongated the front of it, so the distance between his left eye and the left side of his mouth is far greater than the right. He looks like he's fallen from a great height, so much so that for a moment Schroder is reminded of Suction Cup Guy. A piece of rebar with a bloody lump of cement on the end lies next to him. No way of knowing at this point if Church was tortured to give up more information, or tortured for taking Sam Hunter.

"No other cars out there?" Schroder asks.

"None."

Probably Jack Hunter took Church's car, which means father and son have separated. There's an old mattress lying on the floor. Jammed between it and the wall, barely in sight, is a small teddy bear. The bear isn't that old but seems to have had a hard life. He bets Sam Hunter cuddled that bear every night of her life, and wonders what she called it. His own daughter has a bear that she sleeps with. For a second he imagines it was her out here and not Sam, and the image is so strong it makes him want to cry. Jesus—he's so tired.

"You think he found her?" Landry asks on the phone.

"I think so. I think Oliver Church paid the price for taking her."

"He deserved what he got," Landry says. "Deserved it years ago."

"I know. But now I have to lock Edward Hunter up for it. Wasn't his job to find Church, wasn't his job to get his daughter back."

"Wasn't it?" Landry asks.

Even if it was Jack Hunter who pounded in Church's skull, it still comes back on Edward for freeing the old man. Edward has to go to jail now, and that leaves Sam where? Maybe, if he's lucky, he could get a suspended sentence—if he can prove he didn't kill any of the others. Maybe.

Schroder bends down and picks up the teddy bear. Jack Hunter is on the loose and there's already a task force looking for him—but that's not his job, his job is to find the men who robbed the bank, and that job is almost over.

"There's nothing more we can do tonight," Landry is saying. "The girl was there, and she's not there anymore. Edward Hunter got her, has to be him. He'll have taken her somewhere safe, and he'll keep her safe until all this is over. We'll get the rest of the bank crew today, you know we will. Tomorrow at the latest."

He hangs up and walks past the two officers. "Call me if anything changes," he tells them. And with that he gets into his car and heads home, hoping for at least a couple of hours' sleep and some time with his family before he has to start up again, right where he's left off.

chapter fifty-eight

I wake up in the early afternoon with Sam cuddled up next to me. I let her carry on sleeping while I make some coffee and go about waking up some more. I switch on the TV and can't find any news anywhere, as if this city is sick of the news now. There are holiday movies on, a fantasy on one channel, action on another, drama everywhere else, and I wonder what Hollywood would think if one day a Christchurch story showed up on its doorstep—whether it'd think the tale was too dark or too real to turn into a Christmas blockbuster. I prop Sam up in front of one of the movies and she watches it quietly, not laughing or smiling or even saying a word. She misses her mum and she misses Mr. Fluff 'n' Stuff and she doesn't understand why we're spending Christmas Day in a motel room instead of our home, or with her grandparents.

I take Sam to the cemetery so she can spend some time with her mother. With all that's happened, I figure it'll be the last time the three of us are together for a while. I carry Sam out of the car and sit her down by her mother's grave and we hold hands and I tell her over and over that everything is going to be okay. There are plenty of other people out at the cemetery, all of them like me, spending time with the dead; Christmas Day is a day for celebration no matter what world you're in. When I head back to the car with Sam, people keep watching us, and though I'm used to it, this morning it bothers me more than ever. I shield Sam from their stares and drive her back to the motel. She's asleep again before we get there, and I lay her back on the bed and check on her every five or ten minutes, sometimes holding her hand, not sure what I should do next. I leave the TV on and flick channels but nothing of any interest comes up. Outside, Christmas afternoon is looking like a hot one; only a couple of clouds in the sky, the sun beating down on the city. Mine's the only car in the parking lot out front. I figure everybody else has family or a better place to be than this motel.

I sit at the window watching the Christmas day, thinking about what today could have meant, about the presents we didn't get to give, the family time we never got to have, the Christmas lunch and barbecue dinner and the excitement of Santa. I think about my dad, wondering where he is now, what or who he's looking for. I think about the darkness he's trying to satisfy. My own monster is quiet now, and maybe that's the way it'll stay.

My thoughts turn to Schroder when his car pulls in to the motel parking lot. Two patrol cars pull up alongside him, but Schroder is the only one who gets out. A fourth car, a dark station wagon, also pulls in. I watch Schroder go to the office; he disappears inside for about sixty seconds, then comes back out. It's Christmas Day and I figure he'd rather be anywhere else but here, and I'm the same—except there are still a few places worse than this, for me. Jail is one of them. The slaughterhouse is another.

He walks past my window and glances in and sees me but doesn't stop. He heads right to the door and knocks on it.

"Come on, Eddie," he says, going with Eddie instead of Edward, and I figure he thinks it makes him sound friendly. "Open up."

"Leave us alone," I say.

"Eddie . . ."

"It's Christmas."

"You can't keep her here."

"What?"

"You can't keep your daughter here. It isn't right."

"There are plenty of things that aren't right."

"I know that, Eddie."

"You were wrong."

"About what?"

"About a lot of things," I say. "Mostly about this city being on a precipice. It's already fallen, don't you see that?"

"Open the door, Eddie."

I get up and open the door. There's nowhere to run, and no need to. It's all over. I have my daughter back and the police can deal with the rest, they can find my dad, they can find the men who killed my wife. Schroder doesn't look as if he's slept. He steps inside, carrying a brown paper bag.

"Don't take her yet," I say.

"Eddie . . ."

"Please, it's Christmas."

"I know. It's not fair. It's . . . it's just the way it is."

I take a step back. Schroder looks over at the other cars and the station wagon turns around and backs toward the room. Schroder comes in and looks down at Sam, who isn't even aware of his presence.

"Such a beautiful little girl," he says.

"I know."

"I have a daughter of my own," he says. "And a son."

"And?"

"And I don't know, I guess I wanted you to know. Maybe what you said about this city, maybe I should take your advice and get out of here."

"Then who will protect it?"

Two men step out of the station wagon and open the back of it. They lift out a gurney and a sheet.

"Let me take her," I say.

"It's not how it's done."

"Please . . ."

"I'm sorry, Eddie, I'm really, really sorry."

At first I stand back as the two men come inside, and then Schroder has to hold me back as they lay Sam on the stretcher. They unfold a sheet and drape it over her, then carry her away. Schroder opens the paper bag in his hand and pulls out Mr. Fluff 'n' Stuff. He lifts the sheet and tucks it between Sam's arm and her body.

"We'll take good care of her," he says.

I try to say something but can't. It feels like Schroder has extended his fist right down my throat. I cry, and right then Schroder embraces me and I let it all out, crying on his shoulder as the two men take my dead daughter out of the motel room and out of my life.

chapter fifty-nine

Edward sits in the passenger seat saying nothing on the way to the police station. When they arrive, Schroder leads him into an interrogation room and heads back out to grab a couple of coffees and to let Hunter compose himself. The police station is busier than it's ever been on a Christmas day; the task force to find Jack Hunter is operating at full speed, as are the people searching for the final two bank robbers. It's only a matter of time now—but of course everything is always just a matter of time.

Seeing the little dead girl was hard. Once again he imagined it was his own daughter, and once again it brought him close to tears, and when he hugged Edward and held him he had no idea he was about to do it before it happened, and no idea of the impact it would have on him. Hunter sobbed into his shoulder, his entire body convulsing, and they stayed that way for what seemed like ages before Hunter pulled himself away.

It was almost seven o'clock in the morning by the time Schroder got home. His family was awake. They hadn't waited up for him—his daughter had woken early because that's what Christmas was all about, at least for the kids. His wife had let her open just one present; she was waiting for him to get home before opening the rest. He managed to stay awake for another hour before going to bed, and had got almost four hours' sleep before his wife came in to wake him. She handed him his cell phone. He didn't want to answer it but he had to. Witnesses had spotted Edward Hunter that morning at the cemetery where his wife was buried. They'd phoned the police because Edward was carrying his daughter around and his daughter obviously wasn't just sleeping. Before the phone call was over, there was more news—another body had been found.

A week ago Hunter had everything—a wife, a child, a job, he had dreams, the family had Christmas, they all had a future. It makes Schroder sick to know that on any given day your entire future can change.

He makes his way back toward the interrogation room and has his hand on the door handle, the two cups of coffee balanced in his other hand, when his cell phone rings. He steps back from the door and almost drops both coffees while fumbling for the phone.

"Schroder," he says.

"Hey, Carl. I hear it's been a long night," Tate says.

"You got something for me?"

"Yeah. I know who put Roger Harwick up to stabbing Jack Hunter."

"Who?"

"You're not going to believe it," Tate says, but he's wrong, because Schroder does. After all—the last twenty-four hours have been nothing but believable.

chapter sixty

I knew Sam was dead from the moment I saw her in the slaughter-house. I knew it before I had even stepped fully into the room. Felt it, even, if that makes sense. Knew it, felt it, saw it—and then ignored it. Just pushed it out of my mind for as long as I could until somebody—and it took Schroder to do it—came along and shoved the reality back into my face.

Dad's tears weren't tears of joy when he saw her, they were tears of pain. Sam was more like her mother than ever because Mummy's a ghost, and so is Sam now. It was Christmas morning and I took my dead little girl out to the cemetery to see her dead mother while those around me stared and watched, not understanding, wondering what was happening.

Schroder doesn't make me wait long in the interrogation room—maybe five minutes in total, which I figure is pretty good of him. He comes in with a folder tucked under his arm and a couple of coffees in his hand, supported by a small cardboard tray. He sits down opposite me and slides one of the coffees over.

"You need it," he says.

"What I need is to be with Sam."

"Look, Eddie, this is tough—God knows you've gone through more than anybody deserves, but . . ."

He runs out of words. Just like that, like somebody wound him up ten minutes ago and the spring keeping him going has come to a stop.

"I want to be with Sam."

"I know. I know you do."

"Please."

"Soon. Okay? Just—we just need to go over a few things first. Then I can take you to her. Okay?"

I nod.

"Tell me what happened. Do you know where your father is?"

"No idea at all," I say, and then I fill him in on the details. I tell him about the slaughterhouse and how he can find Oliver Church out there, how Dad killed him, how I have no idea where Dad is now.

"Look, Eddie, we already know about the slaughterhouse. You got out there not long before we got there. Truth is you could be facing some serious jail time. We've got bodies stacking up and you're at the center of it all."

"I didn't kill anybody," I say, "except for the guy who made me drown you, and the guy I ran over—but that was an accident. I didn't even kill Bracken. It was the woman."

"We know. We checked the prints on the knife. There was blood on them. Location of the prints beneath the blood showed she was the one holding them when it got used. You're sitting okay as far as that one goes, and maybe for Church too, if you can prove self-defense," he says, "if you hear what I'm saying. You or your dad had to defend against him. But Jesus, Eddie, you helped a serial killer escape. We can't write that one off."

"When she killed Bracken she took away our chance of finding Sam alive."

"Then we need to find her before your father does," Schroder says. "There's another thing, Eddie. Your father. It turns out he's the one who put Harwick up to stabbing him."

"What? What are you saying?"

"It was all a setup. He got Harwick to stab him, to hurt him enough to require hospital treatment but not enough so he'd need a morgue. He knew you'd come and get him. He played everybody. He completely played you."

I wonder at what point Dad decided to use his daughter-in-law's death to his advantage; whether the man knew immediately he could use the tragedy to escape. I wonder if he even cared about what happened to Jodie. I'd like to think it at least took him a few days to think it through, but for some reason I don't think it did. For some reason I think the moment the news was broken to him about the bank robbery he knew in an instant he was going to manipulate me; that he would tell me about the darkness and the monster and would get me to become like him; that the only thing standing between him and freedom was an innocent stabbing of the kind where every major organ was missed, where he could spend the night in a hospital so understaffed that only a single nurse was seen.

"I'm sorry, Eddie."

"You got the rest of the bank robbers?"

"We got the names. One of them we have in custody, one of them we're still looking for."

"And the third?"

"The third was found a few hours ago. He was cut up so badly we were lucky to identify him. We found your father's prints at the scene."

I stare at him without saying a word. My dad got one of the men who killed Jodie. I don't know how I feel about this. I don't know how I feel about anything. I'm numb, too numb, all I have now is all this hurt from Sam not being here.

"Did you tell your dad to kill these men?"

"No."

"But you're glad he's made a start, right?"

"Yes."

"How'd he get the name?"

"I . . . I don't know. Maybe from Church. Maybe he had it all along."

"Maybe."

"What's going to happen to me?"

"For now? Nothing. We can't link you to any premeditated killings. The blood results came in and have cleared you with Kingsly. I'm sorry I didn't believe you earlier—it's just that, well, I was certain you'd killed him."

"The blood cleared me?"

"We ran it against your father's and none of the markers matched, it's a completely different blood type, so whoever killed Kingsly isn't related to your father."

"It didn't match," I say.

"You sound surprised."

"What? No. No, of course not," I say, my mind racing. What does this mean? What does this mean?

"You set your father free, and for that we should be keeping you in custody, Edward, but things having gone the way they have, those who make these kinds of decisions have agreed that you can go home instead. For now anyway. You'll have to answer for it—and not to me, but to a judge. If your dad doesn't hurt anybody innocent and we get him back real soon, I'll do what I can to help you. Of course there are other factors to consider, like . . ."

He keeps talking but I'm no longer listening. All I can think about is the blood type. My blood type doesn't match my father's blood type. If Schroder took blood from me now and compared it to the blood found at Kingsly's house, it would match, only he's got no reason to do that. He's got no reason because he doesn't suspect me anymore. He's got no reason to run the blood found at Bracken's office because he knows it's mine. If he took blood from me now and compared it to my father . . .

It wouldn't match, the monster says, so maybe it hasn't gone quiet at all.

How is that possible?

Come on, Eddie. You can figure it out. And Jack—he has no idea. Poor,

*poor Jack. You and your father are nothing alike and that makes me your
very own creation.*

"Edward? Hey, Edward? You listening to me?"

"Huh?" I focus back on Schroder. "What?"

"I'm telling you there are other things to consider here. Nat and
Diana know the full story. They know you didn't start this . . . war.
But . . . Edward, this is hard, but they don't want you to see them
again. Other than the . . . funeral, they want you out of their lives.
Forever."

"Am I free to go now?"

"I guess."

"Then I want to see Sam," I say, and Schroder drives me to the
morgue.

chapter sixty-one

"This is all very unusual," he says.

"It's an unusual situation."

"Well, yes, I suppose it is, but it's Christmas Day, Detective, and on Christmas Day I don't want to see patients. I want to spend it with my children. My ex-wife had them last Christmas, and this year it's my turn."

"This won't take long," Schroder says.

Benson Barlow sighs. "Then you'd better come in," he says.

The house suggests that psychiatry pays well. There have to be four or five bedrooms in the place, it's two years old at the most, and if Barlow lives here alone except for when he's allowed the children, then it must be a very lonely place to live in. Barlow leads him through to a study where there are books arranged by size and color, and there's a view of a gated swimming pool beyond the bay window that people with emotional hang-ups paid for. The sun is shining down hard on it. He can hear a couple of children laughing from somewhere in the house, and a TV going. Barlow looks different from the other day, he's more like a real person and not a parody. He's wearing shorts with about a dozen pockets and a polo shirt, and his limbs and scalp have reddened from the sun.

"Take a seat," Barlow says, and Schroder notices the study is laid out the same way he imagines Barlow's office in town must be laid out. Barlow takes a seat behind the desk and leans back in his leather office chair. He picks up a pad and a pen, seems to realize his mistake, and puts them back down. He interlocks his fingers and rests his hands on his knees. Schroder sits opposite him in another leather office chair—thankfully not a couch. There are a couple of diplomas on the wall and some expensive-looking art. There's a manual typewriter in the middle of an oak desk, both of which are perhaps from the fifties. There's a closed laptop up on a shelf behind Barlow and a small cactus plant next to it.

"This is no doubt about Edward Hunter?" Barlow asks.

"You've been listening to the news?"

"Yes. I heard what happened. He helped his father escape from the hospital, though I'm not sure why he would do such a thing. Edward despises his father."

"Edward Hunter had his daughter kidnapped by the men who killed his wife."

"Oh dear," Barlow says. "Oh no, the poor girl. And Hunter helped free his dad because he thought his dad could help find her?"

"Yes."

"And did they?"

"They found her, but it was already too late," Schroder says.

"Too late? Oh . . . you mean . . . ," he trails off.

"She was suffocated."

"You have the men who did it?"

"Jack Hunter found him first. It was just one man who killed her."

"And he killed him?"

"Yes. But first he killed a man who used to assault him in prison, and now he's looking for the rest. We picked up Edward this morning. He had his daughter with him. He had taken her to the cemetery to visit his wife, and then he took her to a motel to protect her. He was acting . . . well, I think he was acting like . . ."

"Like she was still alive?" Barlow asks.

"Yeah. I think so."

"You have any idea where Jack Hunter is?"

"No. It's why I'm here. I know you dealt with him all those years ago. Tell me, where do you think he may go?"

"I think he'll find the men responsible for killing his granddaughter."

"Then where?"

"I don't know."

"He stopped taking his medication."

"What?"

"When we searched his cell we found his meds. He hasn't been taking them for days."

"Then if he can't find the men he's looking for, he'll move on to what he knows best—killing prostitutes. He's been in jail a long time, Detective, he'll have desires. The sickness inside him—it will have desires. The problem is twenty years ago he was living two lives, and one of them he was protecting by killing women he didn't think anybody would notice going missing. Now he doesn't have that family life to retreat to, or to hide things from. He may go looking for prostitutes, but it's doubtful he'll restrain himself to only them. Anybody is fair game to him now, Detective, because he's on the run and he knows being free is only a temporary thing. Damn it, why did he have to stop taking his medication!"

"He stopped when Jodie Hunter was shot."

"Yes, yes, I suppose that makes sense. Detective, don't doubt that Jack Hunter heard voices, and he was intelligent enough to hide it, and to deal with it. He knew he had a sickness, and he knew if he stopped taking his medication that sickness, that desire, would come back. You may want to look at the man who stabbed Hunter in jail, you might find it was Hunter himself who organized it. Probably on the same day. He probably figured he could use his son to help him escape."

"I'll look into it," Schroder says, not in the mood to bolster the shrink's ego by telling him that's exactly what happened.

"Hunter is an intelligent man, Detective, and he's still intelligent even off the meds—the difference is that when medicated, he can be controlled. Right now—well, right now he could be anywhere doing anything. Now that you have Edward Hunter in custody, I strongly suggest you let me see him. I told you he was a danger, and last night proved that. I should see him immediately. I can help him."

"He's not in custody."

"What do you mean? You said you picked him up with his daughter."

"And then we let him go. He lost his daughter, he was betrayed by his father, we couldn't keep him after all that. None of this is his fault."

"You need to pick him up."

"Why?"

"What kind of state was he in when you released him?"

"He's a defeated man. We dropped him off at his house. He's not going anywhere. In fact I'm tempted to put a man on him just to make sure he doesn't kill himself."

"He's certainly a candidate for that, but he's also capable of something else. Edward Hunter is a man who holds grudges, Detective, and he's a man who can justify those grudges in different ways. He may not go after the men who killed his wife, but what about the others?"

"Others?"

"From the bank. The bank tellers, the security guard, the media, even the police—anybody who has let him down could be a target."

"He went to the security guard's house."

"What? When?"

"Tuesday night. He got drunk and went there but nothing happened."

"And you didn't think this was important enough to let me know?"

"I just told you."

Barlow takes his hands off his knees and leans forward. "Listen to me very carefully, Detective. You have to go and pick him up. Nothing may have happened when he went to the security guard's house, but his daughter was alive then. This man is a time bomb. Trust me, Detective, if there's one thing I know about, it's time bombs, and this one is about to go off."

chapter sixty-two

It's evening when I get home. Kids are out playing in the street, riding new bikes and new skateboards, yelling and laughing, all is good in their world, all is right and happy and I envy each one of them.

Nothing has changed at all in the house. It's more of a tomb than ever. I walk through the rooms touching things, the walls, the furniture, running my fingers over anything in my path. I sit on Sam's bed for a while and I sit on my bed for a while and I sit in the living room for a while. It's like last week all over again only worse. The unbelievable thing that could never happen has happened— again. I can't even cry. I can't do anything. I sit in the living room with a can of beer but I don't open it. I stare at the TV but don't turn it on. I pick at the stitching on a cushion until it comes apart. The kids outside grow quiet. The day gets darker and they all head inside, some of them bored already with their new gifts. I get up to turn on the light and at the same time somebody knocks on my door. I head over to it, part of me not wanting to answer it, but a bigger part hoping it's the last bank robber, that he's come armed and with the ability to help me join my wife and daughter.

I don't recognize him. He's been severely beaten and can hardly stand, but he's managing to do so by leaning against the wall. My dad is behind him holding the shotgun. He's still wearing the security guard's clothes from the hospital, only now there are large bloodstains on them, mostly dry.

"I got you a Christmas present," Dad says, and he pushes the man forward.

I look at my Christmas present, at the blood on it, the torn and bruised wrapping, and I'm sick at the sight of it. I feel no different looking at Dad.

"Please, Dad, go away. It doesn't matter anymore. This is all over. I've lost everything and they're going to put me in jail for setting you free and the truth is, the truth is . . . I just want this to be over. I want everything to be over."

"This is the man who shot Jodie. This is the man who started it all."

I close my eyes for a few seconds and exhale heavily, tilting my head back, focusing on the loss of Jodie and Sam. I remember the way Jodie fell forward, her face before the gun exploded, where she thought the worst thing that was going to happen to her was skinned palms and knees. I can still feel the weight of Sam in my arms, lifting her from the floor of the slaughterhouse and carrying her outside.

Then I focus on the man Dad brought me. An average-looking man I'd never have paid attention to in the past, maybe somebody who works at a gas station or repairs shoes, anything other than the man he truly is. His face has swollen up, his left eye closed, his right eye bloodshot. The edges of the duct tape covering his mouth are stained with blood. Dad pushes him again and he falls onto his knees in my hallway. His hands are tied behind him so tight they've turned purple. Dad steps inside and closes the door.

"I don't care," I say.

"Yes you do."

Yes. You do.

"I know," I say.

"I got one of the others," Dad says. "I made him suffer. I made this guy suffer too. I was going to kill him when, out of nowhere, I realized how selfish that would have been. I'm sorry about what happened to Sam, son, I really am—and Jodie."

"And this will make it better? Killing him will bring her back?"

"It's not about bringing people back, son."

"You think it's about feeding the monster?"

"That's what it's always about."

"For you, maybe. But not for me."

"This is the man who shot Jodie! Damn it, son, don't you get that? This is the man who killed your wife. This is the path he took that got your daughter killed. My granddaughter." He takes a step back so he's out of range from the man, reaches into his belt, and drags out a knife about half the length of his forearm and hands it over to me. "Now do something about it!"

The man on my floor doesn't even move. There's a shotgun pointing at him and two sets of eyes and all he has the strength to do is look down.

Do it! the monster says.

"No."

"It'll help," Dad says.

Listen to him.

"Listen to the monster," Dad says, struggling to keep the gun pointed ahead while holding the knife. He starts to lower it. "It's telling you to do what I say, isn't it."

"This isn't the way it's supposed to be. It's Christmas Day. I'm going to spend it with Sam and Jodie."

"Son . . ."

"This is the way it's supposed to be. You, him, the monster, none of you are supposed to be here."

I step past them and out the door. There aren't any kids in the street now. Nobody to watch. Christmas lights are flashing from behind windows and from on top of roofs, cars are hidden away in garages and parked up driveways and people are tucking themselves away for the night, tired from too much food, too much sun, too much running around visiting family members and chasing after children. Dad turns toward me. I wonder what Nat and Diana are doing tonight, whether their day has been broken up by small pieces of routine where, for one or two seconds out of every thousand, they forget what happened to Jodie and Sam, only to have it crash back down on them.

"It's in the blood," Dad says. "Don't you feel it? We're the same, son. We're blood men!"

"I keep telling you, Dad, we really are nothing alike. More than you'll ever know."

"You're wrong," he says. "Listen to your voice, Edward," he says, calling me by that name for the first time. "Take the knife. Let the voice guide you," he says, and I take the knife from him. Killing the man inside, that's not the way to go about bringing my family back.

There's another way.

chapter sixty-three

He's not so sure that taking Edward Hunter into custody is the right way to go, and he's equally unsure whether leaving him alone is the way to go. Barlow warned him a few days ago and even though Schroder didn't dismiss the man, he certainly could have paid more attention. He can't ignore the fact that everything that has happened since that meeting, all the deaths, part of the responsibility for that sits with him. Not this time though—he'll pick Hunter up and, no matter how bad he feels for him, he won't let emotion get in the way. It's Christmas Day and he's about to pick up a man who's lost his wife and daughter because a psychiatrist with a comb-over and an ex-wife and a nice pool told him so.

"Jesus," he mutters. There has to be another way. Barlow agreed that if Schroder could get Hunter into custody, he would come and speak to him tonight and try to get a read on his mental condition. As for where Jack Hunter might go, Barlow had no idea.

"Justify it as not really an arrest," Barlow had said to him on the way out the door, "but forced therapy. Give me two hours with him and I'll give you some options. The alternative is to sympathize with him for everything that's happened and do nothing, and if he kills himself or somebody else tonight then those ghosts are with you."

Schroder is passing over the alternative and heading straight to Hunter's house. Christmas Day isn't exactly turning out the way he planned. Thankfully his wife has been good about it. She's the kind of woman who puts things into perspective—and missing Christmas Day with her husband didn't amount to much when compared to what Edward Hunter was missing.

There's not as much traffic on the road as there was last night, but it's still enough to hold him up as he drives through town. People in their teens and twenties are searching for somewhere to be, the bars and nightclubs catering to them. The streets are lit up with neon and fluorescents, and he can't imagine anything worse than being nineteen years old again.

He reaches Edward's house. There's nothing peculiar about the way it looks, no cars parked up the driveway or out front, no broken windows, no open doors, but something about it gives him a bad feeling. Thirty seconds later that bad feeling is confirmed when he steps out of his car and sees the blood on the driveway. It leads toward the door. Two trails of it, one heading one way, the other coming back. He calls for backup. He hasn't had great experiences of late entering people's houses, but he goes ahead and enters this one.

chapter sixty-four

"I first made the newspapers when I was nine years old. I made them in every city across the country, most of them on the first page. I even made them internationally. In them I was black and white, blurred a little, my face turned in to my father's chest, people surrounding us. From then on I was shown on TV, in magazines, in more and more papers, always the same photo. I never wanted any of it, I tried to avoid it, but the option wasn't mine."

I tell her this but she doesn't seem interested. I tell her about my mum and my sister but the words go through her. Her eyes are closed and there's blood all over her. Twenty minutes ago her life was much different, twenty minutes ago she was settling in for the night, a pile of DVDs on the coffee table and a Christmas tree full of blazing lights. I take the car toward town, traffic is thin, everywhere is shut. I'm wearing the clothes from the bank again, the ones with

Jodie's blood on them. I picked them up on the way. This is why I kept them, I realize now. For this moment.

"I was ten years old when the trial began. It was a circus. My mum was still alive, but my sister and me were struggling. Kids would tease us at school. At home, Mum was always yelling at us when she was sober, and crying when she was drunk, and whatever of those two states she was in, you always wished it was the other. Soon the pills and the booze took their toll, but not as quick as she wanted, and when they couldn't finish the job she used a razor blade. I don't know how long it took for her to bleed out. She might still even have been alive when we found her. I held my sister's hand and we watched her pale body, the yelling and the crying gone now."

The woman is conscious enough to cry, the tears mingling with the blood. There's a lot of blood but not a lot of damage. It's all from a head wound. The thing about head wounds is they bleed. A lot. Blood has soaked into the seat, and the woman has wet herself, making it seem like there is much more blood in the footwell than there really is. I tell her about Belinda, about how my sister became a drug addict and died when she was nineteen.

"I was the last of my family," I say. "Dad's monster took them all away."

I keep the car at a constant speed, obeying the law; Edward Hunter was a law-abiding citizen who never did anything wrong in the past and who is now about to correct his future. We reach the center of town. Last time I was here I was running from the police.

"There are people who think that I'm destined to be a man of blood too," I say, "that the same blood runs through both of us. They're wrong," I say.

He wasn't even my father.

And somehow here I am, your very own monster.

I speed up the car that used to belong to Oliver Church, a nice trajectory ahead now, and I hit the wall of glass and it showers everywhere, it rakes against the car, the world sounds full of screams and the car bounces up off the framework and bounces back down and I slam on the brakes but not before I've wedged two desks hard up against the counter. The alarm is instant. The two front tires burst. The front of the car crumples up and the engine stalls. No air bag goes off, but the seat belts stop us from flying out. I look over at my passenger and there are more tears and more blood and I'm pretty sure both of us know that things for her are about to get worse.

chapter sixty-five

"He's gone," Schroder says.

"Maybe . . ."

"And he's killed," Schroder adds.

"Killed who?" Barlow asks.

Schroder steps back outside. "Do you have an idea where he might go?"

There's silence on the other end of the phone for a few seconds. "The cemetery. It makes perfect sense. He'll want to be with his wife. Who did he kill, Detective?"

"I'll call you back."

Schroder calls the station. He organizes a patrol car to go to Gerald Painter's house, to the homes of the bank tellers, to the cemetery, even to Dean Wellington's house. He calls Landry and fills him in on the situation.

"You think Jack Hunter knew all along which bank teller was involved?"

"Maybe," Schroder says. "We need to find out."

The interview Schroder had with the bank teller yesterday was finished off by another detective. Because of all the events last night, nobody had the chance to get around to comparing all the details against each other. Another series of follow-up interviews have taken place over the last six hours, each bank teller difficult to get hold of on Christmas Day, each bank teller reluctant to help out, wanting to spend time with their families instead.

The problem is none of them can remember who loaded the dye packs.

Schroder turns on the sirens and speeds back into town, the houses and cars passing by in a blur. Other police cars come toward him on their way to Hunter's house. When he reaches the station he runs inside to the interrogation room where, ten minutes earlier, Kelvin Johnson was escorted into.

"You've got one chance here to help yourself," Schroder says, and Johnson, the only crew member of the gang who robbed the bank in custody—and now the only one still alive—doesn't even look up from the interrogation table.

"You know everybody else is dead, right? We found Zach Everest a few hours ago, and I just came from looking at Doyle's butchered corpse," he says, Lance Doyle being the last name on the list. "There was a lot of rage there, Kelvin, a lot of rage."

Kelvin says nothing.

"And we know somebody inside the bank was involved."

"You don't know anything."

"Actually I do. I know you're going to jail. I know that you know Jack Hunter has been running around out there killing off your buddies. You know that he'll be in jail soon too, right alongside you," Schroder says, which isn't quite true. "You know Jack Hunter has connections in there—he's been there twenty years so he knows how the place works. You know his daughter-in-law and granddaughter are dead because of something you did, and you know that makes you a target. I know you're going to end up in a jail cell real close to him, and I know your days in there are limited. So both you and I know that the only way you're ever going to live long enough to see the outside world again is if you talk. You tell me who you had on the inside, and you spend your years in jail somewhere you never have to see Jack or Edward Hunter."

"That's bullshit," Johnson says.

"No. What that is is a fact. A one hundred percent fact. So what I'm going to do right now is I'm going to give you thirty seconds to think about it. You're probably thinking that you're a tough guy and can handle yourself in jail since you've done it before. But what you should be thinking about is the desire of two men in this world who right now want nothing more than to see you dead—men who may not be able to do the job themselves, but at least one of them can afford to pay to have it done. Thirty seconds," Schroder says. "And counting."

"Marcy Croft," Johnson says, with twenty-eight seconds still remaining. "Bracken paid her off. She was an easy mark. She needed the cash and she was new there and the plan all along was to shoot her anyway. Bracken wanted her taken out onto the street but instead we took that other woman, the wife."

"Marcy Croft," Schroder says, and he gets a mental picture of the bank teller. She's the one who had the shotgun leveled at her. The one Jodie Hunter died for.

"Did she know people were going to die?"

"She thought it was a simple thing. We'd go in and get the money and get back out. We told her nobody had to get hurt, and for what it's worth that's what I thought too."

"So why didn't anybody try to kill her after the robbery?"

"Couldn't risk it. If we'd touched her after the robbery, you'd have looked into why. You'd have made the connection."

"You weren't worried she'd talk to the police?"

"No. Bracken rang her cell phone about ten minutes after the robbery. Told her that if she spoke to the cops he'd kill her and everybody she loves."

"Did Bracken shoot Jodie Hunter?"

"No. Bracken didn't even say a word in the bank."

"Did you shoot her?"

"No. It was Doyle."

"Okay. That's good, Kelvin. Real good. You can explain that to Hunter when you see him."

"What? You said . . ."

"I lied."

"You son of a bitch," he says, but Schroder hardly hears him as he closes the interrogation door behind him. He checks the messages on his phone. The cemetery was canvassed and no sign of Hunter. No sign of him at the security guard's house. No sign of him at any of the bank tellers' homes. No sign of him at Marcy Croft's house.

He gets in his car and chooses Croft's house. He calls the detectives who spoke to her earlier today and they say she seemed nervous, but put it down to the events of the last week. There's a patrol car parked outside her house.

"Nobody home," the officers say. "Our orders are to wait till she shows up."

Schroder knocks on the door anyway. When he finds her he knows she isn't likely to put up a fight or any fuss. If anything she'll break down in tears and beg for a forgiveness that isn't his to offer. He tries the door. It's unlocked. He opens it.

Marcy Croft lives in a small two-bedroom flat with a flat-screen TV and a Christmas tree filling the living room with blood on the carpet and tipped-over furniture.

"He's got her," he says into the phone. "The bank teller."

"Explain it to me," Barlow says, and Schroder does.

"Does Hunter know the bank teller was in on the robbery?" Barlow asks.

"Maybe. I don't know. It's possible. Jack Hunter may have known. He certainly knew other names."

"It doesn't make sense," Barlow says. "If Edward knew she was in on the robbery, he would have killed her already. You said he took her from her home?"

"There's sign of a struggle and blood on the carpet. Not much," he says.

"Okay. Let's assume he didn't kill her. Let's assume he took her. What for? If he thought this woman was somehow partly responsible for the death of his wife and daughter, he would have killed her already. No reason for him to take her."

"Well, he has her. No doubt there."

"Yes, but why? Let me think . . . are you sure Jack Hunter knew about this woman?"

"I never said I was sure. Could be either way."

"Interesting," he says, then doesn't follow it up. Schroder can almost hear his thinking process. "This woman, he may have taken her for a different reason."

"What other reason is there?"

"It all started with her. This is the woman Edward called out to save. Don't you see? When he saved her, he condemned his wife to death. That in turn condemned his daughter to death. He blames her, Detective, and if he's in as fragile a state as I believe him to be, then he sees her as the catalyst for everything he's lost. Maybe . . . yes, yes, maybe he thinks he can right the wrongs that have happened since then."

"Right the wrongs? You mean he thinks that by killing her he can turn back the clock and save his family?"

"It's possible. And if this is the case, then you'll find he's taken her to—"

"The bank," Schroder finishes, already running toward his car now.

"Exactly."

"Jesus," Schroder whispers, and he turns on the sirens and races back into town.

chapter sixty-six

I get out and move around the car. I open the door and drag the woman out. She's confused. She's scared. This is nothing new for her—she's been confused and scared before, in fact she's been confused and scared in this very place.

She stumbles and falls down and cuts her knees on the glass. She tries talking to me but I can't hear her over the alarm. I can hear a few of the words and can fill in the rest of them myself. She's telling me over and over that she's sorry, but it doesn't matter, not now. Her being sorry isn't going to fix things. I pick her up and drag her to where she almost died last time. The bank alarm keeps going off, and I wonder if things would have worked out different last week if the alarm had gone off like this when the men came into the bank. I get her standing in the same place but when I let her go she collapses back into a heap. Everything is the same as the last time I saw it, only the people are missing. Same posters advertising low interest rates, pictures of happy people paying off twenty-five-year mortgages or borrowing money to buy a boat. The hole in the ceiling has been repaired, the broken office window replaced, the bullet holes in the wall plastered over and repainted, and all the blood cleaned up. No security guard, no front windows now, nobody with a shotgun. Nobody else to call out wait, to stop this woman getting killed, putting his own family in the firing line, nobody with cell phones to capture footage for the news.

"Try to stand up," I say, but she doesn't. I guess it's okay. I can't reenact everything. It's not like I have a shotgun. Just a knife. It'll all work out the same way. This woman for Jodie. For Sam. The woman is crying, sobbing hard now.

"It's the only way," I say.

Do it. Feel it. Feed the urge.

I lean down over her. I hold the knife tightly.

Come on, get it done.

There are footsteps on the broken glass, loud enough to be heard over the alarm. Detective Schroder comes to within a few meters of us, his palms raised to me. He studies the woman before focusing on the knife in my hand.

"Put the knife down, Edward." He has to yell to be heard.

I move behind her and hold it against her throat. She's shaking and she's warm and it'll be over soon, it'll be the way it was meant to be.

"I can't," I yell back.

"Please, please, help me," the woman says, but her voice is low and I don't think Schroder can hear her over the alarm.

"Edward, put down the knife."

"Why are you even here? You weren't here last time."

"I'm here because I don't want anybody else to die."

"How come you got here so fast? Last week nobody showed up for five minutes, this week you're here within seconds. It's not fair."

"I know what you're trying to do," Schroder says. "And it won't work. You can't fix the past, Edward. I know you called out to save this woman and she lived and Jodie died and then Sam died, but you can't bring them back."

"All I have to do is make sure it never happened," I say. "All I have to do is never call out."

"There aren't any takebacks in this world, Edward. No resets."

"Doing this will make everything the way it was supposed to be."

"I wish it were that easy, Eddie, I really do. Life would be so much easier. But it isn't. It is what it is, and killing her won't bring Jodie or Sam back."

"I know it won't. It will stop them from ever being hurt."

"Listen to yourself."

Listen to me. Kill her. It's in your nature. It's who you are.

"Is this what you want?" he carries on. "To become your dad?"

Daddy's a ghost.

"I'm nothing like him."

"You keep telling me you hate what he is, that you hate the rest of us for thinking that you'll become him."

"I'm nothing like him," I repeat.

"Take a look at yourself."

"This isn't about any of that. It's not about what my dad was."

"You're right, Edward, you're absolutely right. This here—this is about you. It's about what you're doing, about what you've already done. You think you're nothing like your father, but look at what you've done tonight. The man who killed Jodie, you got him, Edward. You really, really got him."

"I'm glad I killed him," I say, and it's true. I'm a trader in death.

"And your father? Are you glad you killed him too?"

"He betrayed me," I say of this man who was never my father either way, certainly not for the last twenty years, and certainly not now. "He used me. He used Jodie. All of my suffering was a tool to him. So yeah, he deserved it too." I can still feel the knife going into his chest, can still see the look on his face. I can still feel Belinda's arm around me as we sat on the bathroom floor staring at my mother in the bathtub all those years ago. Blood bubbled up out of my father's mouth instead of words and I thought I could hear air hissing out of the wound in his chest as he stumbled back from the front door of my house into the hallway, he stumbled and fell, and the darkness my father spent his life with finally claimed him. The man he brought to me looked up, and there was hope in his eyes, keen hope that sparkled as bright as a diamond and then just as quickly faded to coal when I put the same knife that had been inside my father into him as well. I put that knife in over and over and when I wanted to stop I couldn't, not right away.

"It's over, Edward. You need to let her go and come with us."

"I can fix this," I say, and Schroder goes blurry and I realize I'm crying. "I can fix this."

"No. You can't."

Yes you can, Eddie. Drag that knife back quick and deep and things will be better, much better.

"Don't be your father," he says. "Put down the knife. Let her go. She didn't do anything to hurt you. You saved her life, you did what nobody else had the courage to do, and the rest of it, none of it is your fault. You didn't kill Jodie, you didn't kill Kingsly, you didn't get Sam killed. You're a good man trying to do the best he can in a world that's taken everything away from him. Don't take everything away from her," he says, nodding toward the bank teller. "Is this what Jodie would want of you?" he asks.

My body tightens and I squeeze my eyes shut, only for a second, only long enough to picture my wife falling forward out on the street. In that same second I picture the rest of our lives together, before and after, the life we lived and the life we were supposed to live. I picture Sam.

"I really don't know," I say.

"I don't think she would," Schroder says. "I very much doubt she wants you to kill in her name, especially somebody who never hurt you. I think she wants what she always wanted from you—to be nothing like your father."

I lower the knife and open my hand.

What are you doing?

I'm not sure what I'm doing. The blade hits the floor, chips the linoleum, and falls on its side. I step back from the woman. She had no strength earlier, but she finds it now to crawl away from me as fast as she can. Two officers come out of nowhere and scoop her up and help her outside. Another two officers move in right behind Schroder, their guns raised and pointing at me. There are patrol cars outside that I didn't even notice pull up.

There's another way to be with Sam and Jodie. Pick the knife back up.

"What?"

"Huh?" Schroder asks.

Pick it up and attack them. Make them open fire. You'll be with Sam and Jodie again. It will all be better. If you're going to be a pussy for your entire life and ignore everything I want, then put us both out of our misery. Grab that knife.

I look down at the knife. Schroder watches me look down at it and comes forward.

"Ain't going to happen," he says, and he kicks it away. "It's the easy way out," he says. "You think it's what Jodie and Sam would want you to do?"

I don't have an answer. He spins me around and handcuffs me and a minute later I'm in the back of a patrol car heading toward my future. Hell, maybe it was even my destiny. Edward the Hunter. I think of the men who wolf-whistled at me at the prison yesterday, I think of seeing the Christchurch Carver, of meeting Theodore Tate. What's left of the accountant in me tries to calculate what kind of jail time I'd have to do, but fails. The city should be rewarding my monster for what it did, not locking it away. I watch the bank grow smaller behind me, knowing I'm nothing like my dad, knowing I have a monster of my own, a monster that is growing inside me, making me wonder what it's going to ask of me when I'm back on the outside again.